HAIL ATLANTIS

Tarren Guy

Books by Tarren Guy

Veritas Rerum Novels
Power of Will

Written in the Stars Novels
The Earth Beneath Us

ISBN: 978-0-6489721-2-9

To Mum, though they may not sail off the edge of the world, you will appreciate the fiction placed within. Happy reading.

Prologue

A shift in the wind promised a cooler night. Curtains that had been previously dormant started to flutter in the afternoon breeze, tracing a course from the Nile river. The room slowly dropped a few precious degrees in the desert heat, a heat she wouldn't miss but would always hold in her heart.

Walking to the window, she gazed out over the land that had been her home for the longest of times. Within the walls of the city, the ground was green with grass, and trees grew tall and strong. Outside, however, there was only sand for as far as anyone could see, except for the life-giving waters of the Nile.

She had built this town up with her husband. The waterways fed both houses and flora, and the marketplace grew over the years. They had established religious halls and learning centers, like the one she was in. The people had praised them over these last thirteen years, but with her husband's passing and the resurgence of old religions causing trouble, she knew her time here was at an end. They may already be on their way.

The shift in the breeze also brought a smell of muddy bog. Her nose twitched uncomfortably, but she soon became used to it out of necessity. The smell emanated from the great river. The dry season had been hard on the waters, and now only a small stream was left. This caused the muddy banks to become exposed and filled the air with the harsh smell. The river was large enough for a small raft, but none of the bigger boats would be getting through. She was safe, at least for a bit longer, as traveling by camel was much slower.

Wiping the sweat from her brow, she lifted the overly large, blue headdress from the table and placed it upon her head. She couldn't allow the children to see her without it. Next to the doorway was a brass gong, and she started hitting it with a small wooden club. The sound of children came from all around the building as little feet started making their way back to the hall. They filed in and sat on the hard-packed earthen floor before her. Each child was sweating and breathing heavily after their break. They would've been chasing each other through the streets surrounding the learning center. One last child ran through the door and sat quickly at the back.

"How was that?" she asked them. "Did you enjoy the break?"

"It wasn't long enough," one of the children said.

"It will never be long enough," she replied. "I could give you twice as long, and you would still be saying the same thing. You wont always get to live happily. You need to enjoy the time given to you with each moment. There is no other way to live." Some of the children nodded in understanding, while some still looked a little confused.

"What will we be learning about this afternoon?" a small girl asked. She knew the girl to be very bright and always ready to take on a challenge. Santiva was the girl's name.

"Today, I am going to tell you a story. It has been handed down through many generations to reach your ears. It's one I hope you will tell to your children and theirs after that. This story is one of adventure and conflict. There are heroes and monsters, love and loss. You may be frightened or moved to feel things you haven't felt before, but know this. The story I will tell you is all true." The children had gone quiet. Their eyes were wide, and they were leaning forward, ready for the saga they were about to hear.

"Ready?" They nodded quickly. "All right then. The story starts with a man darker than the darkest man of our country. He was as dark as the night and lived far away in a distant world. This man had a wonderful ability that many of his people shared. He could fly free from the shackles of his body..."

Chapter 1

Anangu drifted along the currents of the sky, surveying the land of his birth, once lush with vegetation but now unrecognizable. Here it was he had hunted through the woodlands and bathed naked in the rivers. Intuitively, he saw the place where he'd lain with his wife for the first time. Now, the only real indications of his homeland were the caves where he'd learned ancient wisdom from the elders and the rock mountain, Ul-Uru. The land he loved was now swallowed up by bare, cracked earth stretching from horizon to horizon. Having left on bad terms, Anangu never dreamed he would have reason to come back to his tribal homelands. He hadn't wanted to visit, even in spirit as he was now, lest he be called back. He wasn't ready to face his wife or his parents for what he'd done. Seeing what had become of his home, though, broke his heart.

As he fled so many years ago, he happened upon a group of men traveling the river roads. The bronzed race of men, the Uru, had asked that he travel with them. It was rare for a man of the Abori who knew the ancient gifts to be unknown to this race, and they commanded he accompany them. This was a high honor, and Anangu couldn't deny them. He traveled far to the East with the Uru, almost to the edge of the land where they made camp in a high range.

Anangu was tasked with hunting large cat-like beasts that the Uru had lost in an experiment. The Uru were eradicating them before they bred and became a threat to all the people and animals of this land. Anangu had done this task with ease. The Abori wisdom keepers taught him how to float free from his body and fly across the lands. With this talent, he was able to locate the great, black felines quickly.

When the Uru asked him to change his task and search for the reason behind a great upheaval, Anangu used the same tools at hand. Releasing himself from his body, he flew inland. Traveling only a short distance, Anangu was shocked at what he found. The land had started to die. Trees were thinning, their leaves turning brown. The grass died and gave fuel to great fires that ate the land. The rivers that were carved by the great rainbow serpent and flowed with cool, clean water were now dry and forgotten. The banks were corroding, and the river fish's rotting carcasses scattered the riverbed. Only the large, scaled crocodiles that dug into the ground where it was cool still lived.

Flying further inland, Anangu found the land only got worse. Rising higher into the night sky, he saw the land was kissed by the moon in every direction. The silver desert was all he could see, and a terrible dread touched his soul. Floating high, Anangu finally triangulated the central point of the desert to be his tribal homeland and the rock mountain.

Ul-Uru, or "Home of the Uru," stood high above the land untouched. It was of orange tones and sported deep ridges dug out by water running down its side in the rainy seasons. For most tribes, it was a large natural landscape that created a breathtaking backdrop. Most tribes didn't know its secrets though. Beneath the rocky surface lay tunnels and rooms. This was where the Uru experimented. Sometimes lights could be seen hovering over the landscape at night. Other times, loud rumbling noises shook the earth. It was no coincidence the latest trouble upon the land emanated from this point.

Law forbid him from entering the rock formation uninvited. Even in spirit form, the Uru had a way of feeling your presence that seemed unnatural. However, Anangu decided this one time called for an exception to be made. He flew towards Ul-Uru, slowing as he got close to the surface. This made the impact softer than it would have been. Nothing physical could touch Anangu in this form, but his dream flight was halted by an invisible barrier around the perimeter and over the top of the location. His spirit was physically hurt, and he knew that his body would feel it once he returned. He felt around the barrier seeking a place to enter, but nowhere on the surface let him in. Sliding below the sands, Anangu felt the solid barrier sink with him into the earth.

Fifty meters below the surface, his hand finally pushed through where the barrier should have been. Feeling around, Anangu knew for sure this was his way through. After flying into the Uru home, Anangu found a tunnel and started his search. The upper floors were the first to be searched. The topmost floors had been caved in to either stop anyone from entering or lock something inside. It was Anangu's guess that it was the latter, as the cave-in seemed to start from the entrance hall. No one in the vicinity could have survived.

After this, Anangu moved deeper into the earth. As he

searched the empty rooms, he came across signs of life. More accurately, he came across signs of battle and death. Blood bathed the walls, and body parts from Uru were scattered throughout the home. Some of the flesh had teeth marks showing they had been feasted upon. Anangu wondered what could have such massive jaws as the marks suggested.

Exploring further, he came to a room that was active. No life forms could be seen, but within the large round room, metallic objects were slowly moving around the outer walls. Where they touched, water seeped out and into a grate in the center of the room. Anangu realized that they were drawing water from the land and sending it somewhere deep below the surface. This was the cause of the great desert rising up and swallowing the land.

He continued further to determine where the water was going and what caused such carnage in the floors above. On the lowest level, over one thousand meters below the surface, Anangu found where the Uru had finished building. The wall of one area had burst inwards, showing that something had entered from the tunnel beyond. He couldn't fathom what would live so far below the surface of the earth and still be such a threat.

Floating down the tunnels, Anangu's question was answered immediately as he entered a massive cavern. It was easily miles wide and just as deep. Rocky pillars stretched from floor to ceiling, and stone bridges connected them all together. Anangu could see humanoid figures moving on the bridges and into holes carved in the pillars. Movement nearby caught his attention, and he found that one of the humanoids was moving towards him wielding a massive stone club. He knew that they couldn't possibly hurt him in this form, but this didn't stop the fear creeping into his soul. The humanoid figure was easily four meters tall. It wore no clothes, and Anangu could see that it was male. The giant's huge apendage swinging at its knees. The long arms were all muscle and easily lofted the club like it weighed nothing. What disturbed Anangu the most was the way it held its head. The giant was running at him now with its head tilted awkwardly to one side. The mouth was open further than regular humans would be able. The opening almost reached from ear to ear, and saliva was dripping from hundreds of sharp teeth. The giant's eyes never once left Anangu, and just before it reached him,

Anangu fled the area. The giant swung the mighty stone club in the empty air where Anangu's spirit once was.

With fear feeding his retreat, Anangu fled high into the sky and the safety it promised. He had the information he needed and somehow felt he was lucky to get away with his life. As with every dream flight, a golden cable of light anchored him back to his body. He followed it with haste and crashed back into his fleshy form. Pain sparked across every inch of his body as he remembered running into the Uru barrier. Breathing hard, it took a few minutes to recover. Around him stood the three senior Uru who had given him this latest task. They didn't say a word, waiting for Anangu to speak, but Anangu just shook his head. One Uru became impatient.

"What did you see in your dreaming?" The bronze man asked.

Finding himself, Anangu formed the words he needed. "A majority of the land has been swallowed by the desert. Trees are dying, and rivers have dried up," he told them.

"Could you determine what caused this?"

"You did," Anangu said without thinking. He heard hissing like snakes from the three Uru before he realized what he said. "The Uru of Ul-Uru have set something into motion that is drawing water from the earth at an alarming rate and sending it further into the depths of the world." Anangu shivered as he remembered the giants.

"You entered Ul-Uru?" The Uru's face looked deadly. "What did you witness in our home?"

"I had trouble entering. A barrier blocks entry even for the spirit. I needed to enter from underneath and found that the topmost floors were caved in. This was done by the Uru inside so that great beasts couldn't escape. Your people have been slaughtered by a race of giants living deep in the earth. They broke in on the lowest floor. I saw them all."

If the Uru were surprised by this news, they didn't show it. They looked at each other and started talking in a language Anangu couldn't understand. It was low and sounded like hissing accompanied by sharp high-pitched tones. One looked back at Anangu.

"My people will not stay on this continent anymore. The catastrophe that has engulfed this land cannot be stopped without someone inside to open the barrier. Will your people travel with us?" anger sparked in Anangu's belly growing into a bright flame. These people had caused the problem, and now they would run away without trying to help.

"No," he said strongly. "This land will now belong to the Abori people, and we shall fix the problem your people have brought upon us. I cannot speak for all, but know that many will stay."

"So be it," the Uru hissed.

Nudgee was consumed by irritation, a heavy burden weighing upon him as he grappled with his inability to complete the task ahead. When he first embarked on his journey under the tutelage of the elder Towrang, excitement and pride filled his heart. Few among the tribe had the opportunity to delve into the profound wisdom held by the elders, and Nudgee eagerly anticipated the day when he could pass on this knowledge to another promising youth. Recognizing Nudgee's potential, the elders singled him out, separating him from the tribe to spend the next few years with Towrang, delving into their history and the legends surrounding the Abori.

Towrang's guidance extended beyond the confines of their tribe as he assisted a group of Uru in navigating the land, filling Nudgee with excitement at the prospect of encountering these mysterious people up close. Despite only catching glimpses of this bronzed race from afar, little was said about them in the tribes except for warnings to 'stay away where possible.'

As the moon waxed and waned, Nudgee immersed himself in the tales of Abori lore, learning about the man who lived on the moon, lighting fires as he searched for his family taken by the grey spirits to the sky realm. Through these stories, Nudgee gained insights into the origins of fire, rainbow serpents, terrifying yowies, and the legend of the sacred Bullroarer, deepening his connection to his culture and finding immense enjoyment in the process. However, his enthusiasm waned when he was introduced to the concept of the Dreamtime and the dreaming.

Venturing into a cave, Nudgee found Towrang sitting in silence amidst billowing smoke from a small fire, the acrid scent stinging his nostrils. Despite the dampness of the wood, Towrang remained unconcerned. Restless, Nudgee observed the embers dancing from the flames, their fleeting existence extinguished by the surrounding smoke.

13

Towrang's weathered appearance, marked by deeply etched lines and a stark contrast between his white, frizzy hair and dark skin, hinted at his age, yet Nudgee had witnessed his strength firsthand. Steeling himself, Nudgee decided to speak up.

"What will I be learning today?" Nudgee asked, hoping to provoke a reaction from the old man, but he was left wanting. Rising to his feet, he left the cave and ascended to an overhang nearby, a spot where he often waited during Towrang's meditations. Small stones littered the area, and Nudgee enjoyed tossing them at nearby tree branches, testing his aim.

As the sun climbed higher in the sky, Nudgee decided to return to the cave below. The dying embers of the fire cast an eerie glow that danced among the shadows on the rock walls, where generations of Abori people had depicted various scenes and events. Each drawing held its own story, captivating Nudgee's fascination.

"Did you have fun throwing the stones?" the elder asked, startling Nudgee. Although Towrang had often observed him from within the cave entrance, the next line caught Nudgee off guard. "You shouldn't aim for the cockatoos though. You will awaken the wrath of our ancestors." Nudgee knew that Towrang couldn't see him from inside the cave, raising questions about how he knew. Was it a guess? No, it couldn't have been.

"I don't know..." Nudgee began, but he was swiftly interrupted.

"Don't try to deny it. After today's lesson, you will understand. It will be a short lesson today, and then I won't be holding any more until you achieve a specific outcome."

"What is it?" Nudgee asked, his curiosity piqued. "I'm ready for any challenge."

"What I will be telling you is very important," Towrang said, signifying the gravity of the lesson. "Listen carefully, for I will only tell you once. It is for you to decide how to achieve the end result."

"I'm listening, Towrang," Nudgee replied, growing serious. He sensed the importance of today's lesson.

"Today, you are to learn about the Dreamtime and the dreaming. You may have heard that a lot of our stories are from the Dreamtime. Today you will know what this is."

Nudgee had heard the terms used around camp by the adults of the Abori tribes. It was something deeply ingrained in all of their stories and legends, but Nudgee hadn't realized there was more to it than just a name. "The Dreamtime is a balance between the physical and spiritual realms. The dreaming is to leave one's physical body and move into the spiritual body. You understand this?"

"I'd heard that when we pass on, we move into our spiritual form. Are you talking about this?"

"Not quite. What you say is true," Towrang explained. "But there is more to what I'm telling you than just passing on. There are those who have the ability to move into the spiritual body while still living. They can travel anywhere they want and view anything they want. It is how I saw you on the cave top." Nudgee was stunned.

"Do you believe I could have this ability?"

"It is the reason you were chosen to learn the ancient wisdom passed down from Abori elder to Abori man. There are traits in you that show this to be true, but you are the one who needs to bring it out."

"How do I do this?" Nudgee asked, excitement building within him once more.

"You need to remain calm. Allow the world around you to fade away. There should be no sound, no light, and no feeling of this world. Allow yourself to fall into a void of your making, then when you are ready, pull yourself out again. When you come back out of the void, come out into your spirit form. This is all I can tell you. You must find the way yourself."

"That's it?" Nudgee was underwhelmed. "That's all I have to go off?"

"That is all I will be telling you. From this point, you are on your own until you can tell me in the spirit realm that you are ready to learn more."

"But..."

"Do not protest, Nudgee. No one can do this for you. Now leave here and find your path to the spirit realm." Towrang closed his ancient eyes and went back into a trance.

This was the situation Nudgee now found himself in, and it was frustrating. The sun had passed by nine times, and he had failed hundreds upon hundreds of times more than this. It wasn't just that he was failing at the task given to him; he was also hungry. Towrang was the one who had provided for him while he was learning the ancient wisdom. Now he needed to fend for himself, and it was a harsh land. Nudgee had found a goanna two days before, and with a little self-restraint, the meat had lasted until the night before. His small, spindly frame was now weak from lack of food.

Ignoring his rumbling belly and sitting in the shade of a nearby eucalyptus tree, Nudgee calmed his mind. He'd been getting progressively better and faster at closing his mind off to the physical world. Darkness enveloped him as he once more sought that calm clarity somewhere between the two realms. He had scrapped it a few times, but each time Nudgee started to get excited and he fell back into the physical realm. He was not going to make this mistake again, not if he wanted to be fed properly anytime soon.

Nudgee knew the point he sought was coming. The point of clarity that he needed to reach started to envelop him. It crept into every crevice, nook, and cranny that made up the person that was Nudgee, the twenty-year-old man of the Jukembal tribe. He was fit and good with a boomerang. His features were desirable but not handsome, with dark hair, skin, and eyes. At night when he smiled, only his teeth could be seen. None of these mattered at this point. While forcing himself not to be conscious, he tricked his mind into not realizing he was forcing himself. Nudgee did this for as long as he could before his conscious mind came to the surface. He thought immediately of tumbling forward out of his body and then opened his eyes. Disheartened, he was still sitting below the eucalyptus tree. Nudgee rose to his feet and cursed at the tree, turning to hit the trunk. As his punch landed, however, he froze. Before him, sitting on the ground even now, was his body. He was in a meditative trance just as Towrang had been. Raising his hands in front of his face, Nudgee could see through them like murky water. Elation ran through his soul, and he started to jump around.

The next moment, Nudgee found himself spinning out of control into the air. He could not slow the momentum and was helplessly adrift in his erratic ascension. Soon, the outer layers of the Earth's atmosphere passed him by, and he started to become afraid. He moved his head with the spin to view areas for longer periods and predicted the line of movement. He was heading straight towards the moon.

This celestial body resembled Earth in many ways, with its expansive terrain of solid matter consisting of stone and dirt. Despite his search for life, Nudgee found no signs of human presence amidst the desolate landscape. The moon, he realized, was not a vessel for earthly travel but merely a reflector of sunlight, prompting his initial fear to give way to curiosity about its true nature.

He ceased his struggle against the erratic movements and allowed himself to continue spinning towards the moon, hoping to regain control upon reaching its surface. However, that anticipated moment never arrived, as Towrang materialized before him. Like Nudgee, Towrang had transitioned into his spiritual form and pursued him. Upon catching up with the young man, Towrang halted their movements and offered Nudgee guidance to regain control of his body. With Towrang's assistance, Nudgee regained full control and resumed his journey towards the moon.

"Nudgee, stop!" Towrang's urgent cry caused the younger man to freeze in his tracks.

"Aren't you curious, Towrang?" Nudgee questioned. "The moon is nothing like the stories we've been told."

"I am aware of the moon's reality, but you must never venture there. It is too perilous," Towrang cautioned. "The grey spirits of our Dreamtime are genuine. Should you intrude upon their domain, they may mistake your curiosity for a desire to reside there, resulting in the dire consequences of granting your desire."

Shocked and fearful, Nudgee realized the gravity of his near-fatal misunderstanding. "I don't want that," he confessed to his elder. "Why were we not informed of this in our stories?"

"Because people prefer narratives that offer comfort over harsh truths. It's ingrained in our storytelling," Towrang explained.

"So, what can we trust as true and what is false?" Nudgee inquired, seeking clarity amidst the confusion.

"You possess the gift of dreaming, Nudgee. With it, you have the tools to uncover the truths of our world for yourself. But for now, we should return, and I'll meet you where you are currently dreaming," Towrang advised. Nudgee turned his gaze towards Earth, marveling at its vastness, with sprawling land masses and extensive bodies of water.

"How do I return home?" Nudgee inquired.

"From your stomach, you will see a golden cable. Follow it, and it will lead you back to your body, no matter how far you've traveled. I'll join you in the physical realm," Towrang explained before descending.

Spotting the golden cable, Nudgee swiftly began pulling himself back towards his physical form. With determination, he descended rapidly, albeit with little control, until he collided with his body and shuddered to awareness. Gasping for air, Nudgee felt the fatigue and soreness in his muscles, realizing it wasn't just due to hunger but also the result of his rough landing.

Moments later, Towrang entered the clearing, congratulating Nudgee on his achievement. "It took me nearly twice as long to reach the the same point, Nudgee," Towrang disclosed. Although Nudgee felt a twinge of embarrassment, he was proud of his accomplishment. "As you learn to control yourself in the spiritual realm, your returns will become less painful," Towrang assured him.

"I'll practice diligently and master this ability," Nudgee vowed. "I never realized how vast our world truly is. One day, I aspire to explore it all."

Towrang was on the verge of speaking when a movement in the tree above caught his attention. A flash of grey fur alerted him to the imminent danger. He signaled for Nudgee to watch the trees by making a fist and pumping upwards. Nudgee caught the gesture and looked up at the eucalyptus tree just in time to see what Towrang feared.

Two beady, yellow eyes peered down from above a gaping maw adorned with razor-sharp fangs. The creature, covered in grey fur, matched Nudgee in size. Its muscular frame and powerful limbs hinted at its formidable strength, capable of overpowering Nudgee with ease. Crouched on the thick, pale green branches, drool dripped from its jaws as it fixed its gaze upon him.

Despite the pain coursing through his body, Nudgee stood up slowly, his eyes locked on the tree-dwelling menace. He'd grown up hearing stories of the dreaded drop bears, infamous for their ferocious attacks, though commonly known as Koalas. In ancient times, they towered over the Aboriginals, but over generations, they had diminished in size and ferocity, yet remained deadly.

Praying to his ancestors for protection, Nudgee found himself face to face with the fearsome creature, and fear gripped him. He knew that remaining still would mean certain death, so he forced his body to move. With the first

18

step, the beast lunged from its perch. Nudgee dove to his left, rolling heavily as the creature crashed down, its massive paws sending dirt flying as it landed.

Towrang rushed in with a spear, attempting to ward off the beast. However, his efforts were futile as the creature swiped its paw, shattering the spear and leaving Towrang wounded and sprawled across the ground, blood staining the earth.

Ignoring Towrang, the drop bear turned its attention back to Nudgee, emitting a menacing growl as it closed in. Towering over him, it raised its arms, poised to strike with its deadly talons. Despite Nudgee's attempts to evade, his body, weakened by recent events, refused to obey. Closing his eyes, he braced himself for the impending pain.

Like lightning, shining spears shot across the clearing, piercing the soft skin under the beast's arms. Writhing in agony from the new pain, the creature fell back, its thrashing intensified. Two bronze-skinned men strode into the clearing, instantly recognizable to Nudgee as Uru. Each carried another gleaming spear, silver in color and crafted from a material stronger than anything Nudgee had encountered before. He had once held one while an Uru performed a task, noting its weight and unnaturally cold surface that warmed with time. The Uru referred to the material as metal.

As the drop bear rolled in the dirt, attempting to dislodge the metal spear, one of the Uru approached and thrust his second spear cleanly into the beast's head, rendering it lifeless. Retrieving the spears, he tossed one to his companion before turning to face Nudgee and Towrang.

"How could you be so careless as to rest beneath a Koala's home?" the Uru reprimanded in a stern voice. Unlike the Abori people who adorned themselves with animal skin clothing around their waist or chest, the Uru were fully clothed in a soft, woven material. Their garments, white and impeccably clean, hung over their shoulders and fell to their knees, adorned with a trim of gold stitching.

"It was my oversight," Towrang admitted, rising to his feet while applying pressure to his injured shoulder. Though the bleeding had slowed, the pain remained evident on his face. "I was focused on Nudgee during a crucial moment of his learning and failed to recognize the danger lurking above."

"It was a foolish mistake, and next time, we won't intervene in the fight," one of the Uru declared sternly. At that moment, both Uru glanced towards the south, their attention drawn by something unseen and unheard by Nudgee or Towrang. "Patch yourself up. We move at once," they commanded.

Neither Nudgee nor Towrang dared to argue with the Uru, obediently following their orders.

"Nefari!" The voice echoed through the trees, bouncing off branches and whispering through leaves until it reached its intended target. She would undoubtedly ignore him, relishing the freedom she found in evading her caretakers' watchful eyes. Today seemed perfect for a leisurely stroll in the woods. The sun's harsh rays had warmed the land, biting into the skin, but under the canopy of the woodland realm, the gentle breeze soothed the burns to little more than a distant memory.

Approaching a fallen tree barely half her height, Nefari faced a challenge. While others might have easily stepped over it, she delighted in the obstacle. Attempting to grip the moss-covered surface, her hands slipped repeatedly. Spotting a branch that could serve as leverage, she hoisted herself up and began making her way along the trunk.

Halfway across, Nefari encountered a dilemma. In a hollowed section of the trunk lay a spider's web, a scene of life and death unfolding upon its delicate strands. A trapped bug struggled against the sticky grasp of the web's outer reaches, while on the other side, two large legs of a spider dangled from its hiding place. The spider cautiously felt the web, assessing the struggles of its potential prey. It would not strike until it was certain its target was sufficiently ensnared. Revealing its position prematurely risked losing its meal, and deterring other animals from venturing too close.

Nefari found herself torn, her love for all creatures in the woods conflicting with the dire consequences of her actions. If she did nothing, the small black bug would surely meet its end at the spider's fangs. Yet, freeing the bug would not only rob the spider of its meal but could also damage its intricate web, potentially leading to the spider's starvation. It was a weighty dilemma, and Nefari felt tears welling up as she grappled with what to do. Before she could decide, however, nature intervened, and the spider swiftly darted out, seizing the bug's life without hesitation.

"No!" Nefari cried out, though she knew not how she could have acted differently.

"What troubles you, child?" A soft voice inquired from behind. Startled by the unexpected presence, Nefari's tears were momentarily forgotten as she turned to seek the source.

Before her stood a man with the bronze skin of an Uru, a skin tone she shared, though her blood was not pure like his. Recognizing him as one of the three senior Uru, Cecrops, commander of all the Uru warriors, Nefari felt humbled that he would take the time to address her. So overwhelmed was she by his presence that she forgot to reply.

"Are you okay?" Cecrops asked again, noticing Nefari's tears.

Nefari turned her gaze back to the spider devouring the bug and recounted the dilemma she had faced, explaining her struggle to Cecrops. He could see the emotional weight she carried.

"Which of the two creatures did you like more?" Cecrops inquired, seeking insight into her feelings.

"I liked them both," Nefari replied. "I wanted them both to live."

"Life is not always so kind," Cecrops remarked. Kneeling beside her, he placed a reassuring hand on her shoulder. "You will encounter many difficult choices in life. Some you can deliberate on, while others demand swift decisions. Among the hardest are those involving life and death. If you wish to alter the course of events, you must be prepared to act. Otherwise, sometimes it's best to let nature take its course."

Nefari, still upset about the situation, listened intently to Cecrops's words and found herself agreeing with much of what he said. "I will try to be stronger in the future, sir," she promised.

Cecrops nodded approvingly. "I would like to ask you to be strong right now. Can you do this?" he requested. Though Nefari didn't fully grasp his meaning, she nodded vigorously in response. "Good. Stay seated against the fallen tree, and this will be over shortly," he instructed.

Standing up, Cecrops turned his back to her as Nefari complied with his directive. From his side, he drew a short sword of glistening steel, its hilt crisscrossed in red leather, and the blade tapering at the base before widening in the middle with a wicked curve to the point. He stood with relaxed muscles, poised for action. From the depths of the woods, Nefari heard a chilling sound that froze her heart— a cross between a screech and a growl echoing into the clearing. Though she couldn't pinpoint its precise direction, she didn't have to wait long to find out.

From the shadows emerged a great, black, cat-like creature, its large paws flexing long, razor-sharp talons as it circled Cecrops with green slitted eyes. For a moment, Nefari felt a wave of fear wash over her as she watched the formidable feline pacing dangerously close. However, a glance at Cecrops reassured her—radiating confidence and security, she knew he would emerge victorious.

As the giant cat charged, Nefari couldn't help but jump, a small squeak escaping her lips. Meanwhile, Cecrops remained calm, awaiting the opportune moment. With unnatural agility, he sidestepped the beast's attack and swiftly positioned himself alongside it. Bringing his blade up, Cecrops sliced into the beast's belly with precision.

With a mighty cry, the cat hit the ground hard, retreating from Cecrops, understanding him as death itself. Nefari watched in complete awe as Cecrops moved with fluid grace, his dance captivating her. Her tiny blue eyes sparkled with wonderment, momentarily forgetting the danger.

Unaware that the cat had now turned its focus on her and was closing in, Nefari remained unafraid, mesmerized by Cecrops's skill. Without hesitation, Cecrops closed the distance, bringing his blade down and cutting into the beast's side. With a wild cry, the creature retreated to the fallen tree, acknowledging its defeat before leaping over the trunk and disappearing into the forest.

Cecrops, ready to pursue the beast, was interrupted by the sudden arrival of an Abori man rushing into the clearing.

The man wore a kangaroo skin loin cloth and panted heavily as he entered the clearing. Relief flooded his expression at the sight of Nefari, his eyes then falling upon Cecrops, who stood with a bloodied sword, his gaze fixed on the newcomer. Though unsure of what had occurred, the man was grateful to find the girl unharmed.

"Nefari, you gave me quite a fright," the Abori man said,

his tone laden with concern. "You know you shouldn't wander from camp like that." He moved toward her, but Cecrops interposed himself, raising his sword between the man and the girl.

"Who is this man to you, Nefari?" Cecrops inquired, his voice firm.

"I am her minder," the man replied, annoyance evident in his tone as he glared at Cecrops.

"I was addressing the girl," Cecrops retorted, his eyes narrowing into deadly slits. "If you dare to speak for her again, you won't be speaking for much longer. Nefari, who is this man to you?"

"He is my minder, as he said. His name is Ira," Nefari confirmed, her voice steady. Cecrops chuckled at this.

"Your name means watchful, but you have no talent for it," he remarked, raising a hand. Another Uru man entered the clearing, and Cecrops approached Nefari again. "This man is Torven. He will escort you back to my camp. Is that ok?" Nefari simply nodded. "Good. Torven, take little Nefari here to the meeting place and ensure her safety. She is invaluable to the Uru."

"You cannot do this. I was assigned..." Ira began to protest.

"Do you know who I am?" Cecrops interrupted, his tone turning cold as he faced the man. Ensuring Nefari was out of sight, Cecrops prepared to take action.

"You are an Uru who thinks too highly of himself. This position was assigned to me by Brellin, one of the three senior Uru. You are outranked."

"Be that as it may," Cecrops countered, his voice dripping with authority, "Brellin makes mistakes, and if I desired, I could obtain his express permission to dismiss you in an instant. However, I won't do so, not because I need to, but because I choose not to. My name is Cecrops. As a senior, I command all the warriors of the Uru."

Ira visibly paled, a deep sense of dread enveloping him as Cecrops closed the distance between them.

"I won't dismiss you, however. Such an act would be worthless. To me, you are worthless, and thus, your life is forfeit."

Cecrops's mouth stretched unnaturally wide, his teeth multiplying into hundreds of long, slender fangs. Ira's screams were abruptly silenced as Cecrops seized him, sinking his teeth into the dark flesh of the man's throat.

Blood cascaded down Cecrops's chin as he tore out a chunk of flesh, swallowing it greedily. With a disdainful gesture, he let the twitching body of Ira fall to the ground before stalking away, his mouth returning to its normal form.

Nudgee recovered swiftly from the encounter with the drop bear, his youth and fitness aiding in his healing. Towrang, however, required more time. His injured shoulder made sleeping at night and traveling during the day challenging. Struggling to distract himself from the pain, Towrang had grown quiet since the incident, but the Uru showed little concern, urging the Abori onward as if their lives depended on it.

Their journey led them to a vast field encircled by forests and mountains—a landscape believed to have been shaped by a fallen sky, earning the name Warrumbungles, meaning "crooked mountains," by the local Gamilaraay tribe. In the heart of this expanse lay open fields capable of accommodating millions, a sight that led Nudgee to speculate that the Uru numbered nearly as many already. Streams of newcomers continued to pour in through various passes, filling the area to capacity. Nudgee and Towrang found themselves separated from their Uru companions, seated among a group of several thousand Abori.

"What do you think is happening?" Nudgee leaned in, seeking Towrang's insight.

"They often hold meetings in this area. It's not uncommon," Towrang replied calmly, his demeanor reassuring Nudgee amidst the uncertainty.

"I just hope they will be courteous enough to let us know they were going to drag us halfway across the countryside for a meeting next time," Nudgee grumbled under his breath.

An Uru nearby raised an eyebrow in his direction, prompting Towrang to intervene. He nodded apologetically to the man and positioned himself in front of Nudgee.

"Watch what you say, or keep your voice down," Towrang cautioned. "There are too many Uru here who wouldn't hesitate to strike you down."

"Sorry, Towrang. I'm just tired after the trek," Nudgee replied, attempting to lower his voice.

"We have Abori who claim that a great calamity is befalling the land," an Abori nearby interjected. "They say the land itself is turning inside out to take back control."

"That couldn't be true," Nudgee objected. "How can the land do such a thing?"

"I cannot say for sure about the veracity of the rumors," the Abori responded, "but these words came from some of our most trusted elders. They claim to have seen it in their dreams."

Nudgee was taken aback, while Towrang maintained a neutral expression. Before Nudgee could speak further, Towrang placed a hand on his shoulder.

"If the elders speak, we must heed their words," Towrang affirmed to the Abori, who nodded and turned away.

An Uru man rose to his feet at the front of the gathering, accompanied by two others nearby. Though Nudgee had not seen this man before, he recognized the respect he commanded among his people. As the man addressed the crowd, silence fell, with all eyes turning toward him— except for one young girl, perhaps four or five years old, seated at the front. She gazed past the Uru before her, smiling at another Uru further back.

"For those of you who may not know me," the man at the front began, his gaze fixed on the group of Abori. Nudgee's attention immediately snapped back to him. "My name is Glycon. Behind me stand Brellin and Cecrops. Together, we form the ruling body of the Uru people. We have convened this meeting today to address a matter of grave importance—an issue that not only concerns the Uru, but also the Abori people. We have recently received troubling reports indicating that the deserts of our great country are expanding rapidly and uncontrollably. They have already engulfed several tribes and rendered vast swathes of land uninhabitable."

So, it's true, Nudgee thought to himself.

"How did you come by this information?" an Abori man inquired, prompting a shiver to run down Nudgee's spine as a number of Uru grew visibly annoyed by the Abori questioning their leader. They exchanged words in their own serpent-like tongue. Glycon raised his arms in a calming gesture.

"Brothers and sisters, let us not quarrel amongst ourselves," Glycon interjected. "The news is indeed distressing, and it is natural for the Abori to seek clarification."

This response irked Nudgee deeply.

Glycon turned his attention to the Abori who had spoken. "You wish to know how we obtained this information. It was, in fact, one of your own who brought us word. His name is Anangu, known among many Abori as a man of honor and integrity." Many of the Abori nodded in acknowledgment, accepting the news as credible upon hearing the name. Glycon continued, seeking to reinforce the validity of the information.

"He learned of this through his dreams. Venturing far, he discovered that even his own tribe had fallen victim to the encroaching deserts. I would like to clarify that the Uru have not been spared from this catastrophe either. One of our grand cities has been destroyed. Anangu traced the source of this calamity to an ancient foe of all peoples. Deep beneath the earth, a race of giants has proliferated, growing in numbers and strength. They are the ones siphoning moisture from the land, decimating the flora and fauna."

At the mention of the source of the catastrophe, a wave of concern swept through the Uru, unsettling even the most composed among them. Nudgee couldn't help but feel a surge of fear at witnessing the distress of this typically resolute and formidable race. Across the multitude of faces, worry and unease were palpable. It was evident to Nudgee that the magnitude of the problem was immense. Glycon raised his hands, commanding silence, and the massive crowd obediently hushed.

"We are confronted with only two options," Glycon declared, his voice cutting through the tense atmosphere. "The first is to remain here and attempt to confront the giants." His proposal was met with a resounding rejection. "I understand your sentiment. Giants have posed a threat to our people for millennia. Against a formidable force of their numbers, our chances of success are slim. Currently, the largest assembly of giants our race has ever faced lies beneath us, inexorably ascending toward the surface. Soon, we will find ourselves bereft of land and resources, facing an unbeatable enemy. I wholeheartedly concur that the first option is no option at all."

"The alternative I present to you is to vacate this land and seek refuge in safer territories," Glycon continued. Nods of agreement rippled through the Uru assembled. However, among the Abori, confusion and despair lingered. "My Abori friends, I understand your distress regarding this proposal. In these perilous times, I must prioritize the safety of my people. Anangu has already forewarned me that many of you will be reluctant to depart. You have loved ones here whom you hope to reunite with. Therefore, I release all of you from your duties. Those who wish to join us are welcome; we have ample space to accommodate you. To the rest, I wish you strength and resilience in the days ahead. They will be arduous, and survival is unlikely. Make your decision now, as our departure is imminent."

Nudgee found himself faced with a significant decision, one that carried immense weight. He could opt to remain with Towrang, delving deeper into their culture and facing the looming threat posed by the encroaching desert. Logically, it seemed like the right choice, but deep down, Nudgee felt a stirring, a pull towards something else. In his brief experience in the spiritual realm, he had glimpsed the vastness of the world beyond, igniting a profound desire within him to explore every corner, uncover every secret. While Dreamtime offered a means to achieve this, it lacked the tangible experience Nudgee craved. His heart yearned for adventure, for the unknown beyond the confines of his homeland.

"Come, Nudgee," Towrang's voice broke through his reverie, nudging him back to the present. "We should begin our journey back home."

Nudgee hesitated for a fleeting moment, a flicker of uncertainty crossing his features. Towrang, perceptive as ever, caught the subtle shift in Nudgee's demeanor, understanding the silent yearning that tugged at his soul. With a gentle gesture, he placed his hand on Nudgee's shoulder, offering his final words of guidance.

"Your path is about to unfold before you. Venture where your heart leads, and stay safe. Should you ever find your way back to us, know that you will be welcomed with open arms." With a reassuring smile, Towrang turned and departed, leaving Nudgee to grapple with the weight of his decision.

"Thank you, Towrang," Nudgee murmured softly, a mix of gratitude and guilt weighing on his heart as he watched Towrang's retreating figure. With a deep breath, he steeled himself for the journey ahead, his resolve firm as he set his sights on the horizon.

Chapter 2

The exodus across the vast countryside was arduous and unrelenting. Few opportunities for respite presented themselves during the day, and at night, they made camp only when necessity dictated. Each morning, meager rations were distributed, intended to sustain them until the day's end. In the midst of this journey, Nudgee found himself grappling with regret over his decision. Yet, as days turned into weeks, he gradually grew accustomed to the relentless routine, finding a semblance of ease amidst the challenges.

Since their departure from the meeting, Nudgee couldn't shake the eerie sensation of being watched. His gaze often gravitated toward the nearby tree line, and whenever he ventured beyond the safety of the group, he hastened his steps. During the nocturnal hours, as he lay attempting to drift into slumber, the rustling of bushes would unsettle him. On occasion, he glimpsed the glint of malevolent eyes gleaming in the darkness, vanishing as swiftly as they appeared.

On the fourth night, a spine-chilling cry shattered the tranquility of the night, its origin emanating from the depths of the forest. Both Uru and Abori were jolted awake, compelled to investigate the source of this haunting wail.

Into the woods ventured Nudgee, accompanied by a cautious contingent. What they stumbled upon would haunt Nudgee for many restless nights to come. Amidst a gruesome scene lay the ravaged remains of a peculiar and fearsome lizard-like humanoid creature, its form so mangled that discerning its true nature proved impossible. Claw and teeth marks marred its body, still glistening with the warm, crimson hue of fresh blood.

Amidst the chaos, the Uru began barking orders in their unfamiliar tongue, summoning reinforcements wielding torches to scour the area. Illuminated by flickering flames, they scoured the surroundings for clues, guided by the eerie glow. A cry rang out, drawing their attention to a particular spot where paw prints in the soil hinted at the presence of a formidable feline-like predator, comparable in size to Nudgee himself.

Cecrops, a commanding figure, strode into the scene, issuing directives with authority. A squad of five Uru darted into the forest in pursuit of the elusive predator, while another set about cremating the reptilian creature. The acrid stench of burning flesh assailed Nudgee's senses, threatening to overwhelm him, yet he managed to maintain his composure. As the flames consumed the creature, it disintegrated almost instantaneously, leaving behind only wisps of smoke and ash. Upon their return, the Uru dispatched to track the predator returned to camp, their expressions grim, conveying a sense of defeat to Cecrops and his cohorts.

By the seventh day, the exodus had settled into a smoother rhythm, and discussions of the recent unsettling events had dwindled. Nudgee found himself sleeping more soundly, the nagging feeling of being watched dissipating with each passing night. Amidst the Abori group, he had begun forging friendships, their conversations initially revolving around the gruesome discovery but gradually transitioning to discussions about their respective tribes and the motivations behind joining the Uru on their journey.

It was during one such conversation with a group of Abori that Nudgee noticed a lone Uru exhibiting signs of frustration, his gaze darting anxiously towards the surrounding tree line. Recognizing him as the Senior Cecrops, Nudgee hesitated momentarily before deciding to approach and offer his assistance, driven by a sense of duty or perhaps a desire to alleviate the man's apparent distress.

Despite the warnings from other Abori advising against his openness with a senior Uru, Nudgee persisted, approaching Cecrops with his offer. As Cecrops turned to him with a menacing glint in his eyes, Nudgee instinctively lowered his head, addressing him with deference.

"Can I be of assistance?" Nudgee inquired tentatively, his voice laced with respect.

Cecrops' annoyance was palpable as he responded, voice dripping with disdain. "Unless you can fly up and get a view of the area, you won't be able to help," he retorted sharply, his impatience evident. Thinking of his unique abilities honed through training with Towrang, Nudgee hesitated, grappling with the decision of revealing his capabilities.

Cecrops observed the hesitation, pressing him for a response. "Can you help or not?" he demanded.

Summoning his courage, Nudgee tentatively broached the topic of the Dreamtime, hoping to elicit a reaction.

Cecrops seized upon his offer, promptly leading him away from the camp to a more secluded spot. There, he confronted Nudgee, his expression intense as he explained the situation.

"I am searching for a young girl," Cecrops divulged, his grip firm on Nudgee's arm. "Her caretaker proved inadequate and was... dismissed," he added, his tone laden with implications Nudgee dared not dwell upon. "I need you to locate her, as she seems to have vanished from the main migration. Can you tap into the Dreamtime?" Cecrops inquired, scrutinizing Nudgee closely. "You appear rather young for such abilities."

Admitting his limited experience with accessing the Dreamtime, Nudgee confessed, "I have only managed to do so once. I was in the midst of learning when we were called to the meeting. Elder Towrang was guiding me through the process." Pausing, he ventured cautiously, "Is this girl your daughter?"

"No," Cecrops clarified. "She is a valuable asset to the Uru people. She potentially possesses the ability to sustain our race for years to come, although we must wait until she's older."

Unsettled by the peculiar nature of the conversation, Nudgee refrained from delving deeper, fearing what revelations might surface.

"What does she look like?" he asked cautiously.

"The girl has hair the color of woodland leaves in their autumnal change," Cecrops described. "Her eyes are a deep blue, and her skin bears a hue akin to that of the Uru, though traces of Abori lineage may be discernible as well, given her mixed heritage."

Nudgee recalled the girl from the meeting. "She was the one who sat at the front of the meeting, watching you?" he ventured.

"That's her," Cecrops affirmed.

"I'll see what I can do," Nudgee responded, settling himself cross-legged on the grass. He closed his eyes, focusing on entering a meditative state and clearing his mind of all conscious thought. However, the image of the girl persisted, interfering with his concentration. With a frustrated shake of his head, he attempted to dispel the distraction.

"What's the matter?" Cecrops inquired, noticing Nudgee's struggle.

30

"I had some trouble with the steps," Nudgee admitted. "But I'll get it."

Cecrops' expression hardened, his tone ominous. "If you've wasted my time, I'll ensure yours is rather short as well." Nudgee's eyes widened at the threat, his gaze flickering nervously to the sword at Cecrops' side. Hastening his attempts to enter a meditative state once more, he faltered under the pressure, his efforts rushed and unsteady. Cecrops' hand instinctively moved toward the hilt of his sword, a silent warning hanging in the air.

"Give me a minute," Nudgee pleaded, his hands raised defensively. "This relies on how calm I can get, and you're not helping with the threats."

"Make sure you get it done," Cecrops retorted before stepping back, granting Nudgee the space and time he required.

Taking slow, deep breaths, Nudgee felt the tremors in his hands subside as he gradually regained his composure. Finally attaining a sense of inner peace, he prepared himself once more.

This time, the meditation process flowed smoothly. Nudgee was pleasantly surprised to discover that shifting into his spiritual form came more naturally. With each moment, he felt his proficiency grow, realizing that with practice, he would continue to improve. Focusing his concentration, he willed himself to ascend into the air, his spirit obediently following his commands. Delighted by his newfound control, Nudgee soared higher and higher, relishing the expansive view that unfolded before him.

In his spiritual state, Nudgee's senses were heightened, and the clarity of his vision was astonishing. He could discern the details of the landscape below with unparalleled clarity, observing the sprawling clearings and dense forests. In the distance, majestic mountains loomed, forming an imposing range that he recalled standing upon before embarking on this migration. Grasping the vast distance they had traversed in such a short span of time, Nudgee couldn't help but marvel at the journey they'd undertaken. As he focused on the image of the girl in his mind, a peculiar sensation began to stir within his spiritual form, manifesting as a tingling on his right side. Instinctively, he attempted to alleviate the discomfort by scratching at it, but to no avail—the annoyance only intensified. Realizing that it might be a clue, Nudgee chose to follow it, hoping it would lead him closer to the girl.

Flying off in the direction where the tingling lead, Nudgee soon came upon a picturesque scene: a waterfall, its cascading waters creating a mesmerizing display of rainbows dancing in the mist. However, his attention was swiftly drawn to movement at the base of the waterfall, where he spotted the girl, visibly frightened and alone. His heart sank as he observed a formidable black feline with a scar down its side approaching her menacingly. Without hesitation, Nudgee swiftly retreated to his physical body, his landing rough and jarring as he returned to reality.

"Cecrops!" he exclaimed urgently, scrambling to his feet and darting through the trees. It didn't take long for Cecrops to catch up, his expression grave as Nudgee relayed the dire situation.

The day started with such breathtaking beauty, Nefari thought as she watched the large, black cat slowly stalking towards her.

Lost in her own reverie most of the day, the soothing sun warming her bronzed skin, she walked alongside the mass of travellers. Nefari's mind drifting from thought to though to keep herself amused during the trek, though, always they came back to her lost parents. Both had passed away when she was just a child, leaving her to be shuffled between various minders, none of whom she had ever grown attached to.

Her thoughts slowly shifted to the day she encountered the first large cat. She vividly recalled the heroic figure of Cecrops, who had swiftly come to her aid. Now serving as her guardian, Cecrops ensured her well-being, providing her with nourishment and ensuring she rested comfortably. Nefari felt a sense of security in his presence, cherishing the stability he brought to her life.

Nefari realized she had once again fallen behind the exodus, finding herself near the rear of the procession. It was a familiar occurrence, as her slower pace often filtered her to the back by day's end. However, today marked a departure from the norm, as they had halted their journey while the sun still graced the sky. Explained as necessary for the upcoming leg of their trip, this early stop offered a rare opportunity for exploration. Despite the encroaching shadows signaling the waning daylight, Nefari sensed the possibility of venturing out alone—a prospect she had longed for since their journey began, yet had been denied, especially following the recent death found at the edge of the group.

As Nefari entered the camp area, her eyes fell upon a large rock situated to one side. It seemed substantial enough to provide cover for her to slip away unnoticed. Glancing around at the weary faces of the men and women surrounding her, she noted their exhaustion from the relentless trek they had endured. No one paid her any attention as she casually altered her path, veering toward the other side of the boulder before coming to a halt. Casting a cautious glance back to ensure she wasn't being observed or pursued, she waited a few moments, studying the crowd until she felt confident she was in the clear. "That was far too easy," she mused, a grin tugging at her lips as she eagerly skipped off toward the tree line, her energy renewed with the anticipation of her impending adventure.

The forest enveloping her was unlike any she had experienced before. Unlike the dry and barren landscapes she was accustomed to, this forest teemed with life. The air hung heavy and humid, wrapping around her like a warm embrace, causing beads of sweat to form and trickle down her face. The scent of the rainforest was a rich blend of mustiness and freshness, a symphony of aromas that seemed to beckon her deeper into its embrace. Lush vegetation surrounded her, and the dense canopy overhead cast a shadowy veil, stirring a sense of claustrophobia within her. Yet, she pressed on, her curiosity piqued by the distant sound of cascading water. With a burst of agility, Nefari directed her steps toward a beam of sunlight piercing through the foliage, her heart quickening at the prospect of discovering the source of the waterfall.

Finally breaking into the clearing, Nefari couldn't help but feel a twinge of disappointment at its size. She had hoped for something grand, but the sight before her was rather ordinary. Nevertheless, the rainbows that danced around the base of the waterfall, shimmering in the golden sunlight, held a certain charm of their own. Gazing out over the small lake, she suddenly realized how late it had become. Beneath the dense forest canopy, time seemed to slip away unnoticed, and now she worried if she could find her way back before darkness descended. With a reluctant sigh, Nefari tore her gaze away from the tranquil scene, bidding the lake and waterfall a silent farewell. It was then that she saw it.

Crouched low at the edge of the tree line were two green slitted eyes set in a black face, fixed intently on her. The beast's powerful front paws gripped the earth, poised to strike at any moment. Locked in a chilling stare, Nefari barely had time to react before the creature launched itself forward with lethal speed. Stunned for a fleeting moment, she frantically scanned her surroundings for refuge, her heart racing with fear. Spotting a hollowed-out log nearby, she dove towards it, hoping it would provide sanctuary. With only moments to spare, she squeezed herself inside, the tight space offering a sliver of safety against the beast's onslaught.

As the giant cat clawed and swiped at her from outside the log, Nefari's heart hammered in her chest with a mixture of terror and despair. Trapped with no means of escape, she realized the grim reality of her predicament sinking in. With no exits and no hope of rescue, she faced the bleak prospect of either succumbing to starvation or falling prey to the relentless predator outside. And even if someone were to stumble upon this secluded spot, they would have to contend with the ferocious feline guarding it. A wave of desolation washed over her as she realized that the exodus would continue without her, her fate now hanging precariously in the balance.

"Cecrops," Nefari whispered softly, her voice barely above a whimper. With nothing left to do but wait and hope, she prayed fervently that she wouldn't become prey to the lurking predator outside. As darkness descended upon the area, the tension mounted, yet the cat seemed to have retreated, its soft footfalls indicating its presence nearby. It was biding its time, waiting to ambush Nefari when either courage or hunger drove her from her hiding place.

Nefari had witnessed this tactic countless times during Abori hunts. When an animal was startled into its den, the hunters would patiently wait, knowing that eventually, the creature would emerge, believing the danger had passed. But Nefari refused to be so naive.

Suddenly, the cat became agitated once more, its movements erratic as it emitted warning hisses, mimicking the behavior of snakes—the most feared predators in the natural world. It was clear that something else had entered the clearing, posing a threat to both Nefari and the cat. Was it another person who had stumbled upon them, or perhaps something even more dangerous?

Listening intently to the commotion outside, Nefari hesitated, torn between the temptation to investigate and the fear of encountering a greater danger. Eventually, the tumult subsided, replaced by an eerie silence broken only by the occasional rustle of leaves. Should she risk venturing into the clearing? Uncertain and afraid, Nefari weighed her options carefully, acutely aware that her next move could determine her fate.

"Damn beast was the one I fought before we started moving. Look at the scars here and here. I made those," came a familiar voice, breaking through the tense silence. Nefari's heart soared at the sound of human voices, relief flooding her senses. There was more than one person, but most importantly, one of them was Cecrops.

"Show me where the body is, Nudgee. I'll take it back to camp," Cecrops's authoritative voice rang out, instilling a sense of hope within Nefari. They had come looking for her, and they were willing to retrieve her, even if she were dead. Such an honor was not bestowed upon just anyone.

"I'm in here!" she cried out, her voice trembling with emotion. "I'm in here!"

"She's alive!" exclaimed another voice, filled with relief and disbelief.

As the footsteps rushed towards the log, Nefari struggled to wriggle out, but found herself stuck. Cecrops swiftly hacked away at the log's opening, creating enough space for him to reach in and pull her out. With gentle yet firm hands, he extracted her from her cramped hiding place. Nefari, clad in tattered and dirt-streaked clothing, threw her arms around Cecrops's neck, tears streaming down her cheeks as she buried her face into his shoulder.

Easing his arm around the fragile girl, Cecrops lifted her up and began the journey back to camp. Passing by Nudgee, he nodded and bestowed a rare smile upon him—a gesture that Nudgee would remember for a lifetime. Falling in line behind Cecrops, Nudgee guided them back to the safety of the camp, grateful to have played a role in rescuing their lost companion.

The four days that followed passed in a dull haze for Nudgee. Despite his attempts to engage in conversation and find ways to pass the time, he found himself mostly walking like a mindless drone until they reached their nightly campsite. Once settled in, he would relax and consume the meager rations provided, all the while searching for a familiar pair of eyes—the eyes of a young Abori girl around his age. Her smile always brightened when their gazes met, giving Nudgee a glimmer of hope and courage to approach her. Yet, that courage always seemed to elude him, leaving him alone as he retired for the night.

Now, as he stood gazing at the ocean before him, Nudgee felt a sense of anticipation stir within him. Though there was still a half-day's walk ahead of them, the vast expanse of the ocean stretched out to the horizon, its surface shimmering in the golden light of the setting sun. Bright patches dotted the ocean, reflecting sunlight towards the shore. Nudgee strained to make out the objects, but the glare of the sunlight obscured his vision. Whatever they were, they appeared large and emitted a different kind of reflection than the ocean itself. The intense brightness made it difficult for Nudgee to look at them for too long, filling him with a sense of unease and apprehension. He couldn't help but wonder if these objects posed a threat, especially if they were to venture out onto the ocean in their small boats.

For now, Nudgee pushed aside his concerns about the mysterious objects in the ocean as they continued their march. With each step, time seemed to slow, the anticipation of reaching their destination thick in the air. As the scent of sea salt wafted through the breeze, a surprising turn of events unfolded: the girl Nudgee had been watching approached him and fell into step beside him.

"Why haven't you tried talking to me?" she asked directly, her straightforwardness catching Nudgee off guard. She was not one to beat around the bush, and Nudgee felt himself flushing with embarrassment.

"What do you mean?" he stammered, avoiding her gaze.

"You've been staring at me every night before you go to bed. I think I've waited long enough for you to come ask for my name," she replied matter-of-factly, her tone tinged with amusement.

"Sorry," Nudgee mumbled, feeling utterly flustered.

"Well?" she prompted expectantly.

"Well... what?" Nudgee asked, his mind racing as he struggled to keep up with the conversation.

"You still haven't asked my name," she pointed out, a playful smile gracing her lips.

"What... What is your name?" Nudgee finally managed, feeling a sense of relief wash over him as the girl smiled and winked at him in response.

"If you can get onto the ship that I'm on, I might just tell you," the Abori girl's enigmatic words left Nudgee even more bewildered, unsure of her intentions. Before he could respond, she darted off towards the front of the procession, leaving him standing there, perplexed.

"Women," remarked an Abori man nearby, towering over Nudgee with the weight of his years. "Don't try to make sense of what they do. If you do, you are doomed to fail. That one likes you."

"How do you know?" Nudgee inquired, still trying to make sense of the encounter.

"It's written all over her face and the way she moved. Trust me, I have many, many years of experience with the ways of women. I'm starting to grasp a little of what they think. Even if you don't read into all that, she openly invited you to join her on the journey into the new world," the old man explained sagely.

Nudgee mulled over the old man's words, slowly starting to see the situation from a different perspective. Thanking the man for his insight, Nudgee found himself walking on sand as he passed through the trees ahead. Stepping onto the beach, he was met with one of the most breathtaking sights he had ever beheld. The expansive stretch of sand seemed to glow with a pale yellow hue, each individual particle sparkling as sunlight danced upon it. Scooping up a handful of sand, Nudgee watched in awe as it slipped through his fingers, the semi-translucent grains mesmerizing in their beauty. Some of the sand clung to his hands, and he absently wiped them clean on his kangaroo loincloth, feeling a profound sense of wonder at the natural splendor surrounding him.

The ocean was a spectacle up close, with waves crashing onto hidden sandbars at regular intervals, their towering height rivaling Nudgee's own stature. He couldn't help but worry for the young girl, Nefari, who would surely struggle against such formidable waves if she ventured too close. Yet, the deep blue hue of the ocean was mesmerizing, its richness surpassing even the sky above, making it a sight more beautiful than any inland body of water.

Offshore, Nudgee spotted the large objects that had concerned him earlier. Giant ships were docked, accompanied by smaller crafts ready to ferry people out to them. These ships boasted multiple levels and were constructed from the same metallic substance used by the Uru for their weapons. It was this material that had reflected the sunlight so intensely. Each level of the ships appeared to have both indoor and outdoor areas, with Uru bustling about as they embarked and disembarked. Remarkably, the smaller boats moored on the sand seemed unaffected by the crashing waves, effortlessly gliding over any obstacle in their path as people boarded them.

Uru stood near the shoreline, guiding individuals to their designated vessels. Among them, Nudgee caught sight of the Abori girl, her eyes beckoning invitingly as she was directed towards one of the smaller boats. Determination welled within him as he made his way over to the Uru directing the flow of people.

"I want to get on the same ship as her," he declared, pointing towards the Abori girl.

"If you get on the same transfer boat, it will take you to the same ship," the Uru man explained. As Nudgee turned to leave, the man called him back, requesting his name.

"Before you go, let me know your name. They have assigned rooms for everyone. The next person to be stationed on that ship, I will direct to your room. I will also inform the proper people," the man added.

"My name is Nudgee. I am of the Jawjumeri tribe," Nudgee replied.

"Apologies, sir, but you will not be able to join the woman," the Uru man responded without hesitation.

"What do you mean I can't join her? You just told me that I could swap with someone who would be on her ship," Nudgee protested, feeling his frustration growing. "Why would someone request that I be on a specific ship? I'm nobody. Who would do that?"

"That would be me," a familiar voice interjected from behind. Nudgee turned to find himself face to face with Cecrops, the young Nefari clinging to his side.

"What's this about?" Nudgee demanded, his tone sharp with annoyance.

"I have a job for you, Nudgee. You may not like it, but

your skill is an asset I want to keep close. It will also be useful for the task I am assigning you. This is non-negotiable. You will accept it, or you will stay behind on the beach," Cecrops stated firmly, his gaze unwavering.

Nudgee's expression hardened as he processed Cecrops's words. "I know you wanted to spend your time relaxing on the ship with your lady friend, but that will not happen just yet. You will have chances to see her once we have reached our destination. Remember, these are Uru ships," Cecrops continued.

"Just tell me the job," Nudgee replied, resignation evident in his voice.

Cecrops smiled at the abruptness in Nudgee's voice. "Henceforth, you are to be the minder of Nefari, the young girl at my side," he announced, prompting a grumpy look from Nefari as she buried her face further into Cecrops. "She is not too pleased either by this outcome, but I will be busy for the voyage and cannot have her underfoot. She likes to run away, as you know, so use your dreaming to find her on these occasions and keep her out of trouble. Remember, she is important to me. Take her to the transfer boat waiting at the Northernmost point, and the Uru will direct you from there."

With that, Cecrops turned and walked away, leaving both Nudgee and Nefari alone on the beach. Nefari teared up, and after a couple of whimpers, she started to cry.

Nudgee felt a wave of uncertainty wash over him. He wasn't sure how to handle this situation. Should he try to comfort her with words? Offer her a hug? Or perhaps try to lighten the mood with humor? The weight of this sudden responsibility was daunting, and he wasn't sure if he was ready for it.

"Come on, Nefari," Nudgee said in a soft tone, kneeling down in front of her. "Let's get on the ship and get comfortable. You'll have all the time you want to be sad at that point." He reached out to her, but she shied away.

"Come on then," he continued, starting to walk. He glanced back only once to make sure she was following. The sad, little girl with nowhere else to go slowly trudged through the soft sand, dragging her feet the whole time. Nudgee felt sorry for her, realizing that regardless of how he felt, she was hurting more. He caught the eye of the Abori girl on her way out to the ship, but her smile diminished as she realized he was not joining her.

The northern transfer ship was ready and waiting when Nudgee and Nefari arrived. There were fewer people trying to get onto this boat, as it was reserved for the higher-ranked Uru. Nudgee frowned when Nefari defiantly sat at the front of the boat. He wasn't looking forward to this relationship.

Six more Uru boarded the craft, leaving the beach bare in the North. Nudgee looked around for some oars, thinking that he was going to have to row the boat out to the ship, but he couldn't find any. When the boat started to move seemingly on its own, he dove for the side railing and hung on for dear life. This only lasted a short while, and the Uru who were seated in the boat were all staring at him. Nudgee waved them away and looked over at Nefari. She was trying to hold back a smile and turned away when she saw him looking.

The boat itself was perfectly calm. Nudgee expected some motion to be felt from the ocean, like he felt when going through rough water in a canoe. This boat, however, glided over the waves and the ever-moving water as if it wasn't even touching it. He had to look over the edge to make sure they were going through the water. Peels of whitewash rolled off the front of the boat as it paved its way to the large ship ahead. Nudgee couldn't believe how big the ship was up close. Weird symbols on the side of the ship's bow intrigued Nudgee, but he couldn't work out their purpose. An Uru noticed he was looking at the name and smiled.

"The ship's name is Shangri-La. We write the names of our ships on each to determine which is which. See over there," the Uru man said, pointing at another ship. This one, Nudgee noted, had fewer symbols. "That one is named Eden. The ships nearby are Utopia, Zion, Elysium." The Uru was naming off all the different crafts like it was something special. Nudgee did take note that the Abori girl he was talking to was in Heaven. If the voyage went quickly enough, maybe he could pick up where they left off. It was something he could hold onto while the days trudged slowly by. Nudgee followed Nefari up the stairs but was stopped at the top by an Uru. Nefari didn't wander too far.

"From this time forward, we would like you to wear our clothing," an Uru man said. The faces were all starting to merge and look very similar, leading Nudgee to think maybe groups of Uru families inhabited each craft. It made sense to him that family would want to be close to each other. The man handed him some white clothing trimmed with silver.

"You want me to put this on here?" Nudgee asked, uncertain.

"Yes. We ask that you change clothes now, casting your old clothing into the ocean. This is the final thing holding you to your previous life, and it is a very uplifting event. That is what many have said before you." It wasn't embarrassment that stopped Nudgee. He wasn't quite sure that he was ready to cast everything away.

"You can return to your previous life if you still wish," the Uru said with a stern look. Hesitating a moment longer, Nudgee removed his loincloth and placed the well-sized Uru clothing on. It was soft to the touch and very comfortable. He walked to the edge of the ship. There were no railings anywhere in sight, so he kept a foot back from the side. Holding the roo skin loincloth that he had hunted, killed, and crafted himself, Nudgee said one final goodbye. Throwing the clothes far out into the ocean, Nudgee watched as it was engulfed by the waves.

Turning, Nudgee had a single tear in his eye, which Nefari couldn't help but feel for. He walked into the halls of the ship with Nefari trailing. Yet another similar Uru came to meet him.

"Were you all bred from the same mother?" Nudgee asked, not giving thought to how rude the question was.

"Sir, I surely do not know what it is you mean," the Uru replied politely. "I am here to show yourself and the young Nefari to your lodgings for this voyage. If you would follow me." He turned and started walking down the halls. The whole floor was made out of polished wood with a dark dot pattern material spread out across the top of the floor. This material he couldn't identify, but it provided grip and would be useful to prevent any sliding around when the decks were wet.

The walls were a continuation of the outer hull of the ship, a metal substance polished to a crisp reflection. Nudgee found it dizzying to see the endless forms of himself reflected back and forth as they walked alongside him. Even the roof reflected another Nudgee down upon him. Nefari must have been feeling it too, as she reached out and grabbed Nudgee for stability.

The Uru stopped outside a room after a long winding

walk and pointed to the symbol - 1123. "This is the number to your room. It is one, one, two, three. You will see signs at the start of each hall showing the numbers of the rooms that could be found down them. With careful observation, you will find only ten numbers that continually repeat the same pattern, building upon themselves. After a time, navigating the halls will become easier. Until you have become acquainted with them, we are more than happy to guide you back to your room. Areas you may not go to are the whole of the fourth floor. Do not go any lower than this deck either. Any hallway that has locked doors is locked for a reason, so stay out of those also. Anywhere else is allowed. You will find food and fresh water up the stairs at the end of this hall. If you need to know anything else, you can ask any Uru that walks by. Other than that, enjoy."

The Uru opened the door to a large furnished room, unlike anything Nudgee had ever seen before. Nefari ran in and jumped onto a bed close to the opposite wall. The wall itself was made of glass, much like the glass left by lightning storms in sandy areas, but this wall was one large piece and showed a view of the whole ocean. In the middle of the room was a table with two chairs, adorned with large platters of fruit, cheese, bread, and meat. The amount could feed a tribe, and Nudgee scoffed when he realized it was all for Nefari and himself. It was too much.

Thinking about it a little more, however, Nudgee realized that every room would have the same thing. He wondered where they got all the food from and how they had more stored for the trip. He walked over to where his bed was situated. Wide enough for two, it looked so soft. He sat at first, feeling himself sink slowly before he really laid back to get the full experience. To say it felt wonderful was a vicious understatement. Nudgee felt like he was laying on a bed of clouds. The white walls only enhanced this dreamlike sensation. It was a welcome change to the mirrored walls of the ship, and he was able to rest his eyes. He looked over at Nefari, who was sitting on her bed cross-legged, looking out the window at the ocean.

"Is the room to your liking?" Nudgee asked her. She looked around at him and made an effort to show she was looking forcefully away. Nudgee knew it was childish but didn't blame the girl. She'd been passed around from carer to carer all her life, it seemed, and he was just another one whose days were numbered. Soon she would be given to someone else. "It's fine if you don't want to talk, Nefari. When you're ready, I'll be waiting, ok? For now, I might rest a bit. Wake me if you need anything at all."

Nudgee couldn't fight it any longer. The bed was lulling him into sleep. A rest for his weary body that had walked halfway across the known country. Nudgee fell asleep instantly.

With a start, Nudgee woke to a dark room. It took a moment to realize where he was and what had occurred. Glancing over at Nefari's bed, he spied a small lump he assumed was her before he settled back to snooze a little. Nudgee decided that he would use the dreaming to visit the Abori girl. He didn't see it as spying, but he felt it was still borderline.

Closing his eyes and freeing his mind, it was so easy to fall into a trance while lying on this bed. Nudgee also found that he could escape the confines of his body much easier. Shifting into his spirit body, he took one last look at Nefari in her bed before he flew out of the Shangri-La. It didn't take him long to spot Heaven. He had to admit the Uru were onto something when they named their boats. It definitely made things so much easier. As he was drifting across, he noticed that the ships had started moving and the shore was already a fair distance away. It would've only been viewable with the advantage of height his flight gave. He couldn't pinpoint exactly when this had occurred as the ship didn't feel like it was moving at all. The moon hung in a darkening sky as reds and oranges faded from the Western horizon.

He slipped below the surface of the ship to the inner workings of Heaven. It was similar to the ship Nudgee was on, though the walls in the hallways were white and the floor was made of a dark material. He went looking for the Abori girl the same way he found Nefari. He started by thinking of her features and the way she smiled. Immediately, he started to get a tingle in his chest. The way was forward, so he drifted that way slowly, thinking about her constantly. The tingling sensation started to split into five or six separate little pockets with a larger one still at his chest. Curious about what this may be and wanting an explanation for future flights, Nudgee looked into the smaller tingles first.

After following three of them, he found that they always

led to random Uru. Nudgee knew they were the center as he would fly around them and the tingling would follow, pointing at the Uru without fail. Giving up on the smaller tingles, Nudgee headed towards the largest sensation he could find. The smaller sensations must be pointing to humans with a similar DNA strand, confusing the locator.

The room Nudgee found himself in was on the upper deck and was a vast, spacious area. There were tables and chairs all throughout, and Nudgee decided this was the mess hall for the Uru. It must be the same back on his ship, as this was about the same level that was off-limits. With no care for the Uru seated here, Nudgee followed the sensation through another wall past where the food was being served. He floated on by without giving it a second thought. Suddenly, the tingling ran to his back, causing him to pause in confusion before heading back the way he came. Again, it ran to his back.

Looking down slowly at the food with a horrible premonition, Nudgee immediately gagged. He couldn't physically throw up in his spirit form, but he dry heaved. Crudely carved up on the table was the Abori girl's body, along with what he could only say were two others. These had been slowly eaten away for a longer period of time. He realized all too suddenly that the smaller tingles were parts of the girl being digested. He looked around at the Uru in the room, and he was stunned. At the tables sat Uru men and women, along with the same reptilian beasts that Nudgee had witnessed on the exodus to the ships. Worse still, some of the Uru changed from human form to the very reptilian beast he saw scattered about the room. This started to become too much for him, and he willed himself to wake up, thinking it was all just a dream.

An Uru close by shivered as if something ran up his spine, and he looked directly at Nudgee. He smiled wickedly, his mouth becoming longer and full of hundreds of sharp, thin teeth. Nudgee fled for his body, following the golden chord and flying straight back to his room. Though he was traveling at speed, the bed took the force of his re-entry. When he could fully focus again, he emptied his stomach onto the bedroom floor and then tried to calm himself.

"Nefari!" he called, scared for the child's life. No answer came, and he called again. He sat listening, but there was still nothing. It was now in the twilight time of the night between day and the true night. He ran around the room, looking under the bed and in the closet. She wasn't anywhere. He remembered Cecrops' words about her exploring and, if need be, he should use the dreaming to find her. Nudgee lay back on the bed, and on the third attempt, he floated out of the room.

Nefari giggled as she watched out the large glass wall. She looked back at Nudgee to make sure he didn't hear her little slip-up. She didn't want him to think she liked it with him. She was just amused at how everything outside ran at twice the pace. Seagulls dived for fish and flew away as if they were shooting stars racing across the night sky. Clouds rushed by as if a massive storm front was blowing in, and she could almost see the sun coursing across the sky. It was the dolphins, though, that got her. Those joyful creatures jumping and flipping with unnatural speed made her forget where she was, and she let slip the giggle.

Nudgee, sprawled out on the bed, did not hear her. Nefari could see that he was not awake, but he was not asleep either. She walked over to him and waved a hand in front of his face. No reaction. Slowly, softly, she jabbed him with a finger. No reaction. Growing more confident, Nefari decided to shake him. Still, no reaction. Now she became worried and thought he may be dead, but she was relieved to see that he was breathing... No. Not relieved, she thought to herself. She definitely wouldn't be feeling relieved.

Knowing she would be safe on the ship, she decided that she would explore a little. She didn't know which way she should be going, so when she exited the room, she let her feet walk at random. She didn't like the mirrored walls of the hallway. The reflections scared her, and she picked up the pace towards a doorway at the end of the corridor. When she entered, she was surprised to find that it was a storeroom full of food.

"Are you lost, little one?" someone said behind her. She turned to see an Uru standing in the doorway, blocking her only exit. "Or hungry for that matter?"

"I... I wanted to get some fresh air," Nefari said, thinking on her feet. "I just don't know the way." The man moved closer to her, which made her feel ill at ease. He reached towards her, and she closed her eyes in fright.

"Here," he said. Nefari opened her eyes to see him holding out a peach for her. "They say that these are most sweet under the moonlight at sea. Go back two doors, and you will find that it opens onto the corridor leading straight to the deck."

'Thank you,' Nefari said, taking the peach and darting past him. She followed his directions to the deck and found that the sun was just starting to set. As she sat outside, she noticed that time was flowing at its usual pace again. With her legs dangling over the edge, she watched the sun slowly dip below the horizon. The land she had called home all her life was now a small dark outline against the sunset.

'Goodbye,' she said softly to the winds as they swept back to the land. Her message would be delivered without fail. She looked at the peach in her hand and realized just how hungry she was. Glancing at the sun again, she saw that the last of its rays were poking out. 'Go down,' Nefari commanded. She knew she wouldn't make it until nighttime to eat, but she was stubborn enough to wait for the sun to go down at least.

When she felt she was safe, she bit into the red and gold peach. The furry dry skin had a bitter taste to it, but the juicy flesh inside was at its most optimal sweetness. Juicy droplets of nectar ran down her chin, and she wiped them away with her arm. This peach was perfect in every way, and she remembered that there was a whole bowl full of fruit in the room. If everything was as good as this, she was going to be happy. If not, she could still sneak out to the food store.

She got up, ready to make her way back to the room and threw away the pit. Seeing her discard the food, a seagull sitting on an open door flew down for it and startled her, sending her two steps backward and off balance. With no side rails, this was enough to see her falling towards the ocean with a scream, and without anybody knowing where she was how was she going to escape the waters.

Nefari was horizontal to the ocean when she saw him burst onto the deck. The last thing she saw before her face was facing the water was him diving after her.

The pain she felt in her ankle was the most wonderful feeling in the world, knowing that Nudgee's hand was gripping her tightly. She looked up at him and saw the strain and exertion he was putting into saving her. His arm was over the deck with the rest of his body on the ship. He pulled her up quickly, and as she sat on the polished wood, tears started to well in her eyes. She threw her arms around him and cried, happy to be alive.

"There, there," Nudgee said to Nefari as he picked her up and started walking back to the room. He looked at the girl bundled up in his arms, and his heart sank. She was innocent to everything the Uru were, and she needed protection from them. Though she was half Uru, she was also of the Abori tribes and therefore kin. He knew what needed to be done. He would need to live for this little girl and do everything in his power to be there for her. This meant that he could not act on what he saw tonight. He could not let on that he knew about the sick and terrifying secret the Uru held. From now on, it was all about her. Nudgee got her back to the room and placed her in her bed. She wiped the tears from her face.

"Thank you..." Nefari said, realizing that she hadn't put his name to memory, if she had even heard it at all.

"My name is Nudgee," he told her, picking up on the hesitation. "I am of the Jawjumeri tribe. Would you like to know what my name means?"

Nefari nodded, now feeling intrigued by the introduction.

"It means Green Frog." When Nudgee said this, he puffed his cheeks and then made a ribbit noise. At first, Nefari didn't make any movement, but Nudgee saw her face start to crack. He made another ribbit, and Nefari burst out laughing, to which Nudgee joined in. They laughed until their cheeks were hurting and they were short of breath.

Each one was laughing to release a number of pressures and stress that had been holding them back or recently came to the surface. It was refreshing and made the situation they both found themselves in all the more easy to accept.

"Will you let me take care of you and keep you safe?" Nudgee asked Nefari when they finally calmed down. Nefari looked at him with a sincere and honest smile, nodding her head in acceptance of Nudgee as her protector.

"I may not have any experience with looking after younger children, but I will do everything I can to protect you. I will need your help though. We can find our way together," Nudgee added.

"I would like that," she told him. Nudgee pulled her into a tight hug. This action being more for himself, as tears started to roll down his face.

Chapter 3

As the transfer ship glided into the shallows and beached itself on the island, the young Uru felt a surge of pride. His worth had finally been recognized, chosen by his father, Glycon, for an important task. Their mission was crucial for the longevity of the Uru race.

For eighty years, he had listened to his father, waiting for the opportunity to prove himself. Despite his efforts to assert himself, he had often been dismissed and told to cease his actions. But now, his moment had arrived, and he was determined to succeed.

Their goal was clear: to ascend the nearby volcano and drill into its side, tapping into its core to harness its power and provide energy for their entire race. It was a daunting task, but the young Uru was ready to face the challenge head-on.

Being back on dry land felt like a relief for Atlantis. He'd grown restless on the ship, feeling the confinement of the cabins and the monotony of the journey. Despite the time dampeners helping to accelerate the passage of time, it wasn't enough to alleviate his boredom. Perhaps his father had sensed his restlessness and entrusted him with this important task. However, Atlantis knew that the significance of the mission meant it couldn't be assigned to just anyone.

"Hey Atlantis, where do you want the gear?" one of the other Uru asked him. Atlantis looked at their faces—stern, strong, and strikingly similar. Only the higher-ranked Uru were allowed to use different styles of faces; those in lower ranks could only have slight variations of a basic face. The men before him were Cellen, Merbis, and Zell—lifetime friends and trusted comrades. No matter the trouble, these three were always there for him. That's why Atlantis chose them to accompany him on this job. He knew that together they would get it completed.

"Leave it all in the boat, Cellen," Atlantis replied. "We'll attach the wheels and take it all to the dig site that way."

"That's good," Merbis said. "I thought we were going to have to wait for the Vimana airships to pick them up and take them to site."

"No. They're still two days from being functional. The time when they weren't in use took its toll on the operation of the machines. We have some mechanics fixing them up now, but they've forgotten some of the old ways. They're refreshing themselves first. Not to mention that our best scientists were slaughtered at Ul Uru."

"Three hundred years with little practice will do that to you," Zell said. "We were on that continent for too long."

"You're right, Zell," Atlantis said. "It's great to be back to what we do best."

They finished attaching the wheels, and Atlantis started leading them along a set course to the side of the volcano. It was a rough climb over the sharp rocks and slippery terrain. The path they walked was along the side of the volcano that dropped straight to the ocean. When they were halfway up the side, Atlantis decided it was the right time to turn inland and walk around. This was far easier, and he was enjoying the heat he could feel through the earth. He found an old lava flow down the side of the hill. Looking for a natural split, he found the perfect area to dig into and create the base of operations. There was a raised area that any lava coming down the mountainside would naturally divert away.

"Boys, I think we've found the site for our dig," Atlantis told the others.

"About time too," Zell told him.

They started to unpack the equipment and set it up in front of the site. There were three very different machines that they unpacked from the boat. One was a large box on wheels. At the front side was a conical piece that spun extremely fast and would break up rocks while sending excess dirt behind it. The next was another box on wheels, though instead of having a conical piece on the front, this one had a scoop. Its role was to pick up all the excess dirt and place it into the final machine, a large basket on wheels. There were five of these last machines, and their job was to run backward and forward to a dump site. Atlantis decided that the dump site would be off the side of the cliff to prevent a build-up of large piles of dirt and rock. The boys took a little over three hours to set them all up.

"Let's have a meal before we start, little bastards," Merbis said. "I don't want them buzzing around and getting in the way while I'm trying to eat."

"I'll second that," Cellen said. "They don't know boundaries."

"We could always start them and move away a bit," Zell told the others. "They need about three days to finish the dig, and it's better to start them earlier rather than later."

"Let them have their food, Zell," Atlantis said, throwing everyone a cloth-wrapped meal. "We're far ahead of schedule. The job wasn't going to move ahead until the Vimana were ready. I talked them into the boat idea." Atlantis unwrapped a portion of meat from the night befores meal. Soon they would have to go back to different meats. Though filling, they didn't taste anywhere near as good or give him the energy of human meat. He ate slowly, savoring the juicy portions and delighting in the taste.

When he finished eating, he lay back, looking at the sky. He didn't expect to see something looking back down at him. A large humanoid figure stood naked above the dig site on top of the rise. He sat up, and with a clearer perspective, realized a giant stood above them.

"Giants! Watch above!" he yelled. The others got to their feet, producing spears and swords. "Give me cover while I get these machines running."

The giant jumped down from the rise and landed, shaking the land. Small pebbles and loose gravel rolled further down the mountainside as Merbis, Cellen, and Zell ran in, distracting it with their weapons. Atlantis jumped from machine to machine, plunging the quartz crystal ring he wore into a hole of the same shape on each. As he did so, the machines sprang to life and started operating as designed. When he got to the basket-type machines, he heard a cry from Cellen. Merbis had thrust his spear at the giant, who grabbed it and dragged him forward. With the other powerful arm, the giant reached down and grabbed Merbis by the head, imploding it with tremendous force. Blood and brain shot out of the cracks between the giant's fingers and sloshed to the ground. Cellen ran in, slashing a sword across the hand, and the giant used Merbis to swing at Cellen. He was able to roll out of the way but tripped as he fell over the digger. The giant was on him instantly, tearing limb from limb in a bloody massacre. Atlantis just got the third tipper operational when another giant jumped into the fray right next to him. He rolled away, twisting his ankle.

'Zell we have to go now!' he yelled at the only friend left alive before starting at a sprint down the mountainside. He felt the pain from his ankle every time his right foot came down but to stop was certain death. Zell caught up to him quickly and spurred him on to run faster. Part way down he looked over his shoulder and his heart sank as he saw that one of the giants was still giving chase. He knew that he wasn't going to be able to last much longer before he slowed down or took a tumble. He decided he would rather make a stand and fight than let the giant take him as he ran. He pulled the ring from his finger.

'Zell,' he called out, panting heavily as he slowed his pace. His friend looked back as Atlantis threw the quartz ring to him. Atlantis gritted his teeth, feeling the pain throbbing in his ankle, but his resolve remained firm. 'Get that to my father,' he said, his voice urgent. 'I can't run on this foot anymore.'

Zell's eyes widened with understanding as he caught the ring, his expression reflecting the gravity of the situation. He nodded solemnly, clutching the ring tightly before turning and sprinting down the mountainside.

Alone now, Atlantis turned to face the oncoming giant, his heart pounding with fear and adrenaline. As the giant drew closer, Atlantis gripped his sword tightly, ready to give the brute hell.

Zell looked back only once to see a giant with Atlantis's sword stuck in its side pulling the head from his friend's body. The second giant had also joined the chase. Zell ran all the more harder not wanting to let his friend down. He got to the shoreline just in time as the giants had started to close in. He dove into the water as they were a mere twenty feet behind but they didn't follow further. He was safe in the water and slowly swam back to the ships anchored offshore.

Glycon's heart sank as he gazed at the quartz ring lying on the table before him. The weight of grief settled heavily upon him, his mind reeling with the news of Atlantis's death. Zell's silent gesture spoke volumes, conveying the tragic fate that had befallen his son.

For a long moment, the senior Uru remained silent, their expressions reflecting a mixture of sorrow and reverence. Finally, Glycon spoke, his voice strained with emotion. "Why have you presented me this ring?" he asked, the words heavy with disbelief and anguish already knowing the answer to come.

'Your son, Atlantis, returns this to you,' Zell said as the silence deepened.

"And Atlantis's whereabouts?" Glycon asked, his voice

barely above a whisper.

"Your son, along with Cellen and Merbis, are with our ancestors now," Zell replied solemnly.

"How could this happen?" Glycon's voice trembled with a mixture of sorrow and disbelief, his heart heavy with the weight of loss and unanswered questions.

"We had just completed construction of the machines at the dig site when we were attacked by a giant," Zell recounted.

"So they are here as well," Cecrops remarked, his tone grave.

"We knew they were in a number of places. This is as likely as any," Brellin added. "How did you escape, boy?"

Zell relayed the whole story about the fight against the giant and Atlantis's efforts. He told them of the second giant attacking and the orders to flee. Then came the last stand of Atlantis and his wish to get the ring back to Glycon. "If it wasn't for Atlantis, we would all be dead on the mountainside and the machines would all still be inactive. Because of him, work is now underway, and I got the key back with my life still intact."

"But do we still use this site, is the real question," Brellin said. "The giants are going to hinder our efforts at every step." Brellin's question hung heavily in the air, casting doubt on the feasibility of continuing at the current site.

Zell's response was one of disbelief and righteous indignation, his emotions raw from the loss of his friends and Atlantis. "Are we just going to give up after such a sacrifice?" he challenged, his voice filled with pain and frustration.

"You may go, Zell," Glycon's dismissal was firm, cutting off Zell's protests.

"But..."

"Your part in this conversation has ended. Leave," Cecrops told him.

Zell got up and walked out of the room with a dark look on his face.

"We have no other choice than to use this site," Glycon asserted, highlighting the pressing need for Mercury fuel and the uncertainty of encountering giants elsewhere. "The machines are already working, and soon we shall have a base to mine the mercury from the volcano core. We only need to fortify the room."

"We can do that with a barrier field," Cecrops said. "I'll set aside one of mine to protect the mine. I'll change the settings so that it will protect the complete inner workings of the mine and only allow Vimana crafts and inorganic material through. The first load of Mercury will keep the field operational for at least a hundred years. We'll be set at that point."

"Now the only question is how do we get more of our people in and set up the barrier field without the giants knowing," Glycon said.

"I may have an answer for that as well," Cecrops offered. "The dreaming ability of the Abori people could be utilized to locate the giants and consequently avoid them."

"None of the elders embarked on the ships. We lack someone who could perform such a task," Brellin lamented.

"You're correct that no elder joined the voyage. They were too deeply tied to the land they inhabited. However, one Abori with the gift did indeed board the ship. He is currently in the process of mastering the art, having only demonstrated it once prior to our departure. He showcased his ability during Nefari's exploration," Cecrops explained.

"He trespassed into the halls of Heaven," Glycon remarked, his expression clouded with concern. "He knows of our concealment. Has his demeanor changed at all?"

"No," Cecrops assured him. "If anything, he has become even more attentive to Nefari."

"Perhaps you should reconsider your attachment to that girl. She seems to attract trouble wherever she goes. We have plenty of other potential candidates who could provide us with a steady supply of food. Where is the dreamer now?" Brellin asked anxiously. "I hope he hasn't become dinner himself."

"He is currently serving as Nefari's guardian on this very ship. You know well enough that his role affords him sanctuary," Cecrops reassured him. "I'll summon him at once." Cecrops called out to Torven, who was standing just outside the room, instructing him to fetch Nudgee and bring him here immediately.

"As for who will lead our expedition at the dig site?" Glycon inquired.

"Zell would be the most suitable candidate," Cecrops replied. Brellin's reaction was immediate as he spat in disgust at the suggestion.

54

"Zell? An underclassman to lead such a crucial expedition? I would argue that Cygon or even Lavitz would be more suitable candidates," Brellin protested.

"Yes, if you want either of your two sons to join our ancestors, they would indeed be suitable choices. However, Zell has already familiarized himself with the terrain and can navigate back to the dig site. His actions in the recent conflict also speak volumes," Cecrops countered.

"All he did was flee," Brellin retorted angrily.

"No, he did what was necessary to ensure the success of our operation. He made difficult decisions, even at the cost of his companions, all for the sake of the Uru. I nominate Zell as the leader of our expedition," Cecrops asserted.

"I'll support that decision," Glycon interjected. Brellin seemed poised to continue arguing when Torven entered the room, leading Nudgee inside. Nefari accompanied them, ensuring she wasn't left alone.

"You called for me?" Nudgee spoke cautiously, his wariness of the Uru high. He knew that one of them had seen him even in his spirit form. If word spread to the Uru leaders, it could lead to trouble.

"Nudgee, Nefari, please take a seat," Cecrops instructed. "There's no need to be so tense. It doesn't suit you. With me are Glycon and Brellin, Uru leadership. Do you understand why we've asked you here today?" Nudgee sensed a hidden agenda behind the question but simply shook his head.

"Cecrops has informed us of your skill in matters of the Dreamtime, your ability to navigate the dreaming," Glycon explained. Hearing this, Nudgee felt a wave of relief wash over him.

"Yes, what he says is true. I was indeed in the process of learning it before our departure, and I've honed my skills through practice," Nudgee confirmed.

"That's encouraging to hear. Would you be willing to assist us with a small task using your abilities?" Glycon inquired.

"What do you need me to do?" Nudgee glanced at Nefari, assessing her demeanor in the meeting. She seemed engrossed in her interaction with Cecrops, so he felt comfortable leaving her to her own devices for the time being. She could likely keep herself occupied for hours with Cecrops.

"A group of our people recently journeyed to a nearby

volcano to extract fuel for the ships. They encountered some trouble in the form of giants. Only one returned alive, bearing the tale and the key for the excavators. While more men will soon be continuing their work independently, we need to ascertain the location of these giants," Glycon explained the situation.

"So, you need me to gather information about the situation at the dig site," Nudgee clarified, ensuring he understood their expectations.

"Yes, exactly. We need details about the proximity of the giants to the dig site, the location of their dwelling compared to the site, and an estimate of their numbers. We'll need ongoing updates from you as well. Additionally, you'll play a crucial role in ensuring the safety of our people when they return to the dig site," Glycon explained.

"Keep them safe?" Nudgee questioned, seeking further clarification.

"You'll accompany them to alert them of any immediate threats and ensure their safety until they establish the barrier field. Once that's done, you'll return to the ship," Glycon reiterated.

"But what about Nefari?" Nudgee expressed concern. He hesitated to leave her alone. "I can't just leave her."

"Don't worry about Nefari. This task is of the utmost importance. I'll take care of her until you return," Cecrops reassured Nudgee. Nefari's face brightened at the prospect, and she couldn't contain her smile. "Are you alright with this, Nefari?" Cecrops asked her, and she nodded eagerly.

"With all due respect, I'd rather remain on the ship," Nudgee persisted. He knew he was treading a dangerous path with these creatures.

"If you are unable to fulfill the duties we assign to you, we will deem you incapable of performing any task entrusted to you," Cecrops declared firmly, his gaze fixed on Nudgee like a predator stalking its prey. "At that juncture, we will grant you passage to Heaven. You can reunite with your lady friend. Share in her experience. Shall I proceed with the arrangements?" Nudgee's eyes widened in shock. They were aware of his roaming in the Dreamtime. Now they were using it as leverage, threatening him. He glanced over at Nefari, his complexion noticeably draining of color.

"No..." he murmured weakly.

"What's that?" Glycon inquired, sensing a shift in

Nudgee's demeanor. Nudgee took a moment to regain his composure before responding.

"There's no need to make any arrangements. I will undertake the task as needed and resume caring for Nefari once it's finished. There will be ample time to join her when my usefulness has waned," Nudgee replied with determination.

"Well said. Now, if you could gather the requested information," Glycon acknowledged, pleased with Nudgee's resolve.

Nudgee rose from his seat and walked over to the wall, settling himself comfortably as he leaned back against it. He allowed the emptiness to envelop him, a sensation he had grown accustomed to over time. Despite the subtle pressure from the senior Uru, the transition into the fluidity of the spirit came more effortlessly now. He drifted around the room, his form ethereal and weightless. Cecrops glanced up at him, acknowledging his departure into the Dreamtime with a knowing gaze.

"The island isn't too far from here. Once you leave the ship, you'll see it," Cecrops's voice echoed in Nudgee's mind, though it seemed he couldn't hear Nudgee's responses. Undeterred, Nudgee passed through the floors of Shangri-La, observing his surroundings with a sense of detachment. The ocean stretched out before him, its beauty captivating. Today, it was serene, a deep, rich blue that shimmered under the sunlight like a myriad of fairy lights. A gentle breeze caressed his form, tempering the warmth of the region. Slowly rotating in the air, Nudgee located the island with the imposing volcano at its edge. Though not large in size compared to his homeland, it seemed spacious enough for a tribe to call home and live comfortably.

Nudgee soared towards the island, maintaining a height to survey the land below. His keen eyes scanned for any signs indicating a potential dig site. Suddenly, a glint of light caught his attention on the side of the mountain, halfway up. It resembled the reflection he had observed out at sea during the exodus, signaling something metallic. Nudgee instinctively knew this was the location he sought. Drawing nearer, he confirmed his suspicions as he observed machines buzzing around and drilling into the earth, a clear indication of excavation activity. Despite the absence of giants, scattered limbs littered the area, evidence of a recent confrontation. Further exploration revealed a trail of blood leading away from the site, prompting Nudgee to follow it from a safe distance. After a brief walk, the trail led to a crude, unnatural cave entrance burrowed into the earth.

Despite his hesitance, Nudgee pressed on, understanding that this was his purpose. As he floated into the cave, he noticed that the darkness didn't affect his vision, free from the limitations of mortal flesh. Gliding along the rocky pathway, he emerged into a spacious chamber, both tall and wide. Within, four giants lay asleep, surrounded by scraps of flesh and bone. Nudgee surmised that this cave was likely the entirety of the giants' domain, as it could hardly accommodate more of their massive kind.

After thoroughly scouting the area, Nudgee spent almost an hour flying around rocks and exploring smaller caves. Just as he was about to return, he spotted another giant, almost hidden in a small crevice, watching the ships. Nudgee realized that this sentry would alert the other giants if more Uru approached the island. With a sense of urgency, Nudgee hastened back to inform the Uru of his discovery. Upon re-entering his body, he found the experience much gentler and more pleasant than before. Rising, he returned to the table where the others awaited him.

"What did you uncover?" Glycon inquired, the anticipation evident in their expressions.

"I located the dig site. There are several small machines moving around, excavating the earth. I'm not familiar with the technical terms for them," Nudgee explained. "The giants weren't present at the dig site, but they're nearby in a cave. Four of them are currently sleeping there after... after they disposed of the Uru bodies," he added cautiously.

"Speak easy with us," Cecrops urged. "We're aware of their actions regarding the dead." Nudgee nodded in understanding.

"I scouted around the mountain to see if there were more giants residing there, but I only found the initial cave. However, there's one more giant serving as a lookout, watching the ships," he continued.

"That guard will make it more difficult for us to approach undetected," Brellin remarked with concern.

"We'll have the Vimana operational by the time we're ready to move on the site," Cecrops reassured him. "The excavators will require at least three days to prepare the area for our team. We'll need just twenty minutes to establish the barrier field. If we accomplish this, victory is within our grasp."

"Nudgee will keep us informed of the giants' movements upon our arrival. We won't be caught off guard like last time. If we need to make a second attempt to achieve our goal, so be it," Glycon asserted. "Nudgee, when we require your assistance again, we will summon you. Tell Torven outside to bring Zell back to us. You're dismissed."

Nudgee rose from his seat and extended his hand to Nefari, who was seated on Cecrops's lap. Reluctantly, she hugged Cecrops before joining Nudgee at the doorway. However, Brellin intercepted them before they could leave.

"Nudgee, you've witnessed things lately that would terrify most people or provoke anger toward the Uru. Why haven't you acted?" Brellin inquired, his gaze penetrating.

Nudgee met his gaze solemnly, then glanced down at the young girl holding his hand. "She needs me now more than any of my more selfish feelings," he replied to the Senior Uru. "But know this: the anger is there, locked inside me. It will never dissipate. You've deceived and manipulated the Abori people for far too long. I will teach her all the ways of my people. She will carry forth the spirit of the Abori. That is my revenge."

The three Uru exchanged knowing smiles as Nudgee spoke his piece.

"Only time will reveal the outcome of your feeble attempts to outmaneuver us," Nudgee nodded resolutely and walked out the door with Nefari, who was puzzled by the exchange but followed him nonetheless.

Nudgee hovered above the island in his spiritual form, vigilant for any signs of movement. The journey to the dig site was swift aboard the Vimana, yet it filled him with an uneasy dread. As they approached the slender machines, barely longer than two people laying, Nudgee's apprehension grew. The Uru positioned themselves on the Vimana, gripping the handles tightly as they ascended. The first two Vimana lifted into the air with three Uru aboard each, while Zell beckoned urgently for Nudgee to hasten. Seated beside Zell, Nudgee clung tightly as the Vimana surged forward at an alarming velocity, surpassing any speed he had ever known, even in his dreams. The rapid motion churned his stomach, and he struggled to keep down his morning meal as they turned towards their destination.

Upon landing outside the fully excavated cave, Nudgee hastily disembarked, retching on the mountainside. The other Uru, already engaged in constructing the barrier field, mocked his discomfort. "Poor Abori couldn't handle the brief flight across the ocean," one jeered, eliciting laughter from the rest. Zell approached, offering a comforting pat on the back. "You'd best take your position at the cave's edge and commence your lookout duties. If the enemy catches us off guard again, our chances of survival are slim."

Nudgee nodded, making his way to the cave entrance to begin his vigil. The transition to the dreaming state was effortless now, and he swiftly projected his spirit to a vantage point overlooking both the cavern's gaping mouth and the lookout. The sentinel remained stationed, and Nudgee clung to the hope that their approach had gone unnoticed. Ten minutes passed before the giant stirred, rising laboriously to its feet and lumbering down the hillside towards the cave entrance. Nudgee's nerves were on edge; he longed to return to Zell with his observations, yet mere knowledge of their presence wasn't enough. He needed precise details—when they would strike, and the number of giants emerging from the cavern.

Five agonizing minutes passed, each second weighed down by the unbearable tension. Finally, the lookout giant emerged from the cave, triggering Nudgee's heightened alertness. The moment of confrontation had arrived. Four more giants followed suit, though one paused to observe the others before retracing its steps back into the cavern. With urgency, Nudgee swiftly returned to his physical body.

"They're coming!" he urgently exclaimed to the Uru, his heart racing. A curse escaped the lips of the Uru who had mocked him earlier.

"How many?" Zell inquired, his voice tense with anticipation.

"Four," Nudgee responded.

"And how long until they reach us?" Zell pressed.

"Three, maybe four minutes. They're not moving swiftly," Nudgee reported.

"Three minutes. I want this device operational," Zell

commanded, his tone brooking no delay. "We cannot afford to return to this place again."

"It'll be tight," came the reply from the other Uru, their movements quickening as they worked to assemble the device. With rapid precision, they interconnected the pieces, culminating in a completed structure. A button was pressed, initiating a low whirring noise from within as the motor sprang to life. The four Uru hoisted the device and advanced towards the cavern's darkness.

Suddenly, a giant descended from above, crashing onto the back of one of the Uru and sending them sprawling. Nudgee watched in horror as the Uru, ensnared in the giant's colossal grip, were mercilessly thrashed against the unforgiving mountainside. Zell shook Nudgee back to awareness, snapping him out of his horrified stupor.

"We need to get the device inside! More are coming," he urged. "Grab a side." Nudgee's gaze darted back to the giant assaulting the Uru. "Grab a side or face death!" Zell's command propelled Nudgee towards the machine. Together, they lifted it, and Nudgee was surprised by its weight. They began to move, Nudgee propelled by adrenaline coursing through his veins. As they approached the cave mouth, Nudgee spotted three other giants looming above. They leaped down, landing just behind him, spurring him to quicken his pace.

As they plunged into the darkness of the cave, a brilliant blue light emanated from the device, enveloping the entire room and sealing off the entrance. The giants were mere moments behind. Nudgee observed the room bathed in the soothing glow, providing ample visibility.

"Talk about cutting it close," remarked another surviving Uru besides Zell. "I didn't think the Barrier field would activate in time."

"They made significant upgrades back on Eden," Zell informed him. "The device's efficiency was boosted tenfold."

"Remind me to express our gratitude next century when we're replaced," the Uru quipped.

Nudgee trembled as he stood within the cave, the shock of the harrowing experience weighing heavily on him. The presence of the giants outside, futilely pounding against the otherworldly barrier, intensified his sense of confinement. He realized he was now trapped, abandoned by the departing ships. Was this to be his final fate? He glanced back at the Uru beside him. At least they would share a final meal together.

Suddenly, the digger careened through the cave mouth, unaffected by the barrier field. It collided with Nudgee's leg, sending him sprawling.

"Watch out for the little things," Zell cautioned. "They don't care if you're in the way or not."

"What am I going to do?" Nudgee's voice trembled softly.

"What did you say?" Zell inquired, straining to hear.

"What am I going to do?" Nudgee repeated, louder this time, his distress palpable. Overwhelmed by the ordeal, he looked to Zell for guidance.

Zell approached, sensing Nudgee's turmoil, and placed a reassuring hand on his shoulder. "You've made it through the toughest part, Nudgee," he reassured. "You still have over a day before the ships depart, and the giants will likely move on within the hour. Once they're gone, you can return to the coast, where a transfer boat will pick you up."

Nudgee remained unconvinced, his apprehension lingering. "Relax," Zell advised gently. "Take some time to center yourself, and then approach the situation with a clear mind."

With that, the Uru departed, leaving Nudgee to wrestle with his solitude. Alone in the cavern, the distance from his family felt insurmountable, leaving him adrift in a sea of uncertainty. The only solace came from the rhythmic buzzing of the machines as they tirelessly continued their work, burrowing into the heart of the volcano. Observing their relentless efficiency, Nudgee found a strange comfort, realizing how insignificant his worries seemed in comparison.

As the hour passed, the giants grew weary of their futile efforts to breach the barrier and began to retreat. Hope flickered within Nudgee once more as he dared to believe in his escape. Though the thought of leaving the safety of the cave still filled him with dread, it marked a glimmer of progress. He resolved to wait a while longer before attempting to venture out.

However, after just fifteen minutes, the Uru began to gather around him, their intentions unclear.

"See, what did I tell you?" Zell remarked triumphantly. "The giants have cleared out, and you'll be able to return to the ships."

"I want to wait a bit longer before I make the attempt," Nudgee replied cautiously.

"Why?" a second Uru challenged. "Are you scared?" He advanced toward Nudgee, who rose to his feet, backing away until he reached the barrier field, which halted his retreat. The Uru closed in, their proximity unsettling Nudgee.

"I just want to ensure it's safe before I leave," Nudgee explained, his voice tinged with unease.

"Leave him alone, Seb," Zell interjected, stepping between them.

"I think our little friend here needs to depart," Seb retorted, his gaze fixed on Nudgee.

"And what will you do? Eat me?" Nudgee retorted, growing irritated with Seb's aggression.

"Well, since you're offering," Seb replied, his features morphing into a reptilian form. Nudgee recoiled at the sight and the putrid odor emanating from Seb's breath. As Seb lunged towards him, Nudgee stumbled backward, only to realize too late that the barrier field had momentarily lowered. He attempted to regain his footing, but the barrier swiftly reactivated, trapping him outside.

Seb reverted to his human guise, laughing at Nudgee's predicament. Nudgee scrambled to his feet, disoriented, and scanned his surroundings. As he made his way towards the tree line below the cave, a towering giant loomed before him. Cursing under his breath, Nudgee broke into a sprint, the giant in relentless pursuit. He maneuvered across the volcano's terrain, first descending at a slight angle before abruptly changing direction to plummet straight down. His legs burned with exertion, sweat stinging his eyes as he pressed onward. He dared not glance back, yet he felt the giant's presence drawing nearer with every thunderous footfall, each seismic tremor amplifying his sense of impending doom.

Up ahead, Nudgee spotted a natural barricade—a small cluster of trees near the cliff side. It wouldn't halt the giant's advance, but it could buy him crucial moments, perhaps the difference between life and death. Could he reach it? That was the pressing question. He had no choice but to try, he realized, so he aimed for a tree positioned near the outer edge, where the trunk began to fork just above the waist. If he timed his jump correctly, he could sail through with minimal speed loss.

The trees rushed towards Nudgee, the terrain unforgiving beneath his feet. His jump was awkward, and at the last moment, he opted to go feet first. Soaring through the air, a surge of hope flooded him as he cleared the obstacle and landed on the other side, elated. However, his triumph was short-lived as a jolt of agony shot through his left arm, bringing him to an abrupt halt. Unbeknownst to him, his left hand had become trapped in the lower fork of the tree.

Before he could comprehend his predicament, the giant descended upon him, indifferent to his plight. Nudgee watched in horror as its gaping maw loomed closer, its teeth resembling his own—blunt and devoid of sharp edges. Saliva dripped from its mouth as it encircled his wrist. There was no pain as he was freed from the restraint, only a profound emptiness as he witnessed the blood gush forth from the void where his hand once resided.

Staggering to the side, Nudgee teetered on the edge of the cliff before plummeting into the churning ocean below. The impact forced the air from his lungs, but the relentless waves carried him further from shore. As he felt his body growing cold and consciousness slipping away, the water around him turned crimson with his own blood. In the haze of fading awareness, something shimmered across his vision before darkness claimed him.

The room swayed as Nudgee slowly regained consciousness. He felt groggy and disoriented, unsure of his surroundings. Numerous beds filled the room, which was otherwise plain with white walls extending to the ceiling. The only splash of color was a clear bag of red liquid hanging above him, its contents unmistakably blood. A tube connected the bag to his arm, delivering the vital fluid into his veins. As memories flooded back, he glanced at his left hand, only to find it missing, replaced by bloody bandages. Despair gripped him at the loss.

At the far end of the room, a door creaked open, and Cecrops and Nefari entered, making their way to his side. Nefari's eyes were red from crying, and she clutched his right hand tightly. Her distress touched Nudgee more deeply than his own predicament.

"You were fortunate, Nudgee," Cecrops spoke, his voice tinged with relief. "Any deviation and we might have lost you. Nefari has been beside herself with worry these past three days."

"Three days?" Nudgee echoed, struggling to comprehend.

"Yes, you've been unconscious for three days. If not for the timely intervention of the transport boat departing dropping another Uru on shore, the swift action to stop your bleeding, and Nefari's and the Abori's closely matched blood, you wouldn't have lasted ten minutes. Nefari's blood is coursing through your veins now."

Nudgee was surprised by her unexpected role in saving him. Nefari looked up at him, her concern evident, and Nudgee was moved by her care.

"I can see you won't be able to care for Nefari properly with that injury," Cecrops interjected, breaking the somber mood. "We'll need to find someone else to take care of her now."

"No!" Nefari protested. "I don't want anyone else. Nudgee takes excellent care of me."

"He's injured, Nefari. Missing a hand. He won't be as capable as before, and he might need care himself," Cecrops explained gently.

"I won't be a burden, Cecrops," Nudgee assured the Senior Uru. He understood the gravity of the situation. "I'll manage."

"I'll help him," Nefari declared. "We'll take care of each other."

Cecrops hesitated, expressing his concern. "You have a habit of running off and causing trouble. Nudgee won't always be able to save you, especially if you fall off the deck."

"I'll be good, I promise. Just let Nudgee stay with me," Nefari pleaded, her eyes wide with sincerity.

"Alright then, he can stay," Cecrops relented, with a condition. "But only if you promise to behave."

"I swear I will," Nefari agreed happily, turning to Nudgee. Her victorious smile brightened his day, but Cecrops's smile held a different meaning behind the surface. It wasn't about Nudgee's capability; it was about Nefari settling down and acting safer. What was Cecrops's motive? How could she consistently feed the Uru when their sustenance was humans?

"Tell me about the caves," Cecrops inquired, his tone all business. "Were they successful?"

"Only just," Nudgee responded weakly. "We raised the

barrier just in time as the giants closed in on the cave entrance. They were mere meters away. I waited until they had moved on, but one lingered in the trees, and that's where I lost this," he said, attempting to gesture with his missing left arm, the phantom sensation still present.

"Good, now the fleet can proceed," Cecrops stated before departing. Nefari chose to remain with Nudgee.

"I'm relieved you're safe," she said, pressing a kiss to his cheek.

"As am I, Nefari," Nudgee replied, mustering a weak but loving smile.

Over the following fortnight, Nudgee found himself in a horrible state. A fever raged through his body, alternating between scorching heat that necessitated chilling baths and icy chills that defied blankets' warmth. His nights were haunted by visions of the reptilian overseers of the vessel and the towering figures who had robbed him of his freedom, waking him with anguished cries. Only Nefari stood by him, offering solace and care as he endured this harrowing ordeal. Sometimes, he would instinctively reach out to touch her hair, only to be reminded of his missing limb, deepening his sorrow.

Amidst his darkest moments, Nudgee sought refuge in the realm of spirits. Here, he was whole again, his hands restored, and pain and fever banished. In this ethereal sanctuary, he reveled in the freedom of flight and boundless exploration. Once, he soared back to his homeland, yearning to behold its familiar landscapes. As he came upon the shores from which their voyage began, a surge of elation coursed through him. And his joy knew no bounds when he beheld Towrang, suspended in the heavens before him.

"Towrang, it is good to lay eyes upon you once more," Nudgee greeted the elder warmly. "My heart aches for the familiarity of our homeland amidst these turbulent seas."

"I see you've honed your skills in the dreaming," Towrang observed. "How fare your ventures? Do they align with your aspirations?"

"Regrettably, no," Nudgee confessed with a heavy heart. "Since embarking, my journey has spiraled from hardship to despair. I rue the day I left your side."

"Speak your worries, for unburdening your soul may grant solace," Towrang urged gently. Nudgee poured out his troubles, recounting the sinister truth about the Uru, the plight of their people aboard the vessels, the menacing giants, and the loss of his hand.

"The sole silver lining in this bleak voyage is Nefari," Nudgee confessed, his voice filled with reverence. "Though I initially hesitated to care for her, she has become my anchor amidst the storm. I would shield her with my life."

"The Uru were treacherous from the outset," Towrang said. "Driven by greed and tyranny, they coerced our people with fear of reprisal."

"Why did you not caution me against them?" Nudgee inquired, his heart heavy with disillusionment. These were not the revelations he had hoped for in this hour of need.

"Would you have heeded my counsel, Nudgee? I could sense the allure of travel and discovery already ensnaring you. I didn't wish to rob you of that journey, whether its outcome be for better or worse," Towrang explained, his gaze filled with understanding. Nudgee reflected on his past decision, driven by youthful curiosity and a desire to explore the world.

"You're right. I was eager to venture forth and explore. I wouldn't have heeded any warnings," Nudgee admitted ruefully, acknowledging the impulsive nature of his past choices.

"It's the nature of youth. But you've grown immeasurably in these past weeks," Towrang remarked, a mixture of pride and sorrow in his voice.

"I wish to return to my birthplace, to see the land of my upbringing. Will you accompany me?" Nudgee asked, his longing palpable.

"Nudgee, this land is as much your home as it is anyone's," Towrang replied, his tone heavy with reluctance. Nudgee sensed there was more behind this remark. "But I cannot grant you entry," Towrang continued, his expression pained as he gestured towards the land. Nudgee's anger began to simmer.

"What do you mean? Is this punishment for my departure?" Nudgee demanded, frustration boiling within him.

"It's not about you, Nudgee. The Uru left this land in disarray. It hangs precariously between recovery and ruin. The elders toil tirelessly in Dreamtime and the physical realm to restore balance. Any additional souls could disrupt this delicate equilibrium, risking the loss of our homeland," Towrang explained earnestly.

"If you don't want me to return, just say so," Nudgee retorted bitterly. "I understand. I abandoned my home, and now it's abandoning me."

"I see there's still much growth ahead for you," Towrang remarked sadly. "You'll return one day, just not today." Nudgee offered no response, his heart heavy with disappointment. He turned away from Towrang, soaring back towards the ships.

As he approached, he noticed the vessels navigating between two colossal land masses, with no apparent exit except the way they had come. Despite his frustration, Nudgee couldn't help but chuckle at the sight of one landmass resembling a massive leg and foot. His anger momentarily forgotten, he floated back to his physical body, still weak but gradually regaining strength with each passing day.

Opening his eyes, Nudgee found himself in his dimly lit room, his stomach rumbling with hunger. Slowly sitting up, he struggled against dizziness and fatigue. Spotting food laid out on plates, he scanned the room for Nefari, but she was nowhere to be found. Concern crept over him as he called out her name, receiving no response.

Since their return from the volcano island, Nefari had been his constant companion, bound by a promise to watch over him, made in exchange for his protection. Had she ventured out while he was dreaming, assuming he wouldn't notice? Or worse, had something befallen her? Abandoning thoughts of his own hunger, Nudgee laid back on the bed, slipping once more into his spirit form to search for the young girl.

With a strong pull of emotion guiding him, Nudgee made his way towards where he sensed Nefari's presence. His intuition led him to the ship's bow, where a group of Uru had gathered, all fixated on something at the rear of the vessel. Among them stood Cecrops, accompanied by Nefari. Relief washed over Nudgee as he realized that Cecrops had summoned Nefari for some important task.

Turning his attention to the focal point of the crowd's interest, Nudgee observed the ships maneuvering into position, forming a ring. Around this central circle, two additional rings, progressively larger, began to take shape. The vessels glided smoothly into alignment, fitting together seamlessly as if they had been purpose-built for this precise arrangement.

As all movement ceased, Nudgee surveyed the transformed landscape below. It bore a striking resemblance to the targets Towrang had sketched on trees during his spear training: a central circle flanked by two outer rings. Nudgee's spirit buzzed with anticipation as the atmosphere surrounding the ships began to shift. Suddenly, lightning danced around the massive structure, seemingly materializing out of thin air. Then came the deafening roar, a thunderous sound reverberating through the air. Nefari clutched her ears in discomfort, while the bronze-skinned Uru remained steadfast.

Movement resumed aboard the ships, with decks merging seamlessly into one cohesive whole. Bridges stretched across the sections, connecting everything into a vast, unified entity. Canals, though more ornamental than functional, flowed through the sections. However, the most awe-inspiring transformation was yet to come. At the heart of the mass, a colossal pyramid began to rise, towering hundreds of feet into the sky. Its surface gleamed with mirrored metallic walls, reflecting sunlight for miles around. A beacon crowned its summit, casting its light into the night.

Impressed by the breathtaking sight before him, Nudgee realized with certainty that this was now his homeland, crafted by the hands of the Uru.

As a crudely made craft approached, Nudgee observed three men aboard, clad in leather armor and armed with both spears and swords. The tension heightened as they neared the ship, their weapons at the ready. An Uru engaged in a heated exchange with them from the deck's edge, only to abruptly cease and turn towards the central area where Cecrops stood. Nudgee couldn't help but shiver at the thought of silent communication between them. With a swift motion, a rope was thrown down, and the men climbed aboard, guided through the newly formed land to where Cecrops awaited. Though Nefari appeared anxious, Cecrops's reassurance seemed to calm her.

Curious, Nudgee edged closer to eavesdrop on the conversation. To his surprise, he found that the language spoken by these newcomers bore similarities to that of the Uru. However, their appearance was markedly different— powerfully built, lighter-skinned, and adorned with short, cropped beards. The man at the forefront, distinguished by a red cloak attached to his armor, appeared to be their leader.

"Why have you come to our seas?" the leader demanded, his tone authoritative. Nudgee noted Glycon's presence as he stepped forward to engage in the conversation.

"This sea now belongs to us," Glycon declared firmly, taking charge of the dialogue.

"We Hellenes have inhabited these waters for centuries. We fish, we trade, and we thrive through our own strength. Your intrusion is unwelcome," the Hellene leader asserted defiantly.

"Boy, it was I who bestowed upon your people knowledge and means of survival. I am of the immortals whom you worship in your shrines. This land has been under our dominion long before the tribes of your race set foot in Hellas. Will you persist in defiance, or will you acknowledge the return of your Gods?" the imposing figure retorted, his tone commanding.

"You are not my god," the Hellene man retorted, raising his sword in readiness for conflict. Glycon exchanged a glance with Cecrops.

"Look away," Cecrops commanded Nefari, prompting the young girl to shield her eyes. With purposeful strides, Cecrops approached the Hellene, drawing a slender sword akin to the one wielded by his adversary. While Cecrops's blade gleamed like silver, the Hellene's weapon bore the luster of bronze. Without hesitation, Cecrops shed his garments, standing exposed before the bewildered man, who was wholly unprepared for the impending horror.

There was no gradual transition or shimmering illusion. In an instant, Cecrops's form morphed into that of a reptilian being—green, scaly skin, slitted eyes, sharp fangs, and a sinuous tail. The man recoiled in terror, but before he could flee, Cecrops moved with unmatched speed, cleanly severing his head with a single stroke. Wiping his blade on the fallen man's cloak, Cecrops resumed his Uru form, draping his white clothing over his body.

"We are Atlanteans," Cecrops declared firmly, placing a hand on Glycon's shoulder. "This land is Atlantis, home of the Gods." Glycon felt a swell of pride as Cecrops bestowed their homeland with a name honoring his son. "Return to your homes and spread word that the Gods have returned to this land," Cecrops commanded, his voice echoing with authority.

The Hellenes hesitated, uncertain, until Cecrops's thunderous roar spurred them into action. With haste, they retreated to their boat, casting fearful glances back at the Atlanteans. Turning to his fellow Uru, Cecrops raised his voice in a triumphant cry.

"Hail Atlantis!" he exclaimed, the chorus of Uru joining in, their voices resounding across the sea.

"Hail Atlantis! Hail Atlantis! Hail Atlantis!" echoed the unified chant, marking the dawn of a new era in their ancient land.

Chapter 4

The depths of Atlantis were a chilly, forbidding domain, yet Nefari found solace within its embrace. For nearly fifty years, she had become intimately acquainted with the labyrinthine corridors and intricate piping systems that crisscrossed beneath the city's surface. With a mere glance, she could discern her location amidst the darkness. Sparse illumination from dim lights scattered throughout the underworks was her only companion during weeks spent in solitude. Her once bronzed complexion had paled, mirroring the ghostly glow of the moon above.

Over time, Nefari had matured into a striking figure, her Uru heritage bestowing upon her eternal beauty, her features retaining the allure of youth. Auburn-brown locks cascaded to her shoulders, accentuating the richness of her blue eyes. Clad in the attire of a mechanic—dark charcoal garments clinging to her slender frame—she bore the mark of an accident from her youth, rendering her unable to bear children in this realm. It was this pivotal moment that drove her to seek refuge in the depths, dedicating herself to the maintenance and operation of Atlantis.

She recalled the expression on Nudgee's face when she informed him of her prolonged absences in the underworks. He had been a mentor, a fatherly figure to her, and his sorrow was heavy. Though he treated her with paternal care, she sensed the weight of his self-blame for the accident that had altered her fate. Despite her reassurances, he carried the burden of guilt, a burden she wished he would release. Yet, their bond remained unbroken, and she cherished the moments she could steal away to visit him above.

Cecrops had turned away from her at that moment. When the doctors of Atlantis had delivered the news of her inability to bear children, it seemed as though Cecrops erected an emotional barrier between them. This was the deepest wound for Nefari. She had held him in such high regard, perhaps even loved him, yet he abandoned her when she became "broken." Learning that he had ascended to kingship in a distant city named Athens, with a wife and daughters, only intensified her anguish. Despite his apparent accomplishments in Hellas, Nefari couldn't overlook his treatment of her. Nevertheless, Atlantis was her sole focus now, her cherished responsibility, one she vowed to nurture and protect for as long as she lived.

Amid the dimly illuminated corridors, Nefari diligently attended to her tasks, scrutinizing the gauges to ensure peak efficiency. Making minor adjustments as necessary, she confirmed that Atlantis operated at its optimal settings. Returning to the storeroom she had repurposed as her sleeping quarters, she settled into her hammock. In the underworks, time lost its distinction; there was no day or night, only cycles of work and rest. This routine had become her norm, one she had grown accustomed to and had no desire to alter.

Suddenly, a feeling of unease prickled at Nefari's senses. Something felt amiss, though she struggled to identify the source. It began with a faint humming, imperceptible save for the silence of her surroundings. Straining to discern its origin, she pressed her hand against the wall, detecting a subtle vibration coursing through her fingertips.

"No, no, no," Nefari exclaimed, leaping from her hammock and snatching her wrench. Racing through the maze of twists and turns, she navigated with practiced ease, her instincts guiding her toward the source of the trouble. "Why didn't you alert me sooner?" she muttered to Atlantis, frustration evident in her voice, as she rounded a corner to find smoke billowing from an open doorway. Amidst the cacophony of hissing steam and rumbling machinery, shouts of panic echoed within the room.

Surveying the chaotic scene, Nefari quickly assessed the situation. Water gushed from burst pipes, steam obscured visibility, and the machinery groaned under strain, emitting acrid smoke. Though other mechanics scrambled to regain control, she could see their efforts were misguided. Taking charge without hesitation, Nefari issued swift commands.

"Shut down the main lines leading to the motors," she instructed the nearest workers, before turning her attention to another. "Open sub valves eight through twelve to relieve pressure in the pipes. And you," she pointed to a worker with a hand covering their mouth and nose, "don't wait for permission. Maximize the air filters' capacity."

With efficiency born of experience, the crew swiftly executed her directives, trusting in her expertise. As the air cleared and preparations were complete, Nefari ordered the motors to be shut down entirely.

"Wont that destabilize Atlantis?" queried one of the mechanics, voicing the concern shared by many. The motors were crucial for maintaining the city's buoyancy above the ocean's surface.

"You'd need to shut down at least five of these motors across Atlantis before there's any risk of catastrophic failure," Nefari assured, her tone confident. "They designed it with some flexibility."

As the crew tightened the bolts securing the piping, the influx of water and steam gradually subsided, restoring a semblance of normality to the room. Yet, the mystery of the malfunction remained unanswered. Nefari approached the troublesome motor, her keen eyes scanning its inner workings. A glint amidst the cogs caught her attention, prompting her to delve deeper. With careful precision, she disassembled the motor until she uncovered a small piece of fabric lodged within. Retrieving it, she recognized it as belonging to the torn clothing of a young mechanic in the room.

"Does this belong to you?" she demanded, her anger rising as she confronted the guilty party. The young boy averted his gaze, unable to meet her accusing stare.

"Please, Nefari," interjected another worker, stepping forward. "He's still learning, and I bear responsibility for his oversight. We were preoccupied with the crisis, and his actions went unnoticed until it was too late to intervene."

"Keep him away from the motors, Dermak," Nefari instructed firmly, thrusting the torn cloth into his chest. "Shutting down a motor is one thing, but causing an explosion is entirely another."

Resuming her task, Nefari muttered to herself about the foolishness of some people as she meticulously reassembled the motor. Once satisfied that everything was in order, she supervised the start-up process, attuned to any signs of potential damage. With her concerns alleviated, she ordered the crew to clean up the water-laden floor before departing.

Unable to return to the solitude of her makeshift quarters, Nefari's anger lingered, driving her to seek solace in the company of Nudgee. Lost in the passage of time beneath Atlantis, she struggled to recall how long it had been since their last encounter. Regardless, she was determined to find refuge in his presence, if only to temporarily escape the frustrations of the underworks.

74

Nefari reached the access plate and ascended to the upper floors of Atlantis. The harsh daylight assaulted her senses as she emerged, forcing her to squint until her eyes adjusted. Adjusting to the brightness was always the most challenging part of returning to the surface levels. Finding Nudgee's room, she entered, feeling a sense of homecoming wash over her. The familiar surroundings never failed to provide her with a sense of comfort. Nudgee lay in his bed, seemingly lost in slumber. The passage of years had left its mark on him, his once-dark hair and beard now completely grey, his weathered skin marked by countless wrinkles. His breathing was labored, a testament to his declining health. As an Abori, his lifespan paled in comparison to that of the Uru, and Nefari couldn't shake the worry gnawing at her heart.

Deciding to let him rest, Nefari resolved to practice the Dreamtime techniques Nudgee had taught her. He had provided only sparse instructions, insisting that she must discover the path to the dreaming on her own. Reclining on the familiar bed, she focused on quieting her mind and centering her being. Delving into the depths of her consciousness, she embraced the emptiness, allowing herself to exist in a state of pure awareness. Opening her eyes, she was startled to find the ceiling mere inches away. The shock jolted her back to her physical form, waking her from the ethereal realm.

"Well done, Nefari," Nudgee's aged voice broke the silence. "You have exceeded all expectations."

"It's taken me eight years to make progress, Nudgee," she admitted, feeling a twinge of embarrassment. "How long did it take you?"

Nudgee hesitated for a moment before opting for honesty. "I achieved it within days, Nefari," he confessed, his gaze steady.

"Then why do you say I've performed beyond expectations? I would have thought you'd given up on me by now," Nefari responded, her astonishment evident.

"When I was first introduced to the concept of Dreamtime, it was because the elders recognized the innate ability within me," Nudgee explained between harsh coughs, gratefully accepting the glass of water Nefari offered. "Thank you. However, your situation was different. I believed that the Uru lineage within you meant that you would never be able to master the skill. Over the years, my

75

Elder Towrang cautioned me against guiding you down this path, insisting that you were destined for failure. Yet, you have achieved what seemed impossible to many. In that, you have exceeded all expectations. The duration it took is inconsequential."

"But I only just managed to do it," Nefari lamented, her spirits lifting only slightly.

"You have liberated your spirit, Nefari," Nudgee reassured her. "The initial breakthrough is always the most challenging, but from here on, you'll find that things will become easier for you."

Suddenly, Nefari heard a voice in her mind, a sensation that had always made her uneasy. She was uncertain if the communication was one-sided, or if she could also listen in on others. Nudgee recognised the look on Nefari's face and the meaning behind it instantly.

"What have they asked?" Nudgee inquired.

"They're summoning the mechanics to the main hall," Nefari responded. "I'm not in the mood to entertain their requests today; I've just returned home."

"Nefari, I've watched with pride as you've grown into the remarkable woman you are. Your thirst for knowledge and your empathy for others are your greatest strengths. You possess both physical and spiritual fortitude, and you're unafraid to embrace your true self. I cherish you as the daughter I never had, and I'm grateful every day to see you happy. You should heed the call. It may be crucial if they require the expertise of mechanics."

"You know I love you too, Nudgee," Nefari said, pressing a kiss to his cheek. "I'll make an effort to visit more often." With a smile, Nudgee nodded in understanding as she exited the room. Pausing at the doorway, Nefari cast a lingering glance back at the old man, a peculiar sensation washing over her.

After the merging of the ships, Atlantis had undergone a dramatic transformation. Spaces that seemed impossible for a single vessel now sprawled across three or four. The once mirrored hallways now draped over the pyramid beneath which Atlantis resided. Instead of the anticipated darkness, the silver-coated walls unexpectedly allowed in ample light, rendering them nearly invisible except for the skeletal structure of the pyramid and the beacon light above. Nefari marveled at the subtle intricacies of Atlantis, even in its most basic levels where few ventured.

Surveying the main hall, Nefari observed the familiar faces of some and the unfamiliar ones of others, likely from different sectors of Atlantis. All clad in the dark charcoal of mechanics, they numbered around five hundred. Nefari assumed they worked in various sections of the city. Mechanics rarely mingled, a preference Nefari shared as she valued solitude even among her peers.

"Well, if it isn't the White Wrench of the North," a voice nearby interrupted her thoughts. Nefari turned sharply to find a bronze-skinned woman with fiery crimson hair tied up in a bun, the typical choice for mechanics. Unfamiliar with the woman, Nefari raised an eyebrow.

"D'you just call me a Wench?" Nefari was accustomed to the nickname bestowed upon her due to her extended time below deck, resulting in her fair complexion. She took pleasure in toying with those who dared use the term, twisting their words to gauge their reactions. The woman before her was no exception; embarrassment painted her cheeks as her voice squeaked in response.

"No, I said Wrench. Wrench, like the tool we all use," she clarified. But what followed took Nefari by surprise. "I'm sorry, Nefari. I'd heard so much about you, and seeing you now, I was only trying to find a way to break the ice. Everyone said that you loved the nickname."

"Actually, not—" Nefari began, but the woman, named Sanguine, interjected.

"I promise I won't use it again. Is there another name you might like to go by?" Sanguine asked eagerly. Before Nefari could respond, Sanguine continued, "My name is Sanguine, by the way. A lot of people call me Guinea. You can call me Guinea too if you'd like. I've been in the underworks to the south for a good twenty years. No wonder we haven't met, right? Everyone tells me I have so much talent; Atlantis would be sunk without me. I think that you are the reason we still float though. When..."

Nefari breathed a silent sigh of relief as two Uru walked in, drawing attention to the center of the gathering. Grateful for the interruption, she focused on the newcomers.

"Sobek and Shenlong," Sanguine whispered, leaning towards Nefari. Irritation simmered within Nefari at having to stand so close to her. "They are the ones to do the choosing today... Very important job coming up... Work for

Cecrops in Athens..."

Each time Sanguine spoke, she leaned in, her incessant bobbing becoming increasingly irritating to Nefari. As the conversation turned to Nefari's girlhood crush, her gaze shifted towards the two speakers, a detail not lost on Sanguine.

"Fancy him, do you?" Sanguine remarked, pushing Nefari over the edge.

"Quiet, girl! Do you ever stop talking?" Nefari's voice carried louder than she intended, drawing the attention of those around them.

"You're right. Bad habit of mine," Sanguine admitted with a smile. "Can't help but see I hit a sore spot though. What's the history?"

"Girls, if you are finished?" Shenlong's deep voice interrupted.

He towered over them, his imposing figure accentuated by the massive sword strapped to his back. Nefari couldn't help feeling both intimidated and captivated by him. She quickly composed herself and gestured for them to continue as Sobek stepped forward, clearing his throat. Despite his smaller stature, he exuded a sense of authority.

"A generator has gone down in Athens," Sobek explained. "It has resulted in catastrophic failure across a number of our endeavors. The mechs in the city do not have the same skill as you do here on Atlantis, and we need a couple of extra hands to help guide them and bring the generator back online."

"Odd that the fancy pants up there would call us by the term 'mechs,'" Sanguine couldn't resist whispering. "Usually, they are all official and such." Nefari simply nodded in agreement and motioned for them to focus on the front.

"We are happy to take any volunteers who may want to visit the city. There will be free time at the end of each workday to explore," Shenlong added.

"Not to mention the ride on the Vimana," a mechanic chimed in from the side.

"That doesn't sound too bad, does it, Nefari?" Sanguine nudged her with her elbow, but Nefari remained stoic, longing only to retreat to her hammock and sleep.

"Sadly, this will not be the case. The Vimana will be stationed around Athens until the generator is back online. We wouldn't want any rebel forces sacking the city. We leave here from the northern quarter, making land on the nearest shore. From there, we ride two days to the city. Now, who will volunteer?" Shenlong's announcement was met with silence as no one stepped forward, the prospect of the journey dampening their enthusiasm for volunteering.

"I don't think anyone will step up. How about you and I go for it? You can see Cecrops again," Sanguine suggested to Nefari.

"Sanguine, please stop," Nefari interjected, her voice strained.

"Right. You two who've been talking throughout this meeting," Sobek commanded, gesturing towards Nefari and Sanguine. "Front and center. You've just volunteered. Everyone else can file out."

As the others left the room, Nefari cursed her luck, her gratitude to the spirits turning sour. Stuck with Sanguine for a week or more, fixing a generator in Athens, was not how she envisioned her day progressing.

"Names," Sobek ordered.

"Sanguine, sir. Thank you again for this..." Sanguine began before Sobek interrupted.

"Just your name will do," he said, turning to Nefari. "And yours?"

"Nefari," she grumbled.

"The White Wench of the North," Shenlong exclaimed. "I have heard of your skill."

"He called you a Wench," Sanguine whispered, leaning in.

"Did you actually say Wench?" Nefari asked Shenlong, missing the compliment.

"Is that not the name?" Shenlong asked genuinely.

"Just Nefari will be fine."

"Now that that is settled, we leave at once," Sobek declared. "Follow me, girls, and we'll make for the shore."

Today, Cranaus could only spare twenty men. Twenty men against a possible six adversaries, and he knew the task would still be daunting. Success would hinge on the technology the Uru brought and the skill of the mechanics. If they were warriors, he'd feel more confident, but alas, luck seemed to evade him.

Living under the rule of an outsider had become unbearable for Cranaus. This ruler, who had slain his grandfather when Atlantis first settled off the coast, claimed divinity and ruled with an iron fist. But Cranaus cared not for such claims; this man was not a Hellene and had no right to govern them.

Fortunes were shifting in his favor as more Hellenes joined his cause. A victory today would rally even more to his banner, allowing him to advance further. Destroying the generator was merely the first step in a larger plan. When Cecrops felt threatened, he would deploy mechanics to repair it and fortify his defenses. But Cranaus aimed to strike at the heart of his enemy, knowing that the mechanics were the very lifeblood of Atlantis.

"How long are they going to be?" asked Agrippa, settling beside Cranaus on the high hill. Cranaus studied the young man, barely an adult, with a smattering of whiskers on his face. Cranaus himself wasn't much older, only recently having filled out the patches in his dark beard. He'd even entertained the prospect of marriage with three potential partners, until he retreated to the wilderness among makeshift homes.

"Patience, Agrippa," Cranaus replied to the lad. Despite his jealousy of Agrippa's blonde hair, Cranaus continued. "They have not long entered Atlantis. We must wait to see how many men they recruit and plan our assault accordingly."

"Wouldn't it be the same whether they had one or eight men? We would still overwhelm them with our superior numbers," Agrippa reasoned.

"Let's consider that scenario," Cranaus said. "Eight fighting men, along with the two original Uru. We have a two-to-one advantage. Surely we would win with those odds, correct?" Agrippa nodded in agreement.

"With the odds alone, we wouldn't lose, but we would suffer great losses. What is a general?" Cranaus posed the question.

"He tells men what to do on the battlefield," Agrippa replied after a moment's thought.

"Why is he necessary when all one needs is numbers?"

"He uses tactics and strategy to defeat enemies even when outnumbered," Agrippa responded.

"There is more to it than just defeating the enemy. Think about it," Cranaus urged. Agrippa took five minutes to ponder what could be more important than defeating the enemy.

"I honestly don't know, Cranaus," the young man

admitted, shame evident in his eyes.

"It is the men themselves. The general will use tactics and strategies that defeat the enemy while saving the lives of as many men as he can. If you continue to only try to win, eventually you will have no one left alive to stand at your back. You will lose the war," Cranaus explained.

"So then, the ten men, how would you face them?" Agrippa inquired.

"I would split our forces. Once the first group has drawn the enemy in, we shall have a second group attack from the rear," Cranaus outlined his plan.

"Look, they're coming out," Agrippa exclaimed with excitement. Cranaus shaded his eyes from the afternoon sun and counted. Only four Uru were coming ashore. Luck may just be on their side today.

"Only four of them, Cranaus, and they're going to be on horseback. We should just rush them now and be done with it," Agrippa suggested eagerly.

"No. There may only be four, but I still don't trust that big one. I want to get everyone home safely," Cranaus replied, sliding back from the rise to avoid any glint of metal in the sunlight. Agrippa followed suit.

"We'll set up at Caygar's," Cranaus said reworking his strategy. "When they come through the narrow trail, we'll pepper them with arrows from the high ground."

"Is that not cowardly?" Agrippa questioned.

"It doesn't matter whether an action is seen as cowardly or heroic. What matters is the care you take for your men and the final outcome. Right now, this is a different type of warfare than the ones the bards sing about in taverns. Every man is vital. Why did you join the resistance, Agrippa?" Cranaus inquired.

"I've heard what people say in whispers around the inns and taverns. They say how they hate the Uru and that someone should do something. They are, all of them, cowards... I joined your resistance because I want to actually do something. I want to be a hero and not just another drunk sitting alone at a tavern drinking that awful piss they call wine," Agrippa confessed.

"A hero is not born in a day at the right end of a sword. They are born through sacrifice and hardship. It will take you many years to become a true hero of the people, and that is something you must remember. You are doing this for all the cowards, as you call them, back home who cannot act for one reason or another," Cranaus imparted wisdom to Agrippa.

"But they are nothing. No better than the beggar on the street," Agrippa retorted.

"They are everything, Agrippa, and until you see this, your dreams will never be fulfilled," Cranaus responded solemnly.

Their conversation ended there for the day. Cranaus ordered the men out and gave them their destination. Agrippa couldn't understand why the men were smiling. Did they not find this attack cowardly? He wasn't happy about it or the talk with Cranaus.

The resistance group rode out to their destination, arriving just before sunset. They made their camp in the hills surrounding the narrow trail on both sides. Cranaus surveyed the area to ensure their friends were positioned along the trail, noting they were making camp one hundred yards behind. The area was easily defended, situated on a slight rise, and they could see anyone approaching even under the slender moonlight.

"No fires tonight," Cranaus instructed the men. "We can't let them know that we're here. Keep your voices to a minimum also. The sound carries in these hills."

That was all Cranaus had to say, and the men would comply to the letter. Are you a hero? The thought came unbidden to his mind. The boy needed to learn some big lessons in his life, but Cranaus couldn't talk. He was driven by vengeance and any fame that came with it. Women and gold would be his once Cecrops was no longer ruling in Athens. "You are selfish," he told himself before settling down against a rock with his cold meal of bread and cheese.

"The night was going to be a long one," he mumbled to himself.

As Nefari lay on a small blanket, she found herself pondering, "Does Sanguine ever stop talking?" Even in her slumber, the girl seemed to engage in endless monologues with some unseen interlocutor. It all began with a mention of a cow, then veered into discussions about mountains and a dancing squirrel. Nefari, weary of Sanguine's ceaseless chatter, decided she'd had enough for the day. Gathering her blanket, she moved to a spot where the nightly noises would hopefully drown out Sanguine's voice, and settled in comfortably.

Shedding the garments of a mechanic, Nefari lay on her back, using her arms as a pillow. The gentle warmth of the breeze caressed her pale skin, playing with her senses in the darkness. The crescent moon cast a milky hue over the landscape, draining it of color. Amidst the symphony of cicadas in the fields, Nefari imagined them as tiny birds, their chirping lulling her into a trance-like state. She reminisced about the few times she had ventured off the boat, recalling hearing the same sound only once, unable to locate its source.

Her thoughts then drifted to Cecrops, wondering how often he listened to such sounds. Surprised by the persistence of his memory in her mind after so many years, she pondered what entertained him during the nights. Realizing she wouldn't find rest until she expelled him from her mind, Nefari contemplated visiting him in spirit. Attempting to quiet her mind, she focused solely on the rhythmic chirping of the cicadas, using their hypnotic cadence to guide her into an astral journey, away from her corporeal form.

A profound sense of emptiness enveloped Nefari before she found herself hovering in the air above her naked form. With determined willpower, she maintained her spiritual state, resisting the pull to return to her physical body. Confident in her control, she guided herself upward, surveying Atlantis floating off the shore like a colossal island. The beacon atop the pyramid served as a warning to approaching ships, signaling the presence of Atlantis.

Turning slowly, Nefari spotted another distant glow, which she presumed to be Athens, Cecrops' current home. With purpose, she set her course toward it. The lights of Athens loomed larger and brighter as she approached, resembling a distant forest fire until the city enveloped her entirely. Men roamed the streets and filled the bars, their rowdiness often erupting into fights as she glided through the city. Women were a rare sight, mostly hidden in darkened alleys engaged in the more nocturnal ventures that were far more fun to share. The thought of her own infertility weighed heavily on Nefari, a reality seldom acknowledged in her thoughts given her status on Atlantis.

As she pondered Cecrops once more, she concentrated on where she might find him. Like Nudgee before her, she quickly deciphered the meaning of the tingling sensation, sensing a strong and consistent pull guiding her toward him. Trusting her instincts, she followed the direction indicated, soon coming upon Cecrops exiting a temple, cradling a bundle of cloth in his arms. But it was not merely cloth—it was a child wrapped within.

The revelation hit Nefari hard, her mind reeling from the shock. She'd heard rumors among the mechanics of Atlantis about Cecrops having a family, but it'd never truly registered as real until now. Floating ten meters away from the man she'd once yearned to be with, she watched in silence as he carried his child, a sharp, almost painful, reminder of the life she could never share with him.

Nefari couldn't resist trailing after Cecrops, despite the tumult of emotions stirring within her. He navigated several streets until arriving at a house near the Acropolis, surrounded by high walls and adorned with a courtyard and garden. Dense vines draped over the doorway, concealing the back entrance. Cecrops entered through the rear, stepping into a small room secluded from the rest of the house. Inside, only a table and a solitary chair occupied the space, leaving Nefari puzzled by his actions.

As Cecrops placed the child on the table and disrobed, standing naked before her, an inexplicable warmth spread through Nefari's spirit. She suddenly realized her own unclothed state and quickly averted her gaze, focusing instead on the child. But her attention was drawn back as she witnessed a horrifying scene unfolding before her eyes.

The child, once wrapped in swaddling, now turned a deadly shade of purple. Nefari observed with growing horror as Cecrops forced a significant portion of the cloth into the child's mouth. Bewildered by his actions, she stiffened in shock, only to witness a nightmarish transformation take place before her.

Cecrops morphed into a reptilian entity, a being that would haunt Nefari's dreams for years to come. Yellow, slitted eyes loomed above large, fanged teeth within the small head of this green-scaled creature. With a sinuous tail swishing back and forth, it approached the child, its razor-sharp talons tracing down the infant's face. As the child succumbed to suffocation, its eyes rolling back into its head, the beastly form of Cecrops widened its jaws and began to feast upon the child at its last moments of life.

Nefari's scream pierced the night, a raw expression of her horror and disbelief. Startled by her presence, Cecrops glanced in her direction, prompting her to flee, unwilling to face him. Through the ethereal realm, her screams reverberated, echoing her terror.

As she raced back towards her body, hoping desperately that what she witnessed was merely a nightmare, another spirit intercepted her path. Halting abruptly, she beheld Nudgee, not the aged version she had grown accustomed to, but a youthful and robust figure, his eyes filled with determination. Without hesitation, Nefari threw herself into his arms.

"What troubles you, Nefari?" Nudgee inquired, cradling her gently as if she were still a child. "Your screams woke me."

"He's a monster," Nefari sobbed, her tears flowing freely. "Cecrops—he transformed into some sort of scaled creature with slitted eyes and a tail, right before my eyes, and... and he devoured a small baby."

Nudgee's expression hardened with concern, treading carefully with his words. There were truths Nefari wasn't yet ready to confront, and the revelation of a race of reptilian beings within Atlantis, sharing a connection with her, was among them.

"Who do you speak of as a monster?" Nudgee inquired gently, guiding her to share more.

"It was Cecrops. I... I attempted to visit him in the dream realm, and it worked. But when I saw him...," Nefari's voice faltered as she buried her face in Nudgee's chest, her sobs intensifying.

"Forgive me, child," Nudgee spoke softly. "I have been aware of this for some time. I confided in the senior Uru, and they were aware of it as well."

Nefari's tears ceased as the weight of his revelation settled upon her. Pulling away slightly, she confronted him with a touch of anger. "You knew all this time, and you never told me," she accused. "Did you not trust me after all these years? Did you not think I deserved to be warned?"

"Nefari, you know I love you and would do anything to protect you," Nudgee responded gently. "But there were many factors at play in my decision. I have witnessed the remnants of my people, who journeyed with me on these ships, being slaughtered and consumed. My survival has hinged on your importance to them, and my role as your protector. I dedicated myself entirely to keeping you safe and shielded from such horrors. I wished for you to never have to experience fear or distress because of it. But..."

"But what?" Nefari pressed, her anger subsiding slightly.

"I couldn't shield you from the truth forever," Nudgee admitted. "I never gave up on guiding you through the Dreamtime because it is the safest way for you to witness the realities of this world. I had hoped to be there to support you when the time came, but events unfolded too swiftly. Now, you must use what you have learned to your advantage. Keep their secrets close, and wield them when necessary. You have the power to take down empires if you choose." Nefari shook her head, overwhelmed by the magnitude of it all.

'Cecrops already saw me,' she told him. Her eyes started to fill with tears again. 'He knew I was in the room with him and he looked straight at me.'

"Cecrops only sensed your presence," Nudgee reassured her, his voice soothing. "He felt a presence in the room and accurately pinpointed its location. His gaze was likely meant to give the impression that he could see you. He probably assumed it was me, as I am currently the only one within ten days' travel by Vimana who can access the Dreamtime. If he suspects anything and questions you, feign ignorance. He won't press the matter further."

"But how can you be certain?" Nefari asked, her doubts lingering.

"Truthfully, I can't be certain," Nudgee admitted. "But I believe his flaws, particularly his superiority complex, will play to our advantage. He will likely believe he knows best. However, for now, we have more pressing concerns, and I need you to remain calm," he added, his tone turning serious.

Nefari looked at him, puzzled, as he pointed towards a dark area near their campsite. "Do you see that point just there? What can you tell me about it?" Nefari followed his gesture, observing the shadowy spot.

"It's dark, a spot untouched by the moonlight," she replied. However, as she focused her spirit eyes, the darkness seemed to dissipate, replaced by a clarity akin to a full moon illuminating multiple areas of the sky. Suddenly, she discerned a figure clad in dark leather armor, creeping towards their camp with a dagger in hand. Fear gripped her as she realized the imminent danger.

"What do I do?" Nefari's voice trembled with panic,

seeking guidance from Nudgee, who sensed her distress keenly.

"Get a hold of yourself, Nefari," Nudgee's voice carried a firmness. "Your panic serves no one. Find your calm." He waited patiently as Nefari steadied herself.

"Return to your body and inform the senior Uru of the impending threat," he instructed, his tone composed. "Do it discreetly to avoid alerting the intruder. They will handle the situation, either eliminating or capturing him. I strongly advise capture, as it may lead to uncovering any potential accomplices."

"Thank you, Nudgee," Nefari said gratefully, embracing him once more. "You've been the only father figure I've known. I'll come visit you when I return home."

"And you've brought great joy into my life, Nefari... Farewell," Nudgee replied as his spirit faded from view.

Nefari hastened back to her body with urgency, re-entering with a swift motion. As she opened her eyes, she felt the impact ripple through her, resolving to be gentler next time. Rising from the soft earth, she clothed herself and approached Shenlong, who sat by the fire. Seating herself beside him, she struggled to find the right words before blurting out a greeting.

"Good evening, Shenlong."

"Wench," Shenlong acknowledged, using what he thought was her nickname. Nefari was caught off guard by his words.

"Seriously!" she exclaimed, her voice rising as she slapped his arm. "That's not my name. I thought we already went over this on the ship."

"We did," Shenlong admitted calmly. "I just needed to provoke the right reaction from you to catch our friend off guard."

As he spoke, a figure loomed behind Shenlong, wielding a dagger. Before Nefari could react, Shenlong swiftly spun around, seizing the assailant's arm and flipping him onto the ground beside the fire. Nefari recognized him as the same man she'd seen in the Dreamtime, realizing he was nothing more than a scared kid, his wide eyes betraying his fear as his muscles trembled.

"Don't kill me," the adolescent pleaded. "I don't want to die."

Sobek, having heard the commotion, stirred from his sleep. "Why are you here? What was your purpose?" he questioned.

"I came to end your lives and the lives of the Mechanics," the youth confessed. "My friends planned to shoot you with arrows from the hillside when you rode through the narrow trail in the morning. I didn't agree with their cowardly plan, so I decided to take matters into my own hands and become a hero."

"It was very brave of you to come out here alone," Sobek acknowledged. "What is your name?"

"It's Agrippa," the young man replied, his voice trembling with fear.

"You've shown great courage, Agrippa," Sobek continued. "Do your friends know you're here?" Agrippa shook his head in response.

"I believe we should reward you for your bravery. What do you say, Shenlong? Shall we set him free?" Sobek proposed, turning to his companion.

"He's definitely earned it. Agrippa is a hero in the making," Shenlong agreed. Agrippa couldn't believe the enemy's unexpected kindness towards him. A smile spread across his face, and he stood a little taller at the praise. He then turned back to Sobek, awaiting his decision.

"Thank you, Agrippa. You are free," Sobek stated, but before Nefari could process the words, Shenlong swiftly ended the young man's life with a sickening crack from his neck as it snapped easily in two. Nefari gasped in shock, a small yelp escaping Sanguine who had been sleeping moments before.

"Why did you kill him?" Nefari demanded, her voice tinged with disbelief. "You said you were going to set him free."

"I did set him free, just not in the way he anticipated," Shenlong explained calmly. "And what do you think he would have done when he returned to his comrades, intending to ambush us? He would have betrayed us as quickly as he did them to us. He was young and naive in the ways of war."

"But we aren't at war," Nefari protested.

"Every skirmish is a battle, Nefari, every battle a war." Shenlong countered. "But enough about this. We need to move."

"We'll gather the horses and extinguish the fire," Sobek informed Shenlong. "You give them something to wake up to. Prop the body up and leave the head at his feet. I want us well past the ambush point by sunrise. Their complacency will be their downfall."

Then, Sobek turned his attention to Sanguine, motioning for her to come closer. She obeyed, her face pale and shaken from witnessing the violent act.

"Take a good look at that body, Sanguine," Sobek instructed sternly. She reluctantly glanced at the lifeless figure, recoiling at the sight and stench. "If I hear a single word from your lips before sunrise, you'll join him. Understood?"

Sanguine's complexion, already pale, now turned an ivory white as she comprehended Sobek's warning. She nodded silently, her eyes wide with shock, before retreating a few steps away. The turmoil within her overwhelmed her senses, and she doubled over, emptying her stomach onto the ground. The retching sounds thankfully soft against the quiet of the night, a stark reminder of the harsh reality they faced. Nefari watched with concern, realizing the profound impact the events had on Sanguine, who had never encountered such brutality before.

The sun broke the horizon, casting a grim light on the headless corpse before Cranaus. Carrion birds had already begun their feasting, with a solitary crow pecking at an eyeball, causing excess fluids to leak from the torn socket. Cranaus sighed at the young man's tragic fate. The rest of the camp soon joined him, their faces a mix of shock and sorrow.

"Poseidon's balls! Who is that?" exclaimed a burly Hellene, his voice thick with disbelief.

"It's Agrippa," Cranaus replied, his disappointment palpable. "That fool... Mellan, remind me to send a letter to his mother across the Ionian Sea. It's the least we can do."

"Yes, sir," Mellan responded dutifully.

"Cranaus," called another man from across the pass, his voice tense with urgency. "I can still see them. What are your orders?"

"We're going to pursue them," Cranaus declared, his voice firm. "And we'll deal out justice in a manner befitting Agrippa's memory."

"Everyone to the horses and move on the target!" Mellan's voice rang out. The horses had been tethered behind the hills, strategically placed to muffle their sounds. They had been well-fed and groomed, ready for the chase.

And chase they did. The men, clad in sturdy leather armor and armed to the teeth, weighed little to the powerful mounts. Once unleashed, the horses thundered along the path toward their fleeing quarry.

Closing the gap by half, the pursuers watched as the four figures ahead broke into a sprint. Now, the true race began. If the fleeing group could outpace the local steeds bred for speed, they might evade justice at the gates of Athens. But if the pursuers could catch them before then, Agrippa would be avenged.

They rode on tirelessly, without pause. Men and horses alike grew weary from the relentless pursuit. Despite the fatigue, victory seemed within reach as the gap narrowed to eight lengths. But it was a victory Cranaus knew they would never claim. Cresting the next rise, the gleaming city of Athens spread out before them, bathed in the warm glow of the setting sun. The Acropolis, perched high on its hill, seemed to mock them with its brilliance.

"We had them," one man muttered, frustration evident in his voice.

"The moment we came into view of Athens, our chance was lost," Cranaus replied grimly. "We could have caught them on the plains, but it would've meant a fight. The city guard would've intervened before we could finish them off. And our horses wouldn't withstand a retreat."

His words struck a chord with the men, who knew the truth of it. Mellan, ever quick-witted, began issuing orders without hesitation.

"Dismount and give the horses their feed of grain," Mellan instructed. "Tend to them and allow them to rest. When we're ready, we'll walk them part of the way home."

"I'm staying," Cranaus declared. "I'll scout around the city and gather information."

"And your orders for when we return?" Mellan inquired.

"You'll take command, Mellan. Do what you see fit. Rally as many men as possible. I want every road guarded upon their return. We won't let them slip through our fingers again."

"Do we really need that many?" Mellan questioned.

"There's something off about this whole situation. It's as if they were expecting us," Cranaus explained. "Agrippa may have been reckless, but he wasn't foolish. His stealth skills were formidable. Even at my most vigilant, he could've taken me out."

"Perhaps you're letting emotions cloud your judgment. Accidents happen, especially in the heat of the moment," Mellan suggested.

"Maybe," Cranaus conceded, though doubt lingered. "But I can't shake this feeling. Take the men out of sight," he ordered. Mellan nodded and began to carry out the instructions. As the men disappeared from view, Cranaus gazed back at the city where the four fugitives were just entering. "You won't evade me again," he vowed to the gods of Olympus.

Chapter 5

The rough journey finally ended at the gates of Athens. Nefari, inexperienced in horse riding, struggled with the scant instructions received upon disembarking from the transfer boats from Atlantis. She hadn't the luxury of time to acclimate to gripping with her thighs or mastering the reins. Only her sheer determination and tenacity kept her astride the horse that day, though every muscle protested with bruised soreness. She anticipated the pain intensifying over the coming days. Sanguine wore a weary, drawn expression, evidence of the taxing journey. Yet, amidst the discomfort, Nefari found solace in not having to endure Sanguine's chatter throughout the day.

As Nefari entered the city, she cast a backward glance. The looming silhouette on the hill signaled the end of the pursuit. One pursuer lingered on the rise, but Nefari dismissed him from her thoughts. Dismounting with the group, she struggled to remain upright on unsteady legs and collapsed to the ground. Sanguine, panting heavily, slumped down beside her.

"I hope to never repeat such an ordeal," Sanguine remarked between breaths.

"I doubt I'll be able to move for a week," Nefari replied, and Sanguine chuckled, the sound a welcome respite after the day's trials.

"I apologize, Nefari," Sanguine suddenly said, as two young boys approached with water for the exhausted pair. Nefari drank deeply before answering.

"What reason have you for apologizing?"

"I fear I've been a burden to you."

"No," Nefari waved off the notion.

"I have. I know I have. When I meet people for the first time, I get nervous and start talking too much. You especially made me nervous, Nefari," Sanguine confessed.

"Me?" Nefari hadn't met the girl before, so she couldn't fathom why she'd cause Sanguine anxiety.

"You're well known throughout Atlantis as one of the most skillful mechs. I've admired your legend for years, and when I finally had the chance to meet you, it was overwhelming. I know I'm the reason we're on this trip."

"It's okay, Sanguine," Nefari reassured her.

"Please, call me Guinea. I want us to try to be friends."

"We are friends, Guinea," Nefari affirmed, touched by

Sanguine's honesty and vulnerability. "Let's start anew from this moment, okay?" Sanguine smiled and nodded. Sobek approached the girls, unruffled by the challenging journey. They seemed accustomed to such travels, Nefari noted.

"I've arranged transportation to the work site. We can't keep Cecrops waiting any longer. The power needs restoring urgently," Sobek informed them. Nefari felt a pang of sadness at the thought of facing Cecrops after the events of the previous night. She wasn't sure if she could meet his gaze or respond adequately when addressed.

"Come on," Sanguine suggested. "Let's ride one of the litters together. I wouldn't mind being stuck with Shenlong, but Sobek's company would be unbearable."

Nefari smiled at her newfound friend before glancing at the litters. Two large, red-cushioned beds with poles extending from each corner were ready for transport, operated by four strong men. She followed Sanguine to the nearest one and settled herself opposite her friend.

"You're right," Nefari agreed. "It's better that it's just us girls riding one. Look how comical Shenlong and Sobek look on the other." Sanguine glanced across and giggled at the sight of the mismatched pair as the litter ascended into the air. Traveling above the city's bustling streets made Nefari feel somewhat self-conscious.

"I feel like royalty," Sanguine remarked, leaning in. "I know it's a sensitive topic, but would you rather not be riding with Cecrops?"

Nefari's expression darkened instantly. "I'm sorry. You don't have to talk about it," Sanguine quickly interjected.

"No, it's okay," Nefari finally said, opening up. "There was a time when I would have said yes. As a child, Cecrops saved me, and I looked up to him like a hero. It developed into something I mistook for love as I grew older. He used to give me attention, saying I was special not just to him, but to all the Uru. That very few people had my genetics. Then..." She paused, pain evident in her eyes. Sanguine reached out, offering comfort.

"I found out that I couldn't have children. From that moment, it was as if Cecrops didn't know me anymore. He wouldn't talk to me or even look my way. I felt wretched, and that's when I retreated into the underworks of Atlantis."

"Oh, Nefari, I'm so sorry. I didn't know," Sanguine's

eyes glistened with empathy. "I'd thought maybe you two had a fling, and he left you."

Nefari couldn't bring herself to disclose the horrifying truth about her former idol. How could she tell this cheerful, optimistic girl that one of their race's leaders wasn't even human? That he masqueraded as a god to demand sacrificial infants for his consumption? He was a demon, not a deity. So why did she hesitate to expose him to the world?

"I'm sorry, Nefari," Sanguine said after a moment of silence. "I'll drop the subject."

"Honestly, it's okay, Guinea. Is there maybe a special someone in your life?" Now it was Sanguine's turn to blush.

"I see," was all Nefari said.

"You see what?" Sanguine asked coyly.

"Nothing at all," Nefari replied. Sanguine's anticipation became too much for her, and she couldn't contain it any longer.

"There's a cook on Atlantis who used to sneak me sweet things," Sanguine confessed, her face turning crimson. "He wasn't conventionally handsome, but there was something about him that drew me in. Strong hands, warm skin... One night, we found ourselves alone in a quiet walkway, and things sort of... happened. We became intimate."

"You didn't," Nefari exclaimed. "What was it like?"

"It was amazing, Nefari. When the change came over me, it was like worlds colliding."

"What change was that?" Nefari asked, a little confused. "Do you mean when you became a woman?"

"No, when I became so much more," Sanguine said, looking at her suspiciously. "Have you gone through the change yet?"

"Haven't been close to anyone," Nefari admitted.

"My, my, aren't you in for some fun," Sanguine teased.

The litters came to a halt outside an old sandstone building. Conversation dwindled as the men carrying the litter offered the girls a hand up. At first glance, the building didn't resemble a place where generators would be housed. However, they were in the old world now, and the Uru would utilize any available structure. Upon stepping inside, Nefari's perception shifted instantly. The room revealed itself as a vast stairwell descending about ten flights, the walls made of reinforced grey stone that appeared more engineered than natural.

Soft plinks echoed as Nefari descended each step, her hand gliding along the smooth metal railings. She was grateful for the descent; climbing would have been too much for her tired legs, already protesting from the earlier ride. Even now, three-quarters of the way down, the pain from the journey intensified, and her breath grew heavier. Finally reaching the bottom, she leaned against the cold stone wall. A glowing ball of light, reminiscent of those in Atlantis, cast a gentle glow, illuminating the area.

"Nefari, Sanguine, thank you for coming on such short notice," Cecrops greeted them. Nefari had hoped to avoid crossing paths with him, though she knew it was inevitable. Dressed in traditional Hellene clothing—loosely fitted wool draped around his waist and over one shoulder—he approached with open arms. She looked away.

"If you follow me to the generators, you can assess the problem and begin repairs. It's been too long without power already," Cecrops instructed, his tone carrying a sense of urgency.

Cecrops turned and strode into the generator room, with Sanguine leading the way, followed by Sobek and Shenlong. Nefari lingered, taking a moment before entering. Inside, three generators sat silently in the confined space, each occupying a five-by-five-meter area. There was no reassuring hum or buzz, leaving Nefari disheartened. As a mechanic, she knew these machines held potential; she just needed to ignite it. Upon closer inspection, it was evident that someone had tampered with them. The damage couldn't have occurred naturally. However, she decided against mentioning it for the time being.

"You have free rein in this room. Whatever you need is yours," Cecrops informed them.

"We'll revive these machines," Nefari declared, surprising herself with the confidence in her voice. She silently thanked Nudgee for his encouraging words. "We won't let you down."

"Oh, hold me, Guinea," Nefari said, wrapping her arms around her friend's neck, leaning her full weight on her. They both fell to the ground, neither girl having the strength to keep each other standing. They had just come up from the generator room climbing the stairs back to ground level. The sun was setting again, and Nefari laughed.

"What's so funny?" Sanguine asked her.

"It's the sun," Nefari replied. "We rode through part of a night and a whole day. We were exhausted, bruised, and could barely walk—just like now. But when I'm alone in the dark with a machine in front of me, I come alive. Time doesnt matter and pain fades away. I just lose myself in the work. But now, look at the sun." She pointed toward the fiery orange orb dipping between the buildings. "It sets on a second day, and it feels like I've just finished one."

"You have great passion for your work," Sanguine said, smiling gently. "It's beautiful to see." Nefari returned the smile. "Let's head back to the beds at Cecrops estate and rest our weary bones."

"Not tonight, Guinea," Nefari said suddenly. "I haven't finished yet."

"You're not going back down those stairs, are you?" Sanguine asked incredulously. "If you go back down there without good rest and food, you won't be coming back up again."

"No. If that were the case, I would have said my goodbyes at the base," said Nefari. "I want to walk out into the city and explore the streets. I've never been to a place so full of people."

"Then I'll come with you," Sanguine offered.

"We both know you seek your bed for the night. Honestly, this is something I want to do myself. I like to get out on my own, have my own space at times."

"Are you sure?" Sanguine asked one more time. Nefari nodded. "Okay, but don't go near any dark alleyways... and if someone gives you even the slightest unsure feeling, scream as loud as you can. The Uru will come help you."

"I will. Don't worry so much, and go," Nefari said, hugging her friend once more. They got to their feet, and Nefari watched Sanguine walk off to Cecrops' estate, a short way down the road.

The real reason Nefari didn't want to go with Sanguine was Cecrops. She felt strong enough to talk one-on-one to the creature, but she did not want to spend the night under his roof. She would need to find an inn quickly, though, as she was not going to be able to walk around for much longer. Nefari decided to follow the loudest and most rowdy merriment she could hear. This took her two streets over to a tavern of sorts. The sign on the door read The

Turtle Shell.

"As good a place as any, I guess," Nefari said aloud before entering. Men were dancing in the middle of the room, holding large pottery jugs of wine. Their voices were rough and slurred as they tried to match the beat and finely tuned vocal cords of a bard. The stench that hung in the air sent shivers up her spine. It was full and almost alive, rich and pungent. There were meats, wood smoke, and the stale stench of the men all mixed into one smell that hung heavy in the air. Nefari approached the bar.

"Do you..." Realizing the barman was not paying her any attention, she moved closer and waved a hand in his face. The man looked at her with a glum, uninterested expression. "Do you have a room?"

"One obol," the barman said. This was not something that Nefari had planned on. In Atlantis, everything she needed was free to her. She had no need to carry any coins.

"I don't have any money," she told the barman. "I came to work for Ce..."

"Get out of here," the barman yelled at her. "I don't run a charity."

"Excuse me," Nefari said, her temper starting to stir.

"You heard me. Get out."

"Gardi, you don't want this beautiful young girl sleeping out on the streets now, do you," the man next to her interjected. "Not when it could mean your head."

"Speak your meaning, Torres," Gardi said, put off by the comment.

"Recently, Cecrops brought some mechanics from Atlantis to help fix some things for him. She is wearing the garb of a mechanic and so is here on the king's request. She would have told you as much if you let her finish speaking." Gardi looked at Nefari questioningly, and Nefari nodded back.

"She still can't stay for free," Gardi said, though less sure of himself. "Who's going to pay me?"

"I will," Torres said. "Write out her order and I will pay you. I'll have Cecrops compensate me."

"So what shall it be then, Miss," Gardi's whole attitude towards Nefari changed instantly.

"I need a room... With a bath in it. Also, if you could have a meal prepared for me. That would be all," Nefari said.

"That will all equal up to a drachma," Gardi said sternly

to Torres. It was double the amount that someone would usually pay, but if she was really from Cecrops' employ, then why not? Torres handed over the money and waited for a list of costs.

"What is your name, girl?" Torres asked Nefari. "I need to list it on the costing sheet or Cecrops won't compensate me for the coin."

"Nefari. Thank you, Torres," Torres smiled at her.

"All the children of Atlantis are one," he said. Torres scooped up the key from the counter and threw it to Nefari. "Up the stairs and last door is yours. The serving maids will be in shortly with hot water for the bath. Your food will be left outside the door. Now run along, little rabbit."

Nefari thanked Torres once more before moving up the stairs and to her room. The key had trouble turning in the lock, but she finally got it with a sudden clank. The room beyond was nothing fancy but it met all her needs. There was a bed in the corner by a closed window. She walked over to the window and opened it to try and remove the smell of past occupants. A refreshingly cool breeze drifted through, cleansing the room. A bronze bath sat on the far side wall, empty. She would need to wait for the hot water. The only other furniture was a small table and two chairs where people could sit and eat or talk. She moved to the bed and lay down. It wasn't the most comfortable thing she had been on, but her tired muscles were singing their joy at the rest. She closed her eyes for only a moment while she waited for the bath.

A small hand gently shook her awake. Nefari opened her eyes and looked around rapidly. The door to her room was open, and the bath was now filled. Steam rose up into the air. She noticed that the window had been closed and a curtain hung. Looking back at the small figure, she saw that it was a young girl not yet having reached maturity. She pulled a lock of blonde hair back behind her ear as she waited on Nefari.

"Sorry, I must have fallen asleep," Nefari told the young girl.

"That's okay. I heard that you are working for Cecrops and have yet to have a break in the last two days," the girl said. Nefari questioned her with her eyes. "You hear a lot in taverns. My name is Mira. My father runs the bar here. If you need anything at all, let me know."

"Thank you, Mira," Nefari said. Mira's turquoise eyes lit

up under her growing smile. "I see you drew me a bath."

"Yes. When I realized that you were a woman, I added some scented oils and placed up a curtain for your privacy. Also, I thought that your muscles must be aching, so I added some special salts. Merchants bring them from distant lands, and they are said to soothe pain. Many guests have complimented us and even asked for it to be added."

"I am impressed," Nefari said, sitting up. "Not only did you consider my needs after physically seeing me, but you also considered my needs from the stories you have heard. You are a blessing to this tavern."

"Thank you," Mira was now blushing. She extended the towel she was holding. "Use this to dry yourself with. I will have your meal up in one hour. I'll check on you then to make sure you haven't fallen asleep, as you will catch a chill from the cooling waters."

Mira left the room, leaving Nefari in peace once more. She felt better after the quick nap and stood up, walking to the bath. Removing the mechanics' clothing, she tested the waters. A perfect temperature, she thought. Nefari allowed the water to slide over her body, caressing each muscle as she lowered herself into the curve of the tub. She shivered in delight as the warmth penetrated deep into her bruised tissue. The smell of roses and cinnamon was also a delight she would have to take back to Atlantis with her. Nefari never knew a bath could feel so good.

A commotion downstairs started. Nefari thought a fight must have broken out, as there was shouting and a lot of movement. She didn't give it much thought, tucked safely away in the room, when seconds later the door burst open. Nefari was shocked as the man ran in, ripping the curtain from where it hung and opened the window. He turned back and dove under the bed as three more men came running in. Two moved to look out the window as the other approached Nefari. She recognized Torres from earlier.

"Apologies, Nefari, but the man that ran through, where did he go?" Nefari sat with her mouth gaping a moment longer.

"He came in, took down the curtain, opened the window, then dove..." Nefari did not want to lie to the Uru who had helped her, but she did not want to rat out the other man either. She believed stopping there was her best solution. Torres believed her without hesitation, and the three men ran downstairs and out into the night to track down the man now hiding under Nefari's bed.

"I am sorry," Mira said, walking into the room. She had been worried for Nefari, knowing she would be in the bath. "There was no time to stop them."

"It is okay, Mira," Nefari reassured her. "They were men from Atlantis. We are comfortable clothed or unclothed in each other's company. We trust that the other will offer respect and not take advantage."

"I don't believe I could ever be as you are. I was always taught to be modest. I brought you your meal. I made sure they gave you extra to make up for the intrusion. I'll leave it for you on the table and will lock the door this time."

"Thank you again, Mira," Nefari watched the young girl leave and heard the click of the door as the lock fell into place. She waited until she heard the footsteps move away. "Do you plan on sleeping under there?"

The man started to shuffle, trying to slide out from under the bed frame. It looked like he was having some difficulty but eventually got himself clear. Standing, the man walked to one of the chairs, reversed it, and sat facing the bath. Nefari saw the tan from being out in the sun a lot. It suited the strong muscle tone shown by the curves in his dark clothing. He sported a short cropped beard that was full and dark to the point of almost being black.

"I was surprised that I got under there so quickly," he said. "Thank you for not giving away my position to the Uru."

"You don't call them Atlanteans like most people?" Nefari asked. Nestled in the warm bath, only her head and feet could be seen poking out. "Many don't even know the term Uru."

"You learn much when you have ears in the right places. Before, when you were talking to the serving girl, you aligned yourself with Atlantis. Why did you not help the Uru?"

"I did," Nefari said. "I told them everything I saw."

"Yet you stopped at the moment that would have revealed me. If it was Cecrops that was asking for information, would you have stopped then?"

"I would have said you jumped out the..." Nefari paused mid-sentence and settled her mind at the mention of Cecrops' name. Her face became softer again. The man noticed the change but said nothing.

100

"My name is Cranaus," the man said then.

"Nefari," with that, she got out of the bath and retrieved her towel that was now under the curtain. Cranaus was fully aware of the petite, naked form standing before him. His mind raced as he took in all of her curves and lines. He saw the way the water dripped from her short brown hair or traced a path down the edges of her body. The ivory tone of her skin shone like no one else he had seen before.

"Perfect," the words slipped out before he caught himself. Nefari looked up.

"What was that?" She asked, toweling herself down.

"No... No, nothing," Cranaus said, flustered. He watched silently as Nefari placed the towel over her head and rubbed back and forwards getting most of the water. Nefari then draped the towel over her shoulders and took a seat opposite him.

"Would you like to share some food? I know Mira meant well, but there is far too much here for me to eat alone," said Nefari, stretching her tired muscles. They felt exceptional after that bath. Cranaus watched her movements, unable to look away.

"Yekay," he tried to speak and mixed a combination of words. Nefari looked at him with narrowed eyes and realized just what was going through this man's mind.

"I'm making you uncomfortable," she said. "I'll put on some clothes."

"No," he said, reaching out then calmed himself. He looked away for the first time. "No, you don't need to trouble yourself with that. I heard what you said to the serving girl about treating each other with respect no matter the situation. I... Well. I just haven't met anyone that is as beautiful as you are. I am entranced by you." Cranaus looked back at Nefari's ocean blue eyes. She could see the emotion behind his words and was moved by them.

"Not many people where I'm from talk the way you do. Thank you for your kind words," Nefari said as crimson danced upon her cheeks.

"I know that I may be too forward in what I ask, but I cannot leave it be. Would you share a bed with me?" Nefari's hand shot to her mouth, having never before been asked that question. No one on Atlantis ever would in her condition. She didn't know how to react to this and therefore her body chose flight.

"And now I shall put my clothes on," she said, not

meeting his gaze. Cranaus was annoyed with himself for having made Nefari feel uncomfortable. She pulled her clothing back over her head and then sat across from him again. He had an odd expression on his face as if he was thinking deeply about something. Nefari spoke again. "I mean no offense and am truly flattered. Maybe I might have even..."

"You are a mechanic from Atlantis?" Cranaus asked suddenly. "You just got here recently?"

"The news really does travel fast around here," Nefari commented. "I have barely even set foot in this town and everyone knows."

"I need to go," Cranaus said, getting up and walking to the door.

"Please don't," Nefari said. She was enjoying the company, but Cranaus shook his head.

"I must. I shouldn't be here and there are people after me. Thank you for helping me, Nefari. I hope for both our sakes that our paths do not cross again."

Cranaus left the confused and slightly sad Nefari trying to pick up the pieces of what just happened. Were the men of Hellas so fragile that they need to run from a simple rejection? She was even about to tell him that she was not against his proposal but rather not ready to cross that line. The thought of him stuck in her mind as she nibbled on the meats rich in gravy and the chunks of black bread that accompanied it.

It took another four days before Nefari was happy with the generators. In that time she had returned to the tavern only once more having worked in two-day shifts. The barman, Gardi, was far more friendly to her this time and even put her up for free though gave her minimal food. The amount he made from the first visit made up for the loss of an obol or two. Nefari was surprised to find she was disappointed that Cranaus had not returned. She had been harbouring some rather intimate fantasies as she worked.

"Would you like to do the honors?" Nefari asked Sanguine, gesturing towards the generators.

"So, we're finished then?" her friend asked with a relieved smile, wiping the sweat from her brow. Both girls' clothes and cheeks were stained with grease.

"Let's see how it runs, and I'll answer your question then," Nefari replied cautiously, knowing the machines could be temperamental. Sanguine eagerly flipped the switch, starting the generators. Nefari listened intently to the turbines and cogs spinning, discerning every little detail in the motors, but nothing warned her of any issues. Finally, she looked across at Sanguine and nodded. Her friend started bouncing around before rushing over and hugging Nefari, lifting her into the air.

"I'm so happy," Sanguine exclaimed. "We can finally go back to Atlantis, and I can visit my cook. He'd better have something special prepared."

"You'll need to wait one more night before we can set out for Atlantis," Nefari informed her. "I have a feeling it's night time outside."

"Are you going to stay with me back at Cecrops' home?" Sanguine asked, her eyes pleading. "You haven't spent even one of our nights off with me. You've either been here or off exploring the town." Nefari was about to decline when another voice interjected.

"I will have to insist as well," Cecrops said, entering the room. "I was coming down to see how things were progressing, but I see the work is now complete. Thank you both. After your trip in, I've organized a small group to guard your journey back. I will also be coming along as I need to visit Atlantis. We leave first thing in the morning and have no time to pick you up from random taverns."

Nefari felt defeated by Cecrops' insistence and simply nodded, not wanting to risk the consequences of rebellion. Sanguine, observing her friend's demeanor, felt a pang of sadness at how Nefari must be feeling. As they ascended the stairs toward Cecrops' residence, Sanguine linked her arm with Nefari's, silently offering her support. Nefari mouthed a quiet "thank you" in response.

Upon reaching the house, Nefari realized it was the same residence she had seen in her dreams, where she had followed Cecrops. Sanguine entered, and Nefari noticed that Shenlong and Sobek had also joined them. Before following them inside, Nefari paused, her gaze drifting to the side of the house, recalling the disturbing scene from her past. Lost in thought, she appeared almost distressed.

Cecrops, noticing her hesitation, narrowed his eyes before addressing her. "How has your life been living with Nudgee?" he asked, snapping Nefari out of her reverie.

"Good," she replied calmly. "He has always treated me like a daughter."

"Shame about his hand," Cecrops remarked, feigning sympathy. "Life deals both good and bad luck. He just happened to be unlucky on that occasion."

"It was fortunate he came back at all. I consider it a blessing."

"Did he ever impart to you the ways of his people, the people you share the blood of?" Cecrops' question struck Nefari with the weight of realization. It was the moment Nudgee had warned her about. Cecrops must have sensed her thoughts and drawn his own conclusions, suspecting her of spying on him. Nefari strengthened her inner defenses.

"Yes, they were such wonderful and beautiful tales, Cecrops. Not all of them could have been true, but they certainly spark the imagination. Do you know of the stories of my people?" she added, injecting an air of wonderment into her tone.

"I know all the histories of the Abori. I was even there for some of it. How about the stories where the Abori flew over lands and even through space?" Cecrops countered.

"Flying...? Do you mean when the sky people came and took the souls of the Abori to live with them?" Nefari inquired.

"That was a different story entirely," Cecrops conceded. Through Nefari's adept performance, Cecrops concluded that she didn't possess any significant knowledge. Nevertheless, he decided on one last attempt to trip her up. "What caught your attention moments ago? You seemed so lost in thought."

"Oh, that," Nefari replied casually, waving her hand as if the thought were inconsequential. "I was just thinking that it was silly to have pathways down the side of a home. All it does is grant access to the back entrance for anyone who would be thieves." Her answer seemed to satisfy Cecrops.

"The homeowner finds more convenience than not from it. If it wasn't there, a thief would just come through the back with mud on their boots from the gardens behind the house. Come, let us move inside."

The inner rooms of the house were tiled with black marble cut from the same large piece in a seamless manner. The veins running through the dark stone shone like gold. The walls were painted blue and were adorned with pottery vases, each bearing intricate patterns and paintings. Cecrops also used the vases to hold purple flowers, filling the air with the scent of lavender. Nefari took in a deep breath, enjoying the aroma.

"You're smelling the purple flowers in the vases," a voice from the balcony above remarked. The speaker bore the features of Cecrops but appeared much younger, with long, dark hair cascading past her shoulders. She had the air of a confident young woman.

"This is my daughter, Pandrosus," Cecrops introduced her. Nefari felt a twinge of jealousy, quickly reminding herself of the true nature of Cecrops, the monster he was, and consequently, the half-monster Pandrosus must be. "She's been eager to meet you, but you kept eluding her."

"Come with me, Nefari. I'll show you to your room," Pandrosus invited. Nefari welcomed the chance to be away from Cecrops and followed Pandrosus up the stairs, noticing that Sanguine had already headed in that direction upon entering the home.

"My dad and sisters can be such bores sometimes. I always enjoy when we have guests," Pandrosus remarked. "I'm glad you don't talk like Sanguine does, though."

Nefari smiled at the comment. "She means well. Sanguine gets nervous around strangers, so she tends to talk a lot. It calms her, but once she gets to know you, you'll find she's a beautiful person."

"I'm sad that I won't get the chance to know you both well enough. It's already late, and I know you leave first thing in the morning. I just wanted to say a quick hello before you left," Pandrosus expressed her regret.

"I'm sorry I hadn't come back sooner. If you ever come to Atlantis or if I return, we can hang out some more," Nefari offered.

"I would like that," Pandrosus said warmly. She paused in front of a doorway. "This is your room. I hope you find it to your liking." Pandrosus leaned in and hugged Nefari. "May we meet again."

Nefari nodded and entered the room assigned to her... and apparently to Sanguine as well. The room was mostly tidy, with Nefari's bed against one wall, a dresser with drawers, and a bronze mirror. The only thing out of place was Sanguine's bed, positioned right in the middle of the bedroom.

"I dragged it in myself," the redhead declared proudly, sitting cross-legged on the bed, waiting for Nefari. "Welcome to our room."

"Our room?" Nefari raised an eyebrow.

"I wanted to have a girls' night," Sanguine explained with a grin.

Nefari pondered for a moment, then ducked her head out the door and saw Pandrosus entering another room. Calling out to her, Nefari caught her attention.

"Is there something you need? I can fetch one of the housecarls for you," Pandrosus offered.

"Fetch the housecarl and have them bring your bed to this room, then come join us," Nefari instructed Pandrosus.

"What's happening?" Pandrosus asked, surprised by the request.

"Girls' night," Nefari replied with a wink before retreating into the room. She glanced at Sanguine. "I hope you don't mind."

"Not at all," Sanguine said happily. "I've tried talking to her, but I think the conversation was one-sided again. I'll be far more relaxed with you here. The other two wouldn't even talk to me."

"There are two other daughters?" Nefari inquired.

"Yes, three daughters in total. He also had a son, but there was something wrong at birth. He was deformed in some way. He didn't make it," Sanguine explained, noticing the emotions flickering across Nefari's face. "But we don't need to talk about that right now."

Soon, the housecarl entered, dragging Pandrosus's bed sideways into the room. He placed it near Sanguine's bed, and Pandrosus entered in her sleeping clothes.

"So, what shall we do?" Pandrosus asked, still unsure of what was going on.

"I really love your voice, Pandrosus," Nefari said. "It's so unique and musical." Pandrosus blushed, and Sanguine smiled in agreement.

"Tonight is about bonding as women and having fun," Nefari declared.

"Nefari was about to tell me about her adventures around Athens, and we wanted you to join in as well." Nefari glanced at Sanguine, feeling caught off guard and slightly cornered.

"Yes, I'd love to hear about it!" Pandrosus exclaimed, her excitement growing.

"Stories about men and wild times," Sanguine added eagerly. Nefari objected at this point. "So there were no men then."

"Well, I did meet one man," Nefari admitted, recalling Cranaus and his unexpected appearance. Sanguine scooted closer on her bed.

"See, Pandrosus? That's how you get a girl to open up," Sanguine remarked to Pandrosus, who laughed, already enjoying the atmosphere of the night. "Well, continue, Nefari. Elaborate on this mystery man."

Feeling a bit uncomfortable with the sudden attention, Nefari nevertheless saw the wonderment in Pandrosus's eyes and realized that the girl had likely never experienced a night like this before. Gathering her thoughts, Nefari went into great detail about how she found the tavern and secured her room. She recounted her encounter with Mira and the most relaxing bath she had ever experienced. This led to the chase through her room and her conversations with the mysterious man, painting a vivid picture of her recent escapades for her eager audience.

"In the bath!" Pandrosus exclaimed, her eyes widening. "Did you not feel uncomfortable?"

"Things are very different on Atlantis," Sanguine remarked with a mischievous smile. "So, what happened then? Did you maybe..." She let her voice trail off suggestively.

"You didn't," Pandrosus gasped, her hands covering her mouth in surprise.

"No, I didn't," Nefari admitted. "Not that the opportunity wasn't there. I was just embarrassed. When I put my clothes back on, he couldn't get out of there fast enough."

"So, I'm still the only one here who has lain with a man," Sanguine stated. Pandrosus looked at her with shock evident on her face.

"I thought we were talking about kissing," she said. Both Nefari and Sanguine glanced at each other before they burst into laughter.

The girls continued to talk long into the night. As the first rays of the sun hit the windows and their eyes grew heavy, Nefari knew that the day ahead would be a long and arduous struggle. Eventually, Sanguine and Nefari left Pandrosus where she lay, lightly snoring. She had fallen asleep two hours prior, while the other girls kept up their hushed chatter. Outside, the sunlight stung their eyes, making them feel weary.

107

"Let's only do that when we've had a good night's sleep the previous night and aren't about to be riding for two days," Sanguine suggested with a yawn. Nefari couldn't help but yawn herself as she agreed.

"I hope you girls are ready," Sobek said as he brought over both their mounts. He assisted them in getting into the saddles. "Even with the guard, we will still be under threat of attack, as Cecrops will be joining us."

Nefari surveyed the twenty men chosen to guard them. None had the look of an Uru warrior, and all had inferior weapons. They were dressed in bronze armor with bronze-plated kilts, each carrying short swords shaped like thin leaves, similar to the steel one Cecrops wore. Despite their equipment, they all had the air of fighters, and Nefari decided that their capability mattered more than their gear in battle. As Cecrops approached, she braced herself for the encounter.

"The generators are running smoothly. You did your job well," Cecrops acknowledged.

"It is my life," Nefari replied, resolving to mention the sabotage, not for Cecrops's sake, but for the benefit of all those who relied on the generators. "When we fixed them, I decided to reinforce the outer shell, making it harder to break into. Without the proper equipment that only the Uru hold, you shouldn't have the same problem again."

"And what problem would that be?" Cecrops inquired, his eyebrows raised in curiosity.

"Sabotage!" Sanguine interjected, listening intently to the conversation. "Where did you get that from?"

Nefari recounted the evidence of sabotage she had discovered. "There were cables literally yanked from sockets, chipboards snapped in two from immense pressure, and marks indicating someone had placed a large piece of metal in the cogs."

"She is quite right, Sanguine," Cecrops confirmed. "I have been around machines long enough to know when something has been tampered with. I'd just not expected someone so young to see the same thing. You will not speak of this, of course," he told them, leaving no room for arguement. Both girls nodded in agreement. "Good. Now let's start moving. It's going to be a long day, and I suspect you two will want to reach our camp for the night as soon as possible."

Nefari shivered as Cecrops walked around to the back of

the house. Moments later, a ball of light floated around to the front as Cecrops rode the Vimana. They moved through the city at a slow pace, pedestrians giving way to their passing. Once beyond the city limits, the party picked up speed. Nefari remembered the discomfort of the previous horse ride and braced herself for more jolting movements, knowing the yellowing bruises from the last ride would now have their own bruises.

The day wore on as Nefari had feared. She couldn't find the rhythm of the horse's movements and continually came down too hard in the saddle. Yet, this discomfort was the only thing keeping her awake; she knew that falling asleep would mean falling from the saddle. Seeing Sanguine equally uncomfortable eased her frustration. As the sun neared three-quarters of the way across the sky, a noise from the Vimana caught their attention, and Cecrops landed softly on the ground.

"Looks like we make camp here for the night," Cecrops announced, cursing under his breath. Both Sanguine and Nefari breathed a sigh of relief, sliding off their horses. For an outside observer, their dismount would have seemed more like a fall. They sat upon the soft earth, trying to recover from the ride. Though not as harsh as the previous journey, it still left them sore. The pain compounded, and Nefari felt as though she could fall asleep right there on the spot.

"Nefari, Sanguine, I need you over here now," Cecrops commanded. Nefari could see him walking around the Vimana, inspecting the inner workings through the gaps.

"Stay here, Guinea," Nefari told her friend. "He only wants us to fix his stupid toy so that he doesn't have to ride."

"But it may need the two of us," Sanguine said, concerned for Nefari and fearful of disobeying Cecrops. Nefari shook her head.

"I heard the Vimana coming down. One of the valves is sticking. It will take a while to get to the center of the motor, but two people will be fighting for space. It will take twice as long. I'll let Cecrops know what is happening. You set up your tent and get some rest. I'll be in my bed just after nightfall."

"Thank you," Sanguine said, shuffling across and hugging Nefari. "I'll see you in the morning."

Nefari nodded and then moved to where Cecrops was

growing agitated. He looked up, seeing only one girl.

"And Sanguine?" he asked calmly. Nefari could sense that a wrong word now could mean severe punishment.

"I sent her to bed," Nefari replied, just as calm. Cecrops raised an eyebrow.

"I could diagnose the Vimana from the sound when you landed. Two people will only get in each other's way. The problem with fixing a Vimana is that it's a one-person job," Nefari explained. Cecrops nodded.

"How long?" he inquired.

"Until it's fixed? Possibly midnight. I'll get the main components sorted by nightfall. The engines will need to run for a few hours after that. I'll take a nap at that time, and at midnight, I'll come do the final checks," Nefari replied confidently.

"Make it so," Cecrops commanded harshly before walking off. He began issuing orders to move the camp away from the Vimana, as it would be making a small amount of noise for most of the night.

Alone with her tools, Nefari felt a sense of comfort doing what she loved. Even the pain seemed to diminish with a wench in her han... Nefari sent a glare towards Shenlong. With a wrench in her hand. She started working on the Vimana and was pleased to find that her guess about the fault was correct.

Nefari lay in the tent supplied by Cecrops, trying to determine exactly what had woken her. She didn't even remember falling asleep, and her mind felt fuzzy. She noticed the glow on the tent lighting up the eastern walls; the morning sun must have roused her. Suddenly, her senses flared as she realized she hadn't done the final checks on the Vimana. With a sense of urgency, she threw open the tent flap and raced out into a scene of turmoil.

Fires burned all around, casting eerie light and producing low clouds of smoke. The clash of steel on steel filled the night air. As Nefari made her way to the edge of the camp, a Hellene guard crashed into her, sending her sprawling to the dirt. Ignoring her, he rushed into battle.

Struggling to her feet, Nefari's heart clenched as she saw Sanguine locked in combat with a leather-clad man. With horror, she watched as the man threw Sanguine to the ground and raised his sword, poised to strike. Acting on instinct, Nefari grabbed a nearby sword and prepared to charge at the assailant. But it was too late; the man's blade plunged deep into Sanguine's chest, splattering her blood across the earthen floor.

"NO!" Nefari screamed, the words torn from her by sheer emotion. But her cry only seemed to draw the attention of the man before her. He turned to her, his smile wicked and terrifying, a sight that would haunt her nightmares. Trembling, Nefari raised the sword she held in defense, her grip unsteady with fear. The man advanced, his angular face contorted in a bloodlust-fueled grin, his green eyes locking onto hers with an intensity that froze her in place.

The man batted her sword aside, and Nefari fell to her knees, knowing that these would be her last breaths. Her senses heightened as if time had slowed down. She took in the crackling fires sending embers to the stars, the slightly more full moon than the last time she had seen it, and the distant beacon light of Atlantis flashing past the hills. Oh, how she wished she could see the floating city once more.

As the gleaming bronze short sword came up, Nefari closed her eyes, bracing for the end. A metal clang echoed through her ears, but she felt no pain. Opening her eyes, she saw the sword suspended in the air by a second sword inches from her neck.

"What is this, Cranaus?" the man growled. "I will not let you steal my kill. The mechanic must die."

"She is of no concern now," Cranaus replied evenly. "We have Cecrops cornered, and we need everybody we can. His death is most important. Now go!" With a grumble, the man walked off to join a group of others who had formed a fighting ring around Cecrops.

"Are you okay?" Cranaus offered Nefari his hand. She looked up at the man who had just saved her life, her mouth hanging open in disbelief. It was the same man who had broken into her room and hidden under the bed, the same man who had occupied her thoughts and dreams ever since—a nuisance that would not leave her alone. And now, here he was again, at the moment of her death no less. She sat gawking at him without moving, lost in astonishment. Cranaus leaned down and shook her. "Snap out of it, girl."

The moment was shattered, and Nefari found herself back on the battlefield. Her friend was dead, and one of the men who had given out commands had saved her, offering a hand. "Are you okay?" he had asked.

"NO, I AM NOT OK BY ATHENA'S TITS!" she screamed at him, her emotions overflowing, tears streaming down her face. Cranaus pulled her to her feet and urged her to move. At first, she resisted, but her body obeyed, each step feeling involuntary. He guided her to the edge of the camp and fixed her with a serious gaze, demanding her attention.

"The flying thing that Cecrops rides is just over that small rise there. It's running already. Take it and get out of here. You can grieve once you're safe," Cranaus instructed firmly. Nefari looked away, but Cranaus grabbed her chin and forced her to meet his gaze. "If my men come back and find you here, they will kill you. Go and live. Live, if only to avenge your friend."

His words stung Nefari, and a surge of fresh emotions washed over her, anger rising as the dominant force. Composing herself, she wiped the tears from her eyes and took a few steps towards the Vimana. Then, she turned back, determination etched on her face.

"Go!" Cranaus commanded, and Nefari started running. She stumbled over the soft rise, nearly crawling to the Vimana. The engine was running just as she had left it, and she quickly did the last spot checks. Ramming the side plate into place with more force than necessary, Nefari straddled the machine. She wound the engine down and turned it off before adjusting the settings she needed. As she cranked the engine once more, she heard the sounds of men running her way. Fear gripped her, anticipating the attackers who had assaulted her camp.

But when she saw what was rushing towards her, being chased by the enemy, she wished it had been the enemy alone. The reptilian form of Cecrops ran hunched over towards her, his tail swishing from side to side. As the engine reached optimal power output, Cecrops jumped on behind her.

"Go, Go," he urged in a slurred voice, struggling to pronounce the 'G' due to his mouth structure.

With the group of men seeking their blood mere metres away, Nefari took off into the sky. Though she had only a basic understanding of the controls, she had never flown a Vimana herself. They traveled at incredible speed as Cecrops reached over and pointed.

"Pull that small lever there gently until we slow down, then press the grey button on the end of the left handle," he instructed.

Nefari followed his guidance, and the Vimana gradually slowed in the air. When she pressed the grey button, the machine came to a stop twenty meters off the ground. Surprisingly, she found her breathing remained calm, even with Cecrops in his reptilian form right behind her.

"How did you break free?" she asked, turning back to him. But seeing those slitted eyes staring at her up close made her quickly look forward again.

"When I changed forms, many men stepped back. They were stunned long enough for me to make my escape. The rest, you know," Cecrops explained. He stood up on the far back end of the Vimana. "Move back towards me," he instructed, and Nefari complied. With a small leap over her, Cecrops regained control and started the machine moving forward again.

"I don't understand any of it," Nefari confessed.

"You seem mighty calm in my presence, Nefari. Why is that?" Cecrops inquired. Nefari realized her mistake—she had been told to remain calm around Cecrops's human form, not his true form. Her composure betrayed her, and she struggled to find an answer.

"How long have you been able to use the Dreamtime?" Cecrops continued, his tone unnervingly calm.

"The night you ate that child," Nefari replied, her voice edged with defiance. If she was to die at the hands of this monster, she would do so with her head held high.

"There have been many such nights, but I know the one," Cecrops admitted, seemingly unfazed by the implications. "You were wise not to say anything, for your life would have been forfeit. Even now, from this moment, if you say anything about what you have seen, I will kill you myself."

"How do the Uru tolerate you?" Nefari pressed, her eyes narrowing. "Nudgee told me that he had informed the senior Uru about what you were, and they said they were already aware of it. That was before Atlantis was even formed."

"I do not harm other Uru," Cecrops stated simply.

"Yet you would threaten harm upon me," Nefari pointed out.

"You are a half-breed with no true purpose and risk more than you know," Cecrops retorted.

This exchange left Nefari deeply unsettled, and she chose to end the conversation there. As the lights of

Atlantis shone on the horizon, she felt a sense of relief at being home. From that moment on, she vowed never to leave the underworks again.

The moment Nefari's feet touched the hard surface of Atlantis, she felt at ease. She was home now, and everything seemed much easier. Yes, there was still evil and turmoil in the world, but not here. Here, she was safe and could be herself once more, the persona she was before the trip to Athens and being hunted across the countryside. Nefari thought of Sanguine, smiling, but the moment was quickly pushed aside by thoughts of her chest ripped open, drenched in her own blood. She wiped her mind of any such thoughts.

Nefari needed to inform the mechanic's head office that Sanguine had passed. She started making her way to the underworks, navigating the winding maze of halls. She knew every twist and turn intimately, and it wasn't long before she was banging on the office window. It was after hours, but the jerk, Hedas, would be asleep just inside. She heard a scuffling, then the window slid open.

"Who is it?" Hedas, wiping sleep from his eyes, sounded grumpy. "Nefari..? You look terrible."

"Go suck a... Forget it," the fight in Nefari worn away by lack of sleep and recent experiences. He was right, though. Nefari's hair was frizzy, dirt marked her cheeks and clothes, large dark rings under her eyes, her face drawn and lifeless. "I have just returned from Athens. The road was not friendly. Sanguine, Rose of the South, has lost her life." Nefari came up with the name at that very moment but felt it suited Sanguine perfectly.

"Come again," Hedas said, now fully awake.

"Sanguine... Rose of the South... and my friend... has been killed," Nefari spoke slowly and clearly, ensuring he heard her properly. The effort she put into saying those words brought on a flood of emotions she couldn't hold back. Her face crumpled, and she cried into her hands. Hedas stood, gawking at the girl who had always given him so much trouble, sympathy growing within him. Climbing out of the window, he drew Nefari close, wrapping his arms around her.

"Shh," Hedas soothed as he stroked her hair, careful not to get caught in one of her knots. "Thank you for bringing me the news, Nefari. I will inform the proper authorities

114

and the cook, Fruruk." Hearing the name and remembering Sanguine's words about her lover, Nefari cried harder into Hedas's chest. He let her have her moment, and after ten minutes, she started to calm a little.

"Nefari," Hedas said gently. "You've had a tough few days. You're run down and emotional. Take some time to recover and come back when the world doesn't seem so bad."

Nefari nodded, and Hedas kissed her forehead before sending her on her way. She stumbled along, back up the halls, tired and weary. She longed to sleep in her true bed in the room she shared with Nudgee, not just her hammock. When she reached the room, she pushed open the door, greeted Nudgee, and fell face-first onto her bed. Nefari lay there for five minutes, almost falling asleep, but something niggled at her senses. Rolling over, she looked back at Nudgee.

"Nudgee, I'm home," she said, but there was no reply. A sadness filled her chest. "Not you too."

Nefari rolled out of bed and walked slowly towards Nudgee. His face was calm and unmoving. She noticed that his chest wasn't rising and falling with his breathing either. Nefari knew he had passed, and she was sad. She just couldn't shed tears anymore. Looking closer, she noticed someone had cleaned the body and wrapped everything but the face in fine silk. This moved her, and a single tear rolled down her cheek.

Looking out the window at the moon, a thought struck her. She raced over to her bed and laid down, making herself comfortable. Going through the motions, she released her spirit from her body and looked around. There, standing by his own body, was Nudgee. Next to his spirit was a tree that grew in the shape of an arch, making a doorway before him shining green.

"Nudgee," Nefari whispered, running over and jumping into his arms.

"I had feared you wouldn't make it in time," he told her.

"What do you mean?" she asked, worried about the answer.

"My body's lifespan has ended. I passed happily in my sleep soon after seeing you on your way to Athens. We are graced with seven days before we must leave this realm for the next. It gives the spirit a chance to come to terms with what has happened and say its own goodbyes. At the end of the seven days, a door of our making appears, and we are drawn through."

"Please stay," Nefari said softly.

"I have seen your troubles, Nefari, and know you are in pain. I wish I could say more to heal your emotional eclipse, but even now I am being called."

"Let me come with you," she said, grasping him tighter.

"You cannot enter my door," he said, ending the hug by taking her hands in his own. "You do not belong on the other side yet."

"How can I go on?" she asked.

"With each day, new and wonderful possibilities abound. Don't live your whole life locked away in the bowels of Atlantis, licking your wounds. You have far too much strength for that, and even more love to give to this world."

"I don't want to lose you."

"You haven't lost me, Nefari. This is just a parting of ways for a short time. We will meet again one day in this world or the next... I must go... But there is another who wishes to talk."

"Who?" Nudgee pointed behind her, and Nefari swung to see Sanguine. Tears welled in Nefari's eyes, and she turned back to Nudgee. "Farewell, father," she said, kissing him.

"Farewell, daughter," Nudgee replied. He slowly let her hands go, then stepped up to his door. Looking back one last time, he walked through and out of sight. The door faded back to nothing.

"I am sorry for your loss, Nefari," Sanguine said from behind her. Nefari turned to look at the girl before bringing her into a hug as well.

"Guinea, you are just as important to me as Nudgee was. You were my only true friend," Nefari admitted. "You will leave just as big a hole." Sanguine hugged her just as hard.

"The Rose of the South, you said. Thank you for such a beautiful name."

"It was all I could do to honor you."

"You have made me feel special. It is because of you I can now accept my fate and move on to the next realm. I will hang around Fruruk some more, but thank you."

"How did I help?"

"You accepted me when all others kept me at arm's length. I am comforted to know you are still of this world.

116

That you will spread the same joy you gave me and will still create your mark."

"I can't see how that helps," Nefari said, tears welling in her eyes.

"Don't feel sad for me, Nefari," Sanguine wiped away a tear as it rolled down Nefari's cheek. "I was afraid to die when I was alive. Now that I have, the world is such a different place. I have a new adventure to go on and a new life to lead. I got to talk to Nudgee before you arrived. He helped me to understand what was happening."

"Nudgee has been the only man I would have given my life for."

"I can see that. You've been blessed by the people in your life, Nefari. Many would search high and low just to get a small amount of what you had."

"I was blessed when I met you too," Nefari said, trying to smile.

"Naturally," Sanguine said, flicking her red hair. Both girls laughed. "Now go back to your body and sleep. Hedas was right, you look terrible."

"I don't want to leave you. Not now that I got you back."

"I haven't left you, Nefari. I have just shifted into a new form. One day when you also make the journey, we can meet up, and you can tell me about all the adventures that I know you're going to have. Now go rest. I will stay by your side until you're asleep... Then I'm going to haunt Fruruk."

Nefari bowed her head and let out a long, shuddering sigh. She knew it was time to let Sanguine go.

"Goodbye, Guinea, my beautiful and beloved friend. May the world you find yourself in be as pure as your heart."

'Farewell, Wench,' Nefari eyes widened and for a moment she forgot the pain this day had brought. Then her face softened and she smiled, strong and happy.

'From you, I could love the name.' Nefari brought her friend into one last hug.

'Farewell dear, sweet Nefari,' Sanguine whispered into her ear. Nefari drifted down into her body and fell into a deep, dreamless sleep. Sanguine stroked her with her spirit hand. 'Innocent Nefari, may you never learn your true nature.' With a sad smile, Sanguine drifted off to find her cook.

Chapter 6

The sun was setting, painting the clouds in vibrant reds and oranges. A strong breeze swept in from the sea, intensifying the salty smell in the air. Nearby, three seagulls squabbled over the remains of a mangled crab, each desperate for the meal. Cranaus watched the noisy birds with a smirk, their fight almost comedic as they tussled over a crushed shell on the sand.

Close by, fifteen fighting men stood in formation, all dressed in the white garb of the Uru. Cranaus had had to work hard to convince them to join him in an assault on Atlantis. It had taken two days since nearly slaying the monstrous Cecrops to reach this point. As the sunset painted his beard with warm hues, he scratched the sand from it and addressed the men.

"Tonight, we take down Cecrops," Cranaus announced. "Everyone here knows what he is, and we all agree that Athens must be free of him." The men responded with subdued shouts, careful not to let their voices carry on the breeze toward Atlantis. "You all know your roles. Each of you will sneak into Atlantis at different points using one of the three rowboats." He gestured toward the weather-worn crafts on the shore. "Once inside, make your way to the central area and track down Cecrops. If you get a chance to strike, do it. If we're discovered, retreat, and we'll regroup to make new plans. All right, let's go." The men thumped their chests in salute to Cranaus, then dispersed toward the rowboats. Cranaus followed, picking the one on the far left.

"Not one for big speeches, I see," Mellan commented.

"You know I hate that sort of thing," Cranaus replied with a shrug.

"When you're king, you'll need to get used to it." Cranaus laughed, a deep and hearty sound.

"When I'm king, I'll hire a scholar to write my speeches for me."

"Better hire one to teach you to read, too," Mellan replied, sharing in the laughter.

Both men boarded separate rowboats. Two men from each boat pushed them out into the surf, then quickly jumped in. They positioned their oars and began rowing, gaining momentum with each stroke. Clouds obscured the moonlight, and Cranaus hoped they would remain invisible to anyone watching the sea that night.

As they moved with the waves, Cranaus watched Atlantis gradually draw closer. The metallic island city grew larger with every stroke, and he noted the calmness of the night air—no sound drifted on the breeze, and no light was visible from the city. The rowboat Cranaus was on reached the edge of Atlantis, and they were able to find ample footholds to climb. The men scrambled up onto the deck, carefully merging into the shadows of the city. Cranaus knew this was the most dangerous point, and he hoped that their simple disguise would be enough to avoid detection.

As they navigated through the narrow passages, Cranaus used a map drawn by various Hellenes who had ventured to Atlantis over the past fifty years. This map would make the initial stages of their infiltration easier. However, the center of the map was only partially detailed, as no one had managed to gain access to the deeper parts of the floating city. Cranaus shuddered at the thought of how much water lay below them and how this massive metal structure stayed afloat. If it were to sink, no one would survive.

Rounding a corner, they encountered three Uru walking toward them. Cranaus and the five men with him acted casual, walking past the group as if they belonged there. Cranaus fought the urge to reach for the knife hidden at his side, staying focused until the Uru turned a corner and were out of sight.

"It looks like we blend in well enough," Pelleus said. He'd been friends with Cranaus since they were barely old enough to walk. Cranaus remembered the day they climbed an apple tree, and Pelleus fell, breaking his arm. Both their mothers had a heated argument over who should have been watching them, before carrying each boy away. They were told never to see each other again, but the very next day, with Pelleus bandaged and sporting a splint, they were scrambling up the same tree. Cranaus chuckled to himself, wondering what their mothers would think if they saw them now.

"From now on, all conversation is about life on Atlantis," Cranaus said. "We can't risk anyone overhearing anything that suggests we're not from here."

They continued walking through the vast city, speaking little. They were ill-prepared for this part of the plan. Although some people had compiled a map of Atlantis, very few could tell them what sort of conversations the Uru typically had. As they passed another group of Uru, Cranaus started talking about the ocean breeze—or the lack thereof. He mentioned how the night air felt dense without much movement. The Uru passed by as before, but this time, one of them eyed them suspiciously.

Crossing the first central bridge, they made their way through the next section of the city. When they reached the bridge leading to the central area, Cranaus checked the map one last time. They were about to enter a part of Atlantis where the map had no lines or directions. It was a vast, empty abyss they would need to explore to reach their goal. As they approached the pyramid that towered above them, Cranaus ignored the doors leading into it; they needed to stay away from the hallways where the Uru gathered.

Finding a set of stairs, the six men began to descend. Cranaus recognized another group, led by Mellan, descending from a point much farther around Atlantis. He felt relieved to know they weren't alone. With a quick motion of his hand, Cranaus chose a path that curved off in the opposite direction from where the other group was headed. He couldn't believe his luck when, after the hallway straightened, he saw Cecrops standing at the far end, smiling. The men paused in their tracks, unsure of what to do next.

"Cecrops," Pelleus whispered, his voice barely audible. Cranaus felt a sudden chill as a sense of dread crept up his spine. Something was about to go terribly wrong, but he couldn't put his finger on what it was. Despite the sinking feeling in his gut, they moved forward, inching down the hallway. Suddenly, an alarm blared, sending shockwaves through Cranaus's nerves. Cecrops didn't move an inch, his eerie smile unchanged.

"We need to retreat," Cranaus said, coming to a halt. Four of the men stopped with him, but one hadn't heard him and continued toward Cecrops.

"Cranaus, he's right there," Pelleus said. "We can end this now."

"No, something's not right," Cranaus replied, his voice strained with tension. But Pelleus wasn't listening.

"Run away if you want. I'm going to finish what we started," Pelleus said, turning and sprinting after the other Hellene.

"Wait!" Cranaus called, but he couldn't reach his friend in time. As Pelleus and the other man reached Cecrops, armed Uru in steel armor emerged from both sides of the corridor, surrounding the targets. Cranaus knew Cecrops was out of reach, and there was nothing he could do to save his men against the Uru. He couldn't even determine how many Uru there were—they seemed to keep pouring in from all directions.

"Retreat!" Cranaus ordered, and the men began retracing their steps. The last thing Cranaus saw before turning away was the first Hellene going down, followed by Pelleus disemboweling the Uru who killed him, jamming his knife into the man's belly. Two more swords were swinging through the air toward Pelleus, and other Uru were now chasing them through the winding streets of Atlantis.

"I hope one of you has a better memory than I do," Cranaus shouted, "because I can remember nothing about this place." A younger man, barely in his teens, took the lead, guiding them through a mirrored path back to the boats and their escape route.

As Cranaus passed an open door, a sword swung out from it. He dove under the blade, missing its edge by mere inches, then rolled back to his feet. With no time for a full-blown fight, he lashed out, his knife striking the Uru's throat. The man fell to the ground with a gurgling cry.

"Mind the doors!" Cranaus warned, catching up with the others. Twice more, they encountered small skirmishes, barely escaping as the Uru pressed hard on their heels. The young Hellene leading them was killed by an Uru just as he rounded the last bend toward the decks and freedom. The others couldn't stop, and one of them drove a dagger through the eye of the Uru, allowing them to break through to the open air.

Cranaus was surprised to find that the boats hadn't been cut loose, so they all leaped in. Cutting the lines that held them to Atlantis, they rowed toward land. Halfway across, a Hellene yelped and jumped to his feet, nearly rocking the boat over.

"Settle down, Onidas! You're going to tip us all into the ocean," Cranaus said.

"There's a rat under my seat," Onidas replied. The others could see its shadowy form in the dim night.

Nefari tried to be happy, but it was terribly hard. She had isolated herself from people for a long time, but she was never truly alone. The only reason she was getting out of bed at all was because both Nudgee and Sanguine wanted her to keep going. She'd spent the last two days in her room, moping, sometimes in tears, other times completely drained of energy. She even avoided the Dreamtime, fearing that if she saw Sanguine there, her fragile strength would crumble, and she might consider ending it all.

Nefari lay on the floor near the window, naked, watching the sunset. Since the merging of the ships that had brought them to this land, she had arranged for Nudgee to be transferred to a part of the ship on the outer ring, where he could enjoy views of the ocean. Her hair was tangled and matted, dirt clung to her skin from the frantic race across Hellas, and she hadn't bathed or groomed herself in days. She had barely eaten, her only meal a piece of plain bread, which she slowly nibbled.

Suddenly, a face appeared at the window, peering in at her. She instinctively rolled backward as the face retreated. She barely recognized it, placing a hand on her cheek. Nefari's reflection did the same, and seeing herself in this state was a shock.

"Live your life," Sanguine's voice echoed in her mind.

"I will, Guinea," Nefari said aloud, rising to her feet. "I'm sorry it's taken me this long."

Nefari walked to the small door in the corner of her room and stepped into the bathroom. It had running water, a toilet, a bath, and a basin. Every day, used towels disappeared through an opening in the wall and were replaced with fresh ones. White tiles covered the walls from floor to ceiling, while the floor had small matte black tiles. She turned the silver taps, and steaming water immediately began to fill the bath. She dipped her hand in to adjust the temperature, then let it continue filling. She always liked her baths hotter than what Nudgee could comfortably handle.

Remembering something, she dashed back into her room and retrieved a small pouch of salt crystals. Pandrosus had given it to her when she mentioned the baths at the inn, saying the quality was excellent and that even a small amount could wash away all her pain. Nefari thought she might need the entire bag right now, but she wanted it to last, so she added only a little. The crystals melted into the water, turning it a soft pink, and the steam carried aromas of raspberry and apple.

Nefari slowly lowered herself into the hot, relaxing bath. As the warmth rolled up her skin, she shivered from the sensation. As she settled into the curves of the bath, she realized she couldn't remember a bath ever feeling this good. Given her current mood, she couldn't remember much of anything feeling this good. She knew she'd have to thank Pandrosus when she returned to Athens.

"I thought you wanted to hide away on Atlantis and never set foot in that dangerous world again?" her inner voice said.

"I still have friends," she replied, suddenly aware that she wasn't entirely alone, and this sparked a small sense of joy. "I want to see Pandrosus again."

"Is that all?" her mind asked skeptically. An image of Cranaus flashed into her thoughts, and she quickly pushed it away.

"No, there's no one else I want to see," she replied, but she sensed her mind's skepticism. "Seriously," she insisted, as if to convince herself as much as anyone else.

"You forget I see everything running through your mind, Nefari," her inner voice said. Nefari didn't reply. "Let's go for a walk tonight. I need to feel the night air on my skin... And stop talking to yourself. People are going to think you've lost it."

Nefari was taken aback by the fact that her own mind had just reprimanded her, but she nodded, thinking that a walk along the ship's decks might help clear her head. She could look out at distant shores and imagine what her friends might be doing at this moment.

She fully submerged herself in the bath, letting her hair float freely around her. It was oddly relaxing, drifting in the large tub, so she decided to stay that way for as long as she could. She closed her eyes, imagining herself floating as she did in spirit—but this time with her actual body. Each minor movement created gentle ripples around her, but they quickly dissipated. After ten minutes, she surfaced, releasing her breath slowly. Her Uru heritage, with its slower heart rate, allowed her to hold her breath longer than most people.

Nefari drained the bath while still sitting in it, playing with the little whirlpools that formed as the water spun down the drain. When the water was gone, she stood up and wiped away the excess moisture before stepping out and grabbing a towel. The towel was soft and highly absorbent, and she patted her body dry. Grabbing her hair between two parts of the towel, Nefari gently dabbed it to avoid frizz. She kept her hair short because it required less maintenance, and she appreciated that simplicity.

Nefari took out her casual white clothing—the everyday attire of the Uru. She wasn't ready to put on the charcoal-colored outfit of the mechanics just yet. Now that she was clean and feeling more like herself, she felt refreshed. It was amazing how a bath and fresh clothes could boost her energy and make her feel more alive. When she looked outside, night had already settled in. It was the perfect time to go walking during these warmer months, she thought, as she strolled out of her room. What had become a habit over the years was a quick stop by the food storage at the end of the hall before heading out onto the deck.

Nefari thought a peach would be the perfect snack for this walk. She squeezed a few to find one that was perfectly ripe, then smiled when she found the one. As she headed towards the deck, she felt a lightness in her step, a sense of freedom.

Nefari sat on the deck, gazing out into the night sky. She pictured herself as a young girl exploring the ship Shangri-la with a peach in hand. She remembered falling and being rescued by Nudgee—the first moment she accepted him as a friend. She had learned so much about him and loved him dearly, almost like a father. She smiled as she bit into the peach, the sweet, succulent flavor bursting in her mouth. Memories of Nudgee made her smile, even as tears rolled down her cheeks, tears of joy for the time they had shared.

Thoink... Thoink... The sound was soft but distinct. Nefari wiped her tears and looked around, trying to locate its source.

Thoink... Padoink. She followed the sound to the side of the ship and saw a rowboat tied to a pipeline. It seemed out of place—why would anyone on Atlantis use an archaic boat like that? She pondered for a moment, taking another bite of her peach, when suddenly, the alarms around the city sounded.

"Intruders!" The cry went up in the snake-like language of the Uru. Nefari immediately thought of Cranaus. Before she knew what she was doing, she found herself shuffling under a seat in the rowboat. She stayed hidden for a long time, her mind racing with second thoughts. At one point, she even considered abandoning the boat and returning to Atlantis. She froze when she heard running feet approaching. Three men jumped into the boat, cut the line, and quickly started rowing for shore. Nefari didn't move a muscle, now wondering why she had climbed aboard a boat full of people who might want her dead.

Her doubts grew when the man sitting directly above her shifted his foot and it made contact with her. With a startled yelp, he jumped up, rocking the boat dangerously on the rolling ocean. She had been discovered. Another man reprimanded him for his clumsiness.

"There's a rat under my seat," the man replied, grabbing Nefari by the arm and dragging her out for everyone to see.

"Nefari?" Cranaus exclaimed, recognizing her. Nefari's eyes lit up at the sound of his voice. A break in the clouds revealed her features more clearly. "It is you."

"Do you know this wench?" The man holding Nefari asked, yanking her forward.

"I'm starting to wonder if you know me," Nefari mumbled. Onidas, the man holding her, spun her around to look into her eyes.

"What did you say to me?" he demanded.

"Calm down, Onidas," Cranaus said. "She does happen to be a friend of mine. She's... um... she's part of the Uru but on our side." Cranaus couldn't let them know she was a mechanic; otherwise, they might throw her overboard with a slit throat.

"And you are sure of this?" Argus asked. He had been quiet until this point. "How do you know she's not a spy? She just popped up out of nowhere."

"She wants Cecrops dead as much as any of us do," Cranaus replied.

"How do you know this?" Nefari asked, her voice laced with skepticism. She hated Cecrops but hadn't fully resolved that his death was necessary.

"I could see it in your eyes the first time we met," Cranaus said. Onidas struck Nefari across the back of the head, knocking her unconscious. Cranaus's anger flared.

"Why did you do that?" he demanded.

"Your little Uru girlfriend is still an enemy," Onidas replied. "The council will decide her fate. You're getting too close, Cranaus."

The rest of the trip back to shore was silent, Cranaus seething with rage. He noticed another rowboat heading toward the shore behind them. iIt was too light on crew for his liking, a grim reminder of how many had been lost during the mission. It was hard to ignore the growing tension between his group and the Uru, and he knew things would only get worse before they got better.

Nefari slowly regained consciousness, her senses returning in scattered fragments. The raucous squawks of gulls assaulted her ears, the repetitive cries grating against her still-sluggish mind. A smoky aroma mingled with the scent of roasting meat, tantalizing her empty stomach. She felt a sharp pang of hunger and knew it had been too long since she'd eaten. She opened her eyes to take in her surroundings, but it was dim, and she realized she was in a roughly constructed shack. Sunlight seeped through small gaps in the wooden walls, creating thin beams of light that danced across the room. As she moved her head, one of the beams struck her eyes, forcing her to squint and retreat from the harsh light.

Nefari sat up on the makeshift bed—a thin scrap of fabric with soft sand underneath, the only thing making it bearable. Her head throbbed, and she reached back to touch the tender spot where she'd been struck, feeling grains of sand falling from her hair. The dizziness persisted, so she steadied herself by leaning against one of the walls. Once the room stopped spinning, she began to navigate the circular space, searching for a way out.

When she reached the door and tried the latch, it wouldn't budge. Locked in? Why? What threat could she possibly pose? A surge of frustration and confusion washed over her. She'd trusted Cranaus on the boat, even believed they had a sort of understanding. Yet here she was, confined to a shack with no explanation. The other Hellenes' behavior had always been hostile toward the Uru, her people, but she thought Cranaus might be different. It was hard to imagine he'd put her in here, but maybe he had little choice. The other crew members still viewed her with suspicion and distrust. Was Cranaus protecting her or betraying her? The uncertainty gnawed at her as she stood by the locked door, pondering her next move.

Nefari retreated to the small bed, settling into a more

comfortable position. She knew the wooden walls couldn't keep her locked in for long—not when she had a special skill on her side. Silently, she thanked Nudgee for her ability to shift into spirit form. With a deep breath, she let her physical body fade away, feeling the weight lift from her shoulders as her spirit floated free. The aches and bruises melted away, replaced by a lightness that always came with her ethereal form.

She drifted around the shack, phasing through the walls as if they were nothing more than mist. The outside world greeted her with vibrant sounds and scents. Nefari took her time, observing everything around her. It was clear she was in a well-established community, nestled in the hills not far from Athens. She saw rows of modest homes, fields brimming with crops, and small market stalls bustling with activity. There must have been over two hundred people in this hidden settlement, going about their daily lives. The focal point of the community appeared to be a large hall where gatherings and meetings took place.

As she floated through the village, Nefari passed a towering statue of Athena, the goddess of wisdom and war. It made sense; if these people were planning an uprising, honoring Athena seemed appropriate. The statue stood tall, casting a long shadow across the hall's entrance as Nefari glided in.

Inside, she found six men gathered around a large table. At the head of the table sat Cranaus, the man she had trusted, but the others were strangers to her. She moved closer, listening carefully to their conversation. It didn't take long to realize that she was the topic of discussion.

"The girl needs to die, Cranaus," said one of the men, his voice cold and unwavering. He had a long grey beard, a deeply lined face, and a bald head. His presence suggested he was the elder among them. "We can't afford to let a single Uru be part of this uprising. They always end up sympathetic to their own kind and will eventually betray us."

Nefari's spirit wavered for a moment, a chill running through her. The implications of the man's words were stark and dangerous. She'd trusted Cranaus, but now she wasn't sure if he was friend or foe. What would he say in response to this call for execution? Nefari knew she had to stay close, to hear what came next, because her life depended on it.

"That's simply not true, Anatolios," Cranaus replied, his voice steady but firm. "Every war has had people sympathetic to their enemies. People switch sides all the time. I've spoken with Nefari. I've seen into her soul the kind of person she is."

"Then what sort of person is she?" another man asked, his voice less confrontational but filled with skepticism. He was shorter and rounder than the others—clearly a man more inclined toward politics than battle.

"I'll tell you exactly who she is, Titos. Kyros, Flavian, Gregor—you all need to hear this," Cranaus said, meeting each man's gaze in turn.

Nefari listened intently, her curiosity piqued. She floated around the table to position herself opposite Cranaus, standing near Gregor, one of the men she didn't know well.

"Nefari has a gentle nature and a kind soul. She helps those in need even when it means misleading her own people. She's intelligent and self-assured, but there's also a sadness and torment in her. Nothing in her is cruel or deceitful," Cranaus explained.

Gregor, the man nearest to Nefari, suddenly drew a knife from his belt and slashed through the air, with an arc that seemed to pass right through her. He leaped to his feet, glancing around the room and under the table.

"What're you doing, Gregor?" Flavian asked, a hint of irritation in his voice. The others looked at Gregor with a mix of surprise and concern, but he slowly relaxed, with a grin.

"Sorry, I just had a feeling like someone was sneaking up on me. My body reacted on its own," Gregor said.

"Well, let's hope you don't get that feeling in a crowded place," Cranaus replied, his tone more humorous now. "I wouldn't want to have to take you down."

Nefari felt a cold chill in her spirit form, her ethereal body tensing from the shock. The knife had passed through her ghostly form, and Gregor's sudden reaction startled her. She'd barely had time to process the shock when he stood, looking at her with a wicked grin. It reminded her of Cecrops. Could it be that Gregor was an Uru, too? And if so, was he also reptilian, like Cecrops?

She'd have to watch him closely, but now she had a new understanding of the complex dynamics within this group. Cranaus's words offered her some comfort, but Gregor's reaction was unnerving. Would she be able to trust anyone here? As the conversation continued, Nefari knew she'd have to stay alert and gather as much information as possible to understand her place in this complicated and potentially dangerous situation.

"She's already shown a deceitful nature by misleading her own kind to save your life. That proves she's not reliable, Cranaus," Kyros retorted, his voice low but sharp. He was smaller in stature, much like Titos, but that's where the similarities ended. Kyros was all muscle, with a lean, angular face and the unusual trait of a clean-shaven chin. "How can we trust she won't do the same to us at a moment's notice?"

"Do you forget who saved your wife when the lion attacked, Kyros?" Cranaus replied, his voice edged with defiance. "An Uru gave his life even as he took down the lion, just so your wife could live. What was his name?"

"It doesn't matter," Gregor cut in, his tone dismissive.

"What was his name?" Cranaus repeated, this time with more force, ignoring Gregor's interruption.

"Garisi," Kyros answered reluctantly, barely lifting his gaze. "But he was different."

"No, Garisi was an Uru who sacrificed himself to protect a Hellene woman," Cranaus countered. "Not all Uru are bad. Nefari is another Uru who can be trusted. I'd stake my life on her if the moment demanded it."

"You mentioned she's a mechanic?" Gregor asked, raising an eyebrow. Cranaus nodded. "That makes her too dangerous to keep alive. If the Uru get her back, they'll have one more mechanic causing trouble for us. Do we really want to risk that? What do the rest of you think?" Several men around the table shook their heads, while Kyros sat with his arms folded, staring down at the tabletop.

"He's right, Cranaus," Anatolios said, his voice softer but resolute. "You might trust the girl, but if she's a mechanic, she's too dangerous to keep around. Whether she's on our side or not."

"You can't do this," Cranaus said, raising his voice. "I'm the leader of this uprising. I make the decisions here."

Nefari felt a chill run through her ethereal form as the discussion grew heated. Cranaus's leadership was clearly being challenged, and the room was divided on whether to keep her alive or not. It was unsettling to hear them debate her fate so openly, with most leaning toward her death.

Cranaus's loyalty was a comfort, but it might not be enough. Nefari needed to stay alert and find a way to ensure her safety. With these men arguing over her life, she realized she couldn't rely solely on Cranaus to protect her. She would have to use her spirit form to gather more information and plan her escape if things took a turn for the worse.

"One day, you'll be king in Athens, Cranaus. We'll follow your rule, no matter what choices you make. But we agreed when we started this rebellion against Cecrops that, until that day, important matters like this are decided by the many, not the one. It's time to vote," Anatolios said with finality.

Cranaus stood up, defiance in his stance. "I vote to let her live," he said, looking each man in the eye as they cast their votes.

"Death," Gregor said without hesitation.

"Death," Titos echoed, his tone dismissive.

Flavian hesitated, clearly struggling with the decision. His lips pressed together as he spoke: "Death."

"I choose death," Anatolios said, his voice resolute.

All eyes turned to Kyros, who still hadn't given his vote. Without looking up, he waved them away. "You don't need my vote," he muttered.

Cranaus's voice rose, desperate and indignant. "You can't do this! She's an asset! Don't you see?"

"The vote stands four to one. The Uru will be put to death," Anatolios announced, standing up to leave, with the others following suit. Cranaus stormed after them, shouting and arguing, but they ignored his protests. Anatolios gestured for two armed men to follow him, a grim expression on his face.

Nefari felt a wave of cold fear wash over her as she watched the events unfold. She knew she had to act quickly, but the shock and uncertainty paralyzed her for a moment. When she heard the sound of heavy boots approaching, she quickly returned to her body, sitting upright and bracing herself for what was to come.

Thoughts of Sanguine and Nudgee, her friends and mentors, filled her mind. She might soon be joining them in the spirit world. The thought brought a fleeting sense of calm, and she steeled herself for the inevitable.

The door swung open, and bright sunlight flooded the

dim shack. Nefari squinted, blinking rapidly as her eyes adjusted to the harsh light. The two armed men stormed in, grabbing her by the arms. She didn't resist as they dragged her outside and threw her to the ground in front of the councilmen, Cranaus, and a small but growing crowd of onlookers.

Nefari looked up at her would-be executioners, feeling the weight of their judgment. Cranaus's protests were drowned out by the murmurs and whispers of the gathering crowd. The air was tense, and the decision had been made. Would Cranaus be able to turn the tide, or would this be the end for her?

"Cranaus," Nefari acknowledged, turning her eyes to him. He looked troubled, guilt and worry etched across his face. He nodded, but didn't speak. "Anatolios, it's nice to finally meet you in person," she continued, her voice calm. Her words made heads turn toward Anatolios, who narrowed his eyes in confusion. Nefari took this moment to play with the group's nerves.

"Titos, I'm glad you're curious about who I am. Next time, why not come talk to me instead of voting for my death?" she said, her tone challenging. Titos fidgeted in his seat, looking away. "Flavian, you didn't say much during the meeting. I'm curious if you voted with the crowd or if you truly believed I deserved to die?" she asked. Flavian's jaw dropped as if he didn't know how to respond.

Then she turned to Kyros, who stared back at her without an ounce of remorse. "Oh, Kyros. You had the chance to honor the memory of Garisi, the Uru who saved your wife's life. Yet you didn't even vote, knowing it wouldn't have mattered to the outcome. You just shrugged it off. What would Garisi think?"

"How—" Kyros began, but Nefari cut him off by raising her hand and shaking her head.

"No, you dismissed your vote because you thought it wouldn't matter. Why would your words matter to me now?" she said, her voice hardening. She then turned to Gregor, whose eyes were full of malice. Nefari gave him a cruel smile. "Gregor, how long has it been since you left Atlantis?" she asked, watching his reaction. His eyes grew wide, and others around him turned to stare. "I'm sure there are a number of Uru who miss you."

"What are you saying, Nefari?" Cranaus asked, confused. "I've known Gregor all my life."

Nefari hesitated for a moment, then saw the faint smile on Gregor's lips—a smug grin that said he knew he had the upper hand. "I was in the room when you all voted for my death. Gregor's blade passed through my stomach when he sensed someone was there," she explained. The other men exchanged uneasy glances, their expressions a mix of disbelief and intrigue.

Gregor's grin widened. "You think you know something, but you really don't," he said, his tone dripping with arrogance. The way he looked at Nefari sent chills down her spine. Despite Cranaus's initial shock, he was struggling to understand. Had she revealed too much, or had Gregor successfully planted doubt?

This was a dangerous game, and Nefari knew she had to tread carefully. With the group on edge, she needed to find a way to escape before the vote's grim outcome became a reality.

"That's impossible," Anatolios said, his brow furrowing.

"No, it's a fact," Nefari insisted. "I was there because I can leave my physical body. How do you think I know all of this? I am part Uru and part Abori. The Abori were a race that lived alongside the Uru on my home continent. They had this ability to use what we call the Dreamtime—a spiritual state where you can explore beyond your physical form. A dear friend taught me how to do it."

Anatolios seemed taken aback, his skepticism flickering. "You said you're part Uru and part Abori?"

Nefari nodded. "Yes, and the Abori had unique abilities. The Uru have their own traits, like slower aging. Tell me, Anatolios, you're older than Gregor. Have you known him all his life?"

Anatolios thought for a moment, his suspicion growing. "No, I met him maybe thirty years ago," he said, casting a glance at Gregor. "How is it that you haven't aged?"

Nefari's voice was steady. "It's another Uru trait. We don't age like humans. Cecrops is a prime example of this." The name of the old leader sent a ripple through the crowd, and Gregor's expression darkened.

Gregor's rage erupted, and he lunged at Nefari, shouting abuse in the Uru language, his movements quick and dangerous. Nefari braced for the impact, but it never came. Instead, Gregor's eyes rolled back, and he collapsed to the sand, a knife protruding from the back of his head. The crowd gasped, and Nefari looked up to see Cranaus standing with his arm extended in the position of a throw.

Their eyes met, and the weight of what had just happened sank in. Cranaus had thrown the knife that ended Gregor's life, likely saving hers in the process. The intensity in his eyes was mixed with confusion, like he wasn't sure what to believe anymore.

"I don't quite understand everything that just happened, but I'm changing my vote," Flavian said, his voice shaky, breaking the tense silence that followed. Anatolios, Titos, and Kyros exchanged uneasy glances. Cranaus remained rooted to the spot, the implication of his actions still sinking in.

Nefari knew this was her chance. With Gregor's attack and Cranaus's dramatic intervention, the mood had shifted. But there was still uncertainty and a lingering sense of danger in the air. She had to navigate this new tension carefully, proving herself to these people who were now questioning their beliefs and their allegiances. Would Cranaus's defense of her be enough, or would others in the group seek to uphold the original vote? The path ahead was uncertain, but she knew she had to make her case to survive.

"With Gregor out of the running, that makes two votes to two," Cranaus said. "Kyros, your vote is most vital now."

"Nefari, you are a danger to us and all that we stand for," Kyros began. Nefari felt her stomach tighten. "If the Uru use you, we could all face death. None of our plans would remain secret; you'd uncover them all. Being a mechanic also gives them a huge advantage. And with that in mind, my vote is... Live."

Nefari was shocked. She thought she'd misheard him, but Kyros continued. "You are an asset to the Uru, but you chose to leave them. Cranaus spoke up for you, and you helped this village when you could have let it fall into ruin. Gregor was a spy. He would have betrayed us all countless times. I believe you're on the right side of this fight, and despite what you could offer the opposition, I trust you won't let yourself be used like that."

"Thank you, Kyros," Nefari replied, her voice trembling with gratitude. Tears welled up in her eyes. "Thank you for believing in me."

"Now that that's sorted," Cranaus announced, "the tally sits at three to two. Nefari is free to wander our village. We'll keep guards posted, but the matter is now closed." He then looked at the two men who had escorted Nefari. "Take Gregor away and burn him."

As they moved to remove Gregor's body, two balls of light appeared in the sky, speeding toward Athens. Cranaus turned to Nefari. "If you have such an ability as you say, who's aboard the Vimana?"

Nefari took a deep breath, laying down, she focused on the Dreamtime. She left her body again and followed the Vimana to find two figures on board, then returned to her physical form.

"It's Cecrops and Glycon, another senior Uru," she said. "They're heading to Athens."

Cranaus grimaced, rubbing his temples in frustration. "Cecrops returning to Athens is not good news. We need to be ready for whatever he's planning."

The announcement sent a ripple of concern through the gathered crowd. They knew Cecrops as a cunning and dangerous leader. The fact that he was returning to Athens suggested something ominous.

Nefari stood up, her resolve strengthening. "What can I do to help?" she asked. She knew she had to prove her loyalty to the villagers, especially with the shadow of Cecrops looming over them.

Cranaus looked at her, a mix of concern and appreciation in his eyes. "You should stay close, Nefari. Your abilities could be invaluable, but we also need to ensure your safety. If Cecrops is involved, things could get dangerous quickly."

Nefari nodded, determined to stand with Cranaus and his people. The journey ahead would be fraught with uncertainty, but she was ready to face it, knowing she had allies who believed in her.

The crowd of Hellenes gradually dispersed, leaving Cranaus and Nefari alone. She sank to her knees, leaning against the weathered shack, her whole body trembling as the gravity of recent events washed over her. Cranaus sat down beside her, his hand resting gently on her shoulder. His touch felt warm against her skin, his hand large and reassuring. She tried not to dwell on it.

"Are you okay?" Cranaus asked, his voice soft.

"I'm fine," Nefari replied, her voice still quivering. "I haven't thanked you for backing me up during the vote. You helped me a lot, and I was able to gather all the information I needed to talk my way out of trouble."

"You don't need to thank me. Consider it repayment for the time you saved me in Athens."

"You returned the favour when you stopped that sword from cutting me in half."

"Then let's say it's compensation for not being able to save your friend," Cranaus replied, his voice tinged with sadness. The mention of Sanguine's death weighed heavily on Nefari, but the warmth of Cranaus's hand on her shoulder lightened the burden just a little.

"Let's just say we're even," Nefari said, not wanting to dwell on the past. It was best to move forward, not backward.

"Do you really think you can do what you said?" Cranaus asked, his expression skeptical. "It sounds completely crazy, but I have to admit, the things I've seen make me believe almost anything is possible."

"It's true," Nefari said with quiet confidence. She felt she could be completely honest with Cranaus. "It's not something the Uru can do, but they can sense when I'm around. Gregor proved that without me even having to say anything."

"I'll believe you, Nefari," Cranaus said, "but the rest of the Hellenes will want proof. They might not kill you after today's decision, but if you fail, they'll exile you from the village."

"That's their choice, but I'm confident in what I can do," Nefari replied with a faint smile. Cranaus returned her smile, though his eyes betrayed a hint of concern. After a pause, he shook his head and said, "How about we take a walk around the village? I can show you around, since you'll be here a while." He stood and extended a hand to help her up.

Nefari took his hand, and he gently pulled her to her feet. "Steady now?" he asked.

"Yes, thank you. But I have a question," she said, her tone turning serious. "What exactly are you people? You've tried to kill me, Cecrops, and others, not to mention blowing up the generators in Athens."

Cranaus smiled, an impish glint in his eyes. "That obvious, huh?"

"Machines are my life," Nefari replied, her voice flat.

"Well, you won't find too many machines around here, I'm afraid," Cranaus said, shaking his head with an exaggerated pout. Nefari gave him a playful smack on the arm.

"Answer the question," she insisted.

"Why? So you can report everything to Atlantis? I knew you were a spy," Cranaus teased. Nefari narrowed her eyes, showing she wasn't in the mood for games. Cranaus sighed and relented. "Alright, alright. This village is home to everyone who respects the old ways. We want Athens to return to what it was before Atlantis. The Uru don't honor the Gods; they mock them with their claims. Cecrops is not a God."

"It's a noble cause," Nefari said, her tone measured. "But does everyone in Athens share that sentiment?"

"Over there are the sleeping quarters," Cranaus said, pointing toward a cluster of tightly packed houses as they walked the village. "You've already seen our prison. The city of Athens is under Cecrops's control. Most people are too scared to speak their minds. Folks who speak against the Uru tend to disappear. So, while not everyone in Athens is on board with overthrowing Cecrops, I believe they'll come around. Athens as a city doesn't care who's on the throne; it will continue to thrive long after we're gone."

"You're not worried that it might all be for nothing? That the Uru are just too strong?" Nefari asked.

"I think about it, but if we fail, we'll be dead anyway," Cranaus said with a shrug. "And then I'll start my journey to the Elysian Fields."

"You have an odd way of looking at life. I can see that you care deeply for everyone in this village, yet you speak like you don't."

"I want to make a difference," Cranaus replied, his voice growing passionate. "I want to give hope to the sick, comfort to the needy. Every day, more Athenians suffer under the Uru. I want to face them and restore Athens to its former glory. My father spoke of an Athens that once held great—scholars, mathematicians, public speakers, philosophers. But now, I see people begging on the streets, fighting with dogs for scraps of food. The Uru take everything good and keep it for themselves. Their technology and machines have made us lazy, our minds dull..." Cranaus's voice trailed off, his emotions bubbling to the surface. Nefari sensed his internal struggle and laid a comforting hand on his back, much like he had done for her earlier.

136

"Are you okay?" she asked gently.

Cranaus looked at Nefari, a spark of clarity in his eyes. "Don't mind me," he said, regaining his composure. "I get caught up in it all." He pointed toward a row of small shops. "Come, I'll introduce you to one of our shopkeepers. She's about your age—the only girl around your age, actually." Cranaus led Nefari to a small gift shop, filled with brightly colored crystal jewelry, blown glass vases, and soft silks from far-off lands. There were also small daggers, intricately designed.

"Nefari, I'd like you to meet Pedias," Cranaus said, gesturing to a young woman arranging items on a shelf. "She's a beautiful flower in this otherwise dull village." Nefari felt a small pang of jealousy at Cranaus's flattering introduction, but she brushed it aside. "Pedias, this is Nefari," Cranaus continued.

Pedias turned around with a warm smile and greeted them. Nefari felt a mix of emotions—curiosity, jealousy, and a sense of foreboding. Was Pedias just a friendly face, or did she hold more secrets than she let on?

"...in our village," Pedias was saying. "Cranaus mentioned on more than one occasion that you were beautiful. I hadn't believed him, but I'm glad I was mistaken." Nefari liked Pedias immediately. She noticed the discomfort etched across Cranaus's face, and she took a bit of satisfaction from his awkwardness.

"I didn't... I mean," Cranaus stammered, but Pedias gave him a stern look that seemed to say, "just go with it."

"I'm delighted to meet you, Pedias," Nefari replied with a slight tilt of her head. "Cranaus never mentioned you, which is strange, considering you are the nicest and prettiest thing this village has to offer."

"You honor me greatly," Pedias said with a gracious smile.

Nefari glanced at the wares and felt her breath catch. Resting on a bed of blue silk was a small, blown glass frog. The body was a vibrant green, shimmering as if it were wet, with one front leg reaching out as if trying to grasp something. The craftsmanship was so exquisite that Nefari almost believed it was alive. Pedias noticed her reaction and the tears welling in the corners of her eyes.

"That's a green frog from the Uru's homeland," Pedias explained. "I got it from a friend of mine before I came to live in this village."

"May I?" Nefari asked, gesturing toward the glass frog. Pedias nodded, and Nefari gently picked it up, cradling it in the palm of her hand. She peered closely at its delicate black eyes, observing the smooth transition from the green skin to the subtle yellow tones that edged its body. The craftsmanship was remarkable, capturing the vivid detail of the frogs she remembered from her childhood. The memory of her friend Nudgee making frog noises the first time they met came flooding back. She began to laugh, but the sound quickly turned to tears that streamed down her smiling face.

"That must have been a powerful memory," Pedias said softly, her tone filled with empathy.

"The man that carried this little guys namesake," Nefari said, carefully placing the glass frog back on its silken sleeve, "was like a father to me. He passed away just over nine days ago while I was in Athens."

"Please," Pedias said. "Take it as a gift from me. It's not doing much good just sitting in my shop."

"I couldn't," Nefari replied. "It's too precious to be given out of pity." She turned and walked away, but Pedias called out after her. Cranaus started to follow, but Pedias grabbed his arm and pressed a small silken bundle into his hand before letting him go. Cranaus quickly caught up to Nefari and slowed his pace to match hers.

"I'm sorry," Cranaus said, his voice low. "If I had known how much it would affect you, I wouldn't have taken you there."

"No, it's okay," she replied, managing a small smile as she wiped a tear from her cheek. "It was a happy memory, and I'm grateful for the reminder. Pedias is a kind soul. Have you ever... you know, thought about her?"

"I did, once," Cranaus admitted, rubbing the back of his neck. "I chased her for a while, but she has a thing for a descendant of the great Spartan king Eurotas, and I knew I couldn't compete with that. Not in the way I intended, anyway."

"I wouldn't even know how to chase someone," Nefari said, her voice softening with a hint of vulnerability. "Because of a condition I have, I was unable to have relations with any man on Atlantis."

"You're not on Atlantis now, Nefari. You're free from all that," Cranaus said, leaning in a little. "Here, you can take a husband or share a bed for just one night. Your life is yours to choose."

"And are you chasing anyone at the moment?" Nefari asked with a hint of playfulness. "I'd think many women in the village would be vying for a place in your bed." Cranaus chuckled, rubbing the back of his head awkwardly.

"I have my eye on a girl..." He paused, reflecting for a moment. "But I always seem to go for the younger ones."

"Well, that rules me out," Nefari said with a giggle. "I'd be twice your age if I were a day."

"How could that be?" Cranaus asked, skepticism in his eyes. "You don't look a day over twenty, and I'm clearly not ten."

"You forget that I have Uru blood running through my veins," she replied with a cheeky grin. "This blood keeps me younger for longer. It slows down my aging. I haven't kept track, but I lived as a child in the Uru's homeland. That was almost fifty years ago." Cranaus stood there, speechless for a moment, staring at Nefari in shock. He knew the Uru aged differently than the Hellenes, but it had never occurred to him that Nefari might be older than she seemed.

"No, I didn't think about that," he stammered, struggling to find his words. They walked in silence for a while before he finally spoke again. "I wanted to apologize for what happened at the inn. I hope I didn't offend you."

"Which part are you talking about, Cranaus?" Nefari asked, feigning innocence. She hadn't expected the conversation to take this turn. "The part where you wanted to sleep with me, or the part where you left because I said no?"

"It wasn't the reason I left that night," Cranaus explained, his cheeks reddening. "But yes, the part where I propositioned you."

"Why did you leave then?" she asked.

"When you got dressed, I recognized the mechanic outfit. You already know that I was hunting you."

"But you didn't kill me," Nefari observed, not phrasing it as a question.

"Beauty such as yours shouldn't be taken from this world," Cranaus replied, his voice gentle. Nefari blushed at the compliment but remained silent. 'There's another meeting soon. We've had little luck with the Uru lately, and we need to discuss new plans. I should go." Cranaus started to walk away, but Nefari called after him. He turned back to look at her.

"Just so you know," she said, stumbling over her words, "the idea of it—what you asked at the inn—sounds like fun. I was just shocked because no one had ever asked me that before."

Cranaus smiled softly, his eyes showing warmth. He realized he was still holding the glass frog wrapped in silk. He walked back to Nefari, asking for her hand.

"What do you mean?" she asked, a hint of confusion in her voice.

"Just hold out your hand, close your eyes, and count to twenty," he said with a playful glint in his eyes. Nefari complied, feeling the weight of something placed in her hand. It was soft and smooth to the touch, and she rushed through the counting. When she opened her eyes, Cranaus was gone. Her gaze shifted to the object in her hand—the glass frog, wrapped in silk. Her chest grew tight, and her face grew warm as she stood rooted to the spot, unable to do anything but stare at the thoughtful gift.

Chapter 7

Nefari quickly adapted to life in the village. It lacked the technology she had relied on in Atlantis, but it had something better: vitality. She felt more alive when she worked harder to obtain what she needed. Bathing in the cool streams without heated water made her feel more connected to nature, and the sound of crickets at night was more soothing than the creaks and moans of Atlantis's underbelly.

Rain started to fall, its rhythmic patter echoing through the village. Nefari sighed, recalling her earlier conversation with Cranaus. He'd sniffed the air and said it would rain tonight. Nefari had scoffed, saying that you couldn't predict the weather by smell. Cranaus had just smiled and winked, leaving her wondering what else she didn't understand about this place.

She felt foolish. Growing up in the bowels of Atlantis, she'd never learned the ways of the natural world. But that was okay; she had a new journey ahead of her, with so much to discover. She lay back, listening to the growing intensity of the rain. As she relaxed, she felt herself drifting out of her body, effortlessly rising into the stormy sky. Raindrops passed through her as she ascended, while the clouds below darkened and churned with energy. Lightning arced over the hills, casting an orange glow as it streaked through the sky.

Higher she soared, through the tumultuous clouds and into the serene expanse above. The large moon was cresting the horizon, its light creating intricate shadows on the cloud tops. Lightning continued to flicker, though it was softer and more distant. Nefari reveled in this strange, tranquil world above the storm. After a while, she descended back to her body, feeling a sense of peace and anticipation for the journey ahead.

As Nefari descended from the clouds, a flickering light caught her eye. Amid the strong winds and pouring rain, a poor soul was braving the wilderness. Curious, she flew closer and found that the light came from a small fire against the side of a cliff, providing scant shelter from the storm. A man was crouched beside it, wrapped in an oiled leather cloak pulled low over his face. His posture also shielded a small pile of wood from the rain, but the fire sputtered with each gust of wind. The man shivered, and

Nefari sensed his fear and discomfort.

She moved swiftly, her spirit gliding back into her body. As her eyes opened, she rolled sideways in bed, startled by a silhouette standing beside her. Heart racing, she blinked until the figure became recognizable—it was Titos, a member of the village council. His short, round frame was hard to discern in the dim light.

"Did I startle you, Nefari?" he asked, stepping back to show he meant no harm. "I came to bring you to the council, but you wouldn't wake up. I sensed you were still alive, so I waited."

"Sorry," Nefari replied, her breathing steadying. "I was out among the clouds."

"A gift to see such wonders," Titos remarked with a smile. But then Nefari remembered the man by the cliffside. The urgency of the situation made her sit up quickly.

"How hard would it be to send riders out to retrieve someone?" Nefari asked, hoping the storm wouldn't be too much of a hindrance. Titos raised an eyebrow, slightly puzzled by her urgency.

"Retrieve whom?" he asked, a hint of caution in his voice.

"While I was floating around, I saw a man taking shelter by the side of a cliff to the north," Nefari explained. "He was still exposed to most of the rain and didn't look like he was in the best of spirits. If we could bring him here, he'd be much more comfortable."

Titos's expression grew serious as he weighed her words. "And would you take responsibility if he's a spy and ends up killing members of this village or burning the huts down?" Nefari's eyes widened in shock at his harsh response. "We can't trust every traveler that happens by to be friendly. We are a rebel outpost against those that rule in Athens and Atlantis. There will be spies and cutthroats hired to cause us havoc."

Nefari's initial enthusiasm crumbled under the weight of his words. "I'm sorry," she said, her voice tinged with regret. "I'm not used to living as a rebel."

Titos softened his tone, seeing her remorse. "It's okay this time, Nefari," he said with a rare smile. "The man you saw is one of our scouts."

"You knew he was out there?" Nefari said, her voice rising as she shot Titos a stern look. "Why didn't you send someone to help him?"

Titos gave a faint smile. "He was actually out there as a test for you. We wanted to see if your abilities were as you described." He paused for a moment, choosing his words carefully. "I was the only person who knew where he was going. The cliff is one of two in the north, and it was going to be a guide for you. I guess you found him all on your own without being asked."

Nefari was stunned, then her frustration bubbled over. "Well?"

"Well, what?"

"Are you going to go out and retrieve him now, or am I supposed to check on him later and tell you he's hopping on one leg while playing the flute?" she asked, her voice dripping with sarcasm.

Titos burst into laughter, his shoulders shaking with mirth. "I'll send someone out right away. Did you see his flute?"

Nefari just shook her head, exasperated. "Was that all you needed me for?" she asked.

"Actually, I'd still like you to come to the council meeting. We would appreciate your input on some of our plans," Titos said, his tone shifting to seriousness.

"If I can be of service for the hospitality you've shown me, I'm happy to help. To be honest, I was starting to get fidgety without something useful to do," Nefari replied.

"Then let's go," Titos said, motioning for her to follow.

Nefari left the shack behind Titos, watching as he called a man over to give him instructions for retrieving their scout from the cliffside. The man grumbled about going out in the rain but started to saddle his horse without further complaint.

"Won't he need a second horse?" Nefari asked, concerned.

"He should have his own horse. The man I'm sending out is just a messenger," Titos explained.

"I didn't see another horse anywhere near the cliffside," Nefari said with a hint of worry.

"Maybe it got spooked by the storm and bolted. I always tell the men they need to tether their mounts. It's their lifeline in tough situations," Titos replied, then called out to the young man about to ride out. "Argan, take a second mount. We believe Barados is currently on foot."

"Should have tethered his mount better," Argan replied,

shaking his head. Titos gestured with his hand to Argan and then glanced at Nefari, as if to underscore his point. Nefari just nodded and they continued toward the council meeting.

"Some people here are wary of an Uru living among us," Titos said as they walked. "Even if you're a half-breed, like you say. Don't take offense at anything said out of turn."

"I can handle it, Titos," Nefari replied with a confident smirk. "It takes more than a few insults to rattle me."

"Good to hear," he said with a nod.

They walked the rest of the way in silence, entering the structure where Nefari had first soul walked to in the village. The council chamber was filled with the same people she remembered, along with the maps and charts used to plot their activities. The only empty chair was the one reserved for the Uru spy, Gregor. As she entered, Cranaus gave her a brief nod, but she quickly looked away, still embarrassed by her earlier misjudgment about smelling rain.

Anatolios, one of the council members, stood and addressed Nefari, his voice tinged with malice. "It's not my choice that you're here, Nefari," he said. "But since this council believes you may be of use, I must comply. You may take the chair of the Uru spy. I think that's fitting."

Nefari met Anatolios's harsh gaze with a calm smile, allowing Titos to guide her to her seat. She took a deep breath and spoke to the entire council. "Thank you for giving me this opportunity. I promise to do my best to earn your trust." Her eyes lingered on Anatolios for a moment before continuing. "I will do all I can to keep that trust."

"Not so quickly," Anatolios said, his tone cold and condescending. "We do not trust in your ability. You need to prove yourself."

"That won't be necessary," Titos interjected, trying to defuse the growing tension. Anatolios glared at him, his irritation visible.

"We all agreed," Anatolios retorted, his voice rising. "Even Cranaus, who has always stood up for her, said that it would be best to let her prove her skills."

Nefari wasn't surprised by this. She knew that Cranaus had likely agreed to calm Anatolios's volatile emotions. But Titos wasn't backing down. "I didn't mean she shouldn't prove herself," he said.

"Then what?" Cranaus asked, his patience wearing thin.

"Explain your reasoning so we can settle this."

"Nefari has already informed me where Barados is and asked me to help him. She was using her ability and came across him before I arrived," Titos explained. "This is exactly what we wanted her to do, isn't it?"

"Rightly so," Cranaus said, acknowledging the point. "Anatolios, do you have a problem with this?"

"Yes, actually," Anatolios replied, slamming his fist on the table. "She's tricking us and treating us like fools."

The room erupted into chaos as the council members argued amongst themselves. Nefari found it somewhat amusing, watching them squabble over her presence and abilities. Amid the clamor, she caught snippets of conversation, but it wasn't until Anatolios spoke up that she understood what he truly wanted.

"I want to see her use her ability with my own eyes!" he demanded, his voice cutting through the noise.

"Okay," Nefari said, locking eyes with Anatolios. He seemed unfazed, his skepticism as dense as the heavy rain outside. The rest of the room remained a cacophony of overlapping conversations, with no one paying her any mind. Annoyed by the noise, Nefari slammed her fist onto the table, the sudden bang silencing everyone instantly.

"Okay, I'll show you my ability," she declared. "Anatolios, since you have the most doubts about me, I'll let you set the challenge."

Anatolios smirked, convinced that he had just cornered her in her own bravado. He couldn't imagine how she would pull off her "tricks" in a way that would satisfy him.

"You don't have to do this, Nefari," Cranaus said, trying to intervene. "We already believe in you."

"It's okay, Cranaus," Nefari replied, her voice steady. "Anatolios is still unconvinced. I want everyone to have faith in what I can do." Then she turned back to Anatolios. "What's the test? How would you like me to proceed?"

Anatolios had already devised his plan. "I want you to close your eyes and place your hands over them for good measure," he said. Nefari sat down and did as instructed, her hands pressing firmly against her eyelids. Anatolios's smile grew broader as he gave the rest of the room a knowing look.

He tore a small section of papyrus from a map. "I'm going to write three instructions on this parchment, then give it to Cranaus. He'll perform these instructions outside the tent. When he returns, you'll tell us what he did," Anatolios explained.

"Understood," Nefari replied, her voice muffled behind her hands.

Anatolios quickly scribbled a set of instructions on the piece of papyrus, ensuring they would be as humorous and embarrassing for Cranaus as possible. He folded the paper and handed it over to Cranaus, who tucked it into a hidden pocket. "Don't read it until you're outside," Anatolios instructed. Cranaus nodded.

"You can open your eyes, Nefari," Anatolios said. "Let's see if your ability is as impressive as you claim."

Nefari removed her hands and looked at Anatolios. His grin was wide, and he seemed to relish the moment. She could feel the rest of the council watching her, some with curiosity, others with doubt. She returned his smile and took a deep breath, focusing her senses as she prepared to show them the extent of her unique gift.

Nefari waited patiently while Cranaus left the room, her body relaxed, her senses sharp. Once the door closed behind him, she slipped from her physical form and drifted after him, her spirit moving through the camp without a sound. Cranaus pulled out the parchment in a dry area and unfolded it, his expression growing darker with each word he read. Nefari floated beside him, peeking over his shoulder to see the instructions Anatolios had written.

She stifled a small laugh as she read the list of three directives, the second intentionally left out to trip her up. Anatolios was testing her in a condescending way, and she could see why Cranaus might not be keen to follow through with the embarrassing demands. As she returned to her body, she knew her response would leave Anatolios speechless.

Once back in her seat, Nefari opened her eyes. "That was quick," Anatolios said, his grin smug. "Has he already completed the tasks?"

"He doesn't seem inclined to do them," Nefari replied. "I think he was a little embarrassed."

"What would he have to be embarrassed about?" Kyros asked, his curiosity piqued.

"Likely excuse," Anatolios said, waving her off dismissively. "I expected as much. She can't do what she claims, and we should reconsider what to do with her."

"I can't say I'm not a little disappointed," Flavian

remarked. "A race with abilities like hers would be valuable to have."

Nefari interrupted, her voice clear and precise. "One— remove all clothing, get down on all fours, bark like a dog," she said, reciting the first instruction. Anatolios's face went a few shades paler as the room fell silent. "Three— while acting like a dog, run to the nearest building, lift your leg, and relieve yourself. Two— there isn't a two."

The council erupted in laughter. Anatolios's smugness vanished as he was faced with his own absurd test, now exposed for all to hear.

"If he performs these tasks, there's no way a 'turd of an Uru' could possibly guess it, right?" Nefari finished using the final note at the bottom of the instructions. Her gaze locked on Anatolios, who was now visibly sweating.

Quiet descended upon the room, all eyes fixed on Anatolios. His face told the whole story: shock, embarrassment, and a hint of anger. It was the answer everyone needed, and it was too priceless not to enjoy. Titos burst into laughter, soon joined by everyone else in the room, except for Anatolios. Nefari couldn't help but smile.

"No wonder Cranaus wasn't going to perform them," Titos said through fits of laughter. "Nobody would want to perform that, but how did you know what was written?"

"That's exactly what's on the paper," Nefari replied, enjoying the spectacle of the little round man jiggling with laughter. She found herself laughing along with him, the mood in the room lightening considerably.

Suddenly, a scream echoed from outside, silencing everyone who were instantly to their feet, weapons in hand with the fear of an impending raid. Feet pounded toward the door, and Cranaus burst in, trying to pull his damp clothes into place over wet skin. His arrival sent everyone into another burst of laughter and they settled back into their chairs. His blushing cheeks were enough to bring tears to some of their eyes.

"Oh my..." Nefari exclaimed, unable to contain her giggles. "Did you really do what the list said?"

"Weren't you watching?" Cranaus asked, his face turning a deeper shade of red as he struggled with the confusion.

"I guess I didn't stay long enough," Nefari admitted. "You seemed completely against it while I was watching. I just read the instructions over your shoulder and came back."

"I only... how could... Whatever," he muttered before storming back out into the rain. Flavian called after him, but Cranaus kept walking. Nefari quickly followed, leaving the echoes of laughter behind.

"I saw that coming," Titos said as she exited the tent.

Outside, Nefari caught up with Cranaus, matching his brisk pace. He turned to her, an odd expression in his eyes, one she hadn't seen before.

"Did you really do what was listed by Anatolios?" Nefari asked, curious about his motives.

"I did it for you," Cranaus replied, avoiding eye contact.

"For me?" she asked, taken aback.

"I knew that if you didn't pass their little test, you'd be shunned," Cranaus said, meeting her gaze. Nefari felt a pang of embarrassment at his sincerity. "I wanted to give you every opportunity, no matter the task."

"You didn't have to do that for me," she replied. "There are ways I can accomplish what I need to, and I found that way tonight when I thought you weren't going to do as you were asked."

"There was no way for me to know that," Cranaus admitted. "I can't see the way you do." Nefari was ready to explain more, but the situation demanded another approach.

"Thank you," she said, placing a hand on his arm. The simple gesture seemed to break through his defenses, and he took her hand in both of his, looking into her eyes.

"I'm liking you more and more each day, Nefari," he said, his voice softer, filled with unexpected warmth.

"I've grown fond of you too, Cranaus," she replied, feeling a connection she hadn't anticipated. This fueled his confidence, and he leaned in.

"I want to share the night with you, Nefari," he said with determination. "Would you come back with me to my hut?" The directness of his invitation made her pause. She had thought about it before, and the idea wasn't entirely unappealing. She understood how Sanguine must have felt on Atlantis with Fruruk. Yet, she knew she needed to tread carefully.

"No..." Nefari said, her voice gentle but firm. Cranaus's whole demeanor changed, his shoulders dropping as disappointment washed over him. He let go of her hands

148

and started to walk away.

"You're just going to walk off?" Nefari called out, stopping him in his tracks. He turned back, his expression a mix of confusion and hurt.

"I understood that when we were at the inn, you didn't know me. Turning me down was easy then," Cranaus said. "But you know me now. I thought you enjoyed my company, and you said you grew fond of me. I just don't know what you want."

Nefari couldn't contain her frustration as she spoke. "Wow," she said, her voice rising. "Just wow... Yes, I know you better than I did before, and yes, I've grown fond of you. But does that mean I need to jump straight into your bed? I've lived under the rule of the Uru my whole life—for thirty years, I've pushed down my feelings and desires. I'm not ready to just throw it all away. I was going to say that I had thought about doing the same with you. I was going to let you know that I needed only a little more time to get my mind straight. But now, let's just say you won't be up with me all night anytime soon."

With those words, she turned and stormed off, ignoring Cranaus's calls as he tried to apologize and explain.

"Pandrosus," echoed the voice through the manor, drifting out into the streets below. Pandrosus melted deeper into the shadows, watching her sister, Herse, on the balcony. She would need to join her soon, as the three girls were about to visit their father in the town gardens. Herse knew Pandrosus's secret and was signaling her with a gentle warning. Her gaze shifted to the man standing close to her, tracing his strong, stubbled jaw with a fingertip, delighting in the lust glimmering in his dark eyes.

Belen was a kind man from the cities and lands of Hellas, a wanderer without a fixed home. He was welcome everywhere, except in Macedonia, where a careless jest had incurred the king's wrath. He had narrowly escaped once, and that was enough. Since meeting Pandrosus, his desire to roam had faded; she was his focus, though for a time, it was one-sided. Pandrosus, due to her status, seemed indifferent to his presence—an Uru princess and a Hellene traveler had no business mingling. But Belen had a plan.

Gradually, Pandrosus's stoic demeanor began to soften. Mysterious gifts appeared, flowers adorned her window sill, and once, Belen was caught by Herse, who was anything but shy about her own interest in him. Herse, unlike her sister, was confident enough to engage in a casual fling. Yet when it became clear that Belen had eyes only for Pandrosus, Herse chose a different path: playing matchmaker. Soon enough, Belen and Pandrosus grew closer, meeting in shadowed alleys and exchanging secret gestures in public.

Pandrosus had never given away what Belen so eagerly sought. She retained her maiden honor, holding him at bay each time he got too close. It was a struggle, especially as his hands traced over her breasts and down her body, each touch igniting sparks. When he brushed her thighs and massaged the space between, it was like a wildfire, hot and unruly. But each time, just as the flames threatened to turn into an eruption, she would stop him. She wasn't sure what lay beyond this point, but her father's words always echoed in her mind—a warning against this kind of behavior, threatening her with excommunication from the Uru.

"Will you talk to your father tonight?" Belen asked. In recent weeks, he had been bringing up the idea of her becoming a priestess of Aphrodite. As the youngest daughter of Cecrops, joining the Hellene tradition would bring great honor to her family. Her older sisters would marry and continue the family line, while Pandrosus could pursue a different path. As a priestess of Aphrodite, she'd be free to be with whomever she chose, spreading love throughout all of Hellas.

"I shall," she replied. She longed to be free from the chains of her upbringing, and speaking to her father seemed the only way to carve a future with Belen. He leaned in to nibble at her neck, drawing a giggle, but she quickly pushed him away. "I have to go," she said. Belen pouted, but she held up a finger. "No, tonight is important for my family. You'll have to hold back."

"Hurry back into my arms," Belen said, as he did each time they parted.

"With each step, I bid the winds return me," Pandrosus replied. She watched Belen disappear into the main streets, blending with the few revelers already out for the night. She made her way back to the courtyard behind her home, climbing a sturdy vine to access her room. As she was halfway through her window, a handmaiden entered, rushing over to help her up.

"What were you doing at the window, Pandrosus?" the

150

handmaiden asked, her voice tinged with concern. "I've been looking everywhere for you. Aglaurus asked me to make you presentable for the garden visit." The handmaiden glanced over Pandrosus, noticing dirt stains on her dress. "You'll need a change of clothes. A new dress is in order."

"The soft yellow one will do," Pandrosus replied, hoping to avoid any fuss. "Braid my hair and let it hang down; it won't take long."

"Your sisters are both wearing blue tonight," the handmaiden said, hinting at the family's preference for coordination.

"I'm my own person. The yellow will be fine. We're only going to see Father, after all."

The handmaiden knew better than to argue and left it at that. She took the dirty clothes off Pandrosus and retrieved the yellow dress from the dresser. She carefully smoothed the dress out to make it easier for Pandrosus to slip into. Given Pandrosus's tendency to squirm while getting dressed, the handmaidens knew to make the process as seamless as possible for Cecrops's youngest daughter. This time, the dress went on with minimal resistance, and the handmaiden quickly moved on to brushing Pandrosus's hair, not wanting to give her time to change her mind. The brush slid through her soft, brown hair with ease, and soon the braid was complete, resting just below Pandrosus's shoulders.

"Thank you, Cressida," Pandrosus said. "You always do such great work."

"You shouldn't use my name," Cressida chided. "You know how your father gets."

"Yes, but he isn't here right now, and I wanted to let you know that your work is appreciated."

"Thank you for the kind words. Now run along, your sisters are waiting."

Pandrosus left the room and joined her sisters downstairs. They greeted her with remarks suggesting they were waiting a long time for her. It didn't bother Pandrosus much, though; her sisters often treated her differently. They pushed her around and teased her about every little thing. It was surprising that Herse had been so kind about Belen. Pandrosus couldn't help but suspect her sister had some underhanded ploy. But she would have to worry about that later; tonight was their monthly visit with their father in the town gardens. They didn't get to see him too often, as Cecrops was usually tied up with affairs in Athens until late. Despite the irregularity, these scheduled visits were a welcome respite, at least for Pandrosus.

The gardens of Athens were vast, with stone pathways and benches, sculptures of marble and onyx, and trees and plants imported from neighboring countries. In some sections, the air was sweet with the scent of flowers, while in others, the aroma was more textured, hinting at exotic spices. Of all the places they visited, this was Pandrosus's favorite. The three sisters made their way to where their father waited. As they approached, a hedge separated them from the meeting spot, and whispered voices drifted through. Pandrosus realized her father might still be caught up with work, even on a night meant for family.

"We aren't alone," said a voice Pandrosus didn't recognize.

"My daughters," Cecrops replied. "We're done here anyway. You have your orders; you may take your leave." Pandrosus peeked around the hedge and saw only her father standing there.

"What where you talking about, Father, and to whom?" she asked.

"Just a minor incident in town that needed my attention," Cecrops replied. "Nothing that would interrupt our time together. Come, girls, sit with me and tell me about your week."

"I met with the scholars of the city. They're starting to touch on some basic sciences," Aglaurus said, before Herse cut in.

"Doesn't Pandrosus look like a priestess of Aphrodite, dressed in yellow, Father?" Herse asked. Aglaurus scoffed, and Pandrosus shot her sister a dark look.

"Pandrosus is much wiser than to join such a cult and risk excommunication from Atlantis," Cecrops said. "She's still too young to even consider such things."

"She isn't beautiful enough to be accepted anyway," Aglaurus remarked. "The priestesses would cast her out into the gutter where she belongs."

"They would so accept me, Agi," Pandrosus said, using a childhood nickname that Aglaurus despised. "I'm twenty-three now."

"Don't argue with your sister just for the sake of arguing," Cecrops told his youngest daughter, misinterpreting her intention. "You have nothing to prove here."

"I think it would be a good move, Father," Herse said with a sly look. Pandrosus couldn't tell if Herse was on her side or not. "Think of your standing among the people when one of your daughters becomes a priestess." Pandrosus watched her father for his response, holding a small glimmer of hope.

"You are right, it would bring prestige to our line," Cecrops replied, "but I've already taken measures of my own."

"What have you done, Father?" Aglaurus asked, her eyes gleaming. She loved politics and the art of manipulation, and she aspired to rule the city one day.

"I have reinstated the Panathenaea," Cecrops said. "We are a city that worships Athena, after all, and this festival has always been a high tradition of Athens."

"Athens' namesake and our grandmother would be honored," Herse said, moved by the idea. "I never understood why you took it away in the first place."

"I took it away so that I could give it back," Cecrops said with a cunning smile. "I'll use it to draw out some rebels and put an end to their nuisance."

"You always know just what to do, Father," Aglaurus said, her admiration for his tactics evident.

"I'm glad you think so. On the night of the festival, you'll be married off to the future King of Athens."

"What?" Aglaurus's face fell, shock and horror replacing her confidence. Pandrosus couldn't help but laugh at her sister's sudden misfortune.

"And you, my dear Pandrosus," Cecrops said, turning to his youngest daughter. Pandrosus's smile vanished, replaced by anxiety about what might be in store for her. "I will not let you become a plaything for any Athenian who feels the need. You will become a priestess of Athena. You will remain chaste and untainted."

Tears filled Pandrosus's eyes as the implications for her and Belen were made clear, and she ran out of the garden without saying a word. Aglaurus looked at her father, her expression like that of a child who had just lost a beloved toy, before rushing after her sister.

"Did I say something wrong?" Cecrops asked, his voice tinged with confusion as he turned to Herse.

"You know exactly what you were doing, Father," Herse

replied with a laugh. Cecrops smiled at her response, and Herse shook her head in amusement.

"Neither of them are prepared for the life the Uru lead," Cecrops said. "Pandrosus less so. She can be a priestess for fifty years before I even consider releasing her."

"And what plans have you for me?" Herse asked, half-joking. Cecrops shrugged and spread his hands wide. "I don't know whether to be hurt or feel lucky."

"I'll take that," Cecrops said. "Shall we leave this pitiful place and get dinner? A priestess to Thanatos has delivered twins at the temple."

"I would love to," Herse replied with a mischievous smile. Father and daughter left the gardens arm in arm.

The room was thick with tension. The acts forced upon him by Anatolios, along with Nefari's biting words afterward, still weighed heavily on Cranaus days later. It did seem to help bridge the gap between Anatolios and Nefari, but for Cranaus, that was little comfort. His eyes met Nefari's across the room, and she shot him a dirty look. Cranaus returned his gaze to the maps scattered across the table. She hadn't forgiven him for what he'd said.

"Cranaus." An arm shook him. "Cranaus," Titos said again. "Are you with us, or off with the dogs?"

"I am here," he growled, annoyed by the jest. Such moments only soured his mood further.

"What should we do? Cecrops has no plans to leave the city or even his villa for the next four days. We could slip into Athens amid the heavier-than-usual traffic entering the city, or we could look towards Atlantis."

"Not Atlantis," Nefari said. "They are mostly innocent. We shouldn't attack a culture for the actions of one monster."

"We don't attack just because we can," Flavian replied. "Sometimes a tactical strike with minimal casualties helps draw out our true objective."

"He won't come," Nefari said, ensuring everyone heard and understood. "Atlantis isn't ruled by Cecrops alone. Two others hold equal rank, handling the day-to-day affairs of Atlantis. Cecrops manages the mob."

"So we're back to one target," said Titos. "It's always been Cecrops."

"No," Cranaus spoke up, his voice resolute. "Our target

154

is Athens first and foremost. Cecrops has stolen her from the people, so we will free her. If Atlantis has issues with this, they too will be taken from the equation."

"I don't think..." Nefari began to say.

"...We will not take Athens back from Uru rule just to hand her over to the next Uru that wanders in," Cranaus snapped, stubbornly. The fire feeding his resistance was also fed by his foul mood. "If the Uru in you can't handle that, Nefari, then get out of my camp."

The tension in the room grew suffocating. Nefari glared at Cranaus, her eyes alight with fury, while the other council members suddenly found the walls, maps, and floors more interesting. Kyros stood between them, staring at the ceiling to avoid getting caught in the crossfire. But then, Nefari's expression shifted to a smile, though the anger in her eyes didn't wane.

"Such a sad little puppy you are. The moment your toys are taken, you throw a tantrum. I'm not your mother; I won't coddle you and say everything will be all right. You're on the road to ruin, Cranaus." Her words struck a nerve, but she seemed satisfied with the damage inflicted and was ready to move on with the planning. She knew Cranaus would retaliate, but she decided to ignore him for the rest of the afternoon. However, a messenger at the door interrupted Cranaus's opportunity to snap back.

The fire in his eyes hadn't dimmed, but curiosity now mixed with the anger. The man at the door was Corra, the group's most deeply embedded spy, indicating that his news was significant.

"You're sure?" Anatolios exclaimed, though Cranaus could barely hear the messenger's reply.

"Cecrops told me himself," Corra said. "The Panathenaea will be reinstated and held on the traditional day."

"Thank you. Return to Athens and don't let yourself be seen," Anatolios replied. Corra nodded and slipped out. Anatolios returned to the table, and Cranaus leaned forward, intrigued by the news.

"Did I hear correctly?" Cranaus asked. "Is the Panathenaea going to be recognized this year?"

"That is what Corra has told me." The others around the table were taken aback by the revelation. Nefari, however, felt out of the loop since she hadn't even heard of the Panathenaea.

"What is the Pana...?" Nefari started to ask.

"The Panathenaea," Kyros clarified, "is a festival held in Athens each year to honor the Goddess Athena. We haven't been able to celebrate it since Cecrops banned it. It's surprising that he's reinstating it now."

"He's trying to win the love of the people," Anatolios said.

"Will it work?" Flavian asked.

"Many will be swayed by this tactic," Cranaus said. "The people want to find the path back to normality for our great city. Until now, the resistance has been their only hope. We need to be prepared for the fact that those who once sheltered and supplied us may no longer be our allies."

"The people of Athens couldn't be that flimsy, could they?" Nefari asked, her skepticism evident.

"They're just trying to survive. They don't always have the same privileges that others have, so things like this can sway them," Kyros explained.

"This gives us the chance we need to get close to Cecrops," Anatolios said, sensing an opportunity. "We will need a runner."

"Titos looks fit enough," Kyros said, poking the small, round man in the gut. Titos slapped his hand away, triggering a burst of laughter from the others.

"What happens at the Panathenaea?" Nefari asked.

"There will be feasts, worship, and mingling, but the event that Anatolios is referring to is a large foot race held around the streets and foothills of Athens," Kyros explained. "The man who wins that race is honored by the king and presented with the golden helm of Athena."

"I could run the race," Nefari offered, but everyone just smiled.

"Uru normally have a bronze complexion, do they not?" Flavian asked.

"Rightly so," Titos replied. "And by the looks of our little princess here—"

"Princess?" Nefari said, arching an eyebrow.

"She's gotten out of her tower very little," Titos teased. "She definitely wouldn't be fit to run in an event people train for months in advance."

"Why am I getting the feeling that you're all teasing me?" Nefari asked with a pout.

"Because we are, princess," Cranaus replied in a neutral tone, even cracking a small smile. She slumped back in her chair. "The race is for Athenians only. Even Hellenes born in other cities can't compete."

"You could've just told me that to begin with," Nefari grumbled. She wasn't pleased with becoming the butt of everyone's jokes.

"Nefari, could you confirm the information given to us?" Titos asked. Nefari paused for a moment, her eyes closing as if lost in thought. When she opened them, she nodded.

"I didn't have to go far. All of Athens is buzzing with the news of the upcoming festival."

"Then I have the right person for the job," Kyros said. "I'll be out for a day or two while I track him down, but come the festival, we'll be ready."

"You don't mean—?" Cranaus started, but Kyros just winked at him.

The festival day arrived, and Athens' streets brimmed with people. The city pulsed with life and energy, its vibrant heart beating louder than ever. Unlike other days, the gates stood open, allowing anyone to enter freely. Still, small patrols moved through the crowds, ensuring that even in times of celebration, safety wasn't neglected— because there's always one or two troublemakers who might disrupt the joy.

Colorful ribbons and lavender flowers adorned the stone walls and shop carts, creating a visually pleasing spectacle and masking the typical odors of the city. Music filled the air, emanating from various points throughout Athens, its harmonious notes weaving through every alley and street.

Nefari had never seen a festival on this scale before. To avoid attracting attention, the rebels had dispersed and entered the city individually. When it was her turn, she was struck by the vivid sights and the lively sounds. As she navigated through the bustling crowd, her unfamiliarity with the city's rhythm led to a few awkward moments. She bumped into passersby and stumbled when her foot tangled with an Athenian's leg, sending a tray of sweet honey buns flying through the air. Bystanders laughed as the sticky treats landed in unexpected places, but Nefari quickly apologized and moved on. Gradually, she got the hang of the crowd's flow and managed to find her footing.

Over the din of the festival, a metallic clanging sound caught her attention. It was faint but distinct—metal striking metal. Concerned that her comrades might be in trouble, she followed the sound's direction. What she discovered around the corner was unexpected: on a raised platform, two naked warriors circled each other, one wielding a blunted sword and shield, the other a blunt bronze axe. Nefari looked around, puzzled by the lack of concern among the onlookers. No one seemed inclined to intervene. What was going on? This wasn't the battle she had anticipated.

The man with the sword lunged, aiming for his opponent's torso. The axeman deftly stepped aside, closing the distance, and rammed his fist into the swordsman's side. The crowd erupted in cheers, adding to Nefari's confusion. This didn't seem like a typical festival performance. She grabbed the nearest bystander by the arm.

"Why isn't anyone stopping them?" she asked. The man gave her a cold look, then jerked his arm free.

"No one stops these fights, Nefari." The response came from a boy who seemed to appear out of nowhere. He had frizzy brown hair that sprang up from his head, and he was at least a head taller than Nefari, despite looking like he was in his mid-teens. His limbs were long and spindly, adding to his disproportionate appearance. He wore only a loincloth and had a grin that made Nefari uneasy.

"Who are you?" she asked, keeping her voice steady.

"Sorry, you wouldn't know me," he replied, then continued as if she'd never interrupted. "This fight is part of the festival. Men strip down and show their strength to the crowd."

"Why do they need to strip down?" she asked, still confused.

"To prove they have no fear. A dick gets smaller the more they fear. See? look at the man hiding behind the shield? Not so confident," he said, pointing out the swordsman. "Small dick."

Nefari just shook her head."Disgusted are you? Dont like dicks?"

"Nothing like that. I have no issues of being naked in the presence of others, male or female. We of the Uru don't make fun of them or speak so directly about them."

"About dicks? Maybe you arent as comfortable as you thought then."

"Look, kid, whatever your name is, I don't have time for this kind of talk," Nefari said, turning away. "Enjoy your festival."

As she walked off, she passed The Turtle Shell, the tavern exceptionally lively this day. Outside, Mira stood with a tray of small clay cups filled with beer, trying to coax passersby to come inside.

"Mira," Nefari called, waving as she walked over. "How have you been?"

"Nefari! It's been ages since you last visited," Mira replied, her eyes lighting up. "You have to stay with us tonight."

"I'd love to, but I might have other things to take care of," Nefari said, a hint of regret in her voice. She was disappointed she wouldn't be able to stay with her friend.

"I understand," Mira said with a wink. "Enjoy the festival while you can!"

"You too, if you get a break," Nefari said, hugging her friend before moving back into the bustling crowd.

"You stopped just to talk to her? Maybe you don't like dicks after all," came a voice behind her. Nefari spun around to see the lanky boy again, a smirk on his face.

"You're a filthy urchin," Nefari said, now visibly annoyed. "Why are you following me? Don't you have a street corner to beg on?"

"It's fun teasing you," the boy said with a grin.

"And you still haven't told me who you are," Nefari replied, her patience wearing thin.

"I know," he said, his grin widening.

"... Well? Are you going to tell me your name?" she asked, trying to maintain her composure.

"Nope. I like it better this way," he replied, clearly enjoying her frustration.

"I have somewhere I need to be soon, so I'd appreciate it if you didn't follow me or talk to me anymore," Nefari said to the lanky boy. She moved away, heading into the crowd. A quick glance over her shoulder, however, revealed that he was swinging his arms dramatically and keeping pace with her. Nefari stopped abruptly, grabbing him by the shoulders and looking him in the eye. Her voice was firm as she spoke, emphasizing each word. "Leave. Me. Alone."

The boy's eyes shifted past her, and he suddenly seemed less amused. Nefari followed his gaze and saw Cranaus approaching. He hadn't noticed them yet, but he was closing in fast.

"Sure, I can do that," the boy said with feigned

159

indifference, then vanished into the crowd. Nefari exhaled a sigh of relief, but her respite was brief. A hand landed on her shoulder, and she turned to see Cranaus standing before her.

"I thought I'd never find you in this crowd," he said, his voice friendly.

"You were looking for me? I didn't expect to see you so soon," Nefari replied, surprised.

"Come with me. Let's go to the starting line for the race together," Cranaus said, taking her hand and leading her through the throngs of people. Nefari felt a bit uneasy about letting him get close, but at least with him around, the obnoxious boy wouldn't return.

As they walked, Nefari noticed that they were heading to a part of Athens she didn't know well. The alleys grew narrower, and the noise of the festival dulled. The race's starting line was tucked away in the lower part of the city, where stone buildings cast deep shadows. Contestants were warming up, stretching, and adjusting their gear. Nefari was taken aback by their state of undress. It seemed the race would be run naked, a fact that added to the festival's unconventional atmosphere. A line of brightly colored ribbons marked where the runners would assemble.

Cranaus let go of Nefari's hand and motioned toward the ribbon. "The race will start soon. Want to watch it with me?" He seemed eager to stay by her side, but Nefari wasn't sure what to make of him or his intentions. She glanced at the racers, then back at him, deciding how much to trust him.

"Nefari, I wanted to have some time alone with you to apologize for how I've been acting lately," Cranaus said, looking down at his feet.

"What?" Nefari was taken aback. This wasn't what she had expected from him. Cranaus reached into a hidden pocket and pulled out a small box, handing it to her.

"This is for you, as a sign that I want things to be the way they were before... well, before I became a jerk." Nefari opened the box to find a black leather braided necklace with a teardrop-shaped stone. The stone was a deep blue, like the ocean, with veins of gold running through it. It was encased in a delicate spiral of copper wire from top to bottom. The craftsmanship was exquisite, and it reminded her of the glass frog that Cranaus had once given her.

"It's beautiful," she said, admiring the intricate design.

"What kind of crystal is this?"

"It's not technically a crystal but a rock," Cranaus explained, noticing her confusion. "Crystals are a specific type of mineral structure, while rocks can be a mixture of minerals. This one is lapis lazuli. It's said to mend ill will between friends and loved ones. Some believe it draws energy from the throat chakra, enhancing communication and strengthening the spirit."

"So, a perfect all-round stone," Nefari said with a smile. "Will you put it on me?" Cranaus took the necklace and carefully placed it around her neck, tying it securely so that it wouldn't come off easily. Nefari felt the coolness of the stone against her skin and admired its craftsmanship, a feeling of joy spreading across her face.

"Hey, Nefari!" A voice rang out from a distance, causing Nefari's heart to sink. She knew exactly who it belonged to. The lanky boy from earlier was now among the competitors at the race's starting line, slick with oil like the other runners. He was standing naked, legs apart, pointing down at his appendage. "Look, Nefari! My dick's still big! No fear"

Cranaus scoffed at the comment, while Nefari rolled her eyes in exasperation. To deflect the situation, she scanned the line of runners and pointed at a particularly muscular contestant. "If you think that's big, you should see the blonde Adonis three runners up," she remarked with a smirk.

The boy, apparently named Thanos, dismissed her comment with a wave of his hand. "He's only here to flex his muscles," he retorted.

"Eyes on the race, Thanos!" Cranaus yelled, trying to bring him back to focus. Thanos stuck his tongue out playfully, but then turned his attention back to the race, seemingly unaffected by the exchange.

"That's our runner?" Nefari said, incredulous. "He's been following me around and being obnoxious all day."

"That's just how he is," Cranaus replied, shrugging. "Two years ago, he spent an entire week finding ways to get his butt cheeks in my line of sight. Don't take it personally. Kyros probably mentioned you, and Thanos thought it would be fun to give you a 'proper' greeting."

"Why do we even have him as our runner?" Nefari asked, not convinced that Thanos's antics were worth the trouble.

"Because he's fast," Cranaus explained. "Despite his behavior, he's good at what he does. Look, the race is starting."

Nefari turned to watch the runners line up, shoulder to shoulder. They were jostling for position, pushing and shoving to get the best spot at the starting line. The oil coating their bodies made it nearly impossible to get a good grip, which was likely part of the strategy to prevent interference during the race. Thanos stood at the edge of the pack, surprisingly calm, not trying to force his way to the front. Despite his juvenile antics, he seemed ready to take the competition seriously.

"Why isn't Thanos trying to be in the best position?" Nefari asked, watching the starting line where Thanos lingered at the edge.

"He's in the best position for his strategy," Cranaus explained. He saw the curiosity on Nefari's face and elaborated. "Thanos doesn't lead from the front. He sticks behind the third or fourth runner, pacing himself. After about three miles, he starts to move up, conserving his energy for the final stretch. That's when he makes his move, overtaking the front runner. Right now, those at the front are just wasting energy tussling among themselves. That will cost them later."

Nefari nodded, starting to understand the tactics. She glanced at the runners, noting a man who stood slightly behind the pack at the rear. "What about that guy? Is he following a similar strategy?"

Cranaus turned to look where she was pointing and swore under his breath. "That's Giannes," he said, a touch of tension in his voice. "He's an Olympic champion. I didn't expect him to be back in Athens. He's going to be a real threat in this race."

A loud gong echoed through the streets, signaling the start of the race. The crowd cheered as the runners set off at a brisk pace, quickly disappearing from view. Nefari noticed Giannes was still at the back, not making any effort to push forward.

"He'll stay there until about halfway through the race, then move up when they start heading back to the city," Cranaus said, leading Nefari to a table with high-backed chairs. "He's like Thanos but starts from the far rear."

They sat down, and Nefari felt the sturdy chair providing excellent support. She felt a sense of comfort as she settled in.

"It's so open here," Nefari remarked, scanning the area for onlookers.

"It's fine. If anyone gets too curious, I'll tell them you had too much wine and passed out," Cranaus said with a smile. "That should keep them at bay."

Nefari laughed, appreciating his quick thinking. "Thanks. I'll keep an eye on the race and let you know about any key developments." She leaned back into the chair and relaxed her body, allowing her spirit to soar above the city streets, following the trail of the runners as they kicked up dust with each step.

Chapter 8

Thanos stood at the starting line, eyes fixed on the cobblestone trail stretching out before him. The city was eerily silent, with not a soul in sight. He liked it that way. The solitude allowed him to clear his mind, to focus on the task ahead without distractions. No cars, no pedestrians, just him and the open road. It was his time to gather strength, both mentally and physically, before the race began.

In this stillness, his thoughts drifted back to his childhood. He had always been different, his arms oddly large compared to his frail body. The other kids in the neighborhood never let him forget it. They called him names like "rock ape," "freak," and "golem." Some even said if he had been born in Sparta, he'd have been tossed from Mount Taygetus, discarded as unfit. It was cruel, and it only got worse.

At first, the teasing was verbal, just words tossed his way as he walked down the street. But soon, it escalated. Shoving and pushing led to rotten fruit thrown at him. Then came the real violence—the alleyway ambushes where groups of kids would beat him with fists and feet. He had no way to defend himself, and each day he returned home with fresh bruises and cuts.

His mother tried to comfort him, cleaning his wounds and applying ointments, but his father was another matter. He never said it out loud, but the disappointment was clear in his eyes. Thanos could feel it with every glance his father gave him. After a while, Thanos stopped going home on days he was attacked. He preferred to hide in the streets, scavenging for scraps and sleeping in abandoned corners.

Oddly enough, it was during these times of running from shopkeepers and bullies that he discovered something about himself—he was fast. Faster than any of them. What began as a means to escape soon became a skill, one that would eventually lead him to where he stood now.

Having dealt with the painful memories of his childhood, Thanos let them fade.

Another memory surfaced. It was the image of his first race, the backs of multiple runners approaching the finish line. He had stolen a small amount of money and bet on himself, convinced he was the fastest runner around. And he was almost right—almost. As the race started, he surged ahead, leaving everyone else behind by nearly a mile. But somewhere along the course, they caught up and even passed him. Thanos pushed himself harder, but his legs felt like lead, and his breath came in ragged gasps. In the end, he finished eighth out of ten, feeling utterly defeated. That night, he didn't go home. The fights with his father and the sadness it caused his mother were too much.

"Why did you lose?" a rough voice asked as Thanos sat slumped against a wall, still catching his breath. The street had been empty just moments ago, but now a greying old man with a long scar crossing his face stood over him. The scar ran from his forehead, over his blind left eye, and down to his chin.

"They were faster than me," Thanos said, his voice tinged with resignation. He didn't understand why this old man, a stranger, was pressing him about the loss. Wasn't it clear he was already feeling terrible about it?

"No, that's not why you lost," the old man replied with a stern expression. "You defeated yourself."

"I had money riding on that race. Why would I want to lose?" Thanos protested. The old man smiled, a gentle smile that seemed sincere, but to Thanos, it felt mocking.

"You don't know how to run, boy," the old man said, shaking his head. "I saw the body you were given and thought you had great potential. I even bet on you myself, but the moment the race started, I knew I'd made a mistake."

"I know how to run," Thanos insisted. "I was winning for three-quarters of that race."

"And after that, your legs wouldn't listen to you, and breathing became difficult," the old man replied, his voice calm but firm. Thanos couldn't understand how this stranger seemed to know so much about him. "You need to learn how to use those long legs of yours, utilize your arms properly, and breathe in a way that keeps you going. You need to run slower to win."

"Slower?" Thanos exclaimed, incredulous. "Nobody wins a race by running slow."

"Yet those seven runners who beat you kept a steady pace, one slower than your fastest," the old man said, raising an eyebrow.

"They were faster at the end," Thanos argued, but the old man shook his head.

"They conserved their energy for the final stretch. That's where the real race begins. Come with me, and I'll show you how to win."

Thanos felt a mix of confusion and curiosity. Who was this man to offer advice? But there was something about him—perhaps the scarred face or the confident tone—that made Thanos consider it. He nodded, feeling a glimmer of hope.

Thanos let the memory of that day with Argurios, the old man who became the mentor and father figure he never had, drift away. Argurios had taught him well, showing him not only how to run but how to think, to pace himself, and to be strategic. Thanos wished Argurios could be here to see this race, the one that could change the course of history. He took a deep breath, pushing back a swell of emotions. The roar of the crowd grew louder as the race was about to start.

A gong sounded, signaling the runners to begin. Thanos surged forward, feeling the ground beneath his feet and the energy of the crowd around him. He settled into a steady pace, staying away from the dense pack of runners jostling and shoving each other for position. He'd learned from Argurios that it was better to stay on the fringes, keeping clear of the chaos but close enough to make his move when the time was right.

As they ran through the city streets, a runner ahead of Thanos stumbled and fell, rolling onto the cobblestones. Thanos recognized him as one of the favorites to win, the 'Adonis' Nefari had pointed out. The falling runner reached out to grab Thanos's leg, hoping to take him down as he fell. But Thanos was ready, his long legs clearing the man with ease.

Approaching the outer gates of Athens, the crowds began to thin. People gravitated back to the city, eager to witness the runners' final sprint toward the finish. Thanos felt the difference immediately. The air seemed clearer, and the noise level dropped. This was where he excelled. His breathing was steady and controlled, with a rhythm that matched his pace: three steps for inhaling, two for exhaling. He took deep breaths, filling his lungs completely to maximize the oxygen to his muscles. Thanos had learned to breathe from his belly rather than his chest, preventing his shoulders from tensing and wasting energy. This conserved energy made all the difference over a long-distance race.

His legs carried him forward with strength and resilience. He used the swing of his arms to distribute the effort throughout his body, giving him a more efficient stride. These techniques, combined with his natural endurance, made him a formidable runner. But Thanos rarely competed at this level. He was content with smaller races and easier money.

The runners began to spread out as the scree-covered slopes surrounding Athens took their toll. Up ahead, a steep incline led to a crest, signaling the halfway point of the race. Thanos knew this part well—it required precision and skill. After reaching the top, they would descend sharply into a gully before climbing back up another challenging slope. This was where his long arms gave him an edge. He could use them to pull himself up the incline, saving his leg strength for the return journey.

Thanos scaled the slope with ease, passing several runners who struggled with the difficult terrain. It was a little earlier than he had planned to make his move, but he felt confident in his pacing and energy reserves. As he neared the crest, he was surprised to see Giannes, an Olympian, appear almost out of nowhere. Thanos hadn't realized he was this close at the halfway point. He had seen Giannes run before knowing him to be a formidable opponent and knew that this short distance could easily be overcome, even with the slope.

As Thanos crested the rise, he let himself pick up speed, using the steep downhill to propel him forward. Gravity and the rush of adrenaline fueled his muscles as he raced toward Athens. Over the next eight miles, he could feel Giannes getting closer, closing the distance. Thanos fought the urge to run harder, knowing he needed to save energy for the final push. When the terrain allowed, he glanced back, keeping an eye on his competitor. The gates into Athens were within sight, and beyond them, the Acropolis—the finish line. His lungs burned, and his breathing became erratic. Just a little more, he told himself, and then he could go all out.

What Thanos didn't know was that he wasn't alone. Nefari was trailing him, shouting words of encouragement. But her voice was muted to the physical realm. Nefari was growing increasingly worried as she watched Giannes inch closer and closer to Thanos. The gap was now less than a hundred meters. She flew closer, trying to give him a boost with her presence, but there was nothing she could do.

As she flew past the gates, a glint of sunlight caught her eye from ground level. In the bushes, a man held a dagger, poised to throw it. Nefari could see his target—Thanos. Panic surged through her. "No!" she cried, but Thanos ran on, unaware of the danger. "Stop! Please stop!" she pleaded, waving her arms in front of him as she kept pace.

Desperate, Nefari felt the stone around her neck grow warm as she tried one last time to save Thanos.

Thanos felt a mixture of relief and caution as he closed in on the gates. He knew the final leg would be intense, with the crowds pressing in and competitors jostling for position. It was a place where accidents could happen, and he needed to be careful. Movement to his left caught his eye just as Nefari appeared in front of him, her expression filled with fear and urgency.

"Thanos, watch out!" she cried, her voice piercing the noise of the crowd. It was the look in her eyes that struck him the most—the terror and desperation. It was enough to make him hesitate, just for a moment. But it was the moment that saved his life.

Giannes barged into Thanos from behind, sending him sprawling to the ground. The sudden impact jolted through his body, but anger fueled his sore limbs, and he scrambled back to his feet. Nefari was nowhere in sight, and Thanos chided himself for being so careless. He glanced toward the spot where he had seen movement earlier. It was just a spectator with an annoyed expression, likely startled by Thanos's tumble.

"Don't worry," Thanos said, misinterpreting the man's glare. "I'll catch him again," he added, then sprinted into the city. Giannes was within sight, the crowds roaring as they cheered the runners on. The noise grew wilder as people realized it was going to be a head-to-head battle for the finish between these two competitors. Those who'd bet on the Olympian booed Thanos, but he blocked out their voices, focusing only on Giannes's back.

They climbed the slope toward the Acropolis, almost neck and neck. Thanos had caught up to Giannes with just fifty meters to go. They were shoulder to shoulder, shoving each other as they sprinted. Thanos watched Giannes carefully, waiting for the right moment. As Giannes leaned in for another shove, Thanos stepped aside, letting Giannes stumble off balance. That was all Thanos needed. He surged ahead, crossing the finish line as the crowd erupted in a cacophony of cheers and boos.

Cecrops, one of the organizers, was there to greet the victor. His smile was wide, but there was something unsettling about it. Despite the victory, Thanos felt a twinge of unease, knowing that there was more to come later that night at the celebration. He turned away from Cecrops, trying to catch his breath. The crowd was still cheering, and Giannes came over to congratulate him, slapping him on the back.

"That was for you, Argurios," Thanos thought, sending a silent prayer to his late mentor.

Back near the starting line, Nefari regained consciousness with a faint smile on her lips. She had given everything to save Thanos and hopefully ensure his success. Beside her, Cranaus, her guardian spirit, stood watch.

"Thanks to you, we won," she told Cranaus simply.

The city of Athens came alive as night fell, with the sounds of revelry echoing through the streets. Pandrosus stood on her balcony, watching the festivities below. Despite the lively atmosphere, she had been forbidden to join the festival's feasting, drinking, and other indulgent activities. Her father had tightened his grip on her freedom ever since she expressed interest in becoming a Priestess of Aphrodite.

A whisper rose from the alleyway beneath her balcony, and she peered over the edge to see Belen holding a jug of wine.

"I can't tonight," she called down. "My father won't allow it."

"Is your father here to stop you?" Belen replied with a grin. "He's out there mingling with the crowd, probably enjoying the free-flowing wine. I doubt he'll notice you're missing while he's busy with the ceremonies."

"The servants are loyal to him," she said with a sigh. "They'll tell him if I'm not in my room when he comes back."

"Just tell them you have a headache and need to rest," Belen suggested. "They'll leave you alone if they think you're asleep. Once you're in bed, no one will bother you. Then you can meet me."

Pandrosus hesitated, but only for a moment. She nodded and said, "Wait here."

Belen watched her as she left the balcony, his eyes following her every move. She was taking her time, making sure everyone knew she was going to bed, so Belen could hear her voice even from the street below. After a while, the lights in her room were extinguished, and the balcony became a dark silhouette against the city's glow. Belen waited, growing anxious. But soon, Pandrosus reappeared, climbing over the balcony railing. She had changed into more practical clothing for sneaking out, her usual attire replaced with a simple white tunic trimmed with silver

Pandrosus landed lightly on the cobblestones, her feet barely making a sound. She leapt into Belen's arms, and he embraced her tightly. It had been weeks since they'd last seen each other, and her father's strict control over her movements had only grown more oppressive since then.

Belen pressed his lips to her forehead. "I've missed you," he whispered.

"I'm sorry," Pandrosus replied, her voice laced with frustration. "My father has been keeping me locked up ever since I told him I wanted to become a Priestess of Aphrodite. He's completely against it."

"I figured he might react that way," Belen said with a gentle sigh. "But don't worry about it. I understand how protective fathers can be."

"He's too protective," she said, rolling her eyes. "It's like I can't breathe. I can only be myself with you."

"I'm here now, dear heart," Belen's voice was soft and reassuring. "Let's enjoy the festival. What do you want to do?"

Pandrosus hesitated, blushing slightly at her own thoughts. Her father would hate it if she misbehaved during the festival, but she had no intention of taking things too far. She was still trying to be a good daughter. "Let's eat, drink, and dance," she said, her smile widening. "I want to dance!"

"Dancing it is!" Belen said, noting the spark in her eyes. Her father's strictness was working in his favor. If he could keep her feeling rebellious, he'd have more chances to get close to her.

Together, they slipped into the vibrant streets of Athens,

where the festival was in full swing. Dancers twirled, jugglers tossed flaming torches, and musicians filled the air with lively tunes. Pandrosus felt the pulse of the city and wondered why her father was so determined to keep her away from it. She spun into a group of dancers, her movements fluid and graceful, and held out her hand to Belen. He joined her, laughing as they twirled to the rhythm.

The music's energy flowed through Pandrosus, lifting her spirits. The oppressive weight of her father's rules melted away, replaced with the warmth of the festival. This was where she belonged—in the heart of Athens, dancing among the people.

When Pandrosus felt her energy flagging, she signaled to Belen that she needed a break. As the crowds swirled around them, she was lucky to find a table that had just cleared. She waved to Belen, who was scanning the area to find her. He navigated the bustling street with surprising agility, carrying a plate loaded with meats and gravy, another with bread, cheese, and fruit, and balancing two large tankards of red wine.

Pandrosus couldn't help but be impressed by his skill, and she dove into the food with enthusiasm. Belen watched her eat with a grin, his eyes lingering on her lips as she devoured the feast. He reached across the table and gently wiped a streak of gravy from her chin, his touch lingering just a little too long. Pandrosus blushed, her cheeks turning a soft shade of pink. To cover her embarrassment, she reached for her tankard and drank the wine in a single swig.

"Slow down," Belen warned. "You might lose your head if you keep drinking like that." He could already see the flush in her cheeks and the slight glaze in her eyes—the wine was hitting her hard.

"Tonight's about having fun and breaking the rules," she said with a giggle. The sparkle in her eyes was unmistakable, and Belen knew that if she kept drinking at this pace, things could escalate quickly. The thought crossed his mind that one or two more tankards might lead to a bolder Pandrosus, but he pushed that notion aside for the moment.

"You keep eating, and I'll get you a refill," he said, standing up with her empty tankard in hand. He made his way through the crowd toward the nearest tavern.

Pandrosus, left alone at the table, watched the festival with a smile, her attention captured by a fire dancer spinning flaming sticks in a mesmerizing display. She was entranced by the swirling flames, the way they painted patterns in the night air.

She was so engrossed in the performance that she nearly jumped out of her seat when Belen gently shook her arm.

Belen handed Pandrosus her drink, and she took it with both hands, sipping cautiously. The world seemed to sway in time with the music, her senses pleasantly dulled by the wine. She thought back to the last time she had gotten into her father's wine with her sisters—it hadn't ended well, with a rough morning after. But tonight was different; she felt safe and comfortable with Belen. She looked at him, smiling with a warmth that came from more than just the alcohol.

"What are you thinking about?" Belen asked, catching her gaze.

"Just that you're an amazing person, and I couldn't imagine being with anyone else," she replied, her words tinged with the honesty that came with intoxication. Belen smiled back, finishing the last of the food and downing his drink.

"Do you want to go somewhere private?" he asked, his tone suggestive. "I'd like to spend more time with you, alone."

Pandrosus hesitated. She knew the implication of his words, but the warmth in her body and the intoxicating buzz made it hard to think clearly. The rational part of her urged caution, but she found herself agreeing. "I would love to," she said softly.

Belen stood and helped her out of her chair. She swayed a little, but when he put his arm around her waist, the world seemed to stabilize. He led her through the bustling streets, weaving through the crowds until they reached a quieter part of town. They stopped in front of a modest house, and Belen opened the door with a flourish.

"Is this your place?" Pandrosus asked, taking in the rose-scented air.

Belen nodded. "Yes, please come in."

The interior was softly lit, with rose petals scattered across the floor. He led her to a bedroom dominated by a four-poster bed draped with sheer curtains. The mattress looked inviting, and Pandrosus couldn't resist running and jumping onto it. The bed was as soft as a cloud, and she laughed at how plush it felt.

Belen climbed onto the bed, holding himself up with one knee and one arm. With his free hand, he gently brushed the hair from Pandrosus's face. Her giggles faded as she felt the heat in his gaze, her cheeks blushing a deeper red. Belen leaned down and kissed her softly on the lips. His kisses trailed down to her neck, and she felt a shiver as he nibbled gently on her shoulder.

'Stop that,' she giggled before gazing into his eyes.

'Shall we go further?' Belen asked. His voice was now husky and he was to far gone to stop even if she said no. Happily though he got an affirmative, shy little nod from Pandrosus. He hooked his fingers under the hem of her clothing pulling it upwards and over her head. Belen threw this across the room and took in the beauty that lay below him. Two small yet supple, round breasts with cute pink nipples. His hand traced down between them and over her flat belly. He tickled her sides causing Pandrosus to squirm underneath him before continuing down to between her legs. Belen Could feel the warmth radiating from between her legs and he slipped his hand down to her private area. She was moist and smooth. Jolts of excitement ran up his spine as she moaned softly from his warm finger.

'I don't want to wait anymore,' she purred in his ear. Normally with street whores, Belen would tease them long into the night. With Pandrosus he wasnt thinking straight and pulled out his pulsing member lining it up to her opening. There was little resistance as he entered her, the moist lubrication helping him along. All around him she gripped like a velvet vice and he felt like she was trying to pull him further in, engulf him completely.

Pandrosus could feel every inch of Belen inside of her, stretching her. There was no pain like the serving maids had spoken of. Only the warmth and pure joy of Belen. Then he started to move. Feelings she couldnt describe slide off his shaft and coursed through her veins spreading out all over her body. Lights started exploding in her eyes and she felt she was losing control to the rhythm of their lovemaking. Stronger and more intense the feelings became until she felt so full she couldnt contain it anymore. And like a dam filled to overflowing her body burst with waves of ecstacy as the orgasm washed over her. Belen didn't stop feeling Pandrosus tensing in pure

173

pleasure but, rather, thrusted harder and faster, his head tucked in beside hers. As his own orgasm began to grow, he nibbled gentle upon her neck though the skin felt a little rough here.

Pandrosus didn't notice the change that was happening, didn't see the green tinge to her skin or the scales forming. Her mind melted back into a primal state as a tail grew beneath her. The slitted yellow eyes glanced over at the man that was upon her and she opened her mouth wide, saliva dripping over hundreds of razor sharp teeth. Belen was too lost in the love making to know what was happening until Pandrosus bit deep into his neck, ripping out his vocal chords.

The shock and pure terror displayed on Belen stayed with him until the last gasps of air left his lungs. Just as Belen hadnt't stopped, Pandrosus was wild biting into the soft fleshy skin and swallowing chunk after fleshy chunk without chewing.

Twenty minutes later, Pandrosus snapped back to consciousness, her senses slowly reawakening to a gruesome scene. Her surroundings were dim, but the sight of the man she once loved lying lifeless in a pool of blood was unmistakable. His body was mangled, and her own hands—now transformed into something serpentine—were drenched in crimson. A bone, chewed to its core, fell from her grasp as a wave of revulsion washed over her. She tried to scream, but the alien form she had taken had different vocal cords, and all that emerged was a low, guttural hiss.

Panic seized her. She had to get away, as far from this horror as possible. Blood trickled down her chin and stained her chest, a grim reminder of the violence she couldn't remember committing. Without thinking, she fled into the night, her snake-like limbs slithering through the darkened streets. She instinctively stuck to the shadows, darting between alleys and weaving through the maze of Athens' backstreets.

The city's noise and festivities seemed distant now, a blur against the overwhelming sound of her own heart pounding in her chest. Each shadow seemed to twist with sinister intent, each echo a reminder of the monstrosity she had become. Pandrosus didn't know how this transformation happened, or why she turned into a monster, but the weight of her guilt and terror drove her to run as fast and as far as she could.

174

Nefari savored the bustling energy of the festival, her senses awash in the aromas of roasted meats and the distant clamor of lively music. The feast had her eating more than her stomach could comfortably hold, but she didn't mind—the air was electric with celebration. Still, she held her breath as she passed the alleyways, where drunken revelers were using the shadows to relieve themselves. The stench was nauseating, and she quickly moved past.

Her thoughts drifted back to the day's events. It'd been a whirlwind—rekindling her friendship with Cranaus, dancing through the streets without a care, and making new alliances. Their plot against Cecrops was nearly complete. Thanos had won his race earlier, a pivotal moment that would lead to Cecrops presenting him with a golden olive branch later tonight. That would be the signal for Thanos to strike, driving a dagger deep into the heart of the monster king.

Cranaus believed that this night would mark the return of Athens to its rightful order, free from Cecrops's rule. He often spoke of how he would honor the ancient traditions and restore the city to its former glory, all under the watchful eye of the goddess Athena. Nefari knew better. She understood the Uru histories and was certain that Athena was of her race, not the one worshipped by the Athenians. But Cranaus was unyielding in his beliefs, and Nefari saw no point in challenging him. His resolve was as solid as iron.

As the festivities continued, Cranaus nudged Nefari, his eyes fixed on Thanos, who stood across the street, high on a table and addressing the crowd. Thanos was in his element, cup in hand, regaling the revelers with an exaggerated account of his race victory. The onlookers cheered and laughed, hanging on his every word.

"Tell me again how my necklace helped him win the race," Cranaus asked, not taking his eyes off Thanos. The young man was up on a table towering over everyone in the street. He held a copper cup filled with wine he had barely touched but was keeping up appearances before the main event. Thanos was telling a wildly exaggerated story of how he had taken the race from a doomed position. The crowd were lapping it up.

"You said yourself that the stone had properties that

fortified works of the spirit," Nefari replied, her eyes also fixed on Thanos. She smiled as he regaled the crowd with a tale about the goddess Athena appearing before him to offer words of encouragement. "I was highly emotional at the time, and the stone started to glow. I seemed to project myself into the physical world for a moment and warn him of the danger. He still knows nothing about that, of course."

Cranaus furrowed his brow. "Who do you think sent the man? Do they know what we're up to?"

"No," Nefari assured him. "I followed the man, and after the race, he was reprimanded by Giannes."

"That is fortunate," Cranaus said with a sigh of relief. There was no backup plan for tonight. Everything hinged on Thanos. "Would you like another drink?" he asked, noticing her empty cup.

"Okay, but this has to be the last one," she replied, holding up a finger. "I want to keep some of my wits about me. Besides, I'm not used to wine this strong."

Cranaus laughed and wandered off in search of more wine. Many of the food and drink stalls had already depleted their supplies for the night, as Athens reveled in the reinstatement of the Panathenaea festival. The city was celebrating with abandon, and it showed.

Nefari watched the bustling street, her gaze wandering across the festival-goers. A flicker of movement on the roof of a nearby building caught her attention. It was quick, and she couldn't be sure if she had seen it or not. As she relaxed back into her seat, she closed her eyes and projected her spirit upward to get a closer look.

What she saw sent a chill down her spine. On the rooftop sat Cecrops, but not in his usual human guise. He was in his reptilian form, watching her with predatory eyes. He must have shifted to climb the building unnoticed. If he knew she was here, then he likely knew about their plot against him. Panic gripped her. She needed to act quickly.

Returning to her body, Nefari opened her eyes to see Cranaus approaching with two fresh pottery mugs of wine. His cheerful demeanor faded the moment he saw the look on her face.

Cranaus worried at Nefari's concern. "What's wrong?" he asked. "Did something happen while I was gone?"

Nefari mumbled something incoherent and then shook her head. "Our plans may be in ruin. I believe I saw

176

Cecrops just now, watching me."

Cranaus laughed. "Girl, I think you've had enough wine. I just saw Cecrops at the end of the street."

"Are you sure?" Nefari asked, her voice sharp with urgency. "Are you absolutely certain it was him?"

"Yes," Cranaus said with a soft smile. "Two of his men called him by name, and it's not a face I'll forget any time soon. I'm just annoyed I don't get to be—what troubles you?" He noticed her deep in thought.

"There's something I need to check on," Nefari said, getting to her feet. "It could be pivotal to us, or it might just be my paranoia. Either way, I need to check it out. Wait here and keep an eye on Thanos."

"Nefari!" Cranaus called after her as she darted into a side street. She didn't turn back.

Nefari was perplexed by what she'd seen. Was there another monster in their midst, one she didn't know about? She needed to find out. Behind the house where she had seen the creature, there wasn't a soul in sight. She crept closer to the walls, careful to stay hidden.

"Would the creature on the roof show itself," Nefari said, raising her voice slightly but keeping it low enough to not carry beyond the building. She waited a full minute, unsure if anything would respond. She was about to use her Dreamtime abilities to see if the creature was still there when a green scaly head peeked over the edge. It had a red stain on its chin, which she recognized as blood.

"What are you doing, Cecrops?" she asked, her voice filled with suspicion.

The creature's slitted yellow eyes regarded her for a moment before it crawled down the wall, face-first, on all fours. Its movements were fluid, almost graceful, despite its grotesque appearance.

"Why do you..." it rasped, its voice guttural and low, "... why do you attribute this form to my father, Nefari?"

Something shifted in Nefari's perception as she looked into the reptilian eyes before her. The harsh yellow slits softened into a look of deep vulnerability. "Oh, Pandrosus," Nefari whispered, her voice catching in her throat. She stepped closer, but the girl recoiled.

"I don't want to hurt you," Pandrosus said, her voice trembling.

"I don't believe you would," Nefari replied softly. "We're friends, you and I."

"And Belen was my lover..." Pandrosus's voice cracked, her reptilian head jerking forward with a suppressed sob. Nefari saw the tears, and without hesitation, she pulled the girl into a hug.

"Tell me everything," Nefari urged, her own emotions bubbling up.

But Pandrosus could only sob, her body shaking against Nefari's embrace. The girl couldn't speak, just weep as she nestled into Nefari's shoulder. The warmth of human contact filled her with a sense of solace, but a strange tension lingered beneath the surface. The scent of flesh seemed to awaken a primal hunger in Pandrosus's reptilian senses. For a moment, Nefari felt a ripple of fear—but then, just as quickly, another scent overrode the instinct, a smell that carried with it a sense of reverence. It was as if eating Nefari would be a betrayal against the essence of what Pandrosus believed in.

"Shh... You don't have to talk if you're not ready," Nefari said, rubbing Pandrosus's back gently. "I'm here for you."

Pandrosus's tears fell freely now, each sob echoing with a lifetime of pain and conflict. "Oh, Nefari," she cried, her voice full of broken memories and shattered hopes. She started to explain what had happened—the struggles with her father, the desperate desire to break away, and the chaos that led to tonight's horrific events. The words came in fragmented bursts, each one weighted with emotion. Nefari listened quietly, offering murmured words of comfort—"there, there," and "it's okay." She knew these words couldn't heal the deeper wounds, but they might offer a small reprieve from the immediate pain.

"Have you tried to change back?" Nefari asked gently.

"I don't even know if I can," Pandrosus replied, her voice full of concern. "What if I stay like this forever?"

"You will be able to change back to your true self," Nefari assured her.

"How can you be so sure?"

"Because..." Nefari stopped, hesitating. Should she tell Pandrosus the truth about her father? It might bring comfort—or it could create a rift too deep to heal. The girl was already in turmoil; the truth might tip her over the edge.

"What?" Pandrosus pressed. She could sense that Nefari was holding something back. "What aren't you telling me?"

Nefari sighed. There was no turning back now. "Your

father has the same condition. I've witnessed his transformation."

"That's a lie!" Pandrosus hissed, her reptilian features tensing. "He would have told me. He wouldn't keep that from me." Her voice cracked as doubt and betrayal seeped in. "Why did he keep it from me?"

"There could be any number of reasons he didn't tell you," Nefari said, hoping to ease her friend's distress. "He might have believed it would skip you, or that he could protect you from it altogether. He's still your father, Pandrosus. I'm sure he has your best interests at heart."

"So, it's true?" Pandrosus asked, her voice fragile with despair.

"It is true," Nefari replied, nodding.

"What am I going to do, Nefari?" Pandrosus's question was laden with a sense of hopelessness, her eyes now welling with fresh tears. The enormity of her situation hit her, and she seemed lost in the uncertainty of her fate.

"How about we start by getting you home?" Nefari suggested, standing up. "If we need to, we'll hide you until Cecrops returns. In the meantime, we can work on finding a way to change you back." She held out her hand to Pandrosus, who sat motionless, staring into the distance. Nefari couldn't tell what the girl was thinking, her reptilian features betraying little emotion. "Will you come with me?" she asked.

Pandrosus blinked, as if coming back to reality, and took Nefari's hand. Together, they made their way back to Cecrops' estate, careful to avoid drawing attention. The streets were busy, and they had to weave through the more quiet streets, slipping into narrow alleys to avoid being seen. At times, Pandrosus had to scale walls and jump across rooftops to stay out of sight.

As they navigated the twisting side streets, Nefari's mind raced. If Cranaus' plan succeeded and Thanos managed to take down Cecrops, Pandrosus might never be able to learn how to turn back. A deep sense of dread filled her at the thought. What if Pandrosus became a danger to others, driven by the same primal urges as her father? The possibility weighed heavily on her heart.

When they reached the estate, Pandrosus led Nefari to her room, showing her how to climb up to the ledge. The light was off inside, a good sign that no one had checked on her. Pandrosus sighed in relief as she climbed inside and

179

sat on the bed, pulling the covers over her. She faced away from the door, her body curling into a tight ball.

"We need to keep our voices down," Nefari said, her voice low. Though the sounds of the festival filled the night, it was still too risky to speak at a normal volume.

"Why not just talk as Uru can, with our minds?" Pandrosus suggested.

Nefari considered this for a moment. "It has been decades since I used that voice—I almost forgot it existed. On Atlantis, people would send messages with it all the time, but I haven't used it in years."

"Do you think you can't anymore?" Pandrosus asked, switching to telepathic speech. A shiver went through Nefari as the forgotten sensation returned.

"I can," Nefari replied telepathically. "I was just making a light comment about my situation."

"What is your situation?" Pandrosus asked, her voice showing concern for Nefari. "I heard you turned your back on Atlantis and were living in the wilderness with a bunch of men."

"That's not quite true. I haven't turned my back on Atlantis, and it's not just a bunch of men. I've been going through a lot lately and needed time to get my bearings. I mentioned a man who got chased through my room at an inn." Pandrosus nodded. "He's in the village community. I've been spending more time with him."

"That's... that's beautiful," Pandrosus said, tearing up. Nefari berated herself noting she was thinking about Belen again.

"We don't need to talk about that now," Nefari said quickly. "How can we get you back to normal?"

"I don't know, Nefari. I just can't think straight anymore. I keep remembering what happened, and how it should have been one of my happiest moments, but it wasn't. This has been the worst moment of my life."

"Try to calm down," Nefari told her.

"No, it's too hard."

"I know it's hard," Nefari said, taking Pandrosus's hand. "Just look into my eyes and picture the night you, Guinea, and I spent laughing and telling stories. Remember how happy you were, and how much you want to feel like that again." Pandrosus closed her eyes, trying to find a moment of peace, but her frustration broke through, and she shook her head. Nefari gripped her hand tighter. "Look at me,

Pandrosus. Look into my eyes and picture me from that night. Let my face help you focus."

Nefari watched Pandrosus's expression shift as she tried to concentrate. A soft smile formed on Nefari's lips when she saw the green scales on Pandrosus's skin beginning to take on a more human-like hue. But then, suddenly, the door swung open, and a man's silhouette appeared in the doorway. Pandrosus lost her focus and jumped, her skin reverting to its reptilian form. The man entered, and Nefari instantly recognized Cecrops. House servants followed, carrying candles to light the room, then promptly left. Cecrops's eyes widened when he saw Nefari.

"You have a bad habit of showing up at the wrong time, Nefari," Cecrops said, his voice edged with anger. Nefari knew it was because the attempt on his life had failed. Pandrosus just sat under her blanket, not looking at her father.

"I'm not here to play games, Cecrops," Nefari replied sharply. "I've been helping your daughter with a problem she's having."

"Guards," Cecrops called.

"Father, no!" Pandrosus cried, throwing the blankets off. If she expected Cecrops to be surprised, he wasn't.

"As for you," Cecrops said, turning to Pandrosus. "I expressly forbade you from being too friendly with that man. You're too innocent to be doing such things." Pandrosus began to cry, but her father showed no sympathy.

"Leave her alone, Cecrops," Nefari said. Three men burst into the room, brandishing weapons. They wore no armor, having been given light duties for the night. Their bronzed skin suggested they were of the Uru race, yet they didn't seem surprised by Pandrosus's reptilian form. Nefari found it odd. "Your tainted blood has already caused her enough harm."

Cecrops laughed, a rich and powerful sound. "You think it's my fault that Pandrosus is in this state? Her looks come from her mother." He turned back to Pandrosus, still sobbing. "Has your friend told you why she's in the city tonight? She tried to kill me." Pandrosus looked at Nefari, hoping for a denial, but saw only sadness in her friend's eyes.

"It's true?" Pandrosus asked, stepping back from Nefari. "Did you really try to kill my father?"

"She did," Cecrops confirmed. "She thought me a monster and was helping a band of renegades get close to me. They almost succeeded, but I escaped. We've got two of them in the basement, and that's where Nefari will go."

Pandrosus stood in silence. Nefari hoped she would defend her, but the reptilian face grew hard. "Would you kill me too, knowing I'm like my father? Knowing I'm a monster?" The tears had dried up, replaced by anger and defiance. Nefari dropped her head, unable to meet her eyes.

"I couldn't do anything that would harm you, Pandrosus," Nefari said softly.

"Liar!" Pandrosus almost screamed. Cecrops wrapped an arm around his daughter to comfort her.

"I think we've had enough of your company, Nefari," Cecrops said, gesturing for the guards to proceed. As they moved toward Nefari, she looked around for a way out, but they had her cornered too quickly. They grabbed her struggling arms and held her tightly, not giving her a chance to break free. They dragged her out of the room, while Pandrosus's eyes remained fierce, glaring at her friend.

From the outside, Nefari never would have guessed that the house had a number of sub-levels. These levels were below ground and had no natural light. The only illumination came from a few dimly burning candles. Nefari's eyes hadn't yet adjusted to her surroundings, and she kept tripping on the uneven stone stairs. If not for the guards holding her up, she would have tumbled to the bottom. As she descended deeper into Cecrops's domain, a smell filled her nostrils. It was a nauseating stench of putrid, rotting flesh mixed with urine and feces. Nefari doubted she could endure more than five minutes down here. Her stomach churned, and she felt light-headed.

"Little rabbit, what have you done?" One of the guards asked. Nefari recognized the voice immediately.

"Torres?" she said, looking up at him. The bronze-plated leather helm covered his angular face, but she knew it was him. Only Torres would call her "rabbit." "Torres, you have to help me. They don't know what they're—"

Torres backhanded her across the face. The metal knuckle guards tore open the skin on her cheek. She reeled back, trying to lift her hand to the wound, but the guards held her arms tightly. She had to ignore the stinging pain, blinking tears from her eyes as she looked forward, remaining silent. Nefari wouldn't make that mistake again.

"You have no right to talk," Torres said harshly, and the other guard laughed.

Nefari was starting to see better in the darkness and could keep her footing. She remembered descending three flights of stairs to get to this point, and she could see that the stairs continued much deeper but the guards pushed her onto a hallway floor. The corridor stretched ahead of her, with openings set at intervals along the walls, light spilling from various doors.

The floor was uneven, made from oddly shaped stone pavers. As they walked down the hall, Nefari glanced into the first doorway they passed. Inside, she saw Argan. He was strapped to a wooden device that slowly stretched him as a guard twisted a lever. Argan was sweating heavily and looked deathly pale.

"Our men have already gone through that settlement. There's no one there." The interrogation reached Nefari as they twisted the lever to the next notch. Argan screamed loudly.

"I swear, that's where they are," he said through the pain. The Uru in the room shared a glance.

"He knows nothing more. Kill him." Nefari passed the door, but Argan's screams echoed down the hallway, echoing in her mind. The next door she passed that had light inside was empty. Nefari let out a sigh of relief. Voices came from further down the hallway.

"Where are the rest of the resistance?" The voice was a growl. Nefari hoped it wasn't Cranaus. The lack of response from whoever they were interrogating only deepened her anxiety. She leaned forward to get a better look inside. The moment she could see, her heart sank. It wasn't Cranaus, but it was someone she knew.

Thanos was also strapped to a torture device, though it was different from the one Argan was on. Thanos's height would have been too much for the previous device. This one was designed to slowly compress the victim, collapsing vital organs and crushing bones. Thanos's face was contorted in pain, his struggled breathing short and ragged.

Nefari let out a gasp and the sound must have reached Thanos because he looked up at her. Mustering his strength, he managed a smile, defiant yet filled with sadness. He was able to muster two words before she was forced to move past the door. Though she didn't hear the words from Thanos the torturers voice reached her ear.

"What do you mean by 'Big dick'? Am I to take that as some sort of insult?"

Tears rolled freely as the emotional weight of those two words constricted Nefari's chest. "No fear," she sobbed loud enough for Thanos to hear. The metallic wrap across the back of her head worth it.

Nefari couldn't bear to think what else they had in store for him—or for her. But she had learned one thing: if she gave away all the information she knew, they would kill her.

The guards threw Nefari into a dark room a short distance down the hallway. She could no longer hear any sounds from outside and wasn't sure if that was a good thing or a bad thing.

"One of the torturers should be free soon," Torres said. "Enjoy your stay."

The door slammed shut, and she heard the guards' footsteps fading as they walked away. The room was pitch-black, and Nefari had to feel her way around the walls to gauge the space. As she touched the stone, her hand brushed against something small and furry. She jumped back as a rat scurried away, squealing in annoyance for being disturbed. The stench in the room was overpowering—like someone had died recently.

Nefari slid down to the back wall and sat, trying to make sense of how everything had gone so wrong. Thanos had been captured, so his attempt to assassinate Cecrops must have failed. She knew Thanos wasn't foolish; he would have waited for the right moment. So what went wrong? Did someone intervene? Did Cecrops know in advance? She wished she'd been there when the attempt was made. She felt a pang of guilt, wondering if she'd lost a friend tonight. She also wondered where Cranaus was.

Suddenly, a noise from outside indicated a door opening, followed by the sound of a body being thrown into another cell.

"He put up a good fight," a man's voice said.

"Yeah. It's going to be fun breaking him," another voice replied. "Now, let's get the girl."

Nefari realized instantly that they were talking about

her. It was her turn to be strapped to a torture device and endure excruciating pain. She wasn't mentally prepared for this, but the door opened anyway. Despite her best efforts to resist, the Uru guards dragged her off with overwhelming force. Her struggles were futile against their strength.

The room where they brought Nefari was nearly empty. The bright light stung her eyes as she frantically scanned for instruments of torture. All she saw was a heavy chair with leather straps over the armrests and a table beside it. She fought desperately as they dragged her toward the chair. When she was close enough, she tried to kick it over, but it was bolted to the ground. As they began to strap her arms to the chair, she tried to pull free, but one of the Uru punched her hard in the face, causing her nose to bleed and tears to stream from her eyes. The blow left her dizzy and disoriented.

With her arms secured, the second Uru brought in a tray from outside the room and set it on the table. It contained a variety of bizarre instruments that sent shivers down Nefari's spine. She knew she was about to find out their purpose. Alongside the instruments was a small vial filled with a white, milky liquid. The first Uru picked up a thin, flat-tipped tool and slid it under Nefari's fingernail on her right hand. She realized instantly what they were about to do, and her attempts to curl her finger back were useless against their grip.

"Traitor," the second Uru said. "Listen and listen well. I'm going to ask you questions, and you will answer them completely and honestly. If you do not answer or if you lie to us, my friend here will make sure you understand the consequences. Do you understand?"

Nefari nodded, fear filling her eyes. The first Uru gestured to the second, who wasted no time. With brutal force, he drove the thin blade under Nefari's fingernail and ripped it upward. The searing pain shot through her hand, and Nefari screamed, unable to hold back the agony. She clenched her body in response, and her rapid breathing punctuated the intensity of her suffering. This level of pain was unimaginable. It was different from anything she'd experienced before, like the time she had gotten her hand caught in a gear while learning to be a mechanic. The pressure back then had been immense, almost tearing her hand off, but that felt like nothing compared to this single, torn fingernail.

The first Uru leaned closer. "Nefari, I told you to answer my questions," he said. "A head nod isn't enough."

Nefari glared at him, her face showing shock and disbelief at the violence inflicted upon her.

The first Uru spoke to the larger man, Oz, without taking his eyes off Nefari. "You know, Oz, I think our little princess here doesn't quite understand the predicament she's in." Oz shrugged with indifference.

The first Uru crouched down to Nefari's eye level, his voice dropping to a sinister whisper. "You are ours for as long as we care to keep you. No one will help you. No one will save you. Your life is forfeit, and the only thing keeping you alive is our enjoyment. But you should understand that what we enjoy is causing pain. Now, where are the rest of the resistance?"

Nefari glared at the man before her, defiant despite the pain. "Your breath smells," she told him. The man, known as Tseng, signaled to Oz. A second fingernail was ripped away, and Nefari's scream was silent, her mouth open in shock and agony. She clenched her chest, but the pain began to ebb as if she were drawing it away from her injured hand. Nefari looked back at Tseng with a smirk. It felt much like the dreaming only just her hand was detached. It was an odd sensation.

"I think she likes it, Oz," Tseng said. "How about this? If you don't give me an answer, I'll have Oz rip them all off one by one. Where is Cranaus?"

Nefari laughed loudly, genuinely relieved that Cranaus's name came up. It meant he was still alive, and the resistance was still active. "Thank you," she said. "To you, Oz, and to you, even though I don't know your name."

"Take them off, Oz," Tseng ordered. "Take your time."

Oz obeyed, inserting the tool under each fingernail with excruciating slowness. The skin separated as the blade cut through nerves, sending waves of pain through Nefari's body. Blood trickled down her hand, but Nefari kept smiling at her torturers, as if it was nothing. Tseng's expression darkened as he realized his approach wasn't yielding the expected results.

"This isn't working. We aren't getting any answers. Dispose of her," Tseng snapped, waving a hand dismissively. Nefari's heart raced at the sudden shift. Her face grew pale as she realized they were about to end her life.

Oz picked up the vial, looking back at Tseng. "Tseng?" he asked, his voice gruff, with a hint of uncertainty. Nefari wondered what they were planning. Was it the method of her execution, or something else?

"You've been dying to use that ever since the shopkeeper fooled you into buying it," Tseng said with a smirk. "It's only milk."

"Let me try. She's dead anyway," Oz insisted, his eyes fixed on the vial.

Tseng stood and stared at Oz, then waved his hand dismissively. "Fine, do what you like."

Oz's grin was wicked as he moved closer to Nefari. He placed a hand on her head, pulling her back and leaning down to whisper in her ear. "This liquid is going to burn out your eye. Whether it's open or closed won't matter. It will eat away your eyeball, burrowing into it until you're blind." His words were chilling, sending a shiver through Nefari. She'd spent long days in the dark underworks of Atlantis, but losing her sight entirely was a fate worse than death. "You have one chance to save your sight—and maybe your life, if Tseng allows it. Where is the rebel leader?"

Nefari tried to pull forward, but Oz's grip was like iron. Tears welled up in her eyes as she struggled with the choice: to give up Cranaus to save herself or stay silent and face the consequences. It took only a moment for her to make her decision—she couldn't betray Cranaus. "As you said, I'm already a dead girl," she replied, her voice steady despite the tears. She looked around the room, taking in every detail, knowing it could be the last time she would ever see.

Oz removed the stopper from the vial with his teeth and began tilting the bottle toward her left eye. The milky substance spilled onto her eyeball, and an intense burning pain seared through her. It felt like fire tearing through her optic nerve, ripping away her vision. Nefari thrashed violently, the straps holding her barely able to contain her movements. Then, everything went black, her screams fading as unconsciousness took her.

Oz looked back at Tseng with a triumphant smile. "See, it wasn't milk at all," he said, clearly satisfied with his work.

Chapter 9

Cranaus sat against a crumbling wall in the poor quarters, his breath coming in ragged bursts. All around him, the City Guard conducted a ruthless sweep, searching for any trace of the rebellion. He pressed his hand to his shoulder, wincing as the cut pulsed with fresh pain. Though the bleeding had slowed to a trickle, the guard who'd inflicted the wound was now lying lifeless in a darkened alley.

The dilapidated house where he had taken refuge was a known meeting point for resistance members. Cranaus knew his presence would cause a stir, but he couldn't stay out in the open. He also couldn't shake the feeling that someone had tipped off the guards about their operation.

A noise at the door made Cranaus tighten his grip on his dagger. He glanced up and relaxed slightly when he saw the short, clean-shaven Kyros, standing in the doorway. Cranaus slid his blade back into its hidden sheath as Kyros crossed the room and crouched down, carefully examining his shoulder.

"Ow, careful!" Cranaus protested, pushing him away.

Kyros smirked. "I saw the whole thing," he said. "From my vantage point, it looked a lot worse than it is. You'll live."

"I know I will," Cranaus replied, his voice edged with irritation. He took a deep breath to calm himself. "Did you see anyone else?"

"Flavian's fine. He'll be here soon. Thanos got caught, though. The others... I'm not sure."

Before Cranaus could respond, there was another noise from outside, and Titos strolled in as if he owned the place. "Am I late to the party?" he said with a grin.

"You're later than some," Kyros shot back. "Aren't you worried about walking the streets with the City Guard on high alert?"

Titos shrugged. "If you walk with confidence, the guards tend to leave you alone. Besides, I don't exactly look like a fighter," he replied with a wink. "Speaking of guards, I think your girl is in some serious trouble."

"Nefari?" Cranaus said, sitting up with a sudden burst of energy. His worries had already been mounting, and Titos' words didn't help. "What happened? Tell me everything."

"I apologize," Titos said, holding up his hands as if to

calm him. "I saw her leave just before the ceremony and decided to follow her. You know she's an Uru, and I wanted to make sure she wasn't still spying on us."

"She's not a spy," Cranaus retorted, his voice low and menacing.

"People can have their doubts," Titos replied with a shrug, letting the tension linger in the air. "And she was leaving right before everything went down."

"So... is she?" Cranaus asked, unable to contain his curiosity. Titos just shook his head, the faintest hint of a smile tugging at his lips.

"Nefari met another Uru, a girl. Apparently, the girl got into some trouble and transformed into some kind of reptilian being. Nefari offered to help get her back home."

"Another reptilian?" Kyros muttered, swearing under his breath. "I thought that problem was contained to Cecrops alone."

"Ah, but here's the twist," Titos said, holding up a finger with a smug look on his face.

Before he could continue, the back door swung open with a loud bang, making all three men jump. Cranaus dove behind a table, drawing his leaf-bladed dagger, while Titos and Kyros scrambled to find cover. They were silently signaling to each other, preparing to attack whoever came through the door, when they heard an odd voice.

"I could've sworn I heard the others," said a muffled voice from behind an a cloth of sorts.

Kyros peered over the edge of the table and recognized the intruder. "Poseidon's balls, Flavian! You scared us half to death!" he exclaimed, rising to his feet. "And what's with that ridiculous headpiece?"

Cranaus risked a look, only to see Flavian standing there with a tunic wrapped around his head, partially obscuring his face. Flavian gave a sheepish grin and started unwrapping the dark cloth.

"You can't be too careful," Flavian said, as he closed the door. Titos chuckled in response.

"Come over here, Flavian," Cranaus said, waving him over. "A lot's been going on, and we need to talk." He then gestured to Titos to continue. "You were saying something about the Uru girl with Nefari?"

"The place Nefari took the girl to was Cecrops' house," Titos explained. "The girl was apparently a friend of Nefari's and Cecrops' daughter, Pandrosus."

"That explains why she turned into a reptilian," Kyros said. "She'd have the blood of that snake in her veins."

"When the attack failed, Cecrops was escorted back to his house by his guards," Cranaus stated, his concern growing. He had thought Nefari might be hiding somewhere, maybe a bit roughed up. Now, it seemed she was in far more danger than he imagined, in the heart of the enemy's lair.

Titos hesitated, his expression serious. "Nefari was taken to the dungeons for interrogation," he said quietly. "When Cecrops got home, I couldn't hear the whole conversation from where I was hiding, but it seems the friend betrayed her. Cecrops called her a traitor."

"No!" Cranaus slammed his fist on the table in frustration, then winced and rubbed his knuckles. "We've gotta find a way to get them out!"

"The only way is to storm the house and go three floors underground," Titos said.

"How do you know the layout of Cecrops' house?" Flavian asked, raising an eyebrow. "You always seem to have this kind of information just when we need it."

"I'm not making it up, if that's what you're implying," Titos replied, looking at him with confusion.

"That's not what I'm implying. You seem to have information that no one else here could know," Flavian said, letting his words linger. "We follow your lead a lot, but tonight they seemed to know an attack was coming."

"And you did walk in rather confidently," Kyros added.

"We could play the blame game all night if we wanted to," Titos replied. "But personally, I believe our informant, the one who told us the festival would be honored this year, might have been compromised. I get my information from a reliable network of trusted sources."

"A double agent?" Kyros asked.

"Not even that," Cranaus interjected. "He could be feeding us only what the Uru want us to know, while providing them with everything we plan. Let's keep this to ourselves for now until we can confirm it. Right now, we need to focus on getting our... people back."

"We know you have a soft spot for Nefari, Cranaus," Flavian teased. Cranaus blushed, thinking he'd hidden his feelings well. "Thanks for not forgetting our men, too."

"It's not like that," Cranaus tried to defend himself.

"So, buying her gifts and prancing around like a dog..."

190

Titos smirked, earning a scowl from Cranaus. "...is something you'd do for me, Thanos, or anyone else in the resistance?"

Cranaus shut his mouth, earning laughter from Flavian and Kyros.

"Let's get back to the real issue," Titos said, turning serious. "If we need an infiltrator, I know a guy. I can have him on board by morning."

"If you can be quicker, do it," Cranaus said with a nod.

"He works best in daylight. Odd, I know, but he's the best I've ever seen." Titos turned to leave, heading out into the night. As he walked away, the others heard him singing a slurred tune.

"One day he's going to hang for his carefree attitude," Flavian said, shaking his head.

"Just not today," Cranaus hoped sending a plea to the Gods.

Nefari awoke to find herself in a dark cell. The darkness was so complete that, for a brief moment, she thought they'd taken her sight entirely. Panic gripped her chest, and her breaths became short and rapid. Reaching out, she felt nothing in front of her and lost her balance, crashing to the hard stone floor. Her hand got trapped beneath her, and the sudden pain from her ripped-out fingernails shot up her arm and through her body. The searing pain was enough to pull her back from the edge of hysteria.

Gradually, her senses returned, bringing clarity to her chaotic thoughts. The pain in her head centered around her left eye. She gently pressed against her eyelid with her good hand and was relieved to find the eye still there, but even the lightest touch caused searing agony. She vomited from the pain, her stomach heaving violently. Afterward, she wiped her mouth with the back of her hand and made a mental note to avoid the spot on the floor where the vomit lay. The smell of roasted beef and wine from her vomit mingled with the foul odor of the cell, providing a marginal improvement to the air quality.

As her eyes adjusted to the darkness, she noticed faint light seeping through the hairline cracks around the door. But her heart sank when she realized that her vision was severely compromised. The view was half-blurred, distorted. Tears filled her good eye as the reality sank in.

"They took my eye," Nefari sobbed. Her cries grew

louder and more desperate as the weight of what she'd lost crushed her. Death, she could have faced. But this—the loss of sight, the prospect of living in darkness—this was a torture she had never imagined. A dark thought crept into her mind: Would they take her other eye when they strapped her back into the chair?

Nefari felt the dread growing inside her. She knew it was only a matter of time before the torturers returned to finish what they'd started.

Nefari wept for nearly thirty minutes, her tears soaking her cheeks and pooling on the cold stone floor. When her tears ran dry, she simply sat and stared at the thin stream of light that crept through the cracks in the cell door. In the darkness, her thoughts turned to the beautiful things she had once seen. She remembered the delicate glass frog that Cranaus had given her, the rolling hills and grasslands of her homeland, the vast oceans around Atlantis with dolphins dancing in the waves. Memories of her childhood flitted by: colorful birds, lush rainforests, golden sands merging with azure seas. Even the great black feline that once threatened her life now seemed a magnificent creature in her mind's eye.

Her thoughts eventually settled on Cranaus, recalling the day they met, the necklace he had given her, and all the times he had stood up for her. A moment when he was anxiously preparing a list for her challenges surfaced in her memory. The realization of what she had lost, not just physically but perhaps spiritually, filled her with dread. Would her impaired vision in this world reflect in her spiritual journey?

Nefari's body trembled from exhaustion and fear, but she forced herself to focus and calm her racing thoughts. She needed to find a point of serenity amid the chaos. Despite the searing pain in her body, she focused on reaching a meditative state, allowing her spirit to soar. At first, all she saw was darkness, as if the night had engulfed Cecrops's entire domain. No candles flickered, and no torches illuminated the corridors. It was night, yet it felt darker than usual.

Pushing past the oppressive gloom, Nefari willed herself to rise. She burst through the roof of the building, finding herself under the vast, starlit sky. The moon hung large and bright, reflecting the sun's hidden light. The stars spread across the sky like a river of diamonds on deep blue velvet. In the east, the faint glow of the approaching dawn signaled that the sun would soon rise.

Tears filled Nefari's eyes once again, but these were tears of joy. The beauty of the world, as seen by both her eyes, overwhelmed her with emotion. She couldn't contain her happiness as she soared above, laughing wildly at the sheer beauty of the scene before her. It was a sight she would cherish forever.

Nefari looked down at the house below. "You almost broke me," she muttered. "But you won't get that close again. Death doesn't scare me, and anything you do to my body is temporary." She descended through the house, back toward her physical body. As she did, she scanned the other rooms, searching for any other members of the resistance group. The only one she found was Thanos, in the cell directly opposite hers. He was awake but appeared to be in pain, resting against the door with his ear pressed hard against the thick, reinforced wood, as if listening for something.

Nefari returned to her body and called out softly, "Thanos." There was no response. She tapped on the door and called a bit louder. This time, a reply came.

"Nefari?" Thanos's voice held a hint of relief. "I heard your screams, then it went quiet. I thought you maybe passed away."

"No, just... taking a moment to collect myself," Nefari replied.

There was a brief silence, and then Thanos spoke again. "I wanted to ask you something," he said, then trailed off.

Nefari felt the tension in the silence. "What is it, Thanos?"

"When I was coming back into Athens, I had a vision of you standing in front of me," Thanos said. "But it was like a flash—it was gone as quickly as it came. I figured it was just the sun messing with my head." He paused. "Was that—"

"It was me, Thanos," she replied, cutting him off. She realized that no one had explained to him the full extent of her abilities. "I was trying to stop you."

"Stop me?" he echoed, his voice confused. "Why? I was ahead in the race. Why would you try to stop me?"

Nefari took a deep breath. "Because it wasn't safe," she said. "I knew something was going to happen. I wanted to warn you before it was too late."

Thanos was silent for a moment, absorbing her words.

"And that vision—that was you?" he asked, incredulous.

"Yes," she said. "I can project my spirit out of my body and travel. It's how I knew you were in pain, and it's why I was able to see that you were awake."

"That's... amazing," Thanos said, his voice tinged with awe. "But also a bit unsettling." He hesitated. "Does anyone else know about this?"

"Not many," Nefari replied. "And it's best it stays that way." She knew that her ability could be both a blessing and a curse, especially if it fell into the wrong hands.

Thanos nodded, understanding the gravity of the situation. "I won't say a word," he promised.

"Thank you," Nefari said, her voice steadying. The connection with Thanos was a small comfort in the midst of the darkness.

"There was a man in the bushes at the entrance," Nefari explained. "You may not have seen the throwing knife that passed where you would have been, had you not seen me and stopped."

Thanos's memory flashed to the man standing awkwardly by the gates to Athens. "That dirty rat!" he said. "You saved me a lot of trouble, Nefari. Thank you."

"I don't think I saved you all that much trouble, considering where we are because you won," Nefari replied.

"No, I guess you're right," Thanos said, his voice quieting.

"Thanos?" Nefari waited for his response, but the silence stretched. "I want to tell you something about myself and also what awaits us."

"What do you mean?" he asked.

"I'm not a full Uru. I'm a mix of Uru and another race from my homeland called the Abori," she explained. "The Abori have an ability that allows them to fly free from their bodies at any given moment. I've learned this skill over my fifty years from someone I admired like a father. I was watching you race each step of the way and passing on information to Cranaus."

"Why are you telling me this, Nefari?" Thanos asked, his tone edged with concern. "I know I asked, but I don't need such a long-winded answer, especially at the end."

"That's the point," Nefari said. "If this is to be our end, I want you to know where you're going."

"No one could know that for certain," Thanos replied.

"I do," she said with quiet confidence. "At least about your transition. When you die, your spirit lingers for a period of seven days. You have the chance to come to terms with what has happened and say your personal goodbyes to those who are still alive."

"...What happens after those seven days?" Thanos asked, his voice hesitant.

"A door of your own making appears, and you leave this realm for new and greater things," Nefari explained.

"Then why do we fear it so much?" Thanos asked. "Why does it rock us to our core?"

"Because that's part of being alive," Nefari replied. "This world is raw and savage, but it's also beautiful and pure. As you leave your physical body behind, you lose the depth of life. You gain the freedom of soul. You're scared because it's the unknown, and that's hard to shake."

"You're both rather eager for death, it seems," a third voice interrupted. It was the torturer Tseng, his voice a grating reminder of their grim reality. "Cecrops has no more need of you, so let's make it a reality, shall we?"

The cell doors swung open, and Uru guards stormed in to restrain both Nefari and Thanos. Tseng approached Nefari, peering into her injured eye. "Looks like Oz's tonic worked after all," he said with a sneer. "You have a beautiful white eye, though it doesn't seem like you'll be seeing much with it."

Nefari spat in Tseng's face, the glob of saliva rolling down his cheek. He pulled a small cloth from his tunic to wipe it away. "Just returning the favor," she said with a hint of satisfaction.

"Oh, she's feisty, isn't she, Thanos?" Tseng remarked, turning to the lanky man, who stared back with defiance. "Still not talking? Well, that silence will be permanent soon. Darkness will be all you know. Take them," he ordered.

Neither Nefari nor Thanos resisted as the guards led them out of their cells. They knew where they were going and had accepted it. The journey to the room where Nefari would meet her end was both swift and agonizingly slow. Each step felt like it stretched into eternity, yet the moments passed too quickly, a paradox that made the experience all the more surreal.

Nefari's thoughts shifted to Cranaus. She would never get to share herself with him, hold him in a loving embrace, or even kiss him. Her upbringing on Atlantis had taught her to avoid matters of the heart because she was barren, destined to a life without love. If she could do it all over, she wouldn't have hidden away in the depths of that city. She would have explored the world and found joy, not just in the last moments of her life.

"What a wasted life," she muttered under her breath.

"To die with friends is not a wasted life, Nefari," Thanos said, his voice soft as they entered the torture room. A guard kicked him in the back, causing him to stumble forward.

"No talking," the guard snarled.

"Or what? You'll kill me?" Thanos retorted, his defiance unshaken. "In these last moments, you have no power over me, Uru scum." He stood up, looking down at the guard with a fearless gaze.

"You do have power—the power of choice," Tseng said. "And you've chosen to go first. I think you'll remember your friend from yesterday."

Thanos saw the chair where he'd been bound for questioning the night before. It was a large contraption, built for pain, designed to crush his spirit as it crushed his body. He had no fond memories of the thing. "Oh, yes, me and her got well acquainted last night," he said, trying to keep his bravado. "I was starting to miss her tender touch."

A guard grunted and shoved him forward toward the chair. As the Uru prepared the device, Thanos kept his eyes on Nefari. Tears glistened in her eye, and he gave her a faint smile in return.

"Remember what I said," Nefari whispered to him. A guard struck her across the back of the head, and Thanos nodded, smiling through the pain. He mouthed "thank you" to her, then steeled himself for what was to come.

Tseng smiled as he started to twist a mechanism that slowly compacted the torture device, tightening the restraints on Thanos. Nefari was forced to watch her friend slowly being crushed. When she tried to look away, the guards grabbed her head and forced her to witness the grim scene. Each creak of the device was accompanied by Thanos's forced laughter. It was clear that he was using laughter to keep from screaming in agony.

But his laughter became more strained, punctuated by ragged breathing. The bursts grew shorter, more desperate, each one hinting at the escalating pain he endured. Nefari felt her stomach twist as the hours passed. She heard the sickening sound of bones cracking and limbs popping under pressure. It was a relentless, horrifying ordeal. Through it all, Thanos kept a brave smile on his lips, a grim reminder to Nefari that even in the darkest moments, courage could shine through.

"Bastard took his time," Tseng muttered. "Go make sure he's dead, Shao."

Shao, one of the guards, grinned and drew a blade. He took one step toward Thanos's lifeless body, then sheathed his weapon. "No need. His bowels just let go," he said, waving a hand to ward off the stench. "Damn, but he stinks."

The room filled with a nauseating odor, and Nefari's head spun from the intensity. But with the smell came a surge of anger. Fueled by rage and grief, she lunged at Shao, catching the guards off guard with her sudden ferocity. They had not expected this burst of strength from someone who had been calm until now.

Nefari dove headfirst into Shao, her skull connecting with his nose. A sickening crack echoed through the chamber as his nose broke, twisting across his face. Shao reeled back in shock and pain, blood streaming from his shattered nose, while the guards scrambled to regain control of the situation. Nefari's unexpected defiance ignited chaos in the torture chamber, the quiet broken by the sounds of struggle and shouts of alarm.

"Just wait until you die!" Nefari screamed at Shao. "You're going to smell far worse than Thanos with the cesspit you have for a soul!"

"You nasty, half breed whore!" Shao yelled, grabbing Nefari by the throat and squeezing. The air vanished from her lungs, and she felt herself fading into unconsciousness. Her vision darkened as her face turned an unnatural shade.

"Drop her," Tseng ordered. Shao immediately let go, and Nefari fell to her knees, gasping for air.

"Tie the ropes around her ankles," Tseng instructed. "And strip her clothing."

Shao's expression was a mixture of malice and satisfaction as he complied, his broken nose adding to his menacing appearance. "You're going to love your death, whore." He grabbed the front of her tunic and ripped it off, exposing her tanned skin. "Your screams will reverberate throughout the halls warming my heart," he sneered, tossing the torn garment aside.

Nefari felt a rush of cold air against her bare skin. She scanned the room, trying to understand what they were planning, but she couldn't piece it together. The ropes from the ceiling attached to pulleys, leading back to anchor points on the wall. She knew one thing: they were going to hang her upside down.

The guards pulled the ropes, and Nefari's feet were swept out from under her. She barely had time to shield her head from the stone floor as she was hoisted into the air. The ropes pulled her legs slightly apart, her body hanging like a pendulum, only inches from the ground.

She braced herself, unsure of what they intended to do. Given the brutality she had seen and the position she was in, she expected something of a sexual nature was about to start. But Shao's next words were colder than she could have imagined.

"You're an ugly whore," Shao spat. "No wonder no one bedded you. Are you ready to get sawed in half?"

Nefari's eyes went wide as she saw Tseng hand Shao one end of a rusty, jagged-edged saw. The teeth were wickedly pointed, bent either to the left or right, giving them a cruel, uneven edge. Tseng took the other end, and they lowered the blade between Nefari's legs, preparing to saw her from crotch to head.

Suddenly, the sound of running feet echoed from the stairs, causing the men to pause and turn toward the door. An Uru soldier burst in, dressed in full bronze armor, his breath heavy.

"Cecrops has been slain, and the resistance is at our door," he announced.

For a moment, everyone was stunned. The words hung in the air, and then the guards rushed up the stairs, abandoning their grim task. Only Tseng and Shao stayed behind to complete the execution. But just as Shao raised the saw, a knife flashed and lodged in his throat. He fell back, clutching at the hilt, gurgling as blood pooled in his mouth. The saw slipped, grazing Nefari's skin with superficial scrapes.

Tseng turned, his eyes widening in shock as the soldier who had just arrived rammed a short sword into his gut, then twisted and wrenched it upward, ensuring a swift death. Tseng crumpled to the ground, his last breath gurgling through clenched teeth.

The soldier, who called himself Jakaan, quickly cut the ropes holding Nefari, lowering her gently to the floor. He freed her ankles, revealing rope burns where the restraints had bitten into her skin.

"I'm Jakaan," he said. "Titos sent me."

That was all Nefari needed to hear. She staggered toward Tseng's dying body, but Jakaan grabbed her and pulled her toward the door.

"We must move," he said, urgency in his voice. "The guards will be back soon."

Nefari realized that the "bronze" skin beneath the Uru armor was actually a shade of brown, similar to that of the Abori from her homeland. She followed Jakaan's lead but found herself barely able to run. He noticed her weakness and hoisted her over his shoulder. As he took the stairs two at a time, Nefari felt the raw power emanating from him. When they reached the ground floor, he continued up to the next floor, slipping into a room. With a swift motion, he dispatched a servant before an alarm could be raised.

"You've gone up one too many floors," Nefari said weakly.

"Too many guards below," Jakaan replied. "They'll capture us on that floor. Soon they'll return to the lower levels."

Nefari nodded; it made sense. Not long after, the guards from the torture room and additional reinforcements poured back into the lower floors of Cecrops's home. Despite her vulnerability, Nefari felt oddly safe with Jakaan. Her strength was drained, and she needed all her energy just to keep herself from collapsing.

Jakaan moved quickly down the stairs and out a rear door. He carried Nefari down the side of the house, across the street, and began weaving through the maze of alleys and narrow streets. After a while, he rested her against a wall in a secluded alley.

"We should have ten minutes before they raise the alarm. The Uru are prideful," Jakaan said, tossing her a green tunic. Nefari hadn't even noticed when he picked it up. "Put this on."

Nefari struggled to get the tunic over her head, and Jakaan stepped in to help her. Once she was dressed, he picked her up again and continued moving through the labyrinthine streets. He kept to the shadows, peering around corners to ensure no guards were on patrol. By the time they reached the docks of Athens, Nefari had fallen asleep, exhaustion finally overcoming her.

"Nefari," the voice called, pulling her from her dreamless slumber. It was familiar, yet her mind was too heavy to place it. Her memories were fragmented—being carried through the streets of Athens by Jakaan, the smell of the sea, and the distant cries of gulls. Slowly, she remembered the events leading to this moment.

"Nefari," the voice called again, clearer this time. She opened her eyes to see Thanos's face smiling down at her. "How can this be?" she said, her voice hushed with disbelief. "You died in Athens."

"Indeed I did," Thanos replied with a warm smile.

Nefari sat up and looked around, realizing she was in her spirit form. The room was wooden, with one wall curving outward. The walls were damp, and she noticed the slight swaying, indicating they were on a ship. Jakaan must have gotten her off the mainland.

"I'm sorry for what happened, Thanos," Nefari said softly. "I wish I could have done more for you."

Thanos's smile grew wider. "You gave me the courage to face my end. As you said, it's not the end of my life, just my physical form. I wanted to see you before I visit anyone else in my next few days. I know they won't be able to see me like you can, though."

"It means a lot that you came to see me," Nefari replied, tears welling in her eyes. "Thank you for being my friend, even if it was only for a short time."

The cabin door opened, and Cranaus entered, carrying a small tray. He sat in the chair next to Nefari, his presence calming and reassuring. He reached out to stroke her hair, his touch gentle and affectionate. Leaning over, Cranaus kissed her softly on the forehead, then whispered, "I'll be waiting for you when you're ready to wake." His words were comforting, and Nefari felt a warmth spreading through her chest. She smiled, her cheeks flushing with a soft blush.

"He has barely left your side since you were brought on board over a day ago," Thanos told her, his voice echoing like a breeze. "He does love you."

Nefari watched Cranaus, his hand tenderly reaching for hers. "I know... I'm not used to these feelings, but they draw me to him. I think I love him too."

"I believe you do," Thanos replied with a soft smile. He paused for a moment, reflecting. "It's funny. In life, I was scared of so many things. I didn't make friends because I was afraid they'd leave me. I didn't seek love because I thought my long, thin form wasn't attractive. I didn't take risks or strive for anything that seemed difficult, fearing I'd fail. But now, all those fears seem so small. The infinite span of my soul feels so much more substantial than anything I feared in life. Go talk to him. Enjoy your time while you're still here."

"I feel sad to leave you," Nefari said, her voice tinged with regret. She wanted to talk to Cranaus but didn't want to abandon Thanos.

"Don't be," Thanos reassured her. "I just came to say thank you and goodbye. As I said, I have other places to be. Tell the ol' windbag to take care of himself."

Nefari felt relieved not to be torn between her choices. "Wait here a moment longer, okay? I'll be back shortly."

Thanos nodded as Nefari slipped back into her body. She awoke to Cranaus throwing his arms around her, nearly smothering her with his embrace. He was so relieved to see her conscious again that tears streamed down his cheeks. Thanos watched them, feeling the joy in their reunion. He whispered his last words to the room.

"Take care of her, Cranaus. She's truly special."

Thanos floated through the cabin door, into the wider world beyond. It was time for him to move on, leaving behind the chaos and pain of the past, knowing his farewell was as clean a break as it could be.

Nefari pushed Cranaus away. Her arms strained, feeling like jelly, and she was reminded of her injuries—her hand and her eye. Her vision cut in half, a darkness that wasn't quite dark but rather oddly missing. Pain flared in her right hand, making her whimper.

"Sorry," Cranaus said. "Did I hurt you?"

"No, it wasn't you," Nefari replied, waving her good hand. "Thanos is here."

"What do you mean?" Cranaus asked, confused. "Thanos died in Athens."

"Yes, but his spirit is here, in the room with us. He came to say goodbye. If there's anything you'd like to say to him, now's the time. I'll go to his side for a reply."

Nefari didn't wait, slipping into the Dreamtime. Thanos wasn't where he had been floating earlier. She scanned the room, but he was gone. Deep down, she knew this was his farewell.

She turned back to Cranaus, who had already started talking. He spoke about the young Thanos, how he used to run around the streets, knocking over bystanders and making obnoxious remarks. He always seemed furious on the outside, but he had a big smile and a warm spot in his heart for the boy. Thanos embodied mischief and fun, and his passing left the world a darker place.

Nefari thought it was beautiful, and that Thanos would have loved it had he stayed. Returning to her body, she said, "That was beautiful," knowing it was all in vain.

Cranaus sat with an expectant look. When it became clear Nefari wouldn't speak, he pushed further. "Did he have any words for me?"

Nefari was driving herself into a frenzy, her mind racing with worry, when the right words finally came to her. "He said to tell the old windbag to take care of himself."

Cranaus looked off into the distance, his eyes a little unfocused. "He's still calling me that." A single tear rolled down his cheek, a soft smile appearing as he quickly wiped it away, regaining his composure. "Thanos is just as infuriating in death. Is he still around?"

"He's moved on," Nefari replied. She felt that was close enough to the truth.

Cranaus nodded, a faint smile crossing his lips as he remembered something. His gaze drifted, as if he could see a distant memory.

"What are you thinking?" Nefari asked. "That smile of yours—what's behind it?"

Cranaus chuckled lightly. "I was recalling the day Thanos was born. I was visiting a neighboring village with my father. A woman had just given birth days before and was walking around town, proudly displaying her swaddled babe. I was just a kid, maybe six or eight. I can't quite remember the age gap between us. Anyway, when she spotted us, she rushed over to introduce her baby to us. I took one look at that child in her arms, his legs and arms larger than normal and pushing on the cloth, then at my father, and said, 'What a grotesque sight.'"

Nefari gasped. "You said that? To a new, proud and love filled mother?"

Cranaus nodded, laughing at the memory. "I got a thorough scolding from my dad right there in the street.

202

The woman tried to defend me, but my dad insisted that regardless of what I thought, this child was the most beautiful thing in the world to her. He told me that a child's worth is measured by the love it receives, and I had no right to judge. My dad was right, though I was too stubborn to admit it back then. Sometimes, the truth can be a harsh thing, and a little kindness goes a long way."

Nefari let out a slow breath and settled back down on the bed. "That's a good story to remember. Thanos would probably have a snarky comeback to add to it."

"I think he knew, given the way he always found the perfect comeback to my best insults. There will never be another person like him. Wherever he is, I hope he's at peace."

"As do I," Nefari agreed.

Silence settled over them, but it wasn't uncomfortable. Nefari felt at ease in Cranaus's company, and her emotions grew with each passing moment.

"I love you," she said suddenly.

Cranaus blinked in surprise, but quickly composed himself. "I love you too, Nefari. I have for a long time."

"Even with my ruined eye?"

"Even with that," he replied, his voice gentle.

"I'm sorry for losing the necklace you gave me," she said, feeling a pang of guilt.

"It's okay, dear heart," he said. He leaned in and kissed her softly on the lips. She let the kiss linger, enjoying the warmth it brought. A tingling sensation spread across her face, and she wrapped her arms around Cranaus, drawing him in for a deeper kiss. The tingling grew into waves of warmth coursing through her body, more intense than anything she had ever felt before.

She wished the kiss could last longer, but her body began to ache. Gently, she pushed Cranaus away, and he immediately apologized.

"Don't apologize for the kiss," she assured him. "It was wonderful. My body is just still recovering, and I need some rest."

"Take your rest, Nefari. After a short journey, we'll be docking at the Island of Crete. I know people there who will take care of you until you recover and adjust to your new field of vision."

"Will you stay with me?" she asked.

"I can't join you on the island; it's for women only," he

explained. "But I can stay with you here for now."

"That would be nice," Nefari said, smiling as she adjusted her head on the pillow to get comfortable.

Cranaus gently ran his fingers through her hair, stroking it softly. He had just begun to chuckle when he heard her cute little snore, almost like a kitten purring.

The boat rocked gently as it pulled into dock. Nefari, with Cranaus's assistance, made her way to the deck. It felt like a long, arduous journey; the boat's constant sway and her off-balance vision had confined her to bed for most of the trip. She'd tried to walk around the vessel, but it was too disorienting, and the dampness of the bedding did little to help. Staying in bed had seemed like the better option.

Up on deck, Nefari took a deep breath of the crisp sea air. It felt invigorating after the stuffy cabin. She watched gulls and other seabirds diving for food in the azure waters. Glancing around, she took in the sight of Crete, with its high cliffs and rocky hillsides dotted with homes and market stalls. From this vantage point, she could see people, all women, bustling about their daily routines.

Cranaus had explained that this part of Crete was sacred to a half-bull, half-human deity. Nefari hadn't paid much attention to the story, dismissing it as just another mythical monster. But Cranaus had mentioned that men weren't welcome here; if they ventured too far into the town, they would be thrown into the beast's lair.

A foul odor suddenly wafted across the deck with the change of wind, causing Nefari to wrinkle her nose and raise a hand to block the stench. It was unlike anything she'd smelled before, and she looked around, a little alarmed, trying to find the source.

"You're wondering about that smell, aren't you?" Cranaus asked, a hint of amusement in his voice. He'd been to Crete many times and knew exactly what caused it—the blooming dragon lilies. Even on the mainland, he'd come across patches of them, their scent unmistakable.

"Yes," Nefari replied, grimacing. "It's terrible. How can you stand it?"

"I've gotten used to it over time," he said with a shrug. "You'll smell it throughout your stay, but eventually, you won't even notice it."

"What is it? I feel like my eye is going to stumble across a pile of dead bodies any moment now," Nefari said,

204

cringing from the awful smell.

"Do you see those flowers near the shore?" Cranaus pointed toward a cluster of large blooms. Nefari followed his gesture, noting their wide, arrow-like petals with jagged edges curling around a stalk in the middle. The petals were a deep purple, almost black.

"Yes, I see them," she replied, puzzled. She glanced around the flowers, expecting to find something sinister lurking beneath.

"They're called Dragon Lilies." Cranaus explained. "Right now, they're producing that smell you find so unpleasant. It's meant to attract flies and other insects for pollination." Nefari looked at him, not quite believing. Cranaus spread his arms for emphasis but had to quickly catch Nefari as she leaned too far to the side. "It's true. Once they lure the flies in, they trap them inside the flower for hours to spread pollen. It's quite fascinating, really."

"It's disgusting," Nefari replied, wrinkling her nose. She still had trouble accepting that such a smell came from mere flowers.

"Yes, but they have their own beauty," Cranaus insisted.

"I'll be sure to get you a bouquet someday," Nefari said, rolling her eyes.

The boat glided alongside the dock, and the crew began securing it. A slender gangplank was lowered to connect the ship to the salt-weathered wooden pier. Nefari found it difficult to maintain her balance, her gaze shifting from the gangplank to the choppy water below. Cranaus stepped behind her, wrapping his arms around her waist.

"I've got you," he whispered in her ear.

A warm, fuzzy sensation washed over Nefari, filling every part of her body as they carefully descended the gangplank. She felt her cheeks growing warm, blushing strongly as they stopped every few steps to regain their balance. Some of the sailors on the docks noticed the affectionate exchange between them and began whooping and whistling, causing Nefari to blush even more.

As soon as they reached the docks, Nefari tugged Cranaus along, eager to escape the sailors' rowdy teasing. They reached the first street, where Cranaus slowed to a stop.

"This is as far as I go," Cranaus said, gesturing toward the narrow street ahead. Nefari turned back to him, concern in her eyes. "I mentioned that men aren't allowed in the city. This street is the only one where I'm permitted. It's where any male visitors can lodge and get a meal if they get stuck overnight. Beyond this, it's all women."

"What should I do now?" Nefari asked, her worry evident. "I want to stay with you."

"I know," Cranaus replied, his voice soft. "And I want to stay with you, too, but I have to go back and face Cecrops. Nothing's changed, and it's time I deal with the situation head-on."

"I want to help," Nefari said, leaning into his chest.

Cranaus wrapped his arms around her, holding her close. "You need to get better first. Work on that, and when you're ready, come back to the docks and find the boat master, Terban. He's here every second day or so. I've already paid him to take you back to the mainland when you're ready."

Nefari nodded, but her uncertainty remained. "I thought the sway of the boat would have stopped by now, but I still feel off-balance. How am I going to get around this unfamiliar town on my own?"

"The balance issues you're experiencing are related to your eye," Cranaus explained. "Your body is trying to adjust your center of gravity, using your sight as a reference. Since your vision has shifted, so has your sense of balance. But you'll get used to it soon. Also, you might notice your depth perception is off; reaching for things might be a bit tricky at first."

Cranaus squeezed her hand reassuringly. "A friend of mine will come soon to take you to a place where you can rest and recover. She'll take care of you."

"How do you know so much?" Nefari asked, curious about Cranaus's extensive knowledge.

"The resistance has been around for a long time," he replied, his voice carrying a hint of sadness. The melancholy in his tone made Nefari reconsider her next question, and she decided to change the subject.

"The man who rescued me from the torture room— where is he? I'd like to thank him," Nefari asked.

"Jakaan? He's gone back to wherever Jakaan goes," Cranaus replied. "The man is useful, but only Titos knows where to find him at any given time. Just like Thanos. We have many people in the resistance who operate in the shadows. It's safer that way; they avoid being hunted down or becoming a liability in situations like yours."

Nefari nodded, understanding the need for secrecy. "When you see Titos, can you ask him to pass on my thanks to Jakaan? He was exceptional in the way he handled the Uru—always in control and sure of his path."

"Jakaan is one of our best," Cranaus agreed.

A small group of four women came walking down the street at that moment. The people in their way quickly moved aside, a sign that these women were important figures in the town. They were carrying an open litter with silken cushions.

"Your ride to the House of Healing," Cranaus told Nefari. "Be courteous to Melani. She has helped the revolutionaries immensely. I've known her since I was a child, and she will take good care of you."

"I'm already grateful that she's taken me in in my current state," Nefari said, touched by the offer of help.

"I hoped she could come down herself, but she's probably busy with the religious duties of this island. I need to go now, or I might miss the boat."

Nefari's eyes filled with tears. She hugged Cranaus tightly, not wanting to let him go. He returned the embrace, then gently pushed her back and kissed her softly. "We'll see each other again soon," he said before turning away quickly, knowing that if he lingered, he might not be able to leave her.

Nefari watched as Cranaus disappeared around a corner, heading toward the docks. With a sigh, she climbed onto the litter, her body sinking into the soft cushions. The journey had taken its toll, and she hadn't realized how exhausted she was until now. Her muscles ached, the marks on her ankles burned, and her ruined fingernails throbbed as they healed. Surprisingly, her eye felt no pain anymore.

The litter bearers lifted her gently and started walking uphill toward the House of Healing, run by Melani. As they moved past the first street, the town grew more vibrant, with flowers strung along the pathways. Their sweet fragrance helped to mask the awful scent of the dragon lilies. Nefari wanted to take in the sights, but her body rebelled, sending waves of drowsiness that pulled her into a deep sleep.

The litter jolted as it was placed down, stirring Nefari from her slumber. She opened her eyes slowly, reorientating herself. She saw a panoramic view of the town, with the ocean in the distance and a ship leaving the port. It was Cranaus's ship, already on its way back to the mainland. Nefari sighed, feeling a mix of relief and sadness.

She turned her attention to the House of Healing—a grand, three-story marble structure with a large mahogany doorway at the front. Two women stood outside to greet her. One had dark skin and bore no resemblance to the Hellenes of this region. The other was a true Hellene, standing tall with an almost regal demeanor. She wore a long blue tunic, and her auburn hair was loosely twisted over one shoulder.

"Nefertiti," the dark-skinned woman said.

Nefari was momentarily confused. "I'm sorry, my name is Nefari."

"Sabra was speaking in her native tongue," Melani explained. "She hasn't been with us long and doesn't speak our tongue fluently. Translated, 'Nefertiti' means 'A beautiful woman has come.' I'm Melani, and I'll be your host while you recover. If you need anything, just ask me or Sabra."

Nefari was touched by the compliment. "Nefertiti? I like it," she said, nodding to Sabra with a smile. The woman returned the gesture with a warm smile of her own. "Thank you, Melani, for your hospitality. I'm truly grateful."

Chapter 10

Nefertiti looked over her classroom. Two of the students had fallen asleep and were snoring softly, while three others were whispering quietly among themselves, likely plotting some mischief for later. Most of the class, however, was still listening intently, and that pleased Nefertiti. She'd worried that the kids would be bored with her history lesson, but they seemed engaged for the most part.

Her eyes settled on Santiva, a bright young girl with a look of shock on her face. Nefertiti smiled and raised a finger to her lips, signaling for silence. Santiva nodded, understanding the gesture. This girl was too smart for her own good, Nefertiti thought. But perhaps she had dropped some big hints about the story she was telling—the ageless life cycle of an Uru, the spoiled eye, and even the name she had taken in this foreign land. It was enough to pique the curiosity of even the most innocent if they listened and took note.

Nefertiti thought about her own pearlescent eye. It was odd that in the early days, no local sculptor or artist had depicted her as having a white, sightless eye. It took a foreigner to capture her accurately. The piece caused quite a stir, until her husband, Akhenaten, declared it one of the most beautiful works he had ever seen. The man had adored her like no other, and she had felt truly loved.

"We're coming to the beginning of the end," Nefertiti said to the class. "We have our broken heroine, Nefari, and the determined hero, Cranaus. There's the resistance group and the floating nation of the enemy. And behind them all, we have Cecrops—a leader, a king, a warrior, an immortal, a god, and a monster." She paused to let the words sink in. This caught the attention of the three in the back who had been whispering; everyone who was awake was now focused on her.

"Cranaus traveled back to the village of his resistance," she continued. "He knew the fight ahead was perilous, but he was ready to lead his people into battle. The stakes had never been higher, and he was determined to ensure that Nefari, and future generations, would have a world free of Cecrops's tyranny."

The journey back to his village had been hard. Since the

attempt on Cecrops's life, the roads had been heavily patrolled, forcing Cranaus to navigate back trails and goat paths. As he crested the final hill, he looked down at the village he had helped establish. He and a few council members had chosen this location as the base for their resistance. They'd started with basic farms and housing, drawing in others who sought a life away from the city. Now, with a population exceeding two hundred, the village was thriving.

Cranaus descended the slope toward the village, his body weary from nine days of travel, sleeping on damp ground and navigating rough terrain. All he wanted was a warm meal and a good night's rest. But as he entered the village, something felt off. There was an eerie silence, a lack of the usual bustling energy. He stopped and listened, but there was no sound of people or animals. It was as if the life had been sucked out of the place. He began to run through the village, searching for any sign of life. There were no signs of a struggle, and all the structures were intact, yet the village was deserted.

Turning a corner, he came to a sudden halt. Leaning against her empty market stall, seemingly basking in the sun, was Pedias. She hadn't noticed him yet, but Cranaus felt a wave of relief as he saw her chest rising and falling with each breath. He approached her, and she looked up, smiling as he drew near.

"I knew you would return," Pedias said.

"What happened here?" Cranaus asked, his voice tinged with worry. "Where is everyone?"

"They've left," Pedias replied, her tone unnervingly casual.

"Left?!" Cranaus echoed, disbelief and confusion mixing in his voice.

"Cranaus, you've been blinded lately. Since meeting the Uru girl, nothing has gone your way," Pedias told him. "The council is smaller, you've embarrassed yourself in the village, and raids that should've been easy have failed. Your mind has been elsewhere, and the people have noticed. They've lost hope and faith in you."

"Nefari has nothing to do with this," Cranaus replied, his mind racing. Was this the end of the rebellion? "Why did you stay behind?"

"I wanted to see if you were truly lost. I'm glad you left the girl behind." Pedias's voice was flat, her expression

210

impassive.

Cranaus frowned. "Nefari will be back once she's healed. She's special to me," he said firmly.

Pedias's eyes softened briefly, but then her expression hardened. "The council members are waiting for you in the meeting hall. They were going to give you two more days before concluding you'd stayed with her," she said before turning away, disappearing into the house behind her stall.

Cranaus was puzzled by her behavior. Nefari had never harmed her, and on their first meeting, Pedias had even gifted her a glass frog. But he didn't have time to dwell on it now—he needed to face the council.

He headed to the meeting hall. Inside, he found Flavian, Kyros, Titos, and Anatolios playing knuckle dice. They looked up as he entered, and Anatolios cursed under his breath.

"I told you he'd come back," Titos said to the old man. "Pay up." Anatolios sighed, reached into a hidden pocket, and tossed a few coins across the table to Titos.

"Better if he hadn't," Anatolios muttered before turning his gaze to Cranaus. The room fell silent, and the tension was harsh.

Cranaus stood in the doorway, taking in the weary faces of the council members. They looked like men who had already given up the fight. "Tell me everything that has happened," Cranaus said, his voice edged with anxiety.

"There's not much to tell, really," Flavian replied, his voice flat. "The people who followed you slowly lost respect for you. They saw your relationship with Nefari, an Uru, as a betrayal of the cause. Your recent failures, along with fleeing the mainland with her, only fueled the discontent. Rumors spread that you let Thanos die to save Nefari and everyone left."

Cranaus was at a loss for words. He knew arguing wouldn't change their minds or bring back the villagers. "Why did you stay?" he asked quietly.

The council members exchanged glances before Titos spoke. "We thought it would be courteous to say goodbye in person."

"Goodbye?" Cranaus felt a surge of desperation. "What am I supposed to do if you all leave? How can I take back Athens alone?"

"That's not our concern anymore," Anatolios replied sharply. "The Uru have overpowered us and decimated our numbers. Even if we stayed, we'd be no help to you."

Cranaus grabbed the edge of Anatolios's tunic, his voice pleading. "But I need you," he said, looking around the room. "I need all of you."

Anatolios stood and roughly pushed Cranaus's hand away. His eyes burned with anger. "Don't touch me again. You talk about taking back Athens and becoming king, but you're sniveling like a child. We are leaving, Cranaus. A true leader finds his own way, with or without anyone to hold his hand." Anatolios stormed out, followed by Kyros, who didn't even look back.

Cranaus was stunned by the harsh words. The room began to blur as the others gave their farewells and walked out, leaving him alone. He fell to his knees, trying to understand where it'd all gone wrong. Setbacks were part of any campaign, he thought, so how could they lose hope over a few failures? And the hatred toward Nefari simply because she was an Uru—it seemed absurd. How many times had she used her powers to aid their cause, to fight against the forces that had taken Athens?

Desperate for any sign of life, Cranaus ran outside and frantically searched the empty village. He found no one. Falling to his knees, he cursing the gods for his misfortune. His anger was raw and explosive as it echoed through the empty streets. Just as he began to calm down, he was startled by a figure standing in front of him.

A cool breeze drifted through the open window, making the curtains flutter. Nefari welcomed its gentle caress over her body as she lay naked on the bed, her only adornment a lapis lazuli necklace. The wind sent goosebumps across her skin, a refreshing contrast to the pain her body had endured over the past week. The rub marks around her ankles, from where she had been strung up, were healing well. She knew her eye would never recover, so she focused on regaining her balance and depth perception. These, too, were nearly back to normal. Her damaged fingernails, however, were taking longer to heal, and her hand remained too tender to grip anything with force.

On her second day at Melani's healing house, Nefari had asked for Sabra's assistance with moving around the home. Sabra agreed but imposed conditions. She wouldn't carry Nefari or let her lean too heavily on her. This was at Melani's request. Nefari found the terms puzzling, but

212

Sabra explained that they wanted her to regain her balance without becoming overly reliant on others. She could reach out for support if she felt like she was going to fall, but Sabra wouldn't let her lean.

Nefari accepted this and focused on moving independently. To begin with, she had to grab onto Sabra frequently. There was a constant pull to one side, and without the Egyptian woman's stabilizing presence, Nefari would have fallen more than once. Sabra patiently stood by her side, allowing Nefari to regain her balance before they continued walking.

It took three days for Nefari to feel confident enough to move around without Sabra's help. On the day she achieved this milestone, she asked if there was any lapis lazuli in the house. Sabra's eyes lit up at the question, and she quickly guided Nefari down a hallway to a part of the house she had yet to explore

"This is my room," Sabra said, gesturing for Nefari to enter. As the door swung open, Nefari's eyes widened with surprise. Sabra's room was vibrant, with colorful woven fabrics draped from a central ring in the ceiling to the four corners. These could be extended to form a canopy over the simple bed, creating a tent-like enclosure to protect against bugs or create warmth during cooler seasons. The walls were adorned with intricate wall hangings made from a thick, unfamiliar type of paper. The images on the hangings were strange to Nefari, depicting figures in profile with other smaller pictures interspersed. She couldn't make sense of them, so she quickly moved on.

What truly captivated her was the abundance of lapis lazuli in the room. Figurines made of the deep blue stone adorned shelves and dressers, while Sabra's hairbrush and hairpin had veins of lapis lazuli running through them. Nefari felt drawn to a large dresser, where she gently stroked a small beetle-shaped carving. She realized she was trembling with excitement, the allure of the stone almost irresistible. Then, remembering her manners, she turned to see Sabra standing by the door, a warm smile on her lips.

"I'm sorry for intruding, Sabra," Nefari said, blushing as she bowed her head slightly. "I was just... overwhelmed by the amount of lapis lazuli you have in here."

"Think nothing of it," Sabra replied, waving off the apology. "In my country, the stone is plentiful. Almost everyone has some in one form or another. Pharaohs and their queens even adorn their crowns with it. It's a beautiful stone, and I understand why you're drawn to it."

"It's more than just a beautiful stone to me," Nefari said. "Before I was tortured, Cranaus gave me a necklace with a teardrop-shaped lapis lazuli. It was precious to me, but I lost it when I was captured." She left out the detail about its magical properties, deciding it was better to keep that part to herself. Sabra's expression softened, and she walked over to where Nefari stood, gently picking up the beetle necklace.

"Turn around," Sabra instructed, and Nefari complied. Sabra placed the necklace delicately around Nefari's neck. The underside of the beetle was flat, designed to rest comfortably against the skin. Along the chain, three rectangular chunks of lapis lazuli on each side were spaced so that the topmost stones lay across her collarbone.

"It's beautiful," Nefari said, admiring the necklace as she touched the beetle.

"The beetle is called a scarab," Sabra explained. "In my country, it's a symbol of reincarnation or new beginnings. I think it's quite fitting for your situation, don't you? This necklace was meant for you."

Nefari was taken aback. "How so?" she asked, looking up with curiosity.

"The stone has power," Sabra replied, her voice calm but serious. "Even before you entered the room, I could sense it reacting to you. When you came in, you went straight to this piece, and after hearing your story, I was certain."

"What were you certain of?" Nefari asked, intrigued by the sudden turn in the conversation.

"That this necklace belonged to you," Sabra said.

Nefari's eyes widened, and she reached to remove the necklace, but Sabra gently grabbed her hands. "It's too valuable," Nefari protested.

"The stone chose you," Sabra replied with finality. "It wouldn't be right to keep it hidden when it wants to be worn. It suits you, Nefari. Besides, wasn't that why you asked if there was any lapis in the house?"

Nefari chuckled softly. "You're wiser than you look."

Sabra laughed heartily. "It's always good to keep people guessing."

"I didn't want to take anything from you, Sabra. It feels like I'm robbing you," Nefari said, her finger tracing the smooth surface of the scarab pendant.

"Nonsense," Sabra replied, chuckling. "The stone was never mine to keep. It only stayed with me for a while, waiting for you. And who knows? Not to be funny, but you might just be a stepping stone on its journey to where it truly belongs. If you ever feel the stone is meant for someone else, let it go as I have. That's all I ask."

"I will, Sabra. Thank you," Nefari said, pulling her into a hug. "I think that's enough exercise for today. I'm going to rest now."

After receiving the necklace, Nefari began to learn much more about herself. Initially, she had wanted the lapis lazuli to enhance her abilities and perhaps communicate with Cranaus from afar. However, she soon discovered unexpected changes. The first time she left her body while wearing the necklace, she noticed something strange: the damage to her fingers glowed a harsh red, the glow extending up her arm to her elbow before fading back to her natural skin tone. Additionally, a black shadow swirled around her damaged eye, creating a dark void. This curious phenomenon made her hesitant to venture far from her body.

Nefari's spirit form reached out to touch the red glow, but pain shot up her arm, forcing her to pull back quickly. It felt as if she was reliving the torture. After calming her nerves, she cautiously probed the glow again, trying to understand what it meant. Each touch caused pain, but she felt compelled to investigate further.

Within a day, Nefari discovered she could control her body's internal functions. She experimented by speeding up or slowing down her natural healing processes. First, she tested it on minor things like mosquito bites and small scrapes from tripping. Each healed within hours.

She then turned her attention to her damaged eye, attempting to manipulate the nerves, muscles, and blood flow. But no matter how much she tried, she couldn't get any response from the area. Nefari resigned herself to the fact that the eye would never heal. Instead of dwelling on it, she focused on her injured fingers. She worked through the night, her spirit form active while her body remained in a state of rest. By morning, the red glow had diminished to her hand alone. When she returned to her body, the rising sun was just beginning to filter through the window, warming her legs as she opened her eyes. Although she felt mentally drained, her body had a lightness that she hadn't experienced since her days in Athens. She sent a silent thank you to Nudgee for the gift of this newfound ability.

With the red glow now confined to her hand, Nefari decided to take flight and visit Cranaus. She had missed him terribly and had been pushing herself to regain her strength just to see him sooner. Today, the longing was too much to ignore. She needed to see his smile, hear his voice, or even watch him bumble about like he often did.

Nefari's spirit form soared over the oceans, drawn by an inexplicable force. She knew with certainty that Cranaus was at the other end of this pull. Soon, she found him entering the village where they once made a home. But the village felt strange, as if it were a hollow reflection of the place it used to be, a mocking reminder of the life they had built together.

As Nefari followed Cranaus, she listened to his conversations with Pedias and the council members. The tone was somber, filled with disappointment and betrayal. The council members seemed resigned to their fate, disheartened by Cranaus's recent failures and his perceived betrayal with Nefari

It was painful for Nefari to overhear the council members' harsh comments about her, but she understood that as an Uru, she would always face prejudice from those who saw her as an enemy. What truly broke her heart was watching Cranaus, the man she loved, run through the empty village, screaming and searching for any remnant of his old life. His desperation and loss were heartbreaking, and the feelings echoed through the scarab necklace resting on her chest. Nefari focused on her spirit, willing it to become visible to Cranaus. She had to be there for him in this dire moment.

Cranaus sat in shock, his expression vacant. "How?" he asked, almost to himself.

"A friend of mine at Melani's healing house gifted me a piece of lapis lazuli," Nefari replied, stroking the necklace with her spectral hand. She sat beside him, placing a ghostly hand on his knee. There was no sensation, but the gesture seemed to comfort him. "The stones are powerful and have been helping me heal."

"Your eye?" Cranaus asked hopefully, but Nefari shook her head. "I'm sorry."

"Don't be," she said gently. "There was never a chance of

regaining my sight. I've adjusted to life with one eye. My healing is nearly complete, and tomorrow, I will seek out your captain to arrange passage back to the mainland."

A flicker of hope crossed Cranaus's face, but it quickly vanished into despair. "What am I going to do, Nefari? Everyone's left me. Cecrops still holds Athens. I'll never defeat him alone."

Nefari placed a spectral finger on his chest, above his heart. "My dear Cranaus, you have everything you need to defeat Cecrops within you," she said softly. "If I could touch you, I would hold you in my arms and tell you there are no monsters in the world, that you are safe and nothing can harm you. But I'm glad I'm not physically there, because those would be lies. The monsters are real, and you need to face them."

Cranaus sighed heavily, his shoulders slumping. "I'm just one man," he said, defeated.

Nefari laughed. "You once told me about a legendary figure named Gilgamos," she began, her voice dripping with a hint of mischief. Cranaus furrowed his brow, unsure where this was going. "It was foretold that Gilgamos would one day kill the king, his own grandfather, and take the throne for himself. When the king heard the prophecy, he ordered the baby thrown from the highest tower in Babylon."

"Why are you telling me this?" Cranaus asked, growing impatient.

"An eagle caught the child mid-fall, saving him from certain death, and he was raised by a gardener," Nefari continued. "What happened to that child?"

"He fulfilled the prophecy and became king," Cranaus replied, still not seeing the point of this tale.

"Exactly," Nefari said with a grin. Cranaus frowned, struggling to understand.

"I'm not the subject of any prophecy," he exclaimed, throwing his arms in the air. "I'm not some legendary hero. I don't have epic stories about my deeds. I'm just a nobody, with no one to back me up."

"No legend is told before the events that make it legendary," Nefari replied with calm certainty. "Hercules was just a loving husband before Hera killed his wife. David was just a shepherd boy before he faced Goliath. Gilgamos was just a helpless baby before his story became a grand epic. Your legend might be years from being carved into stone, but it can only happen if you start living it today."

"How do I defeat a monster like Cecrops? He's not even human!" Cranaus said, his voice tinged with frustration.

"Do you feel like a single droplet in the tidal wave that is Cecrops?" Nefari asked. Cranaus nodded. "That's what's going to lead to your downfall. You have to put that thought far from your mind. As long as you're breathing, there's hope for victory. Cecrops is likely thinking the same thing—smug in his certainty that he's going to win. That's his weakness. You need to fight him on your terms, with the unwavering belief that you will win."

"And what are my terms?" Cranaus asked, a spark of hope glimmering in his eyes.

Nefari's soft smile spread across her face as she spoke. "I didn't say you should fight on my terms, my love." It was the first time she had dared to use that endearment. She felt a surge of warmth, almost giddy with excitement.

"I don't know what to do," Cranaus confessed, his voice full of uncertainty.

"You will," she replied with reassuring confidence. "I have faith in you. You are to be the king of Athens. Making decisions is part of the journey. Be smart, and think things through." A faint knocking sound interrupted their conversation. Nefari's expression shifted slightly. "I must go. There's someone at my body."

"I don't want you to leave," Cranaus said, reaching out toward her. His hand passed through Nefari's astral projection, the touchless contact reminding him of her intangible presence. He pulled back, feeling a pang of disappointment despite knowing she wasn't physically there.

"I'll see you soon. Be smart. I believe in you," Nefari said before fading away, returning to her body in an instant. The transition was swift, her landing smooth. As her eyes opened, she found Melani standing over her, a familiar face that had been rare during her recovery.

"Sorry to wake you," Melani said. "How are you feeling?"

"Your hospitality has been a great help, Melani," Nefari replied with a smile. "I don't think I could ever repay you for your kindness." Neither of them seemed concerned with Nefari's state of dress—practicality and comfort had become a mutual understanding. "I feel well enough to return to the mainland. Tomorrow I'll speak with the boat master, Terban."

"You Uru heal fast," Melani commented.

"It's not the Uru in me," Nefari explained. "It's the Abori blood."

"Either way," Melani said with a grin, "this calls for a celebration tonight."

Terban, the boat master, was having a terrible day. The storm from the night before had damaged the mast on his ship, forcing him to limp into the harbor. Half of his crew was busy repairing the damage, while the other half was unloading grain from the mainland. Terban knew his crew was prone to laziness, and this led to the trouble he was currently dealing with.

Before him stood a furious Cretan woman, shouting insults, while a businessman named Fernand, who owned the warehouse closest to the docks, watched with a grin. It turned out that Terban's crew, in their haste to get to the tavern, had overloaded one of the pulley nets. The net arm had snapped, sending a quarter of the grain into the Cretan woman's cart of goods. Not only would Terban have to compensate the woman, but Fernand would likely demand a discount on the grain due to its rough treatment. With a grim expression, Terban began to resolve the chaos.

It took three hours for Terban to sort everything out. By then, the sun was high in the sky, and the tide was approaching its ideal level for departure. He decided to set sail immediately, depriving his crew of any time off in Crete. Shouting orders, he stirred the crew into action, eliciting groans and complaints.

"You bilge rats can drink and whore on the mainland for all the trouble you caused today," Terban yelled. "The next ugly, flea-bitten mongrel who complains will be tossed into the Minotaur's labyrinth. Now get to work!"

The crew set about their tasks, pulling ropes and preparing the sails. The main and fore top sails were loosened just enough to avoid catching the light breeze. Once everything was in order, Terban called for the anchor to be raised and the mooring ropes to be released.

As he was about to step onto the gangway, a gentle tug on his sleeve stopped him. He turned to see a young woman with shoulder-length brown hair and striking features. Although she wasn't his usual type, he found himself captivated by her. She wore a plain, faded blue dress that hugged her curves, and a necklace with a rich blue stone lay across her collarbone. Terban's gaze lingered perhaps a bit too long.

"Sorry, lass, ship's about to depart," Terban said with a tilt of his head. "You'll need to find another boat for anything domestic. We're not taking on any travelers."

"Cranaus of Athens said you and he had an agreement," she replied. "He said you'd take me to the mainland."

Terban stopped and gave the girl a closer look. "You're Nefari?" he asked. Nefari nodded with a stern expression. Although Terban had already been paid for the fare—now long spent—it felt like another free ride on an already unlucky day. He hesitated, thinking of rumors that Cranaus had met an unfortunate end. He was inclined to refuse, but his sense of honor as a ship captain made him relent.

"Come aboard, lass, but stay below deck as much as you can," he advised. "The crew is a bit rowdy, and I'd hate to throw someone overboard for bothering such a beauty as yourself."

Nefari blushed. "Thank you," she said, heading up the gangway. Just as she reached Terban, the boat swayed, and she lost her footing. Her face lit up with shock as the water rushed toward her. Terban's reflexes kicked in, and he grabbed her by the scruff of her neck, pulling her back to safety. He held her until she regained her balance.

"Sorry... Thank you, Terban," she said as he released her. He offered his hand, but she waved it away.

"You'll get your sea legs in no time, lass," he assured her before turning back to the crew. "Avast, ye dirty dogs! This is Nefari. Anyone who touches her will be hanging from the mast long before we reach home. She's an Uru, associated with Cranaus. If you escape my wrath, you'll have them to deal with. Understood?"

"Captain!" the crew yelled in unison.

"Set sail!"

Chapter 11

The early morning sun kissed the streets of Athens, casting deep shadows from the homes and shops along the city streets, leaving the alleyways in darkness. All around the city, residents began their morning rituals. Chamber pots were emptied out of windows, spilling their contents Onto walkways that drizzled into the gutter running through the middle of the street. Carts laden with wares trundled toward the marketplace, and bakers, who had been up since well before dawn, were already selling the last of their freshly baked goods.

Cranaus breathed in the city air. He was truly home and vowed never to leave again, come what may. Taking a moment to appreciate the rhythm of this city, he smiled. He didn't want to miss anything on his way to the Acropolis, which loomed above the streets.

Today, Cecrops would be visiting the Acropolis with his daughters and a minimal guard. This was Cranaus's make-or-break moment, a final head-on attack where he intended to throw everything he had into the fight. He knew he wouldn't walk away from this battle, but he hoped to take Cecrops with him. His only regret was not being able to hold Nefari in his arms one last time. She hadn't made it back home in time, and who knew when another opportunity like this would come?

Cranaus began his solitary trek up the slopes of Athens, following the uneven streets. As the Acropolis grew larger in the distance, he wondered if Titos had managed to make any arrangements in such a short time. After speaking with Nefari's spirit, he'd sought out the small round man, but it'd taken a few days to track him down. Cranaus nearly gave up on the search, especially as his confrontation with Cecrops drew near. The last piece of information from their spies needed to be accurate for his plan to work.

Cranaus had found Titos late yesterday, just as the sun was setting. Their conversation was brief—Cranaus simply told him to be ready, that everything would change today. Titos was clever, and Cranaus trusted him, but the question remained: would he have enough time to make it happen?

Cranaus cut across an alley, letting his thoughts drop as he peered around the corner. This vantage point gave him the best view of the Acropolis, and he smiled when he saw his target. The information had proven true: Cecrops was walking with his daughters into the magnificently crafted structure, its pillars of marble encircling an inner sanctum. It was one of Athens' greatest architectural achievements. But the sight made Cranaus grimace. Cecrops had defiled the great hall, even renaming it, so that the citizens now called it Cecropia. That pompous snake thought too highly of himself. "Cecropia," Cranaus spat. It was a name that definitely needed changing.

He noticed a single guard standing watch outside, a massive figure clad the silver armor of the Uru. The guard had a large round hole in the back of his armor, just above the buttocks, whose purpose Cranaus couldn't determine. On his back, the guard carried a sword almost as long as he was tall. Cranaus recognized him instantly: Shenlong. He remembered the night the resistance raided Cecrops' camp, the night he helped Nefari escape. Shenlong had been one of only three Uru to survive that raid, cutting through the resistance ranks with his massive greatsword as if they were thin sheets of paper. It was only when the resistance forces grew too overwhelming that Shenlong retreated. Cranaus had ordered his men not to pursue, knowing the cost would be high. Now, Shenlong was the sole obstacle standing between him and Cecrops.

Cranaus took a deep breath to steady his nerves and sent a prayer to Athena, the patron goddess of Athens, asking for his sword to strike true and for the strength and strategic wisdom to defeat his foes. He stepped out onto the street leading to the front of the Acropolis. Pulling a dark green hood over his head, he walked with strength and determination, as if he had every reason to be there. As he passed Shenlong, the guard eyed him with suspicion.

"Stop!" Shenlong ordered. "You don't respond, so I know you're not Uru. Cecrops is inside. You'll head back down the street and wait until late afternoon."

Cranaus stood with his back to Shenlong as the guard drew the massive sword from his back.

"You will comply, or I'll cut you down where you stand," Shenlong warned.

Cranaus reached up and unfastened the brooch holding his cloak, letting it fall to the ground. He drew his plain, single-handed sword—no adornments, but crafted by a master smith and reliable in every battle. He turned to face his hulking opponent, glad he had opted for leather armor instead of bronze, which would have slowed him down against an adversary like Shenlong.

"Cranaus," Shenlong said with a broad grin. "I've always wanted to be the one to kill you."

"And you'll be left wanting," Cranaus replied, swinging his sword in wide arcs to get a proper grip on the hilt.

Shenlong laughed, a deep, guttural sound. "Come meet your doom, little man. Tonight, you will feed my children, and I shall take your heart." He then began to transform, his body changing to resemble Cecrops—a reptilian being— but with more pronounced features. His green scales stretched over bulging muscles, and his mouth jutted out like an alligator's. His armor expanded to fit his altered form, and a large tail emerged through the hole in the back. Cranaus shook his head.

"Of course, Cecrops' personal guard would be a monster just like him," Cranaus muttered.

"You have no idea, little man," Shenlong replied in a raspy voice, moving slowly toward Cranaus, relishing the suspense.

Cranaus steadied himself, feeling surprisingly calm. He studied Shenlong's approach, noting the guard's lack of readiness. Shenlong seemed to underestimate him—an advantage Cranaus was determined to use.

Cranaus lunged in with an upward slash, moving from right to left. Shenlong deflected it with his left armguard and hammered his right fist into Cranaus's stomach. Cranaus knew that if Shenlong had used his sword at that moment, the fight would already be over. Stumbling back, Cranaus swayed gasping for air. He'd underestimated his opponent.

Shenlong didn't give him more than a moment to recover. The large reptilian swung his massive sword in wide arcs, forcing Cranaus to weave and duck just barely in time. If he blocked with his sword incorrectly, it would snap in two. Shenlong suddenly spun on his heel, bringing the greatsword around in a cross slash with such speed that Cranaus couldn't even see it properly. Instead, he watched Shenlong's hands and leaned back just in time, but the tip of the blade still caught the corner of his mouth, slicing through the edge of his cheek and lips. Blood splattered onto the dirt, and Shenlong paused for a moment, sniffing through his slitted nostrils. Cranaus clutched the side of his mouth and backed toward the Acropolis.

"I do love the scent of fresh blood in the morning," a

voice said from behind Cranaus.

He turned to see Cecrops walking out of the Acropolis, flanked by his three daughters. Two of them smiled as the contest unfolded, but the third stood transfixed, a look of horror spreading across her face as she saw Shenlong in his reptilian form.

"Come to join in, have you?" Cranaus asked, wincing from the pain in his mouth. He knew he could never defeat both fighters at once. He wasn't even sure if he could take down Shenlong—the monster had proven far more formidable than Cranaus had anticipated.

"Sadly, no," Cecrops replied. "The duel has already begun. I will not take the honor from Shenlong."

"How noble," Cranaus muttered, barely opening his mouth. He touched his wounded lip and cheek, trying to ease the pain, but found it distracting. He clenched his jaw and endured the sting until he could ignore it. Shenlong came at him again with a savage swing, forcing Cranaus to dive out of the way. He rolled across the rocky surface and quickly got back to his feet. As he did, he flicked a small throwing knife, grazing the side of Shenlong's neck. A trickle of crimson blood began to flow. Cecrops, standing in the background, smirked. One of Cecrops's daughters, however, screamed at her father, pointing at Shenlong's figure. She mustn't have been aware of what was happening, unlike her younger sister, who stood calmly watching.

"You'll have to do better than that," Shenlong laughed as he advanced. When Shenlong swung his sword in a right cross, Cranaus ducked inside the reach of the blade. He managed to get his sword between the joints in Shenlong's armor, creating a shallow cut. But Shenlong was prepared for this. He dropped his sword and wrapped his massive arms around Cranaus, trapping him in a crushing hold.

"You've made a terrible missstake, little man," Shenlong said, struggling to speak clearly. "You've not realisssed that my teeth are alssso a weapon." Shenlong opened his mouth, revealing rows of long, slender fangs. The stench of his breath made Cranaus almost gag. He knew he would never break free from Shenlong's grip. As the alligator-like maw drew back to strike, Cranaus made his move.

Using the small throwing dagger he had hidden on the roof of his mouth, Cranaus bit down hard on the hilt, holding it in place. He waited until Shenlong lunged at

224

him, then thrust the dagger into the Uru's windpipe. The look of shock that crossed Shenlong's face as his fangs were just inches away from Cranaus's flesh made the risk worthwhile.

Cranaus fell back, watching as the creature shifted between human and reptilian forms, struggling to accept his fading life trying to find a form that could survive. "I think not." Cranaus picked up his sword, and with a single swift swing, he took off the beast's head. It bounced awkwardly before coming to rest a meter away. He gave Cecrops a sarcastic salute and, noting the seething wrath in the eyes of Cecrops's daughters, bowed to them on impulse.

Aglaurus screamed again, her voice shrill and terrifying. Cranaus looked up to see that Cecrops and his other two daughters had shifted into their reptilian forms. Aglaurus backed away, moving close to the cliff edge, then sat on the ground, watching the scene like it was a living nightmare. Cranaus felt a brief pang of sympathy for her but quickly refocused on Cecrops.

"Let me fight him, Father," Herse pleaded, staring at Cranaus like a lion sizing up its prey.

"No, Herse," Cecrops replied. His voice was devoid of emotion. He reached back into the Acropolis and picked up his short sword. "He may look weak, but there's a lot of skill in this young man."

"This ends today," Cranaus said, still struggling to speak with his injured mouth. "Your death or mine—our feud will end here."

"You humans are always so temperamental," Cecrops replied. "Not one of your kind has been grateful for the life we gave you. No one has thanked us for the technology we provided. We are the gods you worship, and yet you stubbornly prefer mist over the truth right in front of you."

"You're a monster and nothing more," Cranaus growled. "Everything you say is a lie. I have nothing left to say to you. Fight me or die where you stand."

"So be it," Cecrops said, his words dripping with disdain.

The taste of blood was less noticeable in Cranaus's mouth as he wiped the sweat from his brow. His muscles ached after the fight with Shenlong, but he kept his body relaxed, knowing he'd need speed and flexibility for this battle. Unlike Shenlong, Cecrops was a skilled warrior—

fast, agile, and seemingly tireless. And unlike Shenlong, Cecrops could be blocked with a sword. This was the real fight.

The two warriors began to circle each other. Cranaus couldn't help but notice how calm Cecrops appeared, even though he wore only a plain Uru tunic with no armor of any kind. This unnerved Cranaus more than any display of brute strength or skill. Cecrops moved with the confidence of centuries of combat, showing no signs of weakness.

Rushing in, Cecrops launched a flurry of cuts and slashes at Cranaus. At first, Cranaus could easily block them, and his confidence grew. Adrenaline coursed through his veins, masking the fatigue from his earlier fight with Shenlong. Just as Cranaus was about to counterattack, Cecrops seemed to speed up, sending a hidden thrust toward Cranaus's unguarded belly. Cranaus saw it at the last moment and twisted away, but not before it grazed his leather armor, leaving a shallow cut.

Cranaus stepped back, resuming the circle, and Cecrops followed fluidly. The Uru leader moved with the grace of a dancer, always in balance, his every step deliberate. Cranaus was momentarily distracted by this display of finesse, losing his chance to counterattack as Cecrops closed in again. Cecrops used a combination of slashes and cuts at varying speeds, disrupting Cranaus's rhythm. One particularly quick stroke slipped through Cranaus's defense, opening a small cut on his arm. Cecrops lunged forward with a savage bite, forcing Cranaus to step back. Cecrops then swept low, tripping Cranaus with his tail, and quickly followed with a downward thrust toward Cranaus's chest as he hit the ground. Cranaus rolled to the side and jumped away just in time.

The duel continued for another fifteen minutes, with signs of wear beginning to show in Cranaus's defense. He had several small cuts across his body, though none were fatal. In contrast, Cecrops bore only a single wound, a lucky strike that Cranaus had misjudged, but Cecrops seemed to move into it as if it had been preordained. After that strike, Cecrops had stepped back and applauded Cranaus before resuming his relentless assault.

Cranaus's breaths grew hard and ragged as the fight wore on. He knew he was reaching his limit; he could no longer keep up with Cecrops's pace. To make matters worse, Cecrops showed no signs of tiring—he seemed as though he could continue fighting all day without breaking a sweat.

As Cecrops closed in, Cranaus decided to play his trump card. He had become familiar with Cecrops's attack patterns and speed manipulations and believed he had found an opening. When Cecrops launched his next flurry of attacks, Cranaus calmly blocked them, biding his time. The instant the opportunity presented itself, he rolled his sword around Cecrops's grip, leaving himself open to attack. Just as he predicted, Cecrops took the opening, allowing Cranaus to use the movement to dislodge and disarm him.

Cecrops reacted with lightning speed, whipping his tail and sending Cranaus crashing to the ground. Cranaus rolled with the momentum, springing back to his feet, just as Cecrops darted left to retrieve his sword. Suddenly, Cranaus heard movement behind him—Herse and Pandrosus, Cecrops's daughters, were rushing toward him. Cranaus grabbed Herse by the throat, lifting her off the ground, and stabbed Pandrosus in the chest with a swift strike. Blood gushed from the wound, and Pandrosus fell, choking on her own blood. Herse, enraged, bit down on Cranaus's arm, who let her go, then swiftly slashed her throat, nearly severing her head.

"No!" Cecrops screamed. "What have you done?"

As Cranaus turned to face Cecrops, he was struck by a powerful psychic force. He suddenly found himself unable to move, as if all control over his body had been stripped away. Gravity pulled him to the ground, where he landed on his side. Cecrops approached and kicked him onto his back, his slitted yellow eyes glaring with rage.

"I have you under my power, you useless worm," Cecrops snarled. "To the Uru, you're just food. You never stood a chance against our might."

Cecrops reversed his short sword, holding it with both hands, and raised it high above his head, the point aimed straight at Cranaus's heart. Struggling against the psychic control, Cranaus couldn't even blink, let alone escape the blade rapidly descending toward him.

Nefari was relieved to hear the ship was bound for port in Athens. She'd spent the entire voyage resting in her cabin, focusing on healing herself. Nefari wanted to be in peak condition when she reunited with Cranaus, and now she felt better than she had in years. Everything around her seemed to glow in the dim light of the cabin—life was incredible.

Despite her best efforts to remain patient, her curiosity got the better of her. Nefari had wanted the next time she saw Cranaus to be face-to-face, but she couldn't wait any longer. She let her spirit drift out of her body, floating through the ship and up into the waking sky. "I need to know where to find him anyway," she thought, trying to justify her actions. The rising sun was always beautiful from her elevated vantage point. It stretched across the rolling land, casting light upon everything it touched. The morning air was crisp, and the earth seemed to shed its darkness like an unwanted robe to become a golden orb under the sun's gaze. Athens was no different; the city bursting in radiance and life, its white walls reflecting the golden light. Everywhere, life began anew with the dawn.

Nefari refocused her thoughts on Cranaus, wondering if he was at the resistance village or somewhere else. She hoped he'd taken her advice and sought out the resistance, taking control of the situation to put his plans into action. She was surprised when her spirit was drawn down into Athens itself. This was not where she expected him to be.

Allowing her spirit to follow the magnetic pull toward Cranaus, Nefari flew down into the city streets. It didn't take long to find him, crouching in an alleyway and watching people go by. He was armed and dressed in leather armor, which worried Nefari. Over his armor, he wore a cloak and hood, concealing his identity. The sneaking about didn't help with her confidence either. Following him closely, Nefari started to guess where he might be heading. As she floated higher, she could see the Acropolis looming nearby and a small group standing at its entrance.

She recognized Cecrops instantly, along with his three daughters and another figure—a hulking man who could only be Shenlong. Dread crept into her as she started to imagine what was about to happen.

Nefari hesitated, unsure of what to do. The moment she paused, she lost the ability to choose. She saw Cranaus stepping out into the open and knew this would be his end.

"This is not what I meant!" she shouted angrily at him, even though she knew he couldn't hear her. Turning, she flew back to her body and found the boat approaching the docks of Athens. As she re-entered her body, Nefari threw off the thin sheet and raced up to the deck. She sprinted to the railing, not waiting for the gangway to be lowered.

"What are you doing, you crazy girl?" Terban yelled. "Get down from there! You're going to hurt yourself!"

"Sorry, Terban, there's trouble and I have to go," Nefari called back as she leaped over the rail onto the dock below. She landed hard but without any lasting damage. "Thanks for the ride."

Nefari ran through Athens, trying to navigate the streets. She hadn't spent much time in the city, which made finding her way difficult. Her worry about Cranaus's fate in his fight with Shenlong didn't help. Fortunately, Cecrops had walked into the Acropolis, or Cranaus would never stand a chance.

After running down a dead end, Nefari doubled back onto the street and grabbed the nearest pedestrian. "Which way to the Acropolis?" she almost screamed. The man was startled and tried to pull away, but Nefari's grip was unyielding. "Tell me!"

"Go back the way you came, three streets, then follow the wider street to the top of the hill," the man squeaked, still struggling to free himself.

Nefari released him without a word and took off running. The man, caught off guard by her sudden release, fell backward onto the uneven stone. He got up, shouting curses. Nefari ignored him, focused on more pressing matters. Her mind was filled with grim images of Cranaus being run through by Shenlong's massive sword or bleeding out in the dirt.

"No!" she told herself sternly. "I can't think like that."

Arriving at the wide street the man had mentioned, Nefari turned and started to climb toward the Acropolis. Her muscles ached, and her lungs burned, but she pushed forward. She didn't want to arrive just moments too late because she stopped to catch her breath. The top of the Acropolis came into view before the road flattened out, giving her a burst of adrenaline that propelled her to run even harder.

However, the scene that awaited her was not what she'd expected. Three reptilian carcasses lay in the dirt—one particularly large, which she assumed was Shenlong's. The question of how many more of these reptilians might be out there crossed her mind, but she dismissed it as she saw

Cecrops looming over Cranaus, sword raised and about to strike. Cranaus's posture was unusual, and Nefari realized he couldn't move. She had heard that the Uru elite possessed some form of mind manipulation, but she'd never seen it in action.

Without hesitation, Nefari tapped into the Dreamtime. Her body continued running, but as her spirit separated, her physical form tumbled to the ground behind her. She sped across the short distance as Cecrops's sword began its downward arc. From Cecrops's head, she could see an almost invisible distortion in the air, as if something was pouring over Cranaus. Throwing her spirit into the stream, she willed it to redirect in every other direction, disrupting the flow. The blade passed through her spirit, and as the distortion's hold on Cranaus broke, he rolled out of the way. The sword point missed him by mere fractions of an inch, embedding itself deep into the dirt.

Cranaus didn't let Cecrops's moment of misjudgment go to waste. Grabbing his own sword, he thrust it into Cecrops's stomach. Cecrops nearly doubled over as the hot lance of pain shot through him. Cranaus gained a better footing, twisted the blade, and ripped it clean out through Cecrops's side. The reptilian fell, convulsing in a pool of his own blood. His body was racked with pain, and it took nearly four minutes for him to die from his wound. But no one gave him much notice; they were too busy catching their breath and taking in the aftermath.

Cranaus moved to where Nefari lay and picked her head up, placing it in his lap. Her eyes fluttered open, and she smiled at him. When he smiled back, her expression changed, and it scared Cranaus more than the fights he had just endured.

"What were you thinking?" she demanded, hitting his arm and chest. "I was so worried about you when I saw what you were doing!"

Cranaus looked at her, confused. "You said Cecrops is just one man, and that I should meet him and fight."

"That's not what I said or meant, you stubborn idiot!" Nefari's eyes blazed. "I just wanted you to step up and form a plan."

"Didn't I win?" he chuckled.

"No, not yet. You still have the Uru patrolling the streets and all of Atlantis to deal with. They're not going to take kindly to someone who killed their war chief."

Fighting could be heard in the distance, coming from Athens. Cranaus smiled. "Well, it looks like those guards you were talking about aren't going to be a problem. Titos must be causing quite a stir. As for Atlantis... that's for another day. We have Athens back." He let out a loud whoop to express his excitement.

Nefari then heard the sound of crying nearby. She'd been too caught up in the relief of seeing Cranaus alive to notice her surroundings. Leaning up, she spotted Cecrops's daughter.

"Who is that?" she asked, though she instinctively knew the answer.

"That's Cecrops's daughter, Aglaurus," Cranaus replied softly. "I don't think she knew anything about the reptilian side of her family."

Nefari got up and moved to kneel beside the girl. Her dress was dirty and had been used to wipe her tears. She placed a hand on Aglaurus's shoulder, causing her to back away suddenly. Her breathing became frantic, and she had a shocked look on her face.

"Stay away from me!" she managed to say through ragged breaths.

"I just want to help—"

"Stay away!" Aglaurus screamed. She backed toward the cliff's edge.

Nefari opened her arms in a gesture of peace and took a step forward. Aglaurus glanced over her shoulder at the steep drop below, and without hesitation, she jumped.

"No!" Nefari cried, rushing forward. She heard Aglaurus's screams as she fell, followed by a sudden, sharp silence. Nefari dropped to her knees in despair. "I was only trying to help you."

Cranaus knelt beside her and pulled Nefari into a comforting embrace. "There's nothing we could've done for her. The shock was too much."

Nefari sat quietly for a moment, her emotions building before she burst into tears. She cried for the end of Cecrops, for Pandrosus who had been her friend, for Cranaus's survival, and for all the little things she wanted to fix but couldn't. Cranaus held her close, softly stroking her hair.

The fighting within Athens had dwindled to a few scattered skirmishes. Across the streets, civilians wielded pitchforks, pots, and whatever else they could find. The Uru hadn't expected the small force that raided the town to be bolstered by the townspeople themselves. They were quickly overwhelmed and defeated.

At the heart of the great city, a band of twelve Uru refused to surrender. They were surrounded by a growing number of Athenians and resistance fighters, forming a defensive circle with a wall at their back. The leader, distinguished by his more elaborate armor, barked orders, indicating he might be a captain or even a general in the Uru army.

Two resistance fighters charged in, but the Uru leader raised his arm, signaling his troops to bring up their shields. The attackers were quickly cut down. Titos, the resistance commander, ordered his men to hold back but maintain the surrounding line. He struggled with a tactical dilemma: if he ordered an all-out attack, many Hellenes would perish, but they would eventually prevail. However, if he held back, how long would it be before the Uru went on the offensive, leading to the same outcome?

Titos felt a surge of relief when Cranaus appeared, followed by Nefari.

"I thought you'd still be days away," Cranaus said, slapping Titos on the back. "Damn, am I glad to see you."

"I figured you'd be ready to make a move," Titos replied with a grin. "Has the king left?"

"Cecrops is no longer a concern," Cranaus nodded. "Atlantis, though, is still an issue. What's the situation here?"

"The Uru at the center are well-trained and effectively led. If we attack, we'll suffer heavy losses. If we stay put, they might strike back and devastate our ranks."

Cranaus paused to consider the options, then stepped into the gap between the Uru and the Hellenes. The Uru leader raised his arm, and the shields came up again.

"Uru leader," Cranaus called out, "what's your name?"

The Uru leader responded without hesitation, his voice laden with arrogance and contempt. "I am Ryujin, 8th General of the Uru army. You insects will soon be dead." As he spoke, he removed his helmet, allowing long, dark hair to cascade down his shoulders. His sharp features and piercing gaze reflected unshakable confidence as he stared down Cranaus.

Cranaus, however, met his gaze without flinching. "I am

232

Cranaus, King of all you see here," he replied evenly. "Cecrops is dead. Shenlong is dead. I killed them both in single combat. You're alive only because I choose it. Your welcome in my city has come to an end. You and your men will leave immediately and return to Atlantis. Don't think about coming back."

Ryujin's expression remained stern and arrogant, but inwardly he felt a hint of uncertainty. He knew Cecrops and Shenlong hadn't responded to his mental summons, but the idea that this wretched bug killed them both in combat was almost too absurd to consider. It had to be a trick.

"Move out," he commanded, and his men began to march away. The Hellenes parted, clutching their weapons tightly, their eyes tracking every movement of the Uru soldiers. As Ryujin became the last to leave, he turned back to Cranaus.

"You're a fool, Cranaus, King," he sneered. "You think you can challenge the might of Atlantis? We have weapons beyond your wildest dreams. You may think you have the upper hand now, but it won't last. You're only alive because Atlantis allows it. I'd advise you to run while you still can."

Cranaus shook his head with a hint of disdain. "I'm not a frightened little snake like you. Tch" he sounded with a slight tilt of his head, signaling for Ryujin to move on. Ryujin glared at Cranaus one last time before following his men out of the city.

"A bold move," Titos said as he walked up behind Cranaus. "Ryujin is going to be trouble once Atlantis gets involved."

"I don't doubt it," Cranaus replied. "For now, my priority is to protect the people. They can fight when they're ready."

"So, we've reclaimed Athens. What's next?" Titos asked.

"Next, we celebrate. Athenians have retaken their city. We have a new king. What else would you suggest?" Cranaus replied, a hint of a smile on his lips. He glanced over Titos's shoulder at Nefari. "Let's celebrate life."

Titos followed Cranaus's gaze and leaned in closer. "Be careful, Cranaus," he warned. Cranaus met the eyes of his long-time friend. "We've driven the Uru out, but the people may not be ready for someone with Uru ties so close to the crown. I'm saying this as a friend and advisor."

Cranaus looked around at the Athenian crowd. People were visibly relaxed, their weapons lowered. Some were smiling and chatting, relieved that the fighting was over. Others were crying, the stress and fear of the battle finally releasing. Cranaus knew they were waiting for him to speak, to explain why they'd risked their lives that morning.

"Brothers and sisters of Athens," Cranaus called out, stepping away from Titos. "This morning, you were roused from your homes by the sound of fighting and confusion. You may not have known the cause or the purpose of the day's events, but I saw each of you stand up and fight. You fought for Athens and the freedom we once held. I am proud of every one of you."

"I will now tell you what has occurred," Cranaus addressed the crowd. "This morning, the resistance made a decisive move to reclaim the city from the Uru. Cecrops and the Uru guards in Athens are dead, and I've taken the mantle of king. If anyone objects, you may speak now without risk of consequence."

Athenians looked around, scanning faces for anyone who might challenge Cranaus's claim. When no one stepped forward, Cranaus continued.

"Thank you for this honor," he said. "You all knew in your hearts that this was the moment to take action. For that, I thank you, and I give you tonight to celebrate." The crowd cheered in response. "But remember, our battle isn't over. We've only just stirred the nest of vipers. Atlantis is out there, floating off the mainland with its beacon tower and shining surface. Below the surface is a race full of hate and terror. They will come for us, seeking to reassert control over our city—the city our fathers and grandfathers once ruled. But I will not submit to them. We all know what it's like to live under another's rule, and I will not let it happen again. Who is with me? Who will fight to keep Athens free from Atlantis?"

An uneasy silence fell over the crowd. Cranaus scanned the faces, a hint of worry in his eyes. He knew it was all for nothing if no one stood with him. Then, a large man in the second row stepped forward, raising his voice. "I will!" he shouted.

Cranaus felt a surge of relief as others followed suit. The first man to step forward was Arylan, a blacksmith over six feet tall, his muscles sculpted by years at the forge. His thick black beard curled outward, stained with soot, and his arms bore the marks of hard labor, barely protected by his leather apron. As the crowd's cheers grew louder, Cranaus nodded to Arylan, who gave him a knowing smile.

"Then let's not waste any time," Cranaus told the crowd. "We have a day to prepare for the celebration. Get to it!" The crowd dispersed, still cheering. "And be cautious of any Uru you come across. If they choose to leave, let them. But if they resist, don't hesitate to take them down."

"What about that one?" an Athenian said, pointing at Nefari. "She's done work for Cecrops on occasion." Nefari recognized the man as Gardi, the patron of The Turtle Shell inn. She was about to defend herself when Cranaus spoke up.

"I know exactly what Nefari has done for Cecrops, Gardi," Cranaus replied, causing Gardi to shrink back, embarrassed by the attention. "But I'm also aware of what she's done against the Uru—her own people. Without her help, the resistance wouldn't have achieved what it has. Anything she's done I have forgiven. I know you may not have yet but let her prove herself over time. That's all I ask. She's no longer Uru; she's one of us."

A murmur rippled through the crowd, but no one voiced further objections. As people dispersed to prepare for the night's celebration, Cranaus turned back to Nefari. The expression on her face showed she was deeply moved by his words. Her gaze held a love that had been there all along, but only now was it coming to the surface. Cranaus smiled back, his cheeks turning a faint shade of red.

"That'll be a touchy subject for months to come," Titos said, breaking the moment. "That is, if we can win this war."

"We'll win," Cranaus assured his small companion. "But there's work to do. Half the Athenians who left here don't know how to prepare for a celebration, and the other half don't have the resources. I need you to use your skills and make sure everything is organized."

"And what will you be doing?" Titos asked.

"I'll be visiting the family estate for some rest," Cranaus replied. "I got little sleep last night and had a busy morning."

Titos laughed. "Make sure to pat the beds down. There's going to be a lot of dust."

With that, Titos left Cranaus and Nefari to organize the night's festivities. Alone now, Nefari jumped at Cranaus and hugged him tightly. She hadn't had a chance to do so earlier, and had been almost jumping out of her skin waiting for everyone to leave. Cranaus enjoyed the embrace. Her body was warm against his, and the warmth seemed to spread through him like a gentle tide. He reached up and softly took Nefari's chin between his fingers. As she looked into his eyes, he pulled her closer, and she closed her eyes and leaned into the kiss. Their lips met just as the sunlight touched the square. Nefari felt the wind swirling around them, tossing her hair about. It was a moment of chaotic perfection, and when they parted, she was left speechless.

"Shall we go find that bed?" Cranaus asked with a smile, then added, "To rest."

"Yes, let's," Nefari replied, linking her arm with his. She felt like she was floating on a cloud, so caught up was she in the man beside her. She didn't even remember the way back to the square as they walked. But she did take note of the building Cranaus called his home.

"Is this the home of a king?" she asked, curious. It was a modest single-story townhouse, narrow at the front and not much deeper on the sides. She spotted a small courtyard, but it only had space for four chairs and a little round table. There were no gardens or flowers, and the place looked rather unlived-in.

"It's the home of my family. A king might rule in Athens, but where he rests his head is entirely up to him," Cranaus replied, his gaze growing distant. He was recalling the day he left fourteen years ago, vowing only to return when Athens belonged to its people once more. Taking a deep breath, he extended his hand to Nefari. "Come, let me show you around."

As they entered, they both stopped. The interior was barren—no furniture, no decorations. Cranaus had expected this, but seeing it in person still saddened him. He showed Nefari the two bedrooms and the dining area. At the back, a modest living space had a fire pit dug into the hard earth floor, meant for a hearth.

"Wait here a moment," Cranaus said, darting out of the house.

Nefari wandered through the home and out the back door. From the street, the backyard had appeared small, an illusion created by poor fencing. But in reality, the yard stretched nearly a hundred meters. It could use some work, but it had potential, and that was enough for her. A scuffle at the front door drew her attention, and she saw Cranaus returning with another man, each carrying an end of a lumpy mattress.

"Nefari, this is Horgdan. He lives next door." Horgdan nodded in greeting. "Horgdan has kindly offered us a bed. We can rest for now, and I'll find more furniture later today."

"That sounds lovely," Nefari replied with a warm smile toward Horgdan. "Thank you for your kindness."

"Oh... no, don't mention it," Horgdan said, waving his hands as he set the bed down. He quickly left the house. Nefari stepped in to help with the mattress.

"I can handle it, Nefari," Cranaus protested, but she didn't let him off the hook. Together, they carried the bed into one of the rooms and laid it down. As they wiggled on the mattress, they managed to find a comfortable spot.

When they were settled, Nefari propped herself up on one elbow. "If you want to spend more than a few moments with me, you'll have to accept that I'm as independent as any man. I like to be physical."

"I can keep you active," Cranaus replied, running his hand up the back of her thigh, edging under her tunic.

"I thought you were tired," Nefari teased, slapping his hand away playfully. Cranaus laughed, then grabbed Nefari around the waist, rolling her across him so she lay on her back on the opposite side. With the upper hand, Cranaus looked down into her eyes, enjoying the intimate position.

They were lost in the moment, a combination of love and desire holding them captive. Finally, Cranaus leaned down and kissed her softly on the lips. Nefari responded by raising her hips into the air. Cranaus grabbed the hem of her tunic and after a moments pause, took a deep breath and removed Nefari's clothing. The girl below him was perfect in every way. Her skin had started to bronze in places but had remained soft and smooth. While on her back, Cranaus noticed that Nefari's petite breasts were still well rounded and perky. The nipples erect, with small pink aureoles.

Sensing the passing of time Nefari opened her eyes to see Cranaus gawking at her. Smiling she reached up to cup his cheek in her hand. 'Did you want to sit and watch me all day?' Nefari asked

Snapped from the trance he shook his head and started to tongue and suck her nipples as his free hand traced the curves of her body. Nefari was feeling uncomfortable with the way he touched.

'Gentle,' Nefari said. Cranaus slowed down giving a greater experience to Nefari. Electricity ran across her skin as he nibbled her neck.

'You are beautiful,' Cranaus whispered into her ear. The kiss that followed was the greatest kiss Nefari had ever experienced. Their tongues played to the rhythm of their lust and as they separated a tendril of saliva still linked them. Cranaus brushed it away.

'Well?' Nefari asked

'Well what? Cranaus replied confused. His mind was caught up in their love and had trouble thinking straight.

'Are you going to take your clothes off? I may not have done this before but I was under the impression both parties clothes needed to be off.'

Cranaus panicked as he rushed to get his clothes off. He got caught trying to take it over his head and was rolling around on the bed wrestling with it. Nefari laughed loudly and shuffled across to him. Resting a hand on his arms she settled him down and took a peek at his body. Strong, well toned, muscles ran across his stomach. Moving lower her eyes spied his organ. It was similar to most of the men on Atlantis and she was comfortable to be near it. Kissing down his stomach she took hold of his penis in her hands and kissed the very tip.

'Athena's tits it's moving,' Nefari almost screamed batting it aside and rearing back.

'You know they'll get harder when aroused, right?' Cranaus said finally getting the clothing off. As she was sitting back, Cranaus crawled up her until he was right at her opening.

'Aren't you going to wait for it to go down or something,' Nefari said worried. 'It would've fit much easier the way it was before.'

'You will find that this is the more pleasurable size and I couldn't make it go back now if I tried,' Cranaus admitted. 'I won't lie though. Your first time can give a little pain until you adjust to it.'

Nefari looked up into Cranaus's eyes. 'All I want is to be together with you always. I love you, Cranaus.'

'And I love you. Even if you are independent and physical, I want to be by your side,' Cranaus had been positioning himself as he talked and as he said side slid deep into her. Nefari let out a gasp as pain raced through her. Cranaus was about to move but Nefari grabbed him shaking her head. Her eyes were shut tight, breath caught in her throat.

Moments passed before she felt comfortable enough to continue. The movements still felt tender but they were mixed with a warmth that felt good. Nefari was enjoying the love making with Cranaus and started to get into the rhythm herself. She couldnt remember at what point the movement changed but they had grown more faster, even wild in their movements and Cranaus changed her position. Grabbing her legs he threw them up over his shoulders so that one leg was on each side of his head.

Nefari felt him deeper than before, his penis touching places she didn't believe could be. The warmth inside started to grow and she felt like there was a dam of feelings about the burst. Standing on the tip of ecstasy Nefari felt Cranaus's release. The hot waves that pulsed from him sent her over the top. She fell into waves of pleasure, lost in what only could be described as true Elysium.

Cranaus opened his dazed and content eyes to the sight of the girl he had just made love to—and screamed. What had been Nefari was now a struggling reptilian creature, her transformation happening without either of them realizing it. Cranaus held on to the legs of the thrashing creature, trying to keep it under control. He considered whether he needed to put it down, but hesitation gripped him.

Suddenly, there was movement elsewhere in the house, announcing someone's entrance. Cranaus, with his back to the door, wasn't able to see who it was.

"Whoa... I, um... I don't think that's normal," said a voice he recognized as Horgdan's.

"Go get the guards—the Athenian guard!" Cranaus ordered, not wanting Horgdan to stumble upon a group of Uru and get hurt in the process.

"Should you still be fornicating?" Horgdan asked, his voice unsure.

"I'm holding... Just go, now!" Cranaus's voice carried an edge of panic, startling Horgdan into immediate action. He ran out of the door, his footsteps fading quickly.

Chapter 12

The room where Nefari found herself was dim and chilly, resembling the dungeon where she'd once been tortured. The only difference now was the soft blue glow that filled the space, illuminating the edges and corners. Her reptilian eyes picked out the shapes and contours in the dark. When she looked at her hands, she saw long, slender, scaled fingers that ended in wickedly sharp nails. She couldn't quite make out the color, but she knew without a doubt that she was green. Her tail swished behind her, flicking back and forth. She was still getting used to controlling those extra muscles.

"The Change," Nefari thought, recalling what Sanguine had mentioned about her and her lover's transformations. How had she not known about this? Fifty years among the Uru, and she'd never heard their secret. Their entire race was reptilian, triggered by their first intimate encounter. How different would her life have been if she'd discovered this sooner? Would she, even now, be honing swords to wage war against Athens? No. Cecrops was only dead because of her assistance. There would be no war. Would she have taken another path? Undoubtedly.

She felt she'd let her entire race down because of her ignorance. She'd helped the Athenian resistance, playing a part in Cecrops's assassination. Even though Cranaus had shown her kindness, it wasn't where she belonged. Her heart longed for Atlantis.

Nefari's spirit soared into the night. Freedom was calling her, drawing her toward the beacon light of Atlantis. The river of stars stretched out above her like a pathway home, and she flew toward it with haste, desperate to leave the world of man behind. Her body didn't matter anymore. The Uru could sense her spirit, and as long as she held onto her lapis lazuli necklace, she would still be able to communicate with them.

Atlantis grew larger as Nefari approached. The ringed city had never looked so beautiful. Moonlight danced on the silver surface, creating a radiant glow against the dark expanse of the ocean. The city's white gleam was like a beacon in the black sea. As she descended beneath the surface, she glided through the living city, passing through rooms and drifting down hallways, seeking a sense of peace.

But the mood of the city was anything but peaceful. At this time of night, the Uru would typically retire to their quarters, but tonight, everyone was awake, crafting weapons and armor. A general was shouting orders, sending people scattering in all directions. Nefari recognized him as Ryujin, and she floated closer. He quickly noticed her presence.

"I've been warned about you, traitor," Ryujin hissed. "Go back to Athens and tell your king that we'll meet him in two days."

"Tell him yourself," Nefari retorted, materializing her spirit into a visible form. Her spiritual manifestation reflected her reptilian nature.

Ryujin's laugh echoed through the corridors. "You slept with him. So, do we still need to go to war?"

"He still lives, if that's what you're asking, and I'm in a dungeon," Nefari replied.

"Perfect," Ryujin said, his voice dripping with sarcasm. "Have you spoken to anyone since your... awakening?"

Nefari tried the word on her tongue. "Awakening. I like that better than 'the change.' And no, I haven't spoken to anyone yet."

"Have you returned to Atlantis, sister?" Ryujin asked.

"This is my home," Nefari replied, surprised by the emotion in her voice. "I've been away too long. I just want the peace I once knew. I want to come home."

"Then I have a job for you, White Wrench." The use of her old nickname made Nefari feel nostalgic. "Go back to your body. Tell them you've infiltrated Atlantis and found a way to defeat the Uru. Say whatever you need to get back on their good side. After all, you managed to get the king into bed, so it shouldn't be too hard."

"To what end?" Nefari asked. "I want to be free from them, not stuck with them."

"On the day of the battle," Ryujin continued, "you're going to feed me all of the Athenians' strategies."

A dark, mischievous smile spread across Nefari's lips— one she'd never worn before, but it suited her reptilian beauty. "The Athenians will be outmaneuvered in every way," she said.

"That's the plan," Ryujin agreed, tapping the side of his head to emphasize his point. "Your intelligence is what matters most in this world. Can I count on you to do this?"

"As much as you can count on any Uru under your

command," Nefari replied with a nod. "I should get back to complete this task if I truly want to come home." Nefari soared upward through the floors of Atlantis and into the night. She paused to take one last look at her home, imprinting the sight in her mind—a reminder of what she was fighting for. Her eyes wandered to the outer ring of the eastern quarters, an area in complete lockdown, accessible only to the most elite Uru.

She dismissed the thought and started back toward Athens, but halfway there, doubts began to creep in. What was so secret that it required constant surveillance? She stopped, her mind wrestling with indecision. In the end, Nefari decided she wanted no more secrets about her race. If it was just a reptilian lounge, at least she'd know what to expect when she came home.

She reentered the eastern section of the building without any issues. With the commotion going on throughout Atlantis, there were few guards stationed here. Nefari found herself in a bare hallway with numerous doors. Above each door was a plaque, this one reading "Egyptian Crossbreeds." When Nefari peeked inside one of the rooms, what she saw left her in shock.

On the far wall were cages filled with pregnant women. Some bore characteristics of Egyptian descent, others resembled the Uru. The cages were stacked, one atop the other, approximately ten rows high and twenty wide. There were hundreds of women at various stages of pregnancy. In the center of the room, an operating table and surgical equipment were set up.

Nefari floated out of the room and into the next. It was the same scene: more cages, more pregnant women. She checked every room along the hallway, all holding the same distressing contents. She floated through the floors, astonished that the pattern continued. Each floor had a different designation: one was labeled "Hellene Crossbreeds," then "Gaul Crossbreeds." She descended another floor, and her blood ran cold. The plaque above the door read "Abori Crossbreeds." This was supposed to be her fate, but for her infertility.

"Let the new girl do it," Nefari heard from a room to the left. She moved to the door and saw an Abori woman on a bed with her legs raised, in the midst of labor. Watching the birth was an unexpected and awe-inspiring experience.

"Cut the cord and give the child to the mother. Let them

bond," the head Uru said. Nefari was surprised to see a hint of compassion, even if only momentarily. She watched as the mother cooed to her newborn daughter, full of joy.

"Okay, that's enough. Bring the child to the washrooms, and I'll show you how to clean them," the head Uru continued. Then, turning back to the other Uru in the room, she said, "Re-inseminate her."

The Uru nodded, picking up a long needle. Meanwhile, the others walked out of the room, and Nefari followed them to the washrooms. The scene inside was shocking: eighteen newborns lay in this single room. Nefari gagged, unable to vomit as a spirit. The babies were placed on benches and hosed down from head to toe with a high-pressure shower nozzle.

"Why do we give the babies to their mothers?" the new Uru asked. "It's not like they'll ever remember it."

"There's a chemical change in a baby that happens during this initial bonding. It makes the meat taste much sweeter," the older Uru replied. "Now, grab your cleaver, and I'll show you how to prepare it."

Nefari's eyes bulged as she fled from the room, unable to bear the fate awaiting the crying babies. It could have been her life. She was nothing more than cattle. Desperate to escape, she visualized her body, and her spirit instantly teleported back to it.

Upon reentering her body, Nefari burst into tears. Her reptilian form made it hard to cry, but the overwhelming emotion couldn't be contained, and the tears wouldn't stop. The door to her cell opened, and Cranaus entered, holding a torch. He stayed near the entrance, not wanting to come any closer.

"Cranaus, they're disgusting," she whimpered, her voice choked with emotion.

Cranaus didn't move toward her. He had a troubled expression as he looked at the woman he knew he shouldn't love. "Where does your allegiance lie?" he asked.

Nefari looked up at him, her eyes filled with pain at the question. The idea of betrayal had crossed her mind just moments earlier, and she realized how close she'd come to siding with the Uru. "Where it always has, with you," she said softly.

"How many Uru are like you?" he asked.

"They all are," Nefari replied. Cranaus's eyes narrowed, but he remained silent. "The whole race undergoes a change when they lay with someone for the first time. Those who haven't changed are unaware of it. It's supposed to happen only with another Uru."

Cranaus nodded and turned to leave.

"Wait! There's more," Nefari called. Cranaus turned back, raising an eyebrow in curiosity. She hesitated, considering how to explain what she was about to reveal. "I've walked the path of a traitor to you," she began. He remained stoic, waiting for her to continue.

"Just before you came in, I left this cell using the Dreamtime. With my recent discoveries about myself and my race, and being confined here, I felt a strong urge to go to Atlantis. Using the Lapis Lazuli necklace, I spoke to Ryujin, the general you released from Athens. He was surprised I had 'awakened,' but believed me when I said I wanted to join the Uru... and I meant it at the time. He told me to regain your trust and then, when the Uru attacked, to use their psychic link to relay your plans to them."

"And why should I believe you're not still following his orders?" Cranaus asked, his voice even.

"My physical transformation wasn't the only revelation I had," she replied, averting her gaze. "I once told you I was treated special as a child, like the Uru had plans for me. I now know what those plans were. The Uru blood in me granted me longevity, but the Abori blood altered my genetics in a way that made my offspring... edible to them."

"What?" Cranaus exclaimed, disbelief etched across his face.

"I was to be placed in a cage and forced to reproduce for the Uru so they would have a steady food supply. But due to my infertility, I escaped that fate. There are hundreds of crossbreeds in the eastern wing of Atlantis from various regions. When I saw them, I knew I'd never help the Uru," Nefari explained, her voice trembling with a mix of relief and anger.

Cranaus didn't speak for a long while. He seemed deep in thought, processing what she'd just revealed and imagining the horrid fate that Nefari narrowly avoided. Finally, he broke the silence. "Do you think you can change forms?" he asked.

"I will learn to," she replied, her eyes holding his gaze.

"Then learn by morning. We shall talk again." With that, Cranaus turned and walked away, leaving Nefari alone in the cell. The door swung shut with a loud clang, followed by the sound of the lock clicking into place. Despite the bleak surroundings, Nefari felt a glimmer of hope. Perhaps this was her second chance—to do the right thing, to right the wrongs of the Uru. She would not waste it.

"Ryujin, I don't see you down here that often," Hedas said as the general stepped through the door to his office. "What brings you to the underworks? Does it have anything to do with the commotion above?"

"Brother, Atlantis is on the edge of war," Ryujin replied. He always held a soft spot for his blood brother. Hedas wasn't skilled with a sword like the rest of his family, but his ability to run the city from the dark depths of the underworks was worthy of respect. "The Athenians have slain Cecrops and taken the city. We're going to take it back. I need you to direct all unessential power to the Pandora Pyramid, ready to open it. Extinguish the beacon light and start cycling the energy."

"Do we really need the destructive power of the Pandora? If we open it now, it will be at least a year before Atlantis will be functioning at full capacity again. The distance to the volcanic islands is too great to replenish the city sooner."

"Athens will have an army. We don't need the Pandora to destroy them, but we need a significant show of force. The psychological effects the weapon will have on the Hellenes will be just as valuable as the destructive force," Ryujin said. "I plan to win future wars with this one attack."

"You always seem to talk in riddles, brother," Hedas replied, knowing better than to argue. "But that's why they made you a general and me the master of the underworks. When will you meet the enemy?"

"A little over a day if they meet us on the field. Two at most if we have to march on the city."

"Okay," Hedas nodded. "I'll begin the procedures in half a day. That way the power will be optimal and won't overexert itself before you're ready. In the meantime, I'll check the system to make sure everything runs smoothly. After that, I'll gather the mechs in the hall for a meeting to explain what will happen and give out special assignments."

"If anyone tells you you're worthless, ignore them," Ryujin said, pulling his brother into a playful headlock and rubbing his knuckles across Hedas's scalp. It was Ryujin's closest approximation to affection. "I feel better knowing you're running the city works."

Hedas wriggled free from the headlock and smiled, but his expression quickly grew thoughtful. "Ryujin... No, it's nothing. Don't worry about it."

"What is it? Tell me," Ryujin pressed.

"It's Nefari," Hedas admitted. "I heard she got caught up with the resistance. I've been worried about her."

Ryujin looked at his brother with a raised eyebrow. "You like her, don't you?"

"No! Well... maybe a little. I don't know. She was always such a nuisance when she came to the office, but she had a way of brightening my day. She had a spark about her that felt warm and full of life."

"Sounds like you like her a lot," Ryujin said with a teasing grin, jabbing Hedas lightly in the side. "You'll be happy to know she's back in Atlantis. I spoke with her just an hour ago."

"She's back?" Hedas asked, his eyes brightening.

"Not physically," Ryujin replied. "She was using that Abori trickery, but she's helping with the war effort. I asked her to pass on information, and once that's done, she'll return to Atlantis. You and she have both been awakened, though she didn't get the full experience. You should share it with her."

"What are you saying?" Hedas blushed, growing bashful. "She wouldn't want to do that with me."

"She's different now, Hedas," Ryujin said, placing a reassuring hand on his brother's shoulder. "Have some confidence. She wouldn't have come to your office every day just to annoy you. She likes you too."

Hedas grew quiet, considering his brother's words. A hint of color rose to his cheeks. "I've got plenty of work to do, Ryujin. I should get to it now. Nefari can wait."

"She's a strong woman and would be a good match for you," Ryujin said as he left the office, heading off to organize the upcoming conflict with the Hellenes. "May you find happiness, brother."

Hedas looked at the pile of paperwork that had kept him occupied all morning and pushed it aside. He was glad to see the end of it—for now, at least. He left the office, navigating the underworks hallways with ease, heading toward a room directly beneath the central pyramid of

Atlantis. He produced the only key for the door, unlocked it, and entered, flicking the light switch as he went.

The room revealed was a large open space with walls coated in a shiny metal. The ceiling was translucent, allowing light to filter through from above and giving the impression that each level above was also translucent, extending all the way to the pyramid's walls. This gave the room a unique perspective, allowing viewers to seemingly see vast distances in every direction. It was the master command center for the weapon, designed for optimal viewing and control.

Hedas moved to the command module that operated the system. It was located at the base of a glass pillar connected to the pyramid's apex. The pillar contained a glowing blue liquid that bubbled unnaturally, as if gases formed randomly at different points. Hedas blew the dust off the command module, then began pressing buttons and tapping gauges. Once he was satisfied that the springs and cogs had loosened up a bit, he pressed the main power button. A low hum began to reverberate through the room as the bubbles in the pillar started to increase in frequency.

As the humming grew louder, small sparks of red lightning began to leap from the pillar, bouncing around the room. The intensity and unpredictability of the lightning increased as the machine stayed in operation, to the point where there was almost no place to stand without having it pass through you. Yet it posed no danger— multiple bolts passed through Hedas without causing him any harm.

Satisfied that the weapon was operating properly, Hedas shut everything down and exited the room. He headed to the meeting halls to organize the mechs for the upcoming battle.

The night had been brutal, and Nefari felt a sense of relief as the sun warmed her skin—skin that she had worn her entire life. Despite repeated attempts, she couldn't figure out the mental state required to revert to her human form. Following her own advice to Pandrosus, she tried recalling joyful moments and happy memories, but this only dimmed the green hue of her scales for a brief moment. She cycled through various emotions, but none of them seemed to work. She was unable to change even a single scale back to its human form.

This led Nefari to analyze her problem. As a member of the reptilian Uru race, she understood their driving motivations. The most obvious was food. To the Uru, humans were prey. Given that, why would her race need to assume human form? They could hunt more efficiently as reptilian humanoids, with their sharp teeth and taloned hands. The only answer she could find was that it was a form of camouflage—a way to infiltrate human society and establish a stable food source without direct hunting.

Reflecting on this grim reality allowed Nefari to regain her human form, though it made her feel nauseated. But even after transforming back, she got little rest. Soon, guards entered her room to escort her to the upper levels, where Cranaus was waiting. The surroundings suggested they were at Cecrops's home.

"Welcome back," Cranaus said. He seemed distant, and Nefari sensed a peculiar vibe from him. "I need you to go to Atlantis again and tell the General that you've successfully infiltrated our ranks once more. He has to believe you."

"I can do that," Nefari replied. Though his behavior seemed off, she attributed it to the stress of an impending war against Athens. "When do you need me to leave?"

"Now would be best," Cranaus replied bluntly. "Titos, Flavian, and the others are on their way. We'll discuss strategy when you return."

"Okay, I'll go now," Nefari replied. Her brow furrowed, concerned about Cranaus's demeanor. He nodded curtly, confirming her unease. Although something seemed off, she pushed it aside and shifted into the Dreaming. She tried an instant jump and was thrilled when she suddenly found herself hovering above the magnificent, floating city of Atlantis. Not knowing where Ryujin might be, she surveyed the scene and saw a crowd gathering at the city's edge near a cluster of ferry boats that transported people to the mainland. Spotting Ryujin among the throngs, she soared down to meet him.

"Ryujin," Nefari called out to get his attention. "It's Nefari."

"I know," he replied, his voice smooth and confident. "Your soul carries a warmth that echoes through the Uru. No one else has that same resonance. I see you're wearing your human cloak. Should I assume...?"

"I've successfully reinserted myself into their ranks," Nefari said with a sly smile. "They don't suspect a thing."

"Excellent," Ryujin hissed, his voice smooth and low. "What did you tell them?"

"I used a bit of twisted truth," Nefari replied, her grin widening. "I told them I'd gone to Atlantis to check on the fallout from Cecrops's death. While there, I claimed that you asked me to spy after seeing me in my reptilian form. I leaned into Cranaus's soft spot for me, and he told me I could prove my loyalty by shifting back to human form."

"I'm surprised you managed that on your own," Ryujin admitted. "There's a reason we don't tell our young too early what they truly are. We need them to understand the human condition, to know their weaknesses, and exploit them. To shift into human form requires the mind of a smart predator. That you came to this realization on your own suggests you've embraced your true nature."

"It just felt right," Nefari confirmed.

"While you're here, I need you to give a message to my brother. Will you do that?" Ryujin asked.

"I can," Nefari agreed, not wanting to upset Ryujin or give him any reason to doubt her loyalty. "Who's your brother?"

"Hedas from the mechanic office," Ryujin replied with a smile. Nefari was taken aback by the connection.

"Hedas!" Nefari exclaimed, recalling how he'd treated her after Sanguine's death. "Hedas is your brother? I've wanted to thank him since the last time we spoke. Where can I find him?"

"Below the Pandoras Pyramid, on the lowest floor," Ryujin said. His gaze seemed to study her intently, and Nefari couldn't shake the sense that he was scrutinizing her reaction. She assumed it was about the weapon, unaware that Ryujin was curious about her feelings toward Hedas. Keeping her composure, she focused on his words.

"Pandoras. A weapon like that could level entire cities. Do you still need the army?" Nefari asked, gesturing toward the gathering Uru around them.

"It's a strategic move," Ryujin explained. "Our soldiers want to fight. The battlefield will offer them a rich feast afterward. The weapon is meant to instill fear in the Hellenes. Now, go see my brother and tell him that I'm leaving. I haven't had the chance to speak with him."

"I'll go now," Nefari said, taking off toward the lower central chamber where Hedas was likely to be. The room was filled with a red glow from pulsing energy surrounding a central pillar. She found Hedas standing alone, absorbed in his work. When he noticed her presence, he looked startled.

"Nefari! How... You're not really here, are you?"

"No," Nefari replied. Hedas pursed his lips and nodded. "Your brother Ryujin sent me to tell you he's leav—"

The door burst open, and an official-looking Uru stormed in. "Ryujin, the 8th General of the Uru, has instructed me to inform you that he's leaving Atlantis."

Nefari floated back, her mouth hanging open in shock. "He did what?" she asked the official.

"Thank you, Zahhak," Hedas said, dismissing the Uru with a handshake, ignoring Nefari in the process. "You can go now." Hedas waited for the man to leave before speaking again. "Zahhak likes to think he's important when given tasks by his superiors, which, for him, is any other Uru on Atlantis. You had a message for me?"

"Not anymore. Zahhak just delivered my message," Nefari replied, incredulous. Hedas narrowed his eyes, then burst into laughter. Nefari stared at him, remembering how infuriating he could be. "What's so funny?" she asked.

"I think my brother wanted to give you a reason to come see me. We were talking about you last night," Hedas explained.

"And why would he do that? Why did he send me to see you?" Nefari demanded, growing irritated.

"Because since you disappeared after our last meeting, I've been worried," Hedas admitted. "When I heard we were going to war with the Hellenes, I asked about your whereabouts."

"That still doesn't explain why Ryujin sent me down here," Nefari said.

"He sent you... because..." Hedas began to blush, his words trailing off.

"Because?" Nefari pressed.

"I... like you, Nefari," Hedas finally confessed.

Nefari's eyes went wide. "But you were always so hard on me."

"That's because I didn't know how to handle my feelings," Hedas admitted. "I just wanted you to notice me."

"I'm sorry, Hedas, but I'm not ready for a relationship. I'm still figuring out who I am." Nefari decided not to mention her relationship with Cranaus—it would only complicate things. Hedas looked disappointed and turned away. "But I do want to thank you," she continued.

"For what?" he asked, turning back with curiosity.

"For the kindness you showed me last time we met. I was really upset, and you made me feel better. If things were different, maybe we could have been together."

"I hope that day comes," Hedas said with an emotional edge to his voice.

"I should be going now."

Hedas nodded, and Nefari faded from sight, returning to her physical body. She realized she hadn't obtained any useful information from Hedas. The worst part was that she missed an opportunity to talk him out of using the Pandoras weapon, especially since she'd be on the battlefield where it might be deployed.

As Nefari opened her eyes, she saw that everyone was already in the room. Anatolios was staring at her while Kyros was speaking.

"We're just not going to get enough troops on the field in time," Kyros said. "We have about a thousand fighters in the city and maybe another two thousand within a day's ride. But the riders we've sent to gather them might struggle to bring them back in time. We just don't have the numbers to match the Uru's strength."

"Even if we had only a thousand men, we'd still have to march at first light," Cranaus said sternly. "The Uru are coming whether we're ready or not."

"He's right," Nefari said, drawing the group's attention. Anatolios kept his gaze locked on her, but she ignored him. Titos wore his usual friendly expression, which she knew concealed his true feelings. Flavian and Kyros looked uneasy, and Cranaus seemed irritated. Given the dire situation, she understood why. "The Uru are already leaving Atlantis for the mainland. Unless you want the battle to spill into the streets of Athens, we need to march soon."

A tense silence settled over the room. Cranaus was the first to speak, breaking the silence.

"Did you accomplish what you needed to?" he asked.

"I spoke with Ryujin," Nefari replied. "He believes I'm on their side."

"Good," Titos said to Cranaus. "This means we can feed him false information on the battlefield."

'It's not going to help,' Nefari told them.

251

"That's enough, Nefari. You can go now," Cranaus said. His eyes bore into hers, almost daring her to argue. Before she could respond, Flavian spoke up.

"I want to hear what she has to say."

"Flavian, I don't want her to accidentally give away our plans because of a stray thought or a question she wasn't prepared for," Cranaus countered. "This plan depends on her control, and I intend to help her maintain it. She can speak her piece, but then she needs to leave."

Nefari felt a wave of isolation wash over her. She'd thought it was due to her transformation, but now she understood it was because of the war. Yet, they could at least talk to her instead of talking around her like she wasn't even there.

"Look at me, Cranaus," she said, her voice laced with frustration. Cranaus glanced at her, his expression filled with irritation. "Don't talk about me like I'm not in the room. This war is going to be hard on all of us, but we should still treat each other with some respect. Otherwise, we're no better than the Uru."

"You have little chance of being anything more," Cranaus snapped.

Nefari's face tightened, and small cracks began to form in her composure. Tears welled up in her eyes, and before she could stop them, they spilled down her cheeks. She turned and ran from the room, sobbing.

A shiver ran through Nefari as the cool night breeze bit deep. It was uncommon to have such cold temperatures this time of year, and she rubbed her arms to stimulate circulation. Staring at the door in front of her wasn't helping, and the longer she stood in the hallway, the harder it was to summon the courage to knock. She hoped someone would walk by, forcing her to make a decision, but luck wasn't on her side. Finally, she knocked on the door leading to Cranaus's sleeping quarters. With the war approaching, all council members needed to stay close, which was why they were at Cecrops's manor.

Cranaus opened the door with a smile on his face, but his expression turned cold when he saw it was Nefari. The butterflies in her stomach quickly turned into a leaden pit of disappointment. She was confused by the shift in his demeanor and wished everything could go back to the way it was when Cecrops was still in charge.

"Can I come in?" she asked, her eyes downcast.

"Do you have something to say?" Cranaus replied, avoiding her question.

"Do you... not love me anymore?"

"No," he said, without hesitation.

Nefari looked up, her eyes filling with tears. "Why? What did I do to lose the love we shared?"

"Do you even need to ask?" Cranaus said incredulously. "You tried to eat me, Nefari! You're a time bomb just waiting to explode. I was lucky to get away with my life."

"I had no control over my actions," she pleaded. "I didn't want to change. I didn't even know I could."

"But it still happened," Cranaus replied, devoid of sympathy. "The memory of that moment is burned into my mind. I can't even look at you without seeing the hideous creature you are. The thought of us together makes me sick."

Each word hit Nefari like a cold dagger, but no more tears came. The pain had gone beyond that point. She turned to leave but then paused at the door.

"I'm on your side, Cranaus," she said without turning around. "I came here tonight to tell you that the Uru are going to use a great weapon tomorrow. It's the Pyramid at the center of the city. They call it the Pandoras Pyramid, and it's like Zeus himself hurling lightning upon your men. They plan to use it sparingly, but it'll cause massive devastation."

She took a deep breath before continuing. "I need to get to Atlantis to stop it. Though the Pandoras Pyramid holds great pain and sorrow, it also holds our only hope. With that device, I can sink Atlantis for good—but I need to be in the command room to do it. There's still a chance for victory, Cranaus. I can save us."

Nefari said nothing more and ran down the hallway, her footsteps echoing as she weaved her way back to her room. Once there, she closed the door, leaned against it, and slid to the floor.

Tonight, Nefari knew the true meaning of loneliness.

Chapter 13

Pedias lay atop the crest of the hill, gazing down over the field. Below, two armies faced each other, preparing for battle. The Athenian army was at a clear disadvantage—they were outnumbered at least five to one, and the Uru had secured a better strategic position. Pedias could see what the Athenians had attempted: they were trying to reach Caygar's Pass, where the narrow corridors would negate the enemy's numerical advantage. But the Uru had beaten them there, and now their forces poured from the mouth of the pass.

The Uru were massed in the center of the field, suggesting they would charge in for close-quarter combat. Their ranks were perfectly aligned, and with the setting sun reflecting off their silver armor, they appeared invincible. The Athenians, meanwhile, had formed a similar line, but their uneven ranks and the small gaps between soldiers indicated their vulnerability. Pedias felt a pang of dread; she knew they were likely to lose.

On the slopes flanking the field, two hundred Athenian archers positioned themselves. From their elevated vantage point, they could rain arrows down on the Uru, but they risked being overrun if any sizeable group of Uru broke off to confront them. The Athenian bronze armor offered little protection against the Uru's superior steel.

"We need to advance," Pedias urged Lacedaemon, the King of Sparta. He wore a bronze breastplate sculpted to resemble a chiseled torso, a red cape, and a bronze helmet with a crimson plume. Beside him lay his spear and shield, with a short sword sheathed at his waist.

Lacedaemon continued to survey the battlefield. "Patience, dear. We don't want to reveal our position too early," he replied. "There will come a time in the fighting when the battle hinges on a knife's edge. If any one thing goes wrong, the entire army could turn and flee. That's when we make our move."

Pedias glanced back at the five thousand Spartan warriors assembled behind her and Lacedaemon. They were all dressed similarly to their king, except they didn't wear the plume on their helmets. "What happens if we misjudge the moment?" she asked.

"Then we go into battle regardless and re-balance the scales," the Spartan king replied. "We still might not match their numbers, but each of our boys can fight as well as four of theirs. Can you see your love from here?"

Pedias had found it easy to convince the Spartan king to join the war. It was no secret that the new king of Sparta had a romantic side. After marrying his niece, Lacedaemon had renamed the former Laconia to Sparta after his wife. Pedias had spun him a story about how she and Cranaus were kept apart due to the conflict between the Uru and the Athenians. Moreover, the Spartans were building a reputation as fierce warriors, and this was an excellent opportunity to bolster that image. Pedias scanned the battlefield.

"There," she said, pointing to the leftmost flank of the Athenian army. "Nefari is there too."

"An odd place for a king to lead his men into battle, and with a woman at his side," some of the Spartans behind Lacedaemon chuckled.

"Cranaus must have a plan," Pedias defended. "The woman is an Uru defector. She's been invaluable to the resistance's efforts. Some even say she can fly with the winds."

"You speak of fairy tales," Lacedaemon retorted. "A woman has no place on the battlefield. You should be grateful I even let you get this close. Once the fighting starts, you will remain here."

Pedias clenched her fists, furious at the king's condescension, but she knew there was no point arguing with him. By right, he was her king, and she owed him her loyalty, especially since he'd agreed to bring the Spartan army to this neighboring state. "Your will, my king," she said through gritted teeth.

They watched as the fighting ignited. Both armies advanced upon each other to a slow, steady beat. Shields were raised and locked, forming a formidable barrier for the men on either side. The Uru faced a tougher challenge as they were bombarded by arrows from both flanks of the hill. With each volley, a handful of Uru soldiers fell, their bodies swiftly replaced and the fallen trodden over without pause. Though the archers inflicted damage upon the advancing Uru, it seemed like a mere ripple in the tide of battle, far from enough to determine the outcome of the war.

Shields clashed together, initiating a power struggle of brute force. Each side sought to push the other back while attempting stabbing thrusts over their shields. The fallen combatants made the ground treacherous and slick for those still locked in combat. The first crack in the Athenian lines appeared mere minutes into the fray. Three men went down simultaneously, and the breach couldn't be sealed fast enough. Two Uru soldiers exploited the gap, widening it as they cut down those around them.

Pedias grasped the grass tightly, her gaze fixed on Lacedaemon. He appeared unperturbed.

"You let your fears consume you, Pedias," he remarked without turning to her. "Observe. It's but a minor setback."

Pedias focused on the breach and witnessed the Athenians rallying. Soldiers positioned at the rear surged forward, bolstering the breach with renewed vigor. The two Uru assailants were swiftly dispatched, and the breach sealed once more. The battle raged on. Three Vimana circled above, raining down fire upon vulnerable targets. The Athenians struggled to counter this aerial assault. Cranaus gestured toward one Vimana, issuing some command, prompting the archers to focus their fire on the pilot. After enduring a barrage of arrows, the pilot tumbled from the craft, which halted in mid-air before slowly descending to the ground.

The sound of a horn echoed from the Uru side, a deep, resonant blast that vibrated in Pedias's stomach. It seemed to come from the very heart of Atlantis. She clamped her hands over her ears, as did many of the Athenians and Spartans, but the horn's power was unrelenting. Those at the frontlines fell, unable to react to the sudden cacophony.

Pedias's face drained of color as she surveyed the battlefield. All the Uru warriors transformed into grotesque reptilian creatures, dropping their formation to spread across the field and into the surrounding hills, encircling the Athenians. Swords became secondary; the Uru now attacked with savage ferocity, using their fanged mouths to tear at the throats of their enemies, leaping on them with predatory instinct. Pedias glanced over to Cranaus and noticed that Nefari had transformed as well, though oddly, Cranaus didn't seem alarmed by it. The two climbed onto a downed Vimana and soared off toward Atlantis without anyone giving chase.

Lacedaemon, the Spartan king, growled, "Your king is fleeing with that monster. What's going on, Pedias?"

"Cranaus has a plan," she replied. "There's always been

talk that Cecrops was a monster, but never the entire race. If Cranaus isn't troubled by Nefari's transformation, then he must have known beforehand. We need to trust him."

Lacedaemon turned to address his men. "Spartans! The enemy has revealed their true demonic faces. But we do not fear. We embrace glorious death on the battlefield. Follow me!" With a defiant roar, the Spartan king charged into battle, leading a spearhead formation of five thousand Spartans behind him.

From her vantage point, Pedias saw the pyramid in Atlantis begin to crackle with golden lightning. The top third split open, and a massive ball of burning plasma shot into the sky, arcing toward the Spartans, who were already racing headlong into the chaos below.

"Nefari, what news of the Athenian armies?" Ryujin's voice whispered in her mind. Though she couldn't see him on the field, she knew he was close by.

"They're weak," she replied, sticking to the plan she and Cranaus had devised. "Many are scared, having heard that the Uru possess shape-shifting abilities akin to the Gods. Some are beginning to see you as divine and question the worth of sacrificing their lives. Still, Cranaus holds sway over their hearts. They will fight, but I'll extract Cranaus from the battle mid-fight. His retreat will sow doubt among the troops."

"Good," Ryujin replied, clearly convinced by her words. "The Pandoras will send them fleeing. Then we feast."

"Don't use the weapon too soon," Nefari cautioned. "I know it drains Atlantis's power rapidly, and to even get a few shots, you've been conserving energy."

"It will be the opening strike," he said with a hint of a smile in his voice. "Their ranks will crumble quickly."

"No," Nefari responded, a bit too quickly. She quickly adjusted her approach. "What I mean is there's a secondary force—a few thousand men—in the hills, ready to reinforce once the Athenians begin to wane."

"Thousands you say?" Ryujin sounded suspicious. "That's an awfully large number to gather so suddenly."

Nefari felt the pressure building, but she had to continue with her fabrication. "It was more luck than planning. A sizable force returned to town yesterday evening after completing a separate campaign."

"Luck has always been a formidable force," Ryujin

replied, his skepticism seemingly easing. "The Pandoras will be deployed the moment they crest the hill. Thank you, Nefari. You've served Atlantis well."

Nefari exhaled, relieved that she'd passed the first hurdle. She saw the Uru ranks begin their advance, and the Athenians moving forward to meet them.

"Did you speak to him?" Cranaus asked in a low voice. "When will their main weapon be used?"

"I spoke to him as planned," Nefari said to Cranaus as they advanced to a point about halfway across the field. She felt increasingly uneasy without a weapon, memories of the night's raid at her camp, previously, flashing through her mind. "They would have used the weapon immediately, but I convinced them to wait. I told them there's a larger force in the hills. Ryujin believed me, so he'll deploy the weapon when the supposed reinforcements attack."

Cranaus grinned. "Smart move. We should be far away by the time they realize there's no other force. Stay back—the Uru shouldn't harm you, knowing you're on their side."

The clash of metal echoed across the battlefield. Athenians and Uru clashed at the center while enemy warriors peeled off to attack the Athenian flanks. Cranaus and several other Athenian fighters rushed to defend the army's vulnerable edges. Cranaus moved with lethal efficiency, his blade a blur as he decapitated one Uru and then thrust through the chest of another in a single fluid motion. Kicking the dying Uru backward, he blocked a savage slash aimed at his own neck, giving an opening for an Athenian ally to dispatch the attacking warrior.

An Uru soldier spotted Nefari and charged. "I am with you, brother. Turn your attention to the Athenians," Nefari communicated telepathically. The warrior hesitated, confused by the mental command, allowing a young Athenian to drive his sword into the Uru's ribs. The Uru fell, dragging the sword with him, and the young man, now weaponless, didn't last much longer—he was struck down, his head cleaved open.

Nefari saw Cranaus knocked to the ground, with an Uru standing over him, ready to strike. Before the reptilian warrior could swing his blade, an arrow pierced his eye socket. The Uru collapsed, dropping his weapon beside Cranaus.

Cranaus cast aside a bronze sword broken near the hilt and picked up the Uru steel. The new blade was heavier, but it had perfect balance. In two swift strokes, he dispatched two Uru warriors, reveling in how the weapon sliced through armor, muscle, and bone. His armor was thick with blood as he scanned for more enemies. The lull in the battle gave him a moment to glance upward, noticing a Vimana hovering over the Athenian army.

"Archers!" he shouted, pointing to the sky. "The Vimana!"

Arrows arced into the air, striking the Uru pilot in the chest. As he tumbled from the craft, the Vimana gently descended, its engine shutting off. Cranaus called out to Nefari, signaling that it was time to move. Nefari smiled and started toward the craft but paused as a deep, rumbling horn echoed across the field. She doubled over, clutching her ears, a wave of pain surging through her body. An unfamiliar feeling arose within her, triggering a transformation she couldn't control. Her scream was a low, hissing cry. She tried to resist the change, but the sensation triggered by the horn was too strong. Regaining her senses, she noticed a blade at her neck. It was Cranaus.

"Are you with us?" he asked simply.

"I am," she replied, her voice strained.

Cranaus lowered his weapon, and they moved toward the Vimana. Nefari took the front, working the controls and lifting the craft into the sky, soaring over Caygar's Pass. Cranaus gripped onto Nefari's altered form for balance, his expression betraying his discomfort.

"Look," Nefari pointed.

Cranaus followed her gaze and saw the Pandoras Pyramid opening at the top, surrounded by crackling golden lightning. A massive plasma ball shot out from the apex. Cranaus looked back and saw a large group of Spartans charging onto the battlefield. The plasma ball veered slightly off course, but its impact was devastating, wiping out one side of the formation. More than a thousand Spartans perished in an instant.

"You knew they were there, didn't you?" Cranaus accused, his voice sharp with anger and suspicion. The only reason he didn't strike her down was that he needed her to get back to the ground. "You're working for the Uru, aren't you?"

Nefari glanced at the battlefield, where the Spartan warriors were regrouping after the devastating plasma attack. The weight of what she'd shared with Ryujin suddenly hit her. "No," she replied, her voice laced with regret. "How could I have known about them?"

"With your dreaming ability. What kind of trap are you leading me into?" Cranaus demanded, his distrust growing with each word.

"Cranaus, you must believe me. I had no idea about the soldiers in the hills. We are on the same side. We're going to destroy Atlantis and free hundreds of slaves," Nefari pleaded.

"We'll see," Cranaus muttered, refusing to grab onto her for support as the Vimana flew through the skies. He struggled to maintain his balance, his anger overshadowing his fear of falling.

Nefari piloted the Vimana to the outer eastern ring, where Cranaus jumped off while they were still a meter above the ground. He landed hard but kept walking, grimacing from the pain. Nefari saw him draw his sword, her heart sinking; after everything they'd been through, he still didn't trust her.

"Walk through those doors," Nefari said, pointing. "Go down the stairs to the bottom, then enter the last room on the left. The password for the panel beside the door is 'Eta Rho Alpha.' This room is where you can disconnect this quadrant from Atlantis. You should encounter little to no resistance inside. I'll give you additional instructions once I've completed my part."

"I should come with you. Your task is far more important," Cranaus suggested.

"I can't get into the master control room for Pandora's Pyramid with a human following me. Trust me to complete this. If we both went, we wouldn't be able to save the unfortunate souls in this quadrant before Atlantis sinks."

"Fine," he grumbled. "Don't fail."

Nefari just shook her head, then steered the Vimana towards the central circle. She didn't bother trying to change back into her human form. This guise was more useful on a ship full of reptilians. Walking with confidence, Nefari descended the stairs, heading for the access tunnels that led to the underworks. She needed to reach the master control room quickly. The longer she delayed, the greater the chance Cranaus would be caught.

As she rounded a corner, she encountered two Uru guards. Nefari realized she wasn't dressed like the Uru—she was wearing leather trews and a white woolen shirt.

Her trews had split at the back to accommodate her growing tail. It had been too long since she'd worn Atlantis's uniform. The Uru guards watched her as she walked by, and Nefari held her breath. Once they passed, she exhaled, thinking she was in the clear.

"Sister, why are you dressed in human clothes?"

Nefari cursed silently and turned to face the two Uru. "I just came from the warfront. I was leaking information to Ryujin. The battle should be over soon. You can find my Vimana up on deck. Could you park it in a side bay? I'll need it later when I rejoin the front. Is Hedas still below?"

One Uru guard narrowed their slitted eyes but said nothing. The other spoke up. "You can find a change of clothes in the linen tubs, three doors down. Hedas is still below. I'll park your Vimana, Nefari," he said with a wink. "There'll be no one around to manage it until the army comes back."

"You know me?"

"I was a mech in the north. You reprimanded me once after my tunic got stuck in the machinery. Dermak took the brunt of it, though. I heard you'd been lost to Atlantis."

Nefari recalled the young boy starting his training as a mech. His face had been a mix of fear and surprise when she scolded him. "I remember," Nefari replied, smiling. "You almost took down the entire power grid. How's your training going?"

"It's coming along well," he replied. "They've let me work on the machines again."

"That's great to hear," Nefari said with genuine enthusiasm. "Truth be told, I was lost to Atlantis for a while. After my Awakening, I knew my place was here, in this remarkable city."

"You better get back to what you were doing" the young Uru said. "I'm glad you're back with us."

The two Uru guards continued toward the Vimana, and Nefari headed to the linen storage where she found a white tunic that fit her. After changing, she was surprised by how comfortable the garment was. It made sense why the Uru wore this kind of clothing—the fabric seemed to dance across her scales.

Making haste, Nefari reached the access point to the underworks that would lead her straight to Hedas's location. She still wasn't sure what she'd say to him to gain access to the master control room, but she hoped something would come to her. The corridors felt familiar, like a home she'd almost forgotten. It wasn't long before she found herself standing in front of the doorway to the Master Control room.

As she reached up to knock on the door, it slid open. The reptilian form of Hedas moving forward, but stumbled and fell, crashing into Nefari. His eyes widened in shock as he found himself tangled up with the very girl he'd been pining for.

"I... I'm so sorry, Nefari. I didn't know you were there," he stammered, quickly rolling away to give her space.

"Hedas, you have nothing to be sorry for," Nefari said, deciding to play along with her good fortune and capitalize on Hedas's awkwardness. "I shouldn't have been standing in the way."

"I feared you were still on the field when I released the Pandoras," he said, waving off her apology. "I'm so glad you're here, though. There's trouble with the machine. I sent two Uru to fix it, but they're taking too long. I need to go myself."

"That might be my fault," Nefari replied, thinking about the young mech and his friend. "I ran into a couple of mechs a moment ago and asked them to move my Vimana. If I'd known they were on official business, I wouldn't have asked."

"Of course they neglected their duty to help you," Hedas remarked, then quickly moved on. "Anyway, I need you to man the control room while I'm gone. I know you can handle it. I'll be back soon, and I'll even let you fire the final round."

"You can trust me," Nefari said, lying easily. This was perfect.

Hedas hurried off down the corridor, and Nefari stepped inside the control room. She quickly assessed the situation. A power fluctuation in one of the lines was causing the controls to behave erratically. This would be tricky, but Nefari knew she could handle it. She stood in front of the control panel, watching the dials and gauges. As soon as Hedas fixed the line, she would need to act quickly to trigger Atlantis's collapse. Hedas had mentioned that there was one round left, so she still had a chance.

The lights on the control panel stabilized, signaling to Nefari that this was her moment. She quickly adjusted the settings on the panel to aim the final shot straight up. The plasma ball would reach its peak and then burst apart, raining down smaller plasma balls across the city. The resulting destruction would cause Atlantis to sink, just as planned. She locked in the settings and set her name as the password to secure them.

Nefari sat back against the control module and entered the Dreamtime, racing to find Cranaus, hoping he hadn't been discovered. Relief washed over her as she found him in the room where she'd instructed him to go. She created a visual form of herself to communicate.

"The shot is set," Nefari said, acknowledging Cranaus's curt demeanor and preemptively addressing his question.

"Good," he replied. "What do you need me to do?"

Nefari detailed the steps required to detach the quadrant from Atlantis, turning it back into a separate ship. Once the instructions were clear, she pointed to a button on the control panel.

"This button will either bring the ship in or detach it from Atlantis," she explained. Cranaus pushed the button, and the halls groaned as the process began. "Good. Now head to the deck, and I'll meet you there shortly."

Nefari quickly returned to her body, knowing she'd spent too much time with Cranaus. As she had feared, Hedas was in the room, leaning over her. He gently shook her shoulders, trying to wake her up. Nefari merged back into her body and opened her eyes.

Hedas let out a deep sigh of relief. "What happened, Nefari? Are you okay?" he asked, his voice laced with concern.

"Hedas, intruders," Nefari said, partly telling the truth. She knew he would never reach Cranaus before she did.

Hedas cursed under his breath. "Let me help you up," he said, offering his hand to lift her from the floor. "As promised, you may push the button to fire."

"Thank you, Hedas," Nefari replied with a smile. She pressed the button to fire the Pandoras. "Quickly, we must find the intruders."

"Don't you want to watch your attack connect?"

"I trust that it will, but Atlantis isn't safe with intruders on board. Come on," she said, racing out the door and heading toward the Vimana. "You search the deck, and I'll see if I can spot anyone from the sky."

Hedas nodded and watched Nefari take off. He noticed her craft descending toward the East and assumed she'd found something. He broke into a jog, following her path.

Behind them, the Pandoras Pyramid surged with golden lightning as its sides began to lower, preparing for the final shot.

Cranaus listened as the ship detached from Atlantis. Although he didn't feel adrift, Nefari had mentioned that Uru ships glide along the water without any noticeable swaying motion. The outer wall of the room turned crystal clear, revealing that they were already fifty meters away from the city. He marveled at the technology, reaching out to confirm that the wall hadn't actually vanished. His hand touched something solid, and he smiled in relief.

But then a dark feeling spread throughout his body as he looked back at the control panel. His hand hovered over a button, his expression hardening. He pressed it again. The ship slowed on its course away from Atlantis, then reversed, heading back toward the dock. As the ship drew nearer, the wall became opaque again, and Cranaus left the room to head back to the deck.

The ship reattached to Atlantis, becoming part of the city once more, and Cranaus saw the Vimana rise into the air and fly toward him. He could make out Nefari's expression as she approached—her reptilian face twisted with rage. She landed on the deck across from him and started screaming.

"What have you done, Cranaus? The slaves are going to die!" she shouted.

"I know," Cranaus replied, his hand resting on the hilt of his sword, though Nefari didn't seem to notice.

"You know?" Nefari's voice hit a high pitch. Her slitted eyes narrowed to thin slits, reflecting her anger. "How could you do something so horrible?"

Cranaus drew his sword, and Nefari hesitated. "Why would I want half-breeds like you running around freely?" he sneered. "They have every potential to be the same monster you are—an abomination to mankind. I don't regret my decision."

A blinding flash filled the air as the plasma ball shot straight up. Nefari knew they had at most two minutes to escape before the plasma rain hit. The smaller pieces would take longer to fall through the atmosphere but would be just as deadly when they landed. Cranaus's words cut deep, severing any ties she thought they shared. Nefari sprinted

264

toward the Vimana, but as she climbed aboard, Cranaus grabbed her by the tail and yanked her back. She hit the deck hard but rolled to her feet, her reptilian scales cushioning her from the worst of the impact.

Cranaus advanced again, sword at the ready. Nefari flexed her fingers, noticing the sharp talons that were now her natural weapons. This man was her prey; she shouldn't be afraid of him. A shockwave shook the city as the plasma ball exploded into thousands of miniature orbs, beginning their descent toward Atlantis. Cranaus swung his silver-steel blade, and Nefari ducked under the slash. She countered with a swipe of her talons, leaving four jagged cuts across his arm, blood spilling onto the deck.

Cranaus, enraged, launched a flurry of slashes, forcing Nefari to retreat. At first, she was confident, but her lack of battle experience quickly became apparent. Cranaus lunged, and Nefari couldn't move fast enough. The blade sliced into her scaly side, and she fell to the deck in pain. Her tail thrashed back and forth, and she found her body unresponsive as the pain took over.

She could escape into the Dreamtime, leave her body to avoid the agony of the final blow. But she chose to stay, to experience every last moment of life while she could.

Cranaus towered over Nefari, laughing maniacally. "Thank you, Nefari. Because of you, I was able to rid the world of your disgusting race. The Spartans will have no trouble taking out the rest of the Uru warriors once Atlantis is gone and their plans are in ruins."

He raised his sword, ready to strike. But before he could bring it down, a figure dashed from the nearby stairs and tackled Cranaus to the ground, sending the sword sliding across the deck. The struggle took both men dangerously close to the edge of Atlantis. Nefari recognized Hedas and felt a surge of relief and gratitude that he came to save her. Then she saw the dagger, as if it had appeared in Cranaus's hand by magic. Cranaus drove the blade into Hedas's ribs, and the reptilian coughed a small amount of blood. As his strength waned, Hedas struck back, driving his taloned hand into Cranaus's chest, just missing vital organs.

Cranaus saw the plasma balls, like falling snowflakes, approaching fast. With a final burst of energy, he pushed the dying Uru off him and leapt over the edge of the ship, disappearing into the ocean below.

Nefari brought the Vimana over to where Hedas lay and

lifted him aboard. As the first plasma balls struck Atlantis, causing massive explosions, she sped away toward the mainland shore. Nefari transitioned into her spirit form, scanning Hedas's wound as she had done for herself in Crete. The area was dark red, nearly black, indicating severe internal damage. She knew she didn't have much time.

Redirecting blood flow around the injured area to prevent further loss, she returned to her physical body. Grabbing the dagger, she pulled it free. Hedas arched his back in pain, his muscles rigid before he collapsed once more. Shifting back to her spirit form, Nefari worked to repair the lung tissue and surrounding areas, knowing it was risky to push him this hard. He could die from the strain, but if she didn't act, he would certainly die.

Once she was sure she had done all she could to stabilize Hedas, Nefari remounted the Vimana and flew away slowly, ensuring Hedas was securely positioned. She glanced back at Atlantis, glad to see it sinking to the bottom of the sea, flames leaping from every crevice. She noticed small black objects in the water and squinted to focus on them. Her emotions swirled between anger and relief when she realized it was the Uru, fleeing the sinking city. They swam through the water like the crocodiles from her homeland. She quickly saw that there were too few to be the slaves from the Eastern quadrant. The Uru had abandoned them.

Feeling a sense of sadness, Nefari directed the Vimana toward the battlefield. Cranaus had been right about the Spartans. They fought with ferocity, pushing the Hellenes to victory. Cheers erupted as the Uru broke ranks and fled in disarray. Nefari shook her head, deciding to head south across the seas, vowing never to return to the lands of the Hellene again.

Epilogue

"Wait, that's it?" Santiva asked as the other children rushed out the door. The bell had rung, signaling the end of the school day. "You left too many questions unanswered."

Nefertiti smiled, feeling a pang of nostalgia. Of all the children in Amarna, she would miss Santiva the most. Glancing outside, she saw that she still had time to answer. "What would you like to know?" she asked.

"What happened to Cranaus?" Santiva began, then added, "And Hedas? Did he die? And General Ryuja?"

"Ryujin," Nefertiti corrected gently. "The Spartan King, Lacedaemon, fought with such skill and courage that the mighty Uru, who had never known fear, turned and fled. Ryujin, however, stayed. He knew Atlantis was gone and could no longer hear the voices of the elders. He lost his life in a final duel against Lacedaemon."

"And Cranaus?" Santiva asked.

"Cranaus survived the ocean swim," Nefertiti said. "I heard he married a Spartan girl named Pedias and had three daughters with her. His reign brought Athens back toward the traditional city it had been before the Uru arrived."

"And Hedas?" Santiva's curiosity was unrelenting.

"Hedas lived through the wound," Nefertiti said. "We spent almost one hundred years of life together. He forgave me for what I did when I explained the story of Atlantis and told him the Uru would survive, as they had for millennia. They would blend in and gather their strength."

Santiva giggled at the thought of them as a couple. "Did you have any children?" she asked.

"Yes, I had a daughter named Sabra," Nefertiti replied. "She took more after the human side of my lineage, so she couldn't change forms, but I taught her about the Dreaming. She took flight within days. When she eventually passed away, Hedas became deeply depressed. He loved Sabra so much that his last words to me were, 'I'm going to protect our daughter in the afterlife.' He left this world shortly after."

"I'm sorry," Santiva said, her eyes welling with tears. "You've been through so much pain, my queen."

"Thank you, Santiva," Nefertiti said, gently cradling the girl's cheek. "It means a lot to me. But don't think that it was all bad. Those hundred years with Hedas were filled with joy. I thought I'd never know love like that again—until I met our late Pharaoh, Akhenaten. He accepted me as I was, even knowing my origins."

"Why does it sound like you're saying goodbye?" Santiva asked, her eyes clouded with worry.

"Because I am," Nefertiti replied. Santiva's expression shifted to shock and sorrow. "My life has been long, full of joy and sadness. But I feel the mortality of my Abori blood calling me. I will return to my birthplace to live out my final years in peace."

"Please don't go," Santiva said, tears streaming down her face. "Who else will teach me?"

Nefertiti embraced the girl, holding her close. "Don't be sad for me, Santiva. You've given me one more thing to be happy about in this life. Dry your tears and go home. Men will soon come for me, seeking to punish me for worshiping a single god. They want to reinstate the old gods of Egypt."

"When are you leaving?" Santiva asked, her voice quivering.

"I have to leave now, or I'll miss my window," Nefertiti said. Santiva nodded, gave her one last hug, and watched as she walked out the door. She saw Nefertiti enter one of the sacred temples. Moments later, a craft rose from the temple's roof and flew toward the southeast. Tears still fell from Santiva's cheeks, but she wiped them away as men riding camels arrived at the school door.

"Is she here, child?" one of the men asked. "Is Nefertiti inside?"

Santiva looked up at him. "Nefertiti, Mistress of the Two Lands, has returned home."

Thank you and I hope to see you again soon.

Books currently in the Aether

Veritas Rerum novels
Pyre of Souls
Veritas Rerum

The Birth of Magic

The Elven King Trilogy

Mage Killer Trilogy

Sword of the Immortal Trilogy
Summoner Mage
Child of Darkness
The Immortal Knight

Novels of the Wandering Swordsman Kiyoshi
A Stolen Sword
Split Personality Swordsman

The Future Past

The Boatman – A book of short stories

Written in the Stars Trilogy
The Stars Above Us
The World Around Us

www.ingramcontent.com/pod-product-compliance
Lightning Source LLC
Chambersburg PA
CBHW032138270626
47172CB00008B/232